TURN ME
LOOSE

ALSO BY ROSALIND JAMES

THE PARADISE, IDAHO SERIES

Book 1: Carry Me Home
Book 2: Hold Me Close

THE ESCAPE TO NEW ZEALAND SERIES

Prequel: Just for You
Book 1: Just This Once
Book 2: Just Good Friends
Book 3: Just for Now
Book 4: Just for Fun
Book 5: Just My Luck
Book 6: Just Not Mine
Book 7: Just Once More
Book 8: Just in Time
Book 9: Just Stop Me

THE NOT QUITE A BILLIONAIRE SERIES

Book 1: Fierce

THE KINCAIDS SERIES

Book 1: Welcome to Paradise
Book 2: Nothing Personal
Book 3: Asking for Trouble

TURN ME LOOSE

Paradise, Idaho: Book Three

ROSALIND JAMES

Montlake
Romance

Published by Montlake Romance, Seattle

www.apub.com

Amazon, the Amazon logo, and Montlake Romance are trademarks of Amazon.com, Inc., or its affiliates.

ISBN-13: 9781503935433
ISBN-10: 1503935434

Cover design by Eileen Carey

Printed in the United States of America

For my sons
Sam Nolting and James Nolting
For soldiering through

FLASH

It was all a series of flashes.

Flash. Stacy was staring at a shower curtain printed with pansies. Purple blossoms, yellow centers. A shower curtain she knew so well. Except . . . not, because it was pink around the edges with mildew, and the bathtub it didn't entirely conceal was brown with dirt. Nasty, and not familiar at all. Her hand groped for her phone in her purse, and she pressed a speed dial she hadn't used much lately, but that her fingers knew all the same.

"I'm so tired," she told her sister. "You aren't here. Why aren't you here? I want to go to bed. I'm scared, Ro."

She listened and tried to focus, but Rochelle's question made no sense. "Your place," she explained, even though it was obvious.

The pounding at the door made her jump, and she hurried to unlock it even as she shoved the phone back into her purse.

"Get out here," she heard. "I'm missing you."

Flash. Back to the party, and she was dancing. Her arms around him, her body sagging against his, and the room coming in and out of focus. She'd felt so good before, but now, she was tired. So tired. "Want to lie down," she said.

"Oh, you're going to lie down," he said. "Let's go."

A disturbance, then, in the room. Shouting, a jumble of words, loud and hard. A girl's voice. Shrill. It hurt her ears. ". . . pregnant. You son of a *bitch*." And then, "All of you. What are you going to do about it?"

"Nothing to do with me," she heard, and then an answering screech that made her wince. She was alone, swaying, finding the familiar couch and sitting down, closing her eyes against the noise.

". . . not going to keep my mouth shut . . ." It was the girl's voice again. ". . . the cops."

She lay back against the arm of the couch and let the voices and the pumping background music wash over her.

The deluge of hard words had ended, then another voice said, "Come on. Let's go outside." And then that was gone, too, and the music faded.

Flash. The furniture was upside down, and her forehead was banging against something. Jeans. Why jeans? And somebody was laughing.

". . . like 'em that way. If they're not conscious, they can't bitch about what you do. Good times."

"Nope." That voice was familiar, too, and coming from someplace very close. "Only woman that can't bitch is a dead one."

That was the last thing she heard.

MEMORY LANE

Rochelle Marks was sleeping—or trying to—with all the windows open and the fan blowing semicool air across her restless form, which was covered only by a pair of blue bikini underwear and a white sheet. Being hot at night would have been just fine if she'd had anybody to be hot with. As it was, there wasn't anyone around to appreciate that those underwear were a size six now instead of a seven. Well, there were people who'd appreciate it. Just nobody she wanted to invite over to appreciate up close.

She'd just drifted off to sleep with the help of a nice fantasy about a rodeo rider who didn't actually have chlamydia, thirty-second staying power, or a wife in Wyoming, because that was the point of a fantasy. And then the phone rang. She groped for her cell, knocked her water glass right smack onto the mattress, and said something very unladylike.

The phone was still ringing, though, so she sat up, edged out of the way of the rapidly spreading pool of water—at least it was cool—shoved the hair out of her face, and said, "If you're a telemarketer or my drunk-dialing ex, I will kick your ass."

"'Lo? Ro?"

The voice was slurred, but she recognized it. Her youngest sister. She sat up straighter. "Stacy?"

"So . . . tired . . ." More mumbling, and then, "I'm scared."

Rochelle was already up, yanking the dresser drawer open and pulling out the first thing her hand landed on: her cutoffs. "Where are you?"

"Wha . . . Your place." At least she thought that was what Stacy had said.

"What? Where?" Rochelle asked, but there was no answer, just some kind of pounding in the background, then a male voice with a dark edge. Something else in the background, too. Music—the raucous, angry shriek of heavy metal. And then silence.

She pulled on a bra and a tank top, thought about her hair and forgot it, grabbed her purse and keys, and took off out the back door, not bothering to lock it behind her. Paradise, Idaho, wasn't generally a hotbed of crime. She climbed into her Toyota, buzzed the windows down for the rush of cool night air, and headed toward downtown and the university.

Your place. Didn't make any sense. She must have misheard. It had been January when she'd moved to her duplex, where Stacy most definitely wasn't, and it was August now. Her cramped Main Street apartment had been rented within days of her leaving it. But just in case, she swung by it on her way to campus.

The narrow front window was dark. Of course it was. Stacy wouldn't have been there anyway, but Rochelle still got out to check.

It was Sunday night, the school year hadn't started quite yet. Which meant a knot of fancy-free college students standing across the street outside Jake's Bar, thinking they were funny but actually only being drunk and loud. She didn't miss living here one bit, especially on a hot summer night.

She headed across the sidewalk to check out the apartment. Her first postseparation place. Her first place of her own, period. Crappy, but at least it had been hers. The front window was open six inches for air, and she heard a fan whirring inside, but that was all. She thought about knocking, and abandoned the idea. Stacy wasn't there.

Your place? Near your place? She crossed the street, registered the "Whoa" from the guys still hanging around outside the bar without any interest at all, and opened the door to the familiar scent of beer and disinfectant and the sight of a few slumped forms on bar stools hanging around until the bitter end for last call. She scored a drunken invitation that she ignored, but certainly no Stacy.

Back to the car again, where the clock on the dash ticked over to 1:43 a.m. as she bumped across the railroad tracks, turned left on Harding, and stopped in front of the three-story block of student apartments. She pulled out her phone and called her sister again. No answer.

She put her finger on the doorbell and kept it there until a hostile blonde in a shortie robe with her hair straggling out of a ponytail pulled the door open with a "What the hell?" Stacy's roommate, Mandy.

"Is Stacy here?" Rochelle asked. She couldn't explain the urgency driving her, or what she'd heard in her youngest sibling's voice—and in the sounds she'd heard after that—that had her here at two in the morning. But she knew it was real.

"Uh . . ." The girl glanced behind her, toward the single bedroom. "No."

"Where'd she go?"

"Party, I think. Something like that." The door was closing, and Rochelle shot a hand out to hold it open.

"A party where?" she demanded.

She got a shrug for that. "I don't know. Not a frat, because I didn't hear about it. With some guy. Do you mind? It's the middle of the *night.*"

"With *what* guy? It's already Monday. Doesn't she have to work tomorrow—today?"

The girl's expression sharpened, and something Rochelle couldn't identify flitted across her face. "I don't know," she said. "You'd have to ask her. And could you leave? *I* have to work tomorrow, anyway."

"When she comes back," Rochelle insisted, "call me, OK?" She pushed past the girl into the apartment, flipping on the light along the way to the accompaniment of an outraged "Hey!" from Mandy. After a quick scrabble for a pen on Stacy's desk, she was writing her own cell number on a piece of notebook paper and shoving it at Mandy. "Here. You have *no* idea? Who's this guy? A student?"

A shrug from Mandy. "I don't know. Hardly met him. Hot."

"Nice. Love the way you've got her back," Rochelle said, and got another blank stare. There was nothing else here, so she left, then sat in her car with her hands on the steering wheel and thought.

Your place. Not the house they'd grown up in, the house where their parents still lived. That would be "our house." Only one place Stacy could have meant, and Rochelle swore at herself for not thinking of it first, however unlikely it seemed.

Heavy metal. She knew that sound all too well. The music she'd always switched off the second she'd walked in the door. She picked up her phone again and dialed a number she'd long since deleted from her contacts, but couldn't erase from her memory.

Four rings. Then voice mail.

"It's me. You know what to do."

She swore again and started up the car. Memory lane, here she came.

◆ ◆ ◆

The only place left to look, and the last place she wanted to go. The little car ate up the miles of dark highway, the route as familiar as breathing after years spent driving it back and forth to work every single day. Only a few sets of headlights flashed by along the way, and once she'd turned off onto the side road and begun to wind up the hill, she saw nothing at all until she was pulling into the long gravel driveway.

Three rigs stood in the yard despite the hour. Not Lake's, but his would be parked behind the shop, as usual. Her sinking heart told her that her instincts hadn't been wrong, because there were both light and noise streaming from the open windows and door. No neighbors to complain, not way out here. Lake was having a party.

Your place.

She headed up the dusty wooden steps of the porch, avoiding the loose board that Lake still hadn't bothered to fix. No porch swing, because she'd taken it. No flower baskets, because ditto. Not that anything would still have been alive by now.

No Lake, either. She walked inside to find Dave Harris lying in Lake's plaid recliner, head back, eyes closed, mouth open, with a couple more guys sprawled on the couch. Beer bottles and plastic cups littered the coffee table, a couple half-empty pizza boxes stood open on the dinette along with more plastic cups, and the whole place stank worse than the bar. Same beer, no disinfectant.

"Hey, Rochelle," Miles Kimberling said, lifting his bottle in a lazy salute. "Couldn't stay away, huh." Beside him, somebody she didn't know said nothing, just stared at her.

Rochelle ignored them and nudged Dave on his booted ankle. "Wake up."

He opened his eyes. "Rochelle? Huh?"

"Is my sister here?"

"Which one?"

"Stacy. And where's Lake? Is he with her? Is she . . . upstairs?"

Oh, no. Lake wouldn't do anything to Stacy, though. Or let anybody else do anything to her, either. He'd known her since she was *six.*

"I don't know," Dave said. "I was asleep. And you don't live here anymore, remember?"

7

She blinked at that. She'd never liked Dave much, but now his voice was . . . hostile. Her phone rang in her purse, and she fumbled for it. She could have set her purse down to look, but there was no surface in her formerly pristine home where she wouldn't have been afraid of catching something. So she didn't.

"She's back," came Mandy's laconic voice over the phone.

"Oh." Rochelle closed her eyes in relief that was surely out of proportion to what had happened. She was overreacting for sure. Must be the heat, or being back here. "She OK?"

"Passed out, that's all. I only called you because otherwise you'd be waking me up again. I got up because I heard the front door, and *somebody* had just woken me up anyway. I went out there, and she was on the couch, and a guy was leaving. Making a ton of noise, just like you."

The alarm bells were ringing again. "Passed out? Wake her up. I want to talk to her."

A gusty sigh came down the line. "She's drunk, that's all. And it's the middle of the *night.*"

"Wake her up. Right now."

Another sigh. "Hang on."

She waited a few minutes with Mandy's voice faint in the background, then Mandy was on the line again, sounding more awake this time, and scared, too. "I can't."

Rochelle's heart was pounding, and she wasn't aware of the mess anymore, of Dave's hostility, the other men's stares, or even the sad state of her former home. "Did you shake her?"

"I did everything. I can't wake her up."

"Call 911."

"She'll get in trouble."

"I don't *care* if she gets in trouble." Rochelle's voice was rising now, and she didn't care about that, either. "If she dies because you didn't call, *you'll* get in trouble. I'll kill you myself. Call 911 right the hell now, and call me when they come. I'm on my way."

◆　◆　◆

The three men in the living room listened to the sound of Rochelle's car crunching over the gravel, then the engine noise receding.

"What do we do?" Miles Kimberling asked. He wished he'd left an hour ago. He had to be at work at seven the next morning. And anyway—he wished he'd left.

"Nothing," Dave said. "So Rochelle came by. So what? What did she see? Some guys partying, that's all."

"What about what her sister saw?"

That got a laugh from Dave. "Stacy? Too out of it to even notice. And, damn, she's turning out fine. Not as hot as Rochelle, but not too bad. Not too bad at all. And the shape she was in?" He sighed. "Yeah. That's what I call party time."

Miles shifted his feet. "Better not let *him* hear you say that."

"Why?" Dave said. "He didn't exactly mind tonight, did he?"

"Sure he did," Miles said. "You heard him."

"Why, that he didn't want her here?" Dave shot him a look of contempt. "That wasn't out of his deep feelings. It was because she's Rochelle's sister, and he knows Rochelle has the biggest mouth in Paradise."

A WHOLE CROP OF STUPID

Four in the morning, and Rochelle still wasn't sleeping. Instead, she was standing in a curtained-off cubicle in Hillman Hospital's ER, looking down at Stacy with a tube in her arm and talking to a doctor who was the furthest possible thing from George Clooney. Hard featured, balding, forty-five, and with no bedside manner whatsoever.

"We've finished running your blood work, Stacy," he said. "You really mixed it up tonight, didn't you?"

Stacy's eyes shifted back and forth once, and then she closed them again. "Too sleepy," she moaned.

"What do you mean?" Rochelle asked. "Mixed it up how?"

"Alcohol, hydrocodone—Vicodin—and Ritalin," the doctor said. "Party drugs. Mix enough of them with enough alcohol, and your party ends up right here." Stacy's eyes were open again. "Want to tell me where you got that?" he asked her. "Raid your grandparents' medicine cabinet? Or from someplace else? We'd all like to know where you're getting your drugs."

"I didn't!" Stacy said. "I just went *out*." She was agitated now, her eyes—their pupils still abnormally small—darting between Rochelle and the doctor.

"With a guy," Rochelle said. "*Some guy.* What guy?"

Stacy got an expression on her face Rochelle recognized. The expression of a girl with five older siblings and a stubborn streak. And she didn't answer.

"Do you remember where you were?" the doctor asked.

"No," Stacy said. "*No. I don't.*" She was looking panicky again. "I don't *remember.*"

The doctor nodded. "Blackout. Vicodin and Ritalin? That's amnesia time. The memory comes back sometimes, usually in pieces, and sometimes it doesn't. You might think about that before you do it again. About what that means, and the neural pathways you've altered forever."

Stacy didn't answer, and Rochelle turned to the doctor and said, "I'll deal with it. Thanks."

He shrugged, the disgust obvious. "We gave her some oxygen, that's about all." His gaze took in all of Rochelle this time, and she knew what he was seeing. Her tank top, cutoff blue jeans, flip-flops, and long, messy blonde hair, not to mention her body. She probably could've chosen her middle-of-the-night wardrobe better. She shifted under his scrutiny, and not in a good way. *Trashy,* he didn't have to say. Dismissing her, the way she'd been dismissed so often. And then she thought, *Hell with you,* straightened her spine, and stared right back at him. What he thought of her? That wasn't her problem.

He glanced away. "I'll get somebody to take that out," he told Stacy, nodding at the IV. "And you can go on home and sleep it off." *Again.* He didn't have to say that, either.

Stacy didn't say much herself until she was dressed again and in Rochelle's car.

"Thanks," she said when Rochelle had started it up and was headed toward campus again. She lay back with a sigh, and Rochelle hardened her heart against the sickness and fatigue she could see in her sister's face. Against the fear and confusion she'd heard in her voice, the little-sister call she'd responded to so many times throughout her all-too-short childhood. Skinned knees and nightmares and wet beds and spilled milk. What you got when you were the oldest of six, when you'd grown up in a three-bedroom house in Kernville, sharing a room with your sisters and helping make breakfast for eight so your mom could get to work. What she was done with, and what she wasn't one bit done with.

"Give me the number for your boss," Rochelle said. "I'll call and tell her you're not coming in today."

"Never mind," Stacy said. "I'll do it."

"No. You'll fall asleep. Give me her number." When Stacy didn't say anything, Rochelle looked at her more closely again, remembering the look on Stacy's roommate's face earlier. "You're kidding. You're going to tell me you got fired. That was a *great* job. That was in the *library*."

"Just because I was late a couple times," Stacy said. "I'll get a new job. It's only been two weeks. I'm really tired. Can we talk about it later?"

Two *weeks?* Stacy had always been responsible. Always the good girl. Something was very wrong. Rochelle pulled into the apartment building's parking lot and stopped with a jerk. "Nope. You've just OD'd. And you can call it whatever you want," she said when her sister opened her mouth to object. "I shelled out for the co-pay. I was there. You OD'd, you got into a situation that could've ended really badly, you lost your job, and school starts in a week. You've hardly even been out to see the folks, and now I know why. You're way off track, and right now, you've got two choices. I call Daddy and tell him what's going on, or you move in with me. You can't pay for this place anyway without a job."

"I *said* I'll get another job," Stacy said. "I'm an adult. I'm allowed to make my own choices."

That was it. That was enough. "Like hell you are," Rochelle said. "You're an about-to-be junior who turned twenty-one six weeks ago and grew a whole new crop of stupid. You really want to disappoint Daddy like this? You're the only one of us to go to college. You know how proud he is of that? You want to see his face when you tell him you got fired? You want to see it in about half an hour, when he stands here in his work boots, ready to get up in that combine all day in this heat, listening to you tell him how you've been screwing up? You think he's still going to be giving you that check every month? You really think so?"

Stacy's mouth opened again, and Rochelle got a rush of anger so strong, she could hardly contain it. "Do not say it," she warned. "Do not tell me that a hundred and fifty dollars doesn't matter. It matters to him. And it should matter to you. You should know what that's costing both of them."

A few tears were trickling down Stacy's pale cheeks now. "All I did was go out. And I'm *sick.* I need to *sleep.*"

"Right," Rochelle said. "Get out of the car. We're packing a few things, you're sleeping it off at my house today, and we're coming back for the rest of your stuff tonight. Congratulations. Your living expenses have just been cut down to the bone. And you know what? You're going to get a new job, too."

◆　◆　◆

Rochelle's day had to get better. Except it didn't.

By the time dawn had begun to tint the sky pink above Paradise Mountain, Stacy was showered and fast asleep under clean sheets in Rochelle's spare room. Rochelle briefly contemplated going back to bed herself, but it wasn't worth it, not for an hour. Instead, she went into her tidy kitchen, featuring every drawer organizer known to man and not a single beer can or pizza box, and made coffee. She lifted her mug toward the tiny terra-cotta pots of herbs lining the windowsill, looked out at the weeping birch that stood in full, glorious leaf at the edge of her backyard, and spoke aloud. "Here's to small blessings. And big ones."

She hadn't had any sleep, true, and for her, calling in sick wasn't an option. She knew—even if Stacy didn't—how much a good job mattered, and her job as the assistant to the dean of engineering wasn't just good. It was *great*. For her. She was tired, but that was all right. She had her day so organized, it would practically run itself. All she needed was her to-do list and her orderly brain. Check and check.

A few hours later, she was starting to cross off tasks exactly as anticipated. She was in the dean's office, running through the week during their usual Monday-morning meeting.

". . . And Dr. Halvorsen is complaining about Mechanical Engineering's conference budget," she finished. "Says the department can't come in under it after all, and he needs a variance. I think you're going to have to handle that one."

"Gotcha," Dr. Olsen said, making a note. He looked at Rochelle more closely. "You OK?"

"Does it show?"

He just looked at her, and she sighed. "Sure. Just something with my sister. Big families. Nothing to worry about. Long night, though. Fortunately, I don't have to wow anybody today. The only thing I've got is the new Computer Science lecturer finally showing up and needing to get situated. At least I hope he's showing up, or there's going to be a scramble."

"Cutting it close," her boss observed. "You got a place set up for him?"

She put her head on one side, feeling a little better. "Now, what do you think?"

"I think you've got a place for him, and an orientation packet, too. Hope he's good at getting oriented. Only time I've ever heard of a faculty member—even a lecturer—being offered a spot, or taking it, for that matter, without ever setting foot on the campus."

"Well, they were desperate down there. Nothing like a last-minute medical leave for classes nobody else is equipped to teach." She closed her notebook and stood up. "And it's only for a semester. You can stand anything for a semester. Or anyone. T. Wayne Cochran. Wayne?

Software geek from San Francisco, willing to take a part-time lecturer job in Idaho for one semester? Talk about desperate. Why?"

"Why indeed," Dr. Olsen said. "But I bet you'll find out."

She snorted at that one. "Only because it's my duty to know all, so you don't have to. Ten bucks says he's got skinny arms and a beard."

He didn't.

A NOT-SO-CHANCE ENCOUNTER

Travis Cochran was hot, sweaty, and a little dirty. He was also late, but who cared.

He'd been cool and clean enough when he'd started out this morning from the University Inn, even though he'd gotten into town late the night before. But when he'd pulled out of the parking lot for the five-minute drive to the university, the old Ford's ride had told him that he had a flat. And by the time he'd jacked it up and changed the tire, he'd been . . . yeah. Hot, late, and with a smear of grease across one sleeve of his blue button-down.

He'd contemplated changing, but his road trip from California had depleted his supply of clean shirts. He'd taken that trip slowly, but then, he'd been taking a lot of things slowly lately. And he didn't care that much about impressing anybody anymore, either. So he didn't change. Instead, he walked back into the motel, washed his hands, rolled up his sleeves to hide the grease, and headed out again.

He took it slow through the edge of town, too, before making the two turns to the university, his windows down against the heat that was already beginning to build.

Not hard to orient himself at all, not here. It was a far cry from the office towers of San Francisco, the cranes and jackhammers of the city's latest building boom, the guys in skinny hipster jeans and black-framed glasses crowding every coffee shop, talking start-up as if they'd invented the concept. Here, puffy white clouds floated like cotton balls in a cerulean sky, huge elms cast dappled shade on the sidewalks, and the few young people in view moved along those sidewalks like they had time on their hands.

He found the parking lot for the massive new brick edifice that was the Engineering Building and headed through the stone portico into a wide hall echoing with summertime emptiness. After consulting the old-fashioned directory board in the lobby, he took the stairs two at a time to the fourth floor. His footsteps rang out against the tile floor of the long hallway that led to the open doorway at the end. He entered a large room with three more doors leading off it, dominated by a central workstation where a young woman sat.

Step one: check in with the dean's assistant and start . . .

Wait a minute. He knew that face. And when she saw him and pushed back from the desk, he knew the rest of her, too.

Rochelle Marks, her nameplate read. But then, he knew that, because he'd been corresponding with her about his living arrangements. He just hadn't connected her with . . . her. Because he'd forgotten her name.

He hadn't forgotten *her,* though, not one bit. And finding her right here, right now? That made his day, suddenly, just about perfect.

Kind of like that first night, when he'd spotted her on the dance floor in a noisy, overheated Spokane bar, her hands up in the air, rocking out to a country band. It had been a dark, cold Friday night in January, and snowing hard. His flight to San Francisco had been cancelled, and he'd been in a dark place, impatient and frustrated after a series of client meetings. About to go to a much darker one, too, although he hadn't known that at the time. That night had been the only bright spot, but it had sure been that.

She'd been a bright spot all by her sweet self, dressed in low, tight jeans that hugged every generous curve, and a wrap-front red sweater that revealed a whole lot of wow. Her long blonde hair had swayed with every movement of her hips in a hypnotizing rhythm, and it had been hard to decide whether he'd rather see the front or the back view, but he'd known he wanted to see more of all of it.

Every guy in the bar had been looking, but Travis had been the one who'd taken her home.

He looked at her now, wearing a sleeveless white blouse buttoned up past all that spectacular real estate, and a print skirt that covered way too much of those man-eating thighs. He remembered sliding one hand inside that cherry-red sweater and closing it over firm, warm flesh. She'd filled his hand and then some, and he had big hands. He'd known right then that his hands, mouth, and every other aching part of him were in for a long, slow road trip, the kind that took you all night long.

His other hand had been wrapped in her hair at the time, as he recalled, tugging her head back for his kiss, and she'd made a noise into his mouth, a whimper that had just about pushed him over the edge all by itself.

She'd liked her legs pulled up high, and that had been just fine by him. There weren't many things in life better than a woman on her back with her legs wrapped around your waist, her arms flung up by her head, her eyes closed, and her mouth open and panting hard.

Oh, yeah. It had been way too long since . . . anything. But especially since her.

Right now, her eyes weren't closed. They were narrowed, accentuating the long, exotically tilted shape she'd inherited along with her high cheekbones, as if some Cossack had wandered into the gene pool at some point. Those eyes were the same vibrant blue as the sky outside, and as unreadable and cool as she'd been warm and wide-open on that January night eight months earlier.

"Hi," he said. "Rochelle."

WELCOME TO PARADISE

Rochelle stared. At the lean face, strong nose, firm jaw—and the lips that had been cut just too damn fine for anyone born with ovaries not to imagine kissing. At dark brown hair that was a bit longer now, long enough that you'd have something to curl your fingers into if you needed to hold on to his head for . . . any reason. And at the way he stood: tall, slim hipped, and loose limbed. His shoulders were broad under his blue button-down, the tanned, sinewy forearms that emerged from the rolled-up sleeves thick with muscle. Thicker, surely, than she remembered. He had one thumb hooked in the front pocket of his Levi's, with the fingers of that big hand splayed along his thigh. He stood like a rancher, like a cowboy, and he moved like one, too.

Travis. He'd come back at last to find her. After eight months, he'd either remembered her, or maybe, just maybe, he'd tracked her down. She hadn't asked for his phone number, and she wouldn't have called him if she'd had it. She didn't want to admit how long she'd waited for him to call *her,* or how it had felt when she'd given up. Now, her mouth had gone dry, and she licked her lips and saw him watch her do it. She didn't know what she was going to do about him, but she had a feeling that at some point, self-control was going to become one hell of an effort.

The dean chose that moment to come out of his office with a stack of papers in his hand. He dumped them into Rochelle's in-box, nodded at Travis, and turned to go.

"Dr. Olsen, I'm thinking?" Travis said. "I'm Wayne Cochran. Your new Computer Science lecturer."

The dean turned back in surprise, then put out a hand. "Brad Olsen. Glad to see you made it. We were wondering."

Travis—Wayne—quirked a corner of that firm mouth as he shook hands. "Yeah. Bet you were. I'm here now, though."

"Has Rochelle got you all set up, then?"

"Nope. Haven't given her a chance. But I'm sure hoping she will."

"Well, I'll leave her to it. Welcome to Paradise."

"Thanks," Travis said. "It's looking good so far."

Rochelle waited until Dr. Olsen had gone back into his office, then said to Travis in a voice she was shocked to find she could still control, "You son of a *bitch*."

"Whoa." He had a hand up. "Hang on."

She'd stood up without realizing it, was hanging on to the edge of her desk and leaning halfway over it. It was all she could do not to charge right around it and punch him in the jaw. Her mama'd done her best to raise her to be a lady. Too bad it hadn't taken. "Travis? *Travis?* You give me a fake name, you lie to me, and then you think it'll be funny not to let me know it's you I'm talking to all these weeks? Think you'll see just how flustered you can make me, showing up here?"

He wasn't looking quite so cool now. "First off," he said, "it's not a fake name. My name's Travis Wayne Cochran. T. Wayne. My family calls me Travis. And maybe I wanted to be Travis that night."

"Oh, yeah. Because it was such a special time."

He started to say something, then seemed to stop himself. "Know what? I'm going to leave that right there. Because the next thing I'm going to say is that I forgot your name, and I lost your number, or I didn't keep it, but that doesn't mean I forgot you. Things got a little . . . complicated in my life after that night. I actually didn't know it was you I'd been emailing with. So, yeah. Son of a bitch? Probably. And one-night stand? Guilty." He must have seen how she winced at that, because he softened his voice. "But messing with you? No. And glad to see you—yes. Definitely yes. *Hell,* yes."

"Well," she said, "that makes one of us." She stalked over to her credenza in her heels, pulled out the shiny red folder she'd stashed there, then walked back over, doing her best to breathe along the way, and handed it to him. Time to do her job. She might not be a lady, but she was a professional. "Here you go. I understand you're paid up on the rent, so all you have to do is call Carol Ritter and pick up the keys to your apartment. Cottage in back of her house, actually. I already checked that it's stocked for you in terms of linens and all. And you'll need to check in with your department, of course. The books are ordered for your class. I made sure of that, since the Computer Science department is doing some scrambling at the moment. The reason for your late hire. They're below us on the third floor, by the way. Otherwise, there's a list of grocery stores and banks and anything else you might need, and a local calendar of things to do." *Not that you'll need help finding those.* She bit her tongue on the words.

"And those things to do wouldn't include you." His brown eyes were steady on hers, his mouth unsmiling.

She straightened her back. And if it shoved her boobs out—well, she'd been faced with that choice since she'd been fourteen. Stand tall and have every guy in eyeball range stare at her chest, or slouch and cower and cover it up. She hadn't cowered then, and she wasn't about to start now. She held his gaze, and he kept his eyes high. But then, he'd already seen it all.

21

"No," she said evenly. "I'm not a fringe benefit."

"Not even an orientation lunch?"

"Not even that."

◆　　◆　　◆

She hadn't needed that much self-control after all. Not one bit, in fact, except for the not-punching thing. She watched Travis's rear view, all broad shoulders, tight butt, and long legs, disappear out the door, and it was like it had all just happened between the two of them. Like she'd just been that stupid, that impulsive, that . . . *not* trashy, she told herself furiously. Why was it only women who were "trashy"? That . . . mistaken. She'd call it that. That completely mistaken.

It hadn't been so bad that first Christmas after her divorce. Then, life had looked like a big wide world of possibilities. She'd just turned thirty, and she'd known that the new decade was going to be her best yet. Her own money, her own life, her own place, with nobody's dirty dishes in the sink and nobody's dirty underwear on the floor. Not to mention the Divorce Diet body she'd exercised into her best shape ever. She'd been out on the town and looking good. A brand-new start.

And then another year had passed, there'd been one more candle on the cake, she was still out on the town, and it wasn't that much fun. She wasn't looking for a good time. She was looking for forever. And when you came from the wrong side of the tracks and you looked the way she did, it wasn't hard at all to get a reputation, especially if you had a wild side. She knew. She'd had exactly that rep as a teenager. Every guy she'd gone out with had had a story to tell in the locker room, and some of them had even been true. She wasn't going down that road again. Times might have changed, but a lot of folks in Paradise hadn't gotten the memo. And she didn't want a bunch of hookups with guys who hung out in bars anyway. She wanted strong and sweet and smart.

She wanted sex, and she wanted it hot, but she wanted babies, too. She was holding out for a full-grown man. She was holding out for a hero, and it looked like she'd be holding out for a while. Fighting her insistent body all the way.

It had been the maid-of-honor stint that had really done it, though. A winter wedding between her good friend, slightly nerdy professor of geology Zoe Santangelo, and Paradise's formerly most eligible bachelor, ex-NFL star Cal Jackson. It had been something about the light in both their faces as they'd claimed each other, not to mention the fact that Rochelle had known that, under the wedding gown she'd bullied Zoe into choosing, her friend had already been five weeks pregnant. And maybe that Luke Jackson, Cal's brother and best man and Paradise's *second* most eligible bachelor, had spent half the ceremony looking at his girlfriend, Kayla, and clearly wishing he could talk her into a double wedding right then and there.

Rochelle had been happy for all of them. Sure she had. And she'd also been jealous as hell.

Which could have been why, a few weeks after that wedding, in mid-January when the weather was at its coldest and the winter at its darkest and bleakest, she'd gone to Spokane to visit her cousin Celine. An hour and a half from home and a hundred miles from everyone she knew. They'd ended up at a country bar on Saturday night with a bunch of make-believe cowboys, some office workers and salesmen in Dockers, and all the guys who'd taken off their wedding rings outside the door. Not too different from Paradise, in other words, minus the college students looking for a cougar.

Except that *he'd* been sitting at a table, his booted feet stuck out in front of him with one ankle crossed over the other, his eyes on her, a beer bottle in his hand, the heat in his gaze making her have to look away fast every time she glanced his way. And she was glancing his way too often, there was no doubt.

She'd been dancing with a dentist when it happened. She'd known he was a dentist because he'd told her so. The third time she moved his hand off her butt, she told him, "I've got great teeth myself. Next time your hand goes there, I'll give you a dental impression you won't forget."

"Mm. Nice," he said. "But I don't think so. I know what women like you want."

"Can't wait to hear that," she said. "Oh, wait. I can." The song was ending. Thank heaven.

"Luckily, it's exactly what I want," he said. "You've got an ass just made for my hand. After that, we can find out what else it's good for."

The music had stopped in the middle of his little speech, and his words fell like stones into the relative quiet. Heads turned around them, although Rochelle barely noticed through the roaring in her own head. Her hand was already rising for the slap that was itching to get out when she heard the voice over her shoulder.

"Way I see it, we've got two choices. I could take him out to the parking lot and kick his ass, or we could ignore him and dance. What's it gonna be?"

"You wish," the dentist said.

"Oh, no." He'd stepped around her now, and Rochelle wasn't one bit surprised to see who it was. "I don't wish. I know. I'm just waiting on the lady here."

"He's not worth it," she said, her breath still coming a bit raggedly. "Let's dance."

"Now, see," he said. "I was hoping you'd be telling me what I wanted to hear."

His sleepy eyes smiled at her, even though his lips barely moved, and she got a hard flutter low in her belly that moved straight on down and set up residence. She forgot all about the dentist, because her guy put his left hand up, and her right one went up to join it as if it had been drawn there by a magnet. She could feel the sigh that went through his body when their hands touched, and his other hand was firm at her waist, letting her know, just like that, that he knew how to dance and all she had to do was follow. Her left hand settled on his broad shoulder, and he smiled down at her for real this time and said, "Oh, yeah. That's what I'm talking about."

She'd have said something smart, but her mouth was too dry. So she just danced, and let him buy her a drink, and danced with him some more. And when the band played a slow one and Travis—his name was Travis, of course, because he wasn't sexy enough already—pulled her up closer, she snuggled right up there until she was molded to his hard body, swaying and rocking and halfway to gone.

"Damn," she heard, and she pulled back a bit to look up at him. His eyes were smiling again, and the tingle that had long since become a buzz sent up a spark so strong, she shuddered.

"Sweetheart," he told her, "that's just too good. Afraid you're the only one I'm going to be taking out to the parking lot tonight."

"Yeah," she managed to say. "Hell of a thing."

"Isn't it, though?" He led her off the floor, and she grabbed her jacket and touched Celine's shoulder with a "Don't wait up."

The wind outside hit them hard, and she gasped, but Travis laughed out loud, a reckless edge to it. "Wow. Lets you know you're alive, huh?"

"Not . . . so much," she said. "Lets you know you're freezing to death."

"Come on." He had an arm around her shoulder, was hustling her across to his car, a late-model SUV, and opening the door for her. Inside, he turned on the engine and blasted the heater, but didn't put the car in gear.

"We . . . waiting for something?" she asked when her shivers had died down and she could speak again.

"Yeah," he said. "Waiting for this." He reached across the console, got one hand under her hair and the other one on her shoulder, pulled her into him, and settled his mouth over hers.

He tasted like tequila and lime. He tasted like 100 percent pure hard man. His lips were firm and warm, and he took his time. One big palm cradled her head, and he kept kissing her, long and slow and fathoms deep, while the motor purred and the radio played one soft country song after another. And still he kissed her. Little butterfly touches on the edges of her mouth, then his mouth drifted over her cheek to her temple, his thumb caressing the other cheek in a rhythm that had her hips moving along.

She shifted in her seat, tried to get closer, and stroked the back of his neck, then sent her hand up, testing the texture of his hair and finding it perfect, short and thick and just right to dig your fingers into. Her other hand was on his shoulder, but there was too much jacket there, and she had to feel him.

"Travis," she gasped.

"Yeah," he sighed, resting his forehead against hers. "Yeah. You want to get out of here?"

"I don't know," she rallied enough to say. "You do it the same way you kiss?"

The faint light from the edge of the lot was enough to show her his mouth curving in a slow smile. "Oh, baby. I'll do it so much better." His hand traced the edge of her jaw, oddly tender. "How do you feel about letting a man undress you?"

"Depends," she said, closing her eyes against the feel of his hand, "on the man."

"Mm." Another kiss on the sensitive outer edge of her mouth, his tongue coming out briefly to trace her upper lip, and she was shivering again. "Then let's go see if I'm the man. I'm thinking slow, with a whole lot of kissing and a whole lot of touching. I'm thinking we make this last all night."

"You got that much to give?"

"I don't know," he said, and she rocked back some. She hadn't been expecting honesty. "But whatever it turns out I've got? I'm going to give it to you."

CONSEQUENCES

He'd done it, too. He'd been all that and a bag of chips.

She'd been startled when he'd driven only ten blocks or so before parking in the garage for the Davenport, Spokane's most exclusive hotel. She'd figured him for a local, and had had some momentary second thoughts about what she was doing here. Another kiss in the car had put an end to those, though, maybe because he still hadn't felt her up. She'd needed more, and she'd needed it in a hurry.

"You a slow mover?" she asked him.

"Could be," he said, with another of those kisses at the corner of her mouth that drove her crazy. "Why don't you come on in with me and find out?"

So she had, and even though she hadn't had sex in months, she remembered enough to know she'd never had it that good. Because he'd turned out to be a very, *very* slow mover. It had been exactly what he'd said: a whole lot of slow undressing, a whole lot of kissing, a whole lot of touching, and a whole, whole lot of "Oh, my God," until she'd wondered, in some hazy corner of her mind, if a person could actually pass out from too much pleasure.

When they were finally lying quietly together, his arms around her, her head on his chest, he said, "Wow," and she couldn't have agreed more.

She smiled, feeling nothing but satisfied and lazy, turned her head to kiss the hard plane of his chest, and said, "Mm."

"You live here?" he asked. "Spokane? Say yes." And that's when she realized that she knew nothing more about him than his first name, however generously he'd shared his body.

"This the getting-to-know-you part of the evening?" she asked. "My mama would be so ashamed of me. Blame it on the Cuervo, I guess."

His hand stroked over the curve of her bottom, and she lit up again despite everything they'd just done. She could hear the smile in his voice as he said, "Well, there's knowing and knowing. We won't tell your mama how well you let me know you, how's that?"

"No," she said, and his hand stilled. "I don't live in Spokane," she went on. "I live in Paradise."

"No kidding. Think I've been visiting there myself."

She laughed against his skin. "It's a town." And then she realized, with a sick jolt, what that meant. "You really *aren't* a local."

"Nope. But I'm likely to be back. No, I'm *definitely* coming back. Count on it."

She sighed at that, pillowed her head more comfortably against his delicious chest, and fell asleep.

In the morning, he tucked the slip of hotel notepaper with her name and number on it into his wallet and said, "Wish I could stay. It feels like we just got started, doesn't it? But I've got too much to do back home. I'll drop you off, for now."

He'd dropped her off back at her cousin's, and then he'd dropped right out of her life. Nobody to blame but herself. If you were looking for something more than a one-night rodeo, you didn't go looking for it in a cowboy bar.

So he was here now. So what? He wouldn't be the only guy in the College of Engineering who had an idea about getting with her, and who wasn't going to be getting anywhere close.

And if he talked? She had to swallow hard at the thought of that. She hadn't exactly held back that night, and neither had he. If he talked—that would make her life so much less comfortable. People said women gossiped, but in her experience, women couldn't hold a candle to men in certain areas. Women didn't usually spread the word in the workplace about the cute guy in the next office they'd taken home from the bar, and exactly how many ways he'd nailed her.

She couldn't do anything about that, though, not right now. So she set it aside and picked up her to-do list. And by the time five o'clock rolled around, she was almost too tired from the lack of sleep, not to mention all the emotion of the night—and the day—to care anymore.

◆ ◆ ◆

Rochelle couldn't even go home and go to bed, because she still had to finish moving her sister. Talk about your Mondays.

"I don't want to live with you," Stacy said from her spot on her bed, where she was planted as if Rochelle would have to pry her fingers loose and drag her out kicking and screaming. Which Rochelle was fully prepared to do.

At least Stacy was looking perkier now. Rochelle guessed that was the benefit to being twenty-one. Her sister wasn't showing any effects from the night before, whereas Rochelle had had to give herself a pretty stern pep talk in the car over here just to keep going. All she'd wanted to do was stretch out on the couch and fall asleep watching a movie.

Mandy had accepted Rochelle's explanation of Stacy's sudden move with a martyred sigh and gone out to leave them to their packing, muttering about "having to find a new roommate now. Thanks *so* much," despite the fact that she'd have no problem at all finding somebody with one week to go before school started, and that she'd be getting double rent as soon as she did. The loss of her company wasn't exactly killing Rochelle, either.

"No offense, Ro," her sister went on. "I mean, thanks for being worried, I guess, but this is all a major overreaction. I'm fine. I didn't even need to go to the hospital, not really. It's not like they had to pump my stomach or anything. OK, I drank a little too much, but everybody does that."

"Yeah? Does everybody take that many pills, too?" Rochelle kept on methodically stacking shirts and jeans into one of the cardboard boxes she'd hastily scrounged from the university's shipping and receiving office. Stacy had packed up her underwear and sock drawers, but now, her efforts were confined to looking mulish.

Stacy let out a gusty sigh. "It's no big deal. Lots of people do it sometimes. And look at me. I'm fine. I'm good. You went way overboard. Let's just forget it, OK?"

Rochelle swiveled on her haunches to look at her. "I wasn't kidding. You're moving in with me. We're done talking about that. But what I want to know is, who gave them to you? Was it the guy you were out with? What's his name?"

Stacy got up and started stripping the bottom sheet. "His name's Shane. And no. Of course not."

"Does he go to school here?" Rochelle pressed.

"He went to college for a while." Stacy seemed to be folding the sheet with extra care. "And now he's got a good job. A lot better than all the college graduates who are working in Starbucks. He says if you want to get ahead, you have to think for yourself. You can't just go rung by rung. You have to jump. Like you." There was defiance in her eyes, and for once, she looked straight at Rochelle. "You've got a great job, and you never went to college at all. You lucked into it, because of your personality and everything. That's how it really works. I'll stay in college," she hastened to add, clearly seeing the expression on her sister's face. "I still have my plan. I'm just saying, there's more to it than that."

That wasn't a warning bell. It was a five-alarm fire. "I didn't luck into a damn thing," Rochelle said. "I started out at the bottom and worked my tail off, and eventually, I impressed the dean enough that filling in temporarily became a permanent job I shouldn't have been qualified for. And since then, I've been making sure he doesn't regret his decision for a single day. This is as high as I'm ever going to get, too. I *don't* have a college degree, and that meant I had to climb every one of those rungs by being better than anybody else he could have found. Everyone *I* know who's gotten anywhere has climbed every rung, too. College degree or not." She shook her head. This was getting them nowhere but sidetracked. "How old is this guy?"

Stacy was folding the mattress pad now. "I don't know. We don't sit around looking at each other's driver's licenses."

"Do not try to weasel out of this. How old? And where's he from?"

Stacy sighed again. "Maybe twenty-five? Thirty?" Like those were exactly the same. "Which means he's mature. I'd have thought you'd like that. And he's from the city. Well," she said with trace of a laugh, "from all over, really. He grew up all over the world, because his dad was a diplomat."

Yeah, right. The sons of diplomats didn't end up in small-town Idaho. Rochelle didn't say that, of course. She wasn't an idiot. "Where'd you meet him?"

Stacy's eyes slid away, but when Rochelle didn't move, just kept staring at her, she finally said, "At the casino, all right? When I went for my twenty-first birthday last month. I was with five other girls, and he could have gone after any of them. He's super hot. But he went for me, because he said I had the sweetest face. So that proves it."

"Proves what? That he was looking for somebody he could sweet-talk into bed? Bet you had the biggest boobs, too. And he didn't get you help last night."

"Nice. Thanks. And yes, he did. He brought me home, didn't he? He must have, because I sure didn't get myself there. And nothing *happened* to me. Seriously, Ro. I'm OK."

Rochelle wanted to say that guys you met in casinos weren't necessarily the best bets, but she didn't have much room to talk. "So he does have a job? He's not skipping that rung?"

"*Yes*. He's got a really good delivery job, picking up lab samples from all around here, plus Union City. All right, he isn't all the way up the ladder yet, but he's going to get there. He invests. He's got a plan. He's got a great rig, too. And you know, sarcasm is the lowest form of humor."

"Thanks. I've made a note. Oops. I did it again." Rochelle grinned at her sister, and Stacy smiled back. Reluctantly, but still.

A driver would be facing random drug tests. Maybe it *had* just been a one-time deal, or the wrong party. Besides, Stacy had a point that she'd gotten home safe. Rochelle had made sure the hospital checked her out to make sure nobody had messed with her. That had been a relief. A guy who was all the way over onto the Dark Side wouldn't have passed up that opportunity.

"Yeah," Stacy said. "Don't *worry*, Ro. I'm sorry you had to get up and everything. I don't know why Mandy even called you."

That made Rochelle pause in her packing. "Wait. You don't remember calling me?" The suspicion that she'd been glad to set aside last night came roaring right back. "Stace. *You* called me. You said you were scared, and you asked me to come get you."

"I did?" Stacy looked truly rattled at last. "I don't remember that."

"You said you were at 'my place.' At least I think that's what you said. You weren't too clear. I was out there looking for you when Mandy called, and it looked like Lake had been having a party. Is that where you were?"

Stacy shook her head. "I don't know. I don't remember. I don't think so."

"And you don't remember who gave you the pills?" If Stacy *had* been at Lake's . . . but Lake hadn't even been there.

Her ex had done plenty of drinking and smoked plenty of weed, but he'd never taken anything harder. At least as far as Rochelle knew. That would've cost even more money, though, so she'd have known. She had a feeling that those kinds of pills didn't come cheap.

Stacy took a cardboard box into the bathroom, and her voice came drifting back to Rochelle. "No. I don't remember. Anyway, it was one time."

◆ ◆ ◆

By nine thirty, Stacy was moved in, Rochelle had sacrificed a few too many dollars and a few too many calories on burritos for dinner, and she was back in her bedroom, the fan trying in vain to cope with today's ration of hot air. She picked up the phone. She didn't want to, but she had to know what was going on.

Again, she dialed the number from memory. Two rings, three, and she was wondering if she could manage to leave a civil voice mail message when she heard the flat, "What."

"Hey, Lake." She tried for brisk and matter-of-fact. "How you doing?"

"How do you think I'm doing? It's harvest. Unless you're calling to tell me you want to come over, get naked, and show me you remember what else that mouth of yours is for, I don't want to hear it."

She held the phone away from her ear at that. "Wow," she finally said. "That's classy. Thanks."

"No, that's what you get when you come barging into my house in the middle of the night without an invitation."

"Yeah," she said, swallowing her anger, because there was no point. This was the man who'd promised to love and cherish her. Well, she didn't love him anymore, either, so that made two of them.

This was the worst part of ending a marriage. The bitter taste it left in your mouth, and the bitterness you sensed in his. "That's what I want to talk to you about," she said. "Was my sister there last night? She came home in pretty bad shape."

"I don't know. It was a big party."

"You didn't notice if my *sister* was there," she said flatly.

"I don't keep track of your sisters and who they run around with. Just like I don't care what you do, or who you do it with. You want to hang around with those stuck-up Jacksons and their bitch wives? You go right on ahead."

She had to stop and blink for a minute, her fatigued, fuzzy brain trying to process all that. Well, it made sense. The farmer Lake worked for wasn't anywhere close to the Jackson brothers in the farming world, and as for Lake himself? He was on a whole different level. "I don't care" was easy code for "It's bugging the hell out of me."

"So you're not going to tell me," she finally said.

"Bingo. If you're through being smart, maybe you'll hang up and let me go to bed. I've got a job to go to tomorrow that doesn't involve sitting on my ass in an air-conditioned office, and it starts early."

PARTNERS

Wednesday. The man was thinking about breaking for a snack, considering his options, when the phone buzzed in his pocket. He pulled it out and glanced at the number.

"Yeah?"

The voice on the other end was low, as always. "I heard you ran into some trouble the other night."

He stuck the phone under his chin and said, "I'm working. I'll call you later."

"No, you won't. You've got some girl threatening to go to the cops. You'll tell me about it now."

"Who told you?" His hand clenched tight.

"Never mind who told me. Just know that I'm checking up on you."

"We're partners. Partners trust each other." It wasn't true, of course, and he filed the information away to deal with later. All his partner had to do was scribble notes on little pads, but people always had to get tricky, to think they should be in charge even when they didn't have a clue how to be.

The voice didn't bother to answer that. "If somebody's dropped a dime, we need to make a plan."

"So you know, it's ridiculous for you to be saying 'dropped a dime.' You're the respectable end of this operation. Don't say 'dropped a dime.'"

"What. Is. Going. On." The voice was flat. "Tell me, or our whole deal is over as of now. I can stop this anytime."

"You can. But you won't. You're too used to the money. And I'm not telling you, because trust me, you don't want to know. You can take it that the problem's solved."

"You sure?"

"You could say it's solved permanently. And I've got to go." He ignored the quack at the other end and hung up.

Another thing to deal with. Later. Well, nobody had ever said entrepreneurship was easy. Lots of people had ambition, and most people never made it, because you had to be strong and smart and ruthless to make the big bucks. Luckily, he was all three. It had taken him some years of wasted time to find his true calling, but he'd found it now.

BAD BOYS AND CAKE POPS

It was Saturday morning, and Main Street was closed for five blocks for the weekly farmers' market. Rochelle had dragged Stacy out of bed at nine to shop, and her sister wasn't one bit happy about it.

"Great! Green beans," Rochelle said chirpily. "And look! The pork guy's here. Pork chops and green beans for dinner tonight."

Stacy stared at her, and Rochelle felt like a cheerleader. *Give me a P! Give me an O! PORK!*

"Too perky, huh?" she asked her sister.

"Just because I should still be in bed, and it's already about ninety degrees, and we didn't even drive? Oh, no. Not so much."

"It isn't ninety. It's barely eighty. And walking's good for my thighs." *And you got in at three this morning, and you look like something the cat dragged in,* she didn't add. Rochelle handed the cashier a five and stuck the plastic bag of beans into her shopping bag. "Did you have a good time last night?" she asked, as casually as she could manage, moving over to the pork booth. "What did you guys do?"

"He took me on a helicopter ride, and then we had a picnic in a vineyard," Stacy said.

"Sarcasm's the lowest form of humor. I feel compelled to mention that. And, yeah. Right. He took you to a bar, and then you went back to his place. You know, if he really likes you, he should at least be feeding you. Just pointing that out."

Stacy heaved a sigh. "I don't want a steady, considerate man who's a good provider. I'm twenty-one, not forty. I've never had a really hot guy. I don't look like you. I've got one now, though, and he's so . . . exciting. Didn't you ever like exciting guys?"

Stacy's mood zoomed up and down so much, it was like living with a yo-yo. Last night, before she'd gone out, she'd been bouncing off the walls, but not today.

"Honey," Rochelle said, picking through the cooler full of pork chops and selecting a package, "I was the bad-boy magnet. If there was a bad boy anywhere in the vicinity, he made a beeline straight for me, and I said, 'Hi there, big boy. Come on in.' That's how I know. You're getting the voice of experience here."

"But Lake wasn't that bad," Stacy said.

"Before Lake. And trust me, Lake got bad enough." Rochelle hadn't felt the need to humiliate herself by sharing all the details with her sister. You could look strong, or you could look weak. She preferred strong.

"Well, yeah," Stacy said, "I know you got divorced, but . . . I don't know. He was always sweet to *me*."

"Sure, he could be sweet. That's the appeal of the bad boy. Not that they're bad all the time, because who'd want that? Because they're wild and crazy and rough around the edges, but they love *you,* because you're special."

She ought to know. Lake had called her the night before. The old formula didn't work on her anymore, but it had rattled her just the same.

"Hey, Ro," he'd said, sounding like the easygoing Lake she'd used to know. "I just wanted to say . . . hey, sorry about the other night."

That's OK, she didn't say, because it hadn't been, and because apologies came too easily to Lake. Lashing out when he'd been drinking, then the rush of making up the next day. Which had once been exciting, and then had just been exhausting. Young girls, the kind of girl she'd used to be, might think it was dramatic and sexy, but who wanted to live like that when they were thirty? Not her, anyway.

"I know," he said. "It was over the top. What can I say, I'm a mean son of a bitch sometimes."

"Well, yeah." Except when he wasn't, like now.

"It was a crappy day," he went on. "The AC went out in the combine, if you can believe it. And the night before, everybody had been over at the place, like you saw, and it went too late and too loud. And you know . . . harvest." The weeks when farmers worked fourteen hours a day, six or seven days a week, and their hired men did, too. "I didn't even know you'd been there until the next day. You came by after I'd crashed, I guess. And I took it all out on you. Old habits die hard, huh?"

"That's gracious." She knew she sounded stiff. *Unless you're calling to tell me you want to come over, get naked, and show me you remember what else that mouth of yours is for, I don't want to hear it.* You could only kick a person in the teeth so many times before they wised up, though, and she'd reached her limit a while back.

"Maybe I've changed," he said. "You might be surprised."

"That was the new you?" She knew she shouldn't get back into it, but she couldn't help it. "Then I'd say—you haven't changed enough."

It hadn't been a great conversation, and neither was the one she was having now with Stacy. "But you don't really *know* Shane," her sister was arguing, sounding exactly like Rochelle herself about six or seven years ago. "Just because *you* picked bad guys doesn't mean *he's* one. And maybe I don't want to learn from your experience, anyway. Maybe I want to learn from mine. Maybe I need to make my own mistakes."

That's good, because that's where you're headed. Rochelle bit her tongue on the words and got in line to pay for her pork chops.

"Last year was awful," Stacy said. "Is it so wrong to have some fun this year?"

It was a good point. Her little sister had broken up with her boyfriend at the beginning of the school year, and Rochelle didn't think her love life had gone too smoothly since then, either. To cap it all off, she'd taken a bad fall ice-skating in March and had suffered a broken ankle that had taken its sweet time healing. But it was also true that through all that, she'd managed to hang on to the scholarship that was supposed to get her through that pre-med degree. Stacy had always been smart, always on the right path.

"As long as you keep up with school," Rochelle said, abandoning the rest of her efforts for the time being. "*And* get a job."

Stacy shook her head irritably. "You're worrying for *nothing*. I'm *doing* it."

Not yet, Stacy wasn't. Besides, Rochelle had finally met Shane the night before, and he hadn't done much to dispel her anxieties. Black hair, piercing blue eyes, a lean, wiry build, and a barbed-wire tattoo peeking out of the edge of his T-shirt sleeve. And then a "Hey, Rochelle. Nice to meet you," a not-covert-enough sweep of her figure, and a slow grin that had made her want to slap him.

She'd known a lot of Shanes. They were dark and dangerous, they raised your heart rate, and they were nothing but trouble.

She wanted to say all that to Stacy, but she knew how effective it would have been if somebody had tried to say it to her. So instead, she said, "Maybe you're right. Could be that everybody needs to make their own mistakes. I know I made plenty. Tell you what. Go grab me another pork chop. We'll invite him over tonight, and I'll be prepared to change my mind."

"He's not going to want to have dinner with my sister," Stacy said.

"No? Maybe he'd be flattered to be asked to meet your family." Or maybe he'd be thinking that this was his night for a sister sandwich. He looked like exactly that kind of guy. Rochelle would settle for him staring at her chest enough that even Stacy would notice. "Why don't you invite him and see what he says? You're telling me he's not a bad guy. Give him a chance to show both of us he isn't." Maybe all it would take was one dinner. Maybe Stacy actually *was* smarter than Rochelle. She was going to be a doctor, after all.

Stacy didn't budge, and Rochelle added, "I promise to grill the meat and not him. I'm your sister, not your father."

"Yeah? Not how it seems," Stacy said. "Anyway, he's busy tonight."

"Really? Saturday night? How much do you actually see this guy?"

"Every week, sometime. What does that matter?"

"That doesn't sound like a boyfriend." Rochelle knew she shouldn't say it, but she did anyway. *That sounds like a fuck buddy. Or just a user,* were the things she *didn't* say, because she was at the front of the line, and she was trying for "classy" these days.

Stacy had colored up. "You don't know anything about him. Maybe you should worry more about your own love life and less about mine. I'd rather be in love and not have it work out than not have anybody at all. *Ever.*"

The pork guy had obviously heard that, because he looked up sharply, then wiped his face clear of expression. He took Rochelle's money and handed her the change, and she turned away, trying to ignore the stab her sister's words had given her.

Stacy muttered, "Sorry. But geez. You don't *know.*"

Rochelle considered explaining that a bad guy wasn't actually better than no guy, but Stacy was right. Some lessons, a woman had to learn for herself.

She shook it off, though, and headed back out into the stream of pedestrian traffic along the crowded street. She had to step aside for a family—a mom pushing a chubby, solemn baby in a stroller, a dad with a three-year-old girl on his shoulders clutching two fistfuls of her father's hair—and her heart twisted in spite of herself.

"Well, hey."

It was Travis, right there behind the family. He was laden with plastic bags, sauntering along in Levi's, a short-sleeved Western-style shirt, and a straw cowboy hat. She'd seen him in the office a couple times during the week, but she'd kept it ruthlessly professional, and he hadn't pushed it. Which was probably proof that he hadn't been that interested after all. She didn't want to admit that she'd been a tiny bit disappointed by that. She was full of mixed messages, even to herself.

Now, she cast an eye over him. She couldn't help it, because his shoulders were still broad, his hips were still narrow, and his legs were still long. And he was still that thrilling eight inches or so taller than her five seven. Color her shallow. Stacy wasn't the only one. And as proof that she wasn't interested, her reaction was a dead loss.

"You gone native?" she couldn't help asking.

She saw a quirk at the corner of that delicious mouth. "Now, why would you think that?"

"Cowboy hat. Et cetera."

"It's hot."

"You're from California."

"Well, you got me there." He looked at Stacy, who was, Rochelle realized, staring back at him with interest. "Hi. I'm Travis."

"Stacy Marks." Sounding perkier than she had all morning. "Rochelle's sister."

"Ah," Travis said. "Pleased to meet you."

Rochelle made a reluctant introduction and said, "We were just finishing up." She ignored the outraged glance from Stacy and the muttered, "Oh, *now* we are."

Travis didn't comment, just walked along with them past another booth crowded with students buying cake pops, something Rochelle was giving a big wide berth to. He gestured beyond the cake pops to a huge display of flowers in the next booth. "I just realized I never sent you flowers. Maybe now's the time. What's your favorite?"

Rochelle just looked at him. "No, thanks. Oh. Peaches." She crossed the street and started filling a paper bag, fighting back a sudden lump that wanted to rise in her throat. He thought she was that easy, that a bunch of flowers would have made the difference. But why wouldn't he think that?

If he really likes you, he should at least be feeding you. The voice of experience? Yeah, right. All Travis had had to do was buy her a few shots of tequila. Of course he thought flowers would do it now. But surely, eventually, even a woman as hardheaded as her could learn her lesson.

FLOWER POWER

"Plant," Travis heard. "Not flowers."

The voice had come from beside him, and he realized that Rochelle's sister Stacy was still standing there. He stopped watching Rochelle, although it was tough, because she was wearing a sleeveless white dress with some kind of holes in the fabric. Innocent, summery, and oh so feminine. No cleavage at all, but her legs and arms looked fine, and so did she. And he'd run smack into a brick wall again. He asked, "Pardon?"

Stacy sighed. "Giving her flowers is too easy. Like, here, have some flowers. I just spent twenty bucks. Yay, me."

"Uh . . ." He fought back a smile. "That won't work?"

The girl was shorter than Rochelle, but still curvy, although without her sister's confidence, without the seductive sway to her step and look in her eye that reminded him irresistibly of those old movies with Marilyn Monroe. Like she knew damn well she was sexy, and she also knew that you were wondering if you were man enough to try. Stacy was a dark brunette instead of her sister's blonde, too, but she had the same blue eyes and high cheekbones.

She wasn't Rochelle, but then, so few women were.

Now, she looked at him pityingly. "It sure won't work with Rochelle. At least it didn't look like it to me."

"So . . . what would be better? Got any ideas? She's upset with me, as you've guessed."

The blue eyes sharpened. Intuition must run in the family, too. "Because you didn't send her flowers? I thought she wasn't going out with anybody. You're *kidding*. *Man*. And she was talking to *me* about that."

He passed that one by. "I said she was upset," he said. "I didn't say we'd gone out."

Stacy obviously wanted to ask more, so he looked at her blandly and prompted, "So not flowers?"

"She loves flowers," Stacy said after a moment, abandoning the topic with obvious reluctance. "She loves to *grow* them. And she's got that new house."

Travis shook his head as if he were removing water from his ears. "I've been left back somewhere by the Elks Lodge. I didn't know she had a new house."

"Oh." Stacy looked surprised, and more interested than ever. "I figured she'd have told you, if you knew her. It's one of her big topics. I mean, it's just a rental, but she's excited about it. The yard was crappy when she moved in, but she's been working on it all summer. She used to have a really nice garden back when she was married."

Travis was still digesting that when Rochelle jerked her head at her sister, and Stacy said, "I have to go." She looked back over her shoulder as she went and said, "But get her something she can plant. It'll work better. She likes that steady thing, anyway. That good-guy thing. House and garden, you know?"

"Wait," Travis said. "How about giving me the address, so I can deliver it?"

Stacy hesitated. "She's had kind of bad luck with guys."

"Yeah," he said. "I know. That's the point."

◆　◆　◆

An hour later, he pulled his truck to a careful stop to avoid tipping over the pot in the bed. It had taken him a while to find her place, because this wasn't so much a street as an alley, gravel and all. And Stacy was right about the gardening. The yard of the unprepossessing duplex, its shabby siding painted a glaring turquoise, was edged by a neatly cut hedge. On the left side, the space inside was filled with rosebushes, with a big white birdbath in the center. Not that side, then, because those had been there a while. On the right side, a sizable vegetable patch boasted neat rows of potatoes, onions, tomatoes, and cabbage, as well as the remains of some bolted lettuce and spinach. Around it, the rest of the small space was dotted with young plants and shrubs. That was more like it. That had to be Rochelle's.

The smell of warm bark mulch drifted into his nostrils, familiar as home, as he hauled the giant bush out of the back of the truck and headed up the walk on the right. He shifted it to one arm and rang the bell, then waited, his heart beating harder than he cared to acknowledge.

The inner door opened at last, and Rochelle was staring at him through the screen door, and through his own screen of huge white blooms.

She seemed to have lost her voice for the moment, so he spoke first. "The flower idea didn't work, so I'm going for plan B. Point me to a shovel and a spot, and I'll plant it for you."

"I said no. No means no."

Danger zone, and no mistake. He thought fast. "Did you? I thought you just said you weren't a fringe benefit. How about if I let you know I heard that, and you let me set this thing down? I was regretting my choice before I got two blocks, by the way. It's a long way to my place from that booth, and I hadn't brought the truck. Plus, I wanted to impress you, so I got the biggest one. Typical guy."

"This is where we don't talk about whether size matters." She was still on the other side of the screen, but he thought she might have been smiling a bit.

"Hey," he said, "I'm ready and willing to have that conversation." This was more like it. "Meanwhile . . . shovel? Spot? Otherwise, best case, I'm going to be putting it out on the sidewalk in front of my place and hoping somebody takes it. Carol will kill me if I plant anything in her garden. Woman's got an obsessive streak a mile wide. You should hear her on the subject of nail holes. And anyway, I don't need a hydrangea."

"You know what it is?"

"My mom has them. She likes them. I took a chance. So, what? Rip it out of the pot and stuff it in my garbage?"

"No!" The word came out too forcefully, and he smiled. He'd known that would do it. Would have worked on his mom, too. She felt the same way seeing plants drooping and dying as some people would have about a thirsty pet.

"It's like they're crying for help," she'd say, and he could tell Rochelle felt the same.

"Wait a second," Rochelle said. "How'd you find out where I lived?"

"I asked somebody."

He thought that was a pretty crafty evasion, but all she said was, "Wait."

He stood there for close to five minutes, and Rochelle didn't come out. He finally set the pot down just as a screen door slammed to his left and a vision emerged.

A lady in her seventies, probably, wearing a brightly printed flowered muumuu, the sun nearly striking sparks off her poofy platinum hair. A pageboy, he thought that was called. Not a hairstyle you saw a lot of these days. A little white dog with a curly coat and legs about four inches long pattered along after her.

Mrs. Next-Door came down the steps, her gait spritely, unwound her hose, turned the water on, and smiled at him. Her red lipstick matched her huge red-flowered earrings, and he smiled back. She was that kind of person.

"Morning," she said, directing the water beneath a rosebush. "Beautiful day." The little dog skittered away from the water in alarm as if it had been a fire hose, which made Travis smile some more.

"It is," Travis said. "Looks like your roses are doing well."

"Not too bad. They keep telling me it's too hot, and I keep telling *them* that there's plenty of time to be cold after you're dead. Roses sometimes need a little tough love."

He laughed. "That so?"

"Roses are babies. Kinda like a handsome man that way. You put up with their nonsense because you enjoy looking at them so much."

Her flip-flop sandals each had a big red flower in the center, he noticed. Matching her earrings. And her lipstick.

He was trying to figure out an answer to that, and deciding that Rochelle might not be coming out and trying to decide what to do about *that,* when she walked around from the back of the house carrying a shovel. She must have done a lightning change, because she was in cutoffs, a T-shirt, and work boots.

He got distracted. His mind went, "Legs," and everything else went on vacation for a moment.

Rochelle looked around, walked over to a spot in the corner of the yard, and stomped the shovel down hard into the dirt. That was distracting too, because she was facing away from him.

He said, "Nice talking to you" to the neighbor, grabbed his pot, and was over with Rochelle in a few strides. It wasn't a very big yard.

"Oh, no," he said, setting the plant down carefully and grabbing hold of the shovel. "That's part two of my big gesture."

She wrestled with him a moment, and he enjoyed it. He got a nice flash of a much better wrestling match, and then she let go of the handle and wrecked his fantasy. "You won't know how to do it, though," she said.

I know how to do it. He didn't say that, of course. "Same depth as the pot," he said. "Three times the diameter."

"How do you know?"

"I could tell you I'm an expert gardener, but you'd find out I was lying. I looked it up."

She glanced at his feet. "When you changed into your boots."

"Yep."

Now, she was looking past him. "You have work boots. And you have a pickup. And none of it's new. I thought you were from San Francisco."

He jammed the shovel into the dirt with his boot. "Everybody comes from somewhere. Even people who've been living in San Francisco."

"Huh. I'm trying not to ask you where. And the ground's hard. Sorry."

"Baked like concrete," he agreed, putting some extra stomp into it. "Because it's been so hot. That's all right. I'm used to hot, and I'm used to hard."

"I thought San Francisco was foggy."

"It is." He kept digging. "But the Imperial Valley's hotter than any-place but the surface of the sun. At least a hundred degrees from June through September. That's why I'm not there. That, and there isn't too much software development going on down there."

"That where your folks are? And all right, I'm asking. Where is it?"

"My mom is." This wasn't the conversation he wanted to have. "She's living in Brawley. Very Southern California, very inland. Never mind. You'll never have heard of it. Your yard's looking good," he continued, changing the subject.

"Not good enough. It needs trees, but I'm not doing trees. Stupid to do all this when it isn't really mine, but I can't help it."

"Not stupid," he said. "Not if it makes you feel settled. Why not trees?"

She shrugged. "When I plant a tree, you'll know I've hung it up."

He shot a quick look at her. "Hung up what?"

"Never mind."

He'd gotten his hole dug now, and he tipped the plant gently and eased it out of the pot, then set it into the hole and started to backfill.

"You do know how," Rochelle said. "I'll get the hose."

He filled the hole halfway with dirt, then waited until she came back to water it down before he went on. As they were waiting for the water to soak in, he said, "Not really supposed to plant them in the heat, so you'll have to keep it well watered."

"You actually did look it up."

"I'm an engineer. Occupational hazard." He finished the backfilling, tamped the dirt down, and, once she'd finished soaking the area, took the hose from her and cleaned off the shovel, giving the caked soil a shove with his boot to loosen it.

He handed the shovel back to her and said, "There you go."

She stood there and sighed. "I'm trying so hard not to find it attractive that you know how to do man things."

He had to laugh out loud. No choice. "Digging a hole's a pretty low bar. You got any shelves you need put up, maybe a fence, and we'll be talking."

"I know how to put up shelves. But you can build a fence?"

"Some say so." She was close enough that he could smell the faint floral scent of her perfume, and he wanted to touch her so badly.

"Well," she said, and visibly shook it off, lifting the shovel. "Too bad I don't need a fence."

"Could you use dinner?"

She didn't answer for a moment, and he tried to pretend he didn't care one way or the other.

"No," she finally said. "Thanks, but no. You're here for a semester. The plant was a nice thought, though. Thanks." And she took her shovel and the pot the hydrangea had come in and disappeared around the side of the house.

MAGPIE HARVEST

The following Saturday, Cal Jackson made the wide turn in the combine that would finish off the lentil field, then headed down along the gap between the buttes towards the next one. He was only a few days away from the end of harvest, and he was ready for it to be done. This year, he had other priorities, and fourteen hours a day cutting was feeling like six hours too long.

He'd been seeing the magpies for a while now. Every time he made a turn around the field, he spotted them in the same place. The black-and-white wings diving, then rising again, a continuous whirlwind. There was something dead in the ditch for sure. Something big, judging by the number of birds. A deer, probably.

He glanced at the birds now, rising into the air as they were disturbed by the vibration from the big combine's wheels. When they cleared the area, he caught sight of something in the weeds, something that was the wrong color. Something blue where there shouldn't have been blue. Blue . . . cloth. Denim.

He hesitated a moment, one hand on the wheel, the other on the gear lever. *Probably nothing.* The stirring in some ancient part of his consciousness wouldn't let it go, though, and instead of driving on, he put his foot on the brake and turned the key.

The minute his head was outside the door and his foot on the step, the stench filled his nostrils. *A deer,* he tried to tell himself again as he walked around the back of the hulking machine. *No need to look.* But he knew it wasn't true.

The weeds were thick in the long ditch that ran between the buttes. There was nothing visible but that one scrap of denim fabric. He forced his feet to keep moving forward, and was almost on top of it before he could see what lay under the weeds.

When he did see, he rocked to a stop.

The magpies had done their job. The shirt had once been pink, you could tell by the tiny cap sleeves, but was mostly a rusty brown now. A color he knew too well after a life as a professional athlete.

Something long and dark streaming along the ground between the weeds.

Hair. Long hair.

The cold had seeped all the way through to his bones. His legs were frozen. He wanted nothing more than to be gone from here, but he couldn't move. All at once, he turned from the waist and was violently sick into the weeds. Gasping and choking on the stink, on the thought.

Then he was leaving the combine behind and pounding down the dirt road to where he'd left his rig. Running hard in the smothering heat, even though there was no amount of speed that could help the thing in the ditch.

Running fast, his boots raising a cloud of dust. Running back into cell-phone range. Back to call the sheriff.

WATER AND CHOCOLATE

About the only thing good Travis could say about his first week of teaching was that nobody had actually fallen asleep or burst into tears of frustration, at least not right there in front of him. He'd thought it would be a piece of cake to teach computer-game design and virtual environments, but he'd realized pretty quickly that knowing the material and teaching it were two different things, even with a syllabus and lecture notes.

Which was why he'd been in the office on Saturday, trying to figure it out before his Tuesday class. Well, that and it was cooler in the office than in his non-air-conditioned apartment. The temperature had fallen some over the past week, but the mercury had started climbing again the day before, and it was supposed to reach ninety-eight today.

Now, though, he'd done the best he could do on next week's lesson plans, and he was thinking he'd check out a reservoir he'd heard about north of town. Swimming outdoors would feel about as good as anything could. Anything he was likely to get, anyway, since he still hadn't solved the problem of Rochelle, and somehow, he couldn't let it go.

It was seeing her around that was messing him up. Every time he'd worked himself up to thinking, *All right, forget that and find somebody else. It's been too long, and you're here for four months,* he'd pass her in the hallway or have to deliver some paperwork—some paperwork he could have put in the interoffice mail—and she'd be looking at him with her cool eyes and sassy mouth, all that body and all those memories, and he'd be right back at square one. He hadn't been hung up on a woman in a long time, but it sure looked like he was hung up on this one. Just another thing that had changed, and wasn't that inconvenient.

He locked his office door, and was headed for the stairs when he heard the *ding* of the elevator. He glanced over to see the doors opening, and just like that, he was pivoting and stepping inside.

Because there was Rochelle, in a flippy yellow skirt and a soft, stretchy shirt. Not something his feet were ever going to be carrying him away from. Rochelle, holding a cardboard box that looked heavy.

She glanced at him, then looked away. Bad start.

"Here," he said, reaching for the box. "Let me. Taking this to the car?"

"No. Basement storage." She let go, though.

"Oh." He realized that he hadn't hit the "1" button, shifted the box into one hand, and did it. The elevator hesitated, then continued down with a sickening lurch.

"Whoa," Rochelle said, rocking on her feet at the jolt.

The car stopped, and Rochelle kept her eyes on the doors. But Travis still had her box. That gave him maybe five minutes, if he took it to the basement for her, which he had every intention of doing. She liked men who could do man things? Well, he was volunteering here and now to do every single man thing there was. Starting with carrying this box.

It took a few seconds to register that the doors weren't opening. And that both the "1" and the "B" were still lit up on the floor indicator. Rochelle punched the button once more, and the car lurched again, then stopped. The lights flickered and died, and there was darkness for a split second before some kind of emergency lighting came on.

Rochelle sucked in an audible breath, but Travis had already set the box down and was pushing the "Door Open" button. The elevator didn't move, but at least it wasn't lurching anymore.

"Huh," he said.

She was reaching around him and punching buttons herself now. Every one of them. And the car still wasn't moving.

"How high up do you think we are?" she asked.

He considered. "Twenty-five, thirty feet, maybe."

"Oh." She let out her breath in a long, controlled sigh. "Don't really want to fall, then."

"We aren't going to fall. We're good, I promise. When was the last time you heard about an elevator falling?"

"*Die Hard.*"

He couldn't help smiling. "Movie."

"Still. It made an impression."

Damn, but she made him laugh. He pulled his cell phone out of his pocket and looked at it. "No service. How about you?"

"They don't work in here." She paced a step forward, then had to stop. Nowhere to go. "All right. Calming down."

He put a hand on her back and rubbed once, and she jumped. "Hey," he said softly. "We're all right. I promise. It's going to be fine."

Her head swung around, and he said, "What? That was wrong?"

She sighed. "Never mind. You confuse me."

He might be trapped, but he wasn't feeling too bad at all. "Makes two of us. Let's try something else. It's a little obvious, but . . ." He opened the door in the wall panel and pulled out the receiver, then waited until he got an operator.

By the time he hung up the phone, Rochelle wasn't looking happy.

"Hour and a half at least," he said. "They dispatch out of Spokane."

She was pressed against the far wall with her arms crossed over her chest, nothing about her body language suggesting she was stuck in an elevator with her dream man.

"Want to sit down?" he asked. "Since we'll be here awhile."

She looked at him, her eyes narrowed. "You didn't arrange this somehow, did you?"

He had to laugh. "Not enough skills, sorry. And I don't usually trap women. Not even ones I like as much as you." He got an involuntary jerk of her head for that. "The elevator getting stuck—that's bad luck. Me getting stuck in it with you? That's maybe not such bad luck. From my point of view."

"You always take the elevator to go down a couple flights?"

"Only when somebody special is in it." He got an almost-smile for that one that she instantly wiped off her face. "And I've got . . ." He slung the backpack he'd been carrying over one shoulder around to the front, opened it, and rummaged around in there. "A bottled water and a candy bar. What do you think? Picnic?"

She'd uncrossed her arms, anyway. "What kind of candy bar?"

"Snickers."

She sighed. "Had to be my favorite."

"I do like a woman who enjoys her chocolate." He indicated the floor. "Shall we?"

She dropped down to the tiled floor, and he sat down a careful couple feet away from her, both of their backs against the wall. He could tell that, if she'd had a moment of weakness during their hydrangea episode, she'd had plenty of time to think it over since, and he hadn't come out on the winning side of the equation.

"Stupid building. Stupid budget cuts," she muttered. "Did I mention that this freaks me out?"

He yanked the top open on the water bottle and handed it over to her. "We'll be all right. Sit tight and wait, that's all. Of course, if I were really a hero, I'd be figuring out how to get out of this thing and rescue you. Or I'd already know how from my Navy SEAL training."

She looked at him in astonishment. "You were a SEAL?"

"Nope. That's why I'm not rescuing you. We need any emergency computer programming, though, we're all set." He held up the Snickers bar and waggled it. "Got this, though."

"Almost as good." She smiled at him, finally, and he grinned back, broke the candy bar in two, and handed her half.

They sat and chewed a minute in silence. This was his big chance, and he didn't want to blow it. "So," he finally settled on. "You always work on Saturday? I'm surprised." *Neutral topic.*

"I like to start off the year ahead of the curve. Get everything organized. Surprised why? That I take my job seriously?"

Not so neutral. "No. You're a capable woman. Pretty hard not to notice that."

"I wish you'd quit it."

"What?"

"Being nice."

He laughed out loud. "What else would I be doing?"

"Oh, you know." She shrugged and didn't look at him. "Grabbing me. Or at least telling me that you knew how we could spend the next couple hours. Like that'd be my big treat, being put on my back on a floor that gets mopped about once a month."

That sobered him up fast. "You don't have a real high opinion of men, do you?"

She started to speak, then stopped and thought, and he watched her face. "Depends on the man," she finally said. "I like some men just fine. I like my dad. My brothers and most of my cousins, too. A few others. But you know, if they're related to you, they're not thinking with their . . . well."

He stopped chewing for a moment, then swallowed, and she handed him the water bottle. "Yeah," he said. "There's that."

"And I know," she said, "that I did the same thing with you. There were two of us making that decision. And this would be the part where I tell you that I don't usually do things like that, and you pretend to believe me."

"Oh, I don't know," he said. "You don't strike me as much of a liar. So go ahead."

"Well . . ." She fussed with her shirt, pulling it down, then settling it around her waist. He watched, which was a mistake, because looking at Rochelle's shirt was way too distracting. It was light purple, with some kind of swirly pattern, and it was thin. If he looked closely, he could almost see through it to the pale skin beneath. Not that he was trying to see through her shirt. Much.

"I don't," she said. "Do that. For the record."

He took another sip of water and thought a second. "Right. Minefield. I'm going to say, I'm still glad you did it with me. And that I'd be happy to know I was the only one." *Then and now.*

"Politically incorrect," she said. "Possessive, with no right to be."

"Guilty again. Or just a man willing to tell you the truth."

"Which would be why, of course . . ." *You said you'd call me and you didn't.* She didn't say it, but she didn't have to.

"No. That would be me being stupid. In all sorts of ways. So, since we're here talking anyway—why *did* you do it? How did I get that lucky?"

He wasn't sure she was going to answer at all, but she finally said, "Just the usual thing. I guess I don't always think with my higher powers myself. I sure wasn't doing it that night. But I'd done so much holding back, not wanting to get another reputation in this town after my divorce. When you look like me, it's not that hard to do."

"Plenty of guys volunteering to help you take the fall, I'm sure. Divorced, huh? So tell me. Why would a man who had a woman like you let her go?"

She glanced quickly across at him, then away, and he said, "Yeah, I know. I did that. But I've just told you I was stupid, because you're . . ." He took a breath and went for it. Might as well put it on the line. "You're smart, honest, funny as hell, obviously hardworking, and about the hottest thing I've ever seen." She shifted slightly, and he thought back over what he'd said. "Am I not supposed to say you were hot? That you're still hot? I'm trying hard here. Give me a clue. Help me out."

The way she was sitting, with her knees drawn up, had that little skirt falling up her thighs a bit, and he couldn't help a quick glance. They looked exactly as good as they had nine months earlier. They looked terrific. He didn't dare look down her shirt, because it was a V-neck. Not a low one, but it didn't matter. There was no way that glance would be quick. A man could drown in her body, and be happy to go.

"I'm not going to talk about my ex," she said, and he forced his mind back to their conversation. "No bad-mouthing the ex."

"True," he said, "if this were a date. But we've gotten that out of the way. There's not much you could say that would make me lose interest. So come on. We've got a couple hours here. Let's tell stories."

"You going to tell me yours, too?"

"If you're into bad drama," he said, and she laughed, her blue eyes lighting up, and he smiled back at her.

"Right," she said. "My ex. You asked for it. My daddy didn't like him, but I'd had a crush on him since the eighth grade. I thought he was hot. Which used to be a problem of mine. In the past. So eventually, I married him, and he spent a few years proving my daddy right. He had the same job as my dad, you see."

"What job is that?"

She looked him in the eye. "Hired man. And because you're not from here, I'll clue you in. There's a wide world of difference between a farmer and a hired man. Except not with my dad, there isn't." She looked fierce now. "There aren't many men in this town more stand-up than my dad, and everybody knows it. But sometimes, when you've got a good dad, you don't realize that not all men are that good. You don't get it. I didn't get it."

"I can see that," he said. "I had a good dad myself. Always thought I'd grow up to be like him, I guess, like it was inherited. Like it was automatic. I found out it wasn't that easy."

"Yeah? How?"

He shook his head. "You first."

She looked like she still wanted to ask, but she went on. "It wasn't the best, but I did what you do. Told myself it wasn't so bad, that this was real life, that nobody was perfect. I was coming around to it, but I was coming around slowly, because my parents have been married thirty-two years, and I wanted that. Anyway, I don't like to give up."

She reached for the water bottle. Her hand brushed his, and the hair rose on his arm at the contact. He watched her take a long swallow, her head back, her throat working, and he was in two places at once. He was listening. He was. She had his attention, and her words had even touched that still-aching spot in his heart. But he was watching her swallow, and . . . damn.

She put the bottle down, not seeming to notice. "Until the day I went to a work with a fever of a hundred and one, and my boss sent me home again. It was winter, and Lake was home, too. I thought I could climb in bed and he'd bring me soup or something. Ha."

"And what happened?"

"Walked in on him and a waitress from down at the Kozy Korner doing the horizontal tango, that's what."

"Ouch."

"And you know what was the worst? What he was doing to her, he'd been too lazy to do to me for a good long time. There he was, though, going out of his way, giving her the good stuff."

"Ah." He glanced down her body again. He couldn't help it. "That your favorite?"

He could tell she was remembering exactly the same thing he was. "Not too many women out there who don't enjoy that, I'll bet. Which you already knew."

His heart had been beating harder ever since he'd stepped into the elevator with her. Now, his pulse rate kicked up into another gear as he remembered her on that white hotel bed, gloriously naked, his body sliding down hers before his hands went to those thighs and pushed them slowly apart. He remembered the way she'd moaned before he'd even started, the way she'd shifted under his hands, unable to wait, and the rush it had given him. And how determined he'd been to make it good.

If he got the chance again, he'd be making it better. "Good to know," he said, his voice coming out strangled in spite of his best efforts at casual. "Just in case."

She shook her head, the blonde hair swaying. "You get me off track."

"You aren't the only one." He fought to remember what—what *else*—they'd been talking about. "We've got an hour to go, easy, so you may as well tell me what happened next."

"Well—I think there are two kinds of people. The kind who see something like that and run, and the kind who make somebody else run."

"Ha. Kicked his ass out?"

"Right out into the snow. Both of them. Barely gave them time to grab their clothes. Until I remembered that the house went with his job, and I didn't want it anyway. But not before I set fire to my wedding gown in the burn barrel out back, along with his collection of concert T-shirts."

His laugh bounced off the elevator walls. "Bet that hurt."

She sighed in reminiscence. "Don't piss me off. Especially when I have a fever."

"I'll remember that. What kind of music?"

"Heavy metal. You like metal?"

"I hate it. Sounds like screaming to me. Makes me agitated. Life's agitating enough as it is. That the right answer?"

She took another swallow of water, and he watched her again, but this time, he was smiling as well as watching. "Yep," she said. "That's the right answer. So I moved to town, got my own place, and to my everlasting surprise, my life got better. The divorce was a whole lot easier than the marriage. Didn't have to pretend I wasn't kicking butt at my job so he wouldn't feel bad, didn't have to watch my paycheck disappear on beer and weed. I had it all. Except, of course, that my eggs are drying up by the day."

That one caught him off guard. "Wow. Sucker punch to the gut there."

She looked right at him. "No point messing around. Literally. No *time* to mess around. I'm thirty-one. The other reason I don't go home with guys I meet in bars."

"Got it."

"So," she said. "With that in mind, want to reconsider our chat here?"

"You know what?" He smiled at her, got a smile in return. "I'm going to keep on going. Guess I like to live dangerously."

"All right, then. Unfortunately, so do I." She straightened her legs, wriggled closer to the wall, and tugged her skirt down her thighs.

He watched her do it and said, "You're killing me here. You do realize that."

She flipped one corner of the skirt up, revealing most of that luscious thigh, and he about had a heart attack. "It's a skort," she said. "I rode my bike, and I didn't want to flash the whole town. So you can wipe that picture right out of your head."

"You know what picture I had in my head?"

"What, that wasn't it?"

"The skirt one? Keeping our clothes on in case somebody showed up early, except for a couple strategic items? Yeah. That was pretty much it. But I was going to be chivalrous. I was going to be the one on the floor on my back. It was going to be a sacrifice, though. So you know."

Her eyes widened. "Oh, nice. You always have to be on top?"

"No. I sure don't. The sacrifice would have been being in the perfect spot to watch you, and not taking off your clothes."

It took her a second, but she fired right back at him. "You just hang on to your fantasy."

"Thanks. I believe I will." He smiled at her, and he could swear her pupils dilated. Just like that, he got a kick of lust down low in his belly that had him shoving a knee up fast.

"So," she said after a minute. "I looked you up, you know. You come by that in-charge thing the honest way, I guess. And there I was hoping it was because you were a rancher."

"How's that?" *Let's stay with the clothes,* he didn't say. *Or without them.* He could remember exactly how she'd sucked in her breath that first time he'd slid his hand inside her shirt. He wanted to hear that noise again.

She made a wide circle with the water bottle she still held. "Come on. Keep up. Rich start-up guy? Owned your own company? Invented some . . . some . . ."

"With a partner," he said. "Yeah. I did that." *OK. Not the clothes. Alas.* "An internal communications app for companies that turned into a whole software bundle. We were trying to develop a multiplayer game—a *great* game, by the way—and the app was a by-product that turned out to be the thing the market wanted. I could tell you more about it, but you'd want to run screaming from the room, and that's not an option, so . . ."

"Because I'm not smart enough to understand?" Her eyes were flashing now.

"No. Because it's boring."

That made her smile, but she pressed on. "So why aren't you still doing it? Why would you be taking about ten thousand dollars to teach a couple classes for one semester in north Idaho? It's hardly even minimum wage, and it's nobody's road to the big time."

He put a hand to the back of his head, gave it a scratch, and grimaced. "Sure you don't have a few softball questions we could warm up with?"

"Hey. You went straight to my marriage."

"That's true. I did. Well, we'll call this two birds with one stone. Because it'll also explain why I took off on you the way I did. I got back to San Francisco and walked right into a big ol' mess. Which was my fault."

She didn't answer, just kept looking at him, and after a minute, he went on. "That partnership of mine ended in a bang, not a whimper. And then some other things happened."

When she still didn't say anything, he sighed. "You're going to make me tell you the whole story, aren't you?"

"Nope. Not if you don't care about getting to know me better."

"Right. The whole story, then. Except I haven't told this to anybody, and I have a feeling it isn't going to help me much to tell it now."

"I'm real big on honesty," she said, and he looked into those blue eyes and knew she was telling the truth.

"We'll see how big you are on it when you hear this. But I'm pretty big on honesty myself these days, so what the hell, I'll give it a shot."

He stopped a minute, and she sat there and waited some more until he finally spoke. For an outspoken woman, she sure could shut up when she had to. She knew how to push a man to talk. By not filling in the gaps.

"I had this partner," he said. "I guess you know that, if you looked me up. Steve Harrison. Flashier guy than me, the public face. He was married to somebody he'd been with since before we'd started, when all we had a wild idea and no capital at all. I'd known *her* since the beginning, too. I liked her, even if I thought she deserved better than him. Fidelity-wise."

"Oh, boy," she breathed. "I have a feeling you're right. I'm not going to like this story."

"Yeah. Steve had really gotten into the whole tech-star thing, you know. Well, I probably had, too, to be honest. Hadn't kept my feet on the ground nearly as well as I'd tried to believe. I hadn't been a real stick-to-it kind of guy when it came to women lately, either. Not exactly the faithful type myself. Not the *unfaithful* type," he hurried to add, "just . . ."

"Never mind," she said. "I get it."

"I didn't even know the two of them had been having trouble until this one night, though, right before that trip when I came up to the Northwest. When I met you."

"Uh-huh," she said into the silence. "This one night."

"Anyway, Claire—his wife—she showed up at my place that night crying, so I poured her a glass of wine, and then I poured her another one, and we killed that bottle and opened another one, and she told me all about it."

"I think I can tell the rest of this story," Rochelle said.

"You said you were big on honesty."

"Maybe not as big as I thought. But go ahead. You're helping me stay strong. So you know."

Well, wasn't *that* good news? *No.* He plowed on. No choice, now. "They'd split up, and I guess it was a low point for her, the way it can be, I suppose."

"Uh-huh. Been there."

"So she was telling me she'd wasted her life. Asking me, did I think she was still pretty, did I think anybody would . . . want her."

He shrugged convulsively, more of a shudder, remembering. Exactly how wrong he'd played it. And the nagging suspicion that maybe he'd been pissed enough at Steve that he'd thought, *How about if I did your wife? What would you think about that?* And what that made him.

He didn't say that to Rochelle, of course. He wasn't a complete moron. "And I said, sure, of course, she was still beautiful, and she was going to find somebody better who deserved her. Maybe laid it on kinda thick. She *was* pretty, and we were both a little drunk. And she came up closer and said . . . had I ever wanted to kiss her."

"I got it," Rochelle said. She didn't sound happy about it, either.

"So we . . . yeah," he went on. "We started fooling around, and it was getting serious, going pretty far, and then she sat back and looked at me and . . . and asked me."

Big brown eyes swimming with tears and passion, or maybe just wine and desperation. Claire, whom he'd always had a thing for, lying back against the arm of his couch, her shirt gone, her breasts swelling soft and round above the cups of the lacy bra, the abrasion of his beard burn showing red on her white skin, her breath coming hard from her pretty pink mouth.

"Please, Wayne. Let's do it. Please."

He wasn't looking at Rochelle now. He was staring across at the steel doors, remembering.

"The way she said it," he said slowly, "it snapped me back. It made me see that it wasn't about me. It was about her trying to prove something to herself, and to Steve, even if he'd never know. It should've been with somebody who cared about her, not somebody who was willing to nail anybody who showed up. Steve was my partner, too, even though I wasn't liking him too much at the moment, and she was way too vulnerable right then, and I'd be an asshole both ways."

He couldn't look at Rochelle. Why had he started this? But he had. It was like, once he'd stopped pretending, he couldn't help it anymore. The truth just came out.

"So I told her no," he said, "and it seemed like that was even worse than if we'd done it, because I was rejecting her, like the making out hadn't been good enough, like she hadn't been sexy enough. When in reality," he went on, knowing that saying this was an even worse idea, "hell, I'm a guy. It was plenty good enough, because there she was, halfway to naked, and she looked good that way. She cried and ran out, and the whole thing was pretty damn horrible. And the next day, I breathed a great big sigh of relief and flew to Spokane and thought I'd been an idiot, and thank God that was over."

"And then you found somebody without all that tricky baggage, somebody you didn't have to say no to."

"Oh, hell." He should have known that that would be how she'd take it. He hadn't told anybody this, and he shouldn't have done it now. "No. That wasn't it. My flight was canceled, I was frustrated and stuck, and nothing seemed like it was going right with my life, even though I should've been on top of the world. And then there you were, and you were exactly that. Right. I should have . . ." He stopped, waited, breathed. "I can't say it well enough. I told you, I'm not good at talking."

"Well, no, you're not wowing me right now."

"I know I'm not, but I'm telling you anyway. I screwed up, and I kept on doing it. The plane landed, I went into the office, and Steve punched me in the face."

"She told him."

"Yep. They'd made up, and he'd 'confessed' all the cheating he'd been doing, and I guess she wanted something to confess, too."

"She wanted to make him jealous, to make him want her. So she said she'd slept with you."

"She sure did. And how could I say no, I didn't? That she'd come on to me, and I'd turned her down? When that was her big thing she could hold over his head? It would've been like slapping her in the face all over again, and he wouldn't have believed me anyway. And in any case, it didn't matter. All it did was make the end come faster between us."

"How long were you partners?"

"Eight years. Which is about two dinosaur ages in the software world." A lot of history to vanish in a day, but vanish it had.

He told her the rest of it, then. How they'd agreed that Steve, the public face of the company, would buy Travis out, because he wanted it more. And if Travis thought Steve would have a hard time keeping it going without him, or keeping his shaky marriage intact—well, either Travis would have the satisfaction of being right, or it was wishful thinking. Anyway, it didn't matter anymore.

"You're right," Rochelle said. "That's a sad story. And you come out of it a lot better than I thought, by the way. That was stand-up of you not to tell him. And not to sleep with her, too."

"Better if I hadn't come so close."

"You want a list of the dumb mistakes I've made? It's long."

"You're generous."

"I'm alive. Anybody who hasn't made any mistakes by the time they get to this point? Either they're lying to themselves, or they haven't ever tried anything. And if you're going to forgive other people, I guess you'd better be able to forgive yourself."

He sat for a moment and took that in. "The rest of it's sadder," he warned her. "And worse. As far as how I come out of it."

She just looked at him some more, and he turned the water bottle in his hands and wondered how much to tell her. Why was he telling her at all? Because they had a bunch more time to spend in here, and spending it making out wasn't an option. Because it was the only way she was going to trust him. Or maybe even because he wanted her to know who he was. Some sort of protective layer seemed to have been scraped off him these past months, or some self-delusional one. He'd made his mistakes, he'd faced them and done his best to atone for them, so what difference would it make to admit them?

"It takes a while," he finally said, "to dissolve a partnership in a successful company. To work out the details. It takes lawyers."

"The payout," she said.

"Yep." He had the feeling she wasn't going to be impressed by how much money he had. In fact, that would probably make her warier than ever. "So in the midst of all that, my mom called, said my dad was having another bad spell, and maybe I should come home. And I was impatient again, because I'd just been home at Christmas, and I was busy, and that was the last thing I needed. So I said I'd come home when I was done, but it was going to be a while."

He closed his eyes for a moment and remembered.

"Be better if it was now, baby," his mom had said on the phone.

He'd sighed. "Is he actually in the hospital?"

"No. But I think you should come anyway."

Another flare of impatience. When his dad had had the first episode of shortness of breath and chest pain and the doctor had diagnosed congestive heart failure, Travis had been as worried as everybody else. His parents had sold the farm and moved to town, though, and his tough-as-leather old man had had valve replacement surgery and had come through it OK. After that, his parents had settled into a new normal, a quiet life punctuated regularly by more of his dad's "episodes," which had resolved every time. Travis hadn't been able to keep running home for every episode. He'd had a business to manage.

"I'll come," he'd promised. "For a day or two. As soon as I'm done with this."

He and Steve had been within a few uncomfortable days of final signatures when his mom had called again. He'd picked up the phone, and before she could say anything, he'd said, "I'll be there as soon as I can, if you still need me. I said I'd come visit, and I will. But this is important."

He hadn't told her what it was about. Time enough for that when he got there. He wouldn't tell them what was behind it, even then. They didn't need to know that, or he didn't want to see the look on their faces when he said it. Especially not on his dad's. His dad thought the world was black and white, good and bad, and, most of all, right and wrong. What Travis had done would've been nothing but wrong, no matter what anybody else had done, and he hadn't wanted to hear it.

"Oh, baby." His mother's voice had broken, and all of a sudden, he'd been sitting up straight, ice running down his spine. "Daddy died."

HOLDING ON

Rochelle sat still, her hand at her heart. "Oh, no."

When they'd first gotten stuck in this elevator, she'd been plenty uncomfortable. Travis had relaxed her, and after that, he'd turned her on. He'd talked to her about *not* taking her clothes off, had smiled at her, and the tingle had turned to a buzz. Exactly like before.

And then, of course, he'd started talking about cheating. By the time he got around to *not* cheating, her emotions had been up and down so much, you'd have thought this elevator was actually working. And when he'd said, "She told me he was dead," her heart was in the basement.

Her hand went out to touch his own, lying relaxed on his knee. His knuckles, she realized, were as decorated with the white crescents and dings of scar tissue as any she'd ever seen. That hand was altogether too big, too hard, and too banged-up to belong to an office worker. Travis was a walking, talking contradiction. If he hadn't been here teaching computer science, she'd have assumed he was lying.

He turned and looked at her, his expression set. "Yeah. All that time I'd been dicking around, thinking I was doing the important stuff—I'd been missing seeing him for the last time."

"But you couldn't have known. You said it was sudden, a turn for the worse."

He shrugged impatiently. "Sure I could've. If I'd listened. Anyway. I went home for the funeral, and I thought, all right, here you go, Cochran. Lost your dad without a chance to say good-bye. Lost your partner. Lost your company. Not doing so hot, are you, big shot? Time to try something different."

"So what did you do?" She'd thought she hadn't wanted to hear his story, because it hadn't fit her model of her dream man. But there were no dream men. He was just a man. Just a man screwing up and determined to try again. Just like her.

"I did a lot of things."

"The pickup," she realized. "That rig you're driving. Was it . . ."

"My dad's? Yep. I thought about why he was driving something that old, and . . ."

"Oh. Because your mom would get the newer car," she realized.

He looked startled. "How do you know?"

"Because that would be my dad, too. Besides that my dad's a farmer, and farmers don't get rid of something if they can keep it running."

"Yep. Farmers hold on." He leaned his head back against the wall, and for once, she wasn't looking at the strong brown column of his throat and thinking how much she'd like to kiss it. Well, she was, but she was thinking something else, too. About how much pain there was in the twist of his mouth.

"So you . . . what?" she asked. "Sold your car?"

"Traded rides. Left mine with my mom."

"What did you have?"

A different twist of his mouth now, a humorous one. "You'll laugh."

She smiled back at him, her heart lifting at his change in mood. "Try me."

"I had my teenage self's dream car. Nothing anybody in San Francisco would ever be impressed by."

"Camaro," she guessed. "Firebird. The painting on the hood and everything. Black."

He laughed, the sound sudden and rich in the confined space. "Close. Black Mustang ragtop, black leather interior. Man, I thought I was all that, didn't I?"

"And now your mom is."

"She is one dashing widow," he agreed. "Not that she cares. She thinks it's impractical. Especially black. 'A black car in the desert?'" he mimicked. "'Honey, no.' She won't sell it, though, in case I want it back. No matter how many times I tell her it's hers."

"So it really *is* hot where you're from." She had her head on her knees, her arms wrapped around her legs. She was smiling up at him, forgetting to be wary, forgetting to be sexy and make him sorry, just because Travis had a mom who sounded too much like her own. And because he'd loved his dad.

"Down near the Mexican border. The Sonoran Desert. And, yeah. I grew up on a farm myself. Not a rancher, though. Sorry about that."

Contradiction time again, or maybe the reason she'd been so drawn to him. Because something familiar in him had called to her, and something in her had answered. Or maybe that had just been the tequila. "What did your dad farm?" she asked, trying to pull her wayward heart back under control.

"Lots of things. Alfalfa, cantaloupe, watermelon. Not one of the big, rich farms like around here. Making a living, that's all. Owing the bank."

"So you really *are* a country boy."

"Maybe. When you scratch the surface. Maybe."

"So why Wayne?"

He blinked. "Huh?"

She circled her hand again. "Hey. You're supposed to be the smart one. Keep up. Wayne? Travis?"

"Oh. Yeah." He leaned his head back again. "Travis was too country, and when I went to college, I decided Wayne sounded classier. Like somebody who'd be rich someday."

"Travis is hotter," she informed him.

He turned his head and grinned down at her, and she laughed back into his face and thought, *Nah. Don't care what your name is. I want to lick you.*

"So then what did you do?" she asked.

"Huh?" he said again. "And yeah, I'm being slow. Can't help it. *A,* you turn my head around. You smell too good, for one thing. And *B,* you're the quick one here."

"I didn't go to college," she said, trying to ignore the sneaky fingers of desire that kept trying to creep into places they shouldn't. "I didn't even take one class. I don't think in outline form, either."

"That's got nothing to do with it," he said. She searched his face and decided he meant it, and smiled a bit more.

"What did you do," she elaborated, "after your dad died? How did you end up here?"

"It's kind of a story."

"Thought we were telling stories. Thought that was the whole idea."

Just then, she heard something. A metallic clang that echoed through the elevator shaft and made her jump; a judder through the mechanism. Travis's arm went instantly around her, and she was holding her breath, and realizing that she was holding his thigh, too. That she had her hand clamped above his knee and was hanging on.

And then the voice. "Hey! You all down there?"

"Yeah," Travis called back. "Right here. Between two and one, I think."

"Hang on," the voice said, and that was all.

She took her hand hastily off Travis's thigh, and after a second, he pulled his arm away.

"Guess the rest of your story will have to wait," she said, and realized her voice had come out shaky.

He handed the water bottle back to her. "Here. Finish it off. He's not going to let us fall now. He'd lose his job."

She laughed, although it didn't come out exactly right, and took a long drink, then dropped the empty bottle beside her.

There was more clanging coming from the shaft, and Travis took her hand and held it tight. "Almost there," he said. "Almost out. Hang on." And she did.

VISITORS

Rochelle had never felt more conflicted. On the one hand, she wanted to get out of here. Her shirt was clinging damply to her skin, she needed to pee, and the clanging that echoed through the elevator shaft had brought back all her nerves. She squeezed Travis's hand and focused on breathing, and he sat beside her, big and solid and strong, and gave her something to hold on to.

That was the other half of the deal. She wanted to hear the rest of his story. She didn't want to leave their metal . . . *not* coffin. Their . . . cocoon, where it wasn't about real life, her bad past choices, or their uncertain future. Where it was about sitting next to Travis and listening to him talk, slow and deep and steady. And maybe holding his hand, too.

Like it or not, though, the elevator was descending again, steadily this time, and then the doors were opening with a rush of cool air and a guy was standing there in dark blue Carhartts and boots, saying, "Everybody OK?"

Travis was on his feet already, pulling her to hers, and the guy was staring at her, clearly having lost his train of thought. Her skirt had ridden up as she'd stood, her shirt was sticking to her, and Mr. Maintenance was checking it all out. She pulled everything down, tossed her hair back, and said, "Yep. We're all good. Thanks for coming."

"I was on a call down in Cheney," the guy said. "That's why I could get to you so fast." He finally tore his gaze from her and glanced at Travis. Travis moved a fraction of a step closer to her, and Rochelle could almost hear the antlers lock.

"Yeah," Travis said, his voice flat. "Thanks, man. We're all good." He bent down, picked up the water bottle, and handed it to Rochelle, then picked up her file box. "Ready to get out of here?" he asked her.

"Sure." She smiled and felt the tremble around the edges. "Thanks again."

Travis led the way down the basement steps, and she followed him, directed him to the storage room, stowed the box, and headed upstairs again. They walked down the echoing main hall, and both spoke at once.

"Can I—" he said.

"I'm just—" she said. "Oh. Go ahead."

"No. You first."

"I'll just . . . duck in here." She indicated the ladies' room. "If you want to wait a sec."

In reality, it was more like ten minutes before she could get herself presentable again. Her first glance in the mirror had her reaching for the paper towels and her purse in horror. Melting your makeup off in an elevator wasn't on anybody's list of beauty tips.

And then she had to make a call. She ducked into the back of the restroom to do it so Travis wouldn't hear her. "Hey, Kayla?" she said. "I know I'm really late. It's a long story. I got stuck. But could I bring somebody to lunch with me?"

"Sure." Her friend sounded surprised. "It's fine. We went ahead without you. Zoe couldn't wait. It's just sandwiches, anyway. Who are you bringing? Your sister?"

That made Rochelle laugh, and she realized how shaky she still was and leaned against the cool tile. "About the furthest thing from it. A guy. His name's Travis. Or Wayne. Or something. He probably eats a lot, and like I said, we've been stuck, and I'll bet he's hungry. And I'm rambling, I know. We've had an adventure, you could say. Can I bring him?"

"Oh, good. That *does* sound like a story. Of course you can. Whatever his name is. I'd like to hear more."

"Later. Maybe. Depending." Rochelle hadn't told anybody about Travis when it had happened. She hadn't even said much to her cousin. She wasn't sure she was ready to start spreading the news of her hookup among the blissfully newlywed.

When she came out of the restroom, Travis was standing there, relaxed as ever.

"You could at least look a little wrecked," she told him. "I had to do major damage control in there."

"Oh, yeah?" She got another of his slow smiles for that, just a lightening of the eyes and a movement at the corners of his mouth. "You looked all right to me. I was thinking, you said you'd ridden your bike up here. It's hot, and you're shaken up, and maybe almost as hungry as me. Let's toss the bike in the back of my truck and go grab lunch, and then I'll give you a ride home."

She cleared her throat. She could still hear the faint sounds from down the hall that meant the elevator guy was doing his thing. At least it'd be fixed for the school week. "I'm late for lunch with friends, actually. But if you'd like to come along . . ."

He gave her more of that crooked smile. "Is this a trick question?"

"I didn't say get down and dirty," she cautioned, trying to keep her heart from lifting. "I said lunch. With friends."

"I heard what you said. And I'll take it."

◆　◆　◆

Careful, Travis told himself as he set her bike in the bed of his truck and slammed the tailgate shut, then opened the passenger door and held it for her. *Slow and steady.* He still had a long way to go to earn her trust.

He might have watched her step up and swing her legs in, and he might have enjoyed it. Just like he'd enjoyed seeing that maintenance guy's eyes slide away from her body once he'd gotten the message. All sorts of primitive things were going on here, and what was worse, they were fine by him. He'd left the city behind for sure.

She directed him through town, up the Maple Street hill, and around to a house on D Street at the north edge of town.

"Nice spot," he said when she led him around the back of the house, where a deck overlooked the view of the last few straggling streets and the fields beyond.

It really *was* "lunch with friends." A man, two women, a boy, and a baby, all sitting in the shade of a blue awning over a wide deck. And to complete the domestic picture, a border-collie mix who came forward wagging a feathery tail.

Rochelle crouched down and gave the dog a pat, saying, "This is Daisy."

The guy had stood up. "Luke Jackson," he said, shaking hands with Travis. "My wife, Kayla." A pretty, petite blonde. "And my sister-in-law, Zoe." Another short woman, a brunette this time. The baby was next to her, asleep in a carrier on the ground. A very *tiny* baby, the kind that made Travis nervous, all fragile arms and legs and a visible pulse beating through the soft spot at the top of its head under some wisps of brown duck-down hair. The baby was wearing only a one-piece undershirt. He couldn't even tell if it was a girl or a boy, because the undershirt was yellow, with a duck on it.

"And our son, Eli," Luke said, nodding at the boy next to him. Travis saw the motion, sensed Luke's kick on Eli's ankle, and had to smile. Exactly what his own dad would have done. The boy scrambled to his feet and shook hands.

"This is . . . um, I don't know," Rochelle said with a laugh. "Travis Wayne Cochran. Who likes to change his name."

"Travis," he said. "Among friends."

"Please," Kayla said. "Sit down and have something to drink, and a sandwich. Rochelle said you'd had an adventure."

"Travis is a new lecturer in Computer Science." Rochelle sat down and poured herself a glass from a pitcher of iced tea. "You might have met Zoe, if she wasn't on maternity leave," she told Travis.

"Geological Sciences," the brunette said as Travis seated himself across from her. "Once upon a time, back when I was smart. Right now, I'm mostly trying to teach Advanced Topics in Sleeping. And failing badly."

"How old is your baby?" he asked.

"Thirteen days. This is our first real social outing. She's on her best behavior, as you see. Don't let her fool you, though. She's evil. But tell us about the adventure. Entertain me."

"She actually loves her baby," Rochelle informed Travis. "Who has a *name*. Geez, Zoe."

Zoe laughed, and her face lit up and changed entirely. "Her name is Alice. And sorry. I'm shocking, I know. Cal—my husband—is harvesting, so I'm refusing to let him help me out at night, and my nobility is killing me. Wheat doesn't wait, and neither do babies. Never mind. I'm good. Tell me the story."

"It wasn't that exciting. Stuck in an elevator," Rochelle explained, her hand waving, glancing at him from time to time out of the side of those laughing eyes. Travis lay back in his chair, sipped his iced tea, ate a sandwich, and watched her. The conversation flowed effortlessly around him, and he relaxed and listened and thought, *Works for me.*

"How's your sister doing, Rochelle?" Zoe asked after a bit.

She shrugged, suddenly not looking quite as animated. "Stacy," Travis said. "Nice girl."

"You've met her." Luke's eyes were watchful, as they had been ever since Travis had showed up with Rochelle.

"Wait." Rochelle was sitting up straighter. "You *didn't*. She *didn't*."

"She didn't what?" Travis asked before finishing off his sandwich and dishing himself up some salad. "Thanks for this," he told Kayla. "Exactly what I needed after my grueling adventure with Rochelle."

"You're not going to worm your way out of this," Rochelle said. "You got my address from my *sister*."

"That'd be telling. Couldn't we say that I really wanted it, and I'm a persuasive guy, and leave it at that?"

"He brought me a plant," Rochelle said. "A hydrangea. And then he *planted* it." She was glaring at him as if it had been a body.

"He did, huh." Zoe's eyes were big, round, and brown. *Deceptively innocent*, Travis would have called them. She didn't look like she was suffering any loss of brain cells to him. "Why?"

"Maybe because it was all I could think of," he said.

"Or maybe," Rochelle said, "because my *sister* told you I liked to garden, and what to get me."

"Like I said, some people find me persuasive."

"You are so . . ." she began. "Both of you."

He sighed. "One minute I'm the elevator hero. The next I'm the goat."

"Hey," she said. "Did you *once* try climbing out the top?"

"Nope. I sure didn't. Shared my Snickers bar, though."

She laughed at that, and he grinned back, and she told Zoe, "I'm not sure how Stacy is. Better, I guess. Up and down."

"She get a job yet?"

"I hate when you zero in on the exact thing I don't want to talk about," Rochelle complained. "Nope. She hasn't. Not too easy, when you got fired from your last one for not showing up, and it was at the university. Means I can't use my contacts, because they check no matter what I say."

"I was hearing our new waitress saying they're hiring at Macho Taco, out in the mall," Kayla put in. "She didn't want it, because it's not the best, but . . ."

"Hmm," Rochelle said. "Yeah. They might be desperate enough. Thanks. And I *will* haul her butt down there every day if I have to." She looked like she meant it, too.

"I could use somebody," Travis offered.

Rochelle just looked at him, and he said, "Teaching assistant. You know, do my . . ." He cast about for an idea. "Grading," he finished lamely.

"No," she said.

"Hey. Why not?"

"You know exactly why not. You've got two very small upper-division classes. If you needed a teaching assistant, you'd have asked for one."

"You know," he said, "you could make this easier. I'm just saying."

"Oh, I don't know," Luke said. "Easy might be overrated."

"Thanks," Travis said. "That's helpful."

Zoe was smiling, and then she wasn't. That's what he noticed. Her eyes widened even more, and then she was standing, and Travis was turning to see what she was looking at.

A big man in dirty jeans, work boots, and a feed cap had come through the side gate, moving fast, followed by a big, ugly dog. Everyone went quiet as the guy came up onto the patio and went straight for the baby, lifted her out of her little seat, tucked her securely into one big arm, and nuzzled the top of her head, then kept his face there.

Ah. The dad. Zoe's husband, Cal. But something was off.

"Honey," Zoe said, her hand on his arm. "What is it?"

Cal lifted his head from the baby, and Travis got a jolt down low in his gut at the bleakness in his face. "I just needed to smell her."

Silence engulfed the group as Cal looked around the table, his gaze landing on the kid.

"Eli," Kayla said quietly, "you're excused."

The boy looked from his mother to Cal, his expression much too old for his age. He didn't answer—but then, he hadn't said anything so far—just picked up his plate and left the table with Daisy trotting along behind.

Meanwhile, the ugly dog had sat himself down next to his master as if he needed to stay right there. Just like Zoe did.

"What happened?" Luke asked his brother. He, too, had stood. "Bad? The folks? Or what?"

Cal sat down, still holding the baby, who hadn't woken. He took one of her little hands in his own large one, the gesture incongruously delicate, and ran his thumb over the fragile knuckles, the tiny nails. "I found a dead girl."

Kayla's hand was at her mouth, but Zoe, who still had her hand on Cal's arm, said, "Where?"

He took a deep breath, blew it out. "Harvesting. Just finished that first lentil field over near Black Butte. She was down in that ditch, under the weeds."

"How'd you spot her?" Luke asked.

"Magpies. I just had to . . . I had . . ." Cal's Adam's apple bobbed in his strong throat as he swallowed, and the hand holding Alice's was shaking. Zoe took the baby from him, got up, and put her back in her seat. Then she scooted close to her husband and put her hand on his broad back, smoothing over it in slow circles.

Cal said, "Sorry, Kayla. I didn't get a shower." He looked down at himself as if noticing for the first time that he was still in his work clothes.

"No, you're good," Luke said. "Could you tell who it was?"

A violent shake of the head at that. "Too many birds. Coyotes, too, I'd say. But . . . a grown girl. Not a . . . not a child. Long, dark hair." His face twisted. "Sorry. I've been with the cops. Quite a while. It was just—it kinda hit me, just now." He put his elbows on his knees and rubbed his hand over his face.

Kayla uttered an inarticulate noise, and Luke put his arm around her. Next to Travis, Rochelle sat still and silent.

After a moment, Cal sat up again and took another deep breath. "Yeah. Well. I went on back and called the sheriff. Jim Lawson came out first, then all the rest of them."

"Jim's his cousin," Rochelle told Travis in an undertone. "Deputy."

"They say anything?" Luke asked.

Another shake of the head from Cal. "You know how they are," he said, sounding steadier now. "Just asked me some questions. Had I seen anybody, any rigs out there? No, but I hadn't been out there. Had I noticed the birds before today? Of course I hadn't. Wasn't harvesting there before. But she'd been there awhile."

"I haven't heard of any missing persons," Luke said. "And I'd think I would have."

"Could've been dumped there from anywhere," Cal said.

"No way of telling how she . . ." Luke began.

"No. But she didn't get there by herself. Not all the way up that farm road, then off over all that rough ground, and in the ditch, with the weeds over her. Arranged over her to hide her, I'd bet. Has to be murder. Has to be. I kept thinking, her folks . . ."

His voice cracked on the final word, and Zoe said, "Cal . . ."

He looked at her and said, "Baby, let's go home. I'm done for today. Even if I weren't, they won't let me move the combine. The whole place is a crime scene now. You about ready?"

"Of course I'm ready. And of course you're not going back to work today."

"You need to rest anyway," he told her.

"Oh, Cal," she said with a broken laugh. "You're so . . ." She rubbed her cheek against his shoulder and said, "Come on. We'll go home. We'll rest together."

Cal picked up Alice's car seat, and Zoe gathered her things then headed around the side of the house with her family, the big dog trotting along behind.

A short silence fell over the group still sitting at the table after their departure.

"Hell of a thing for a new dad to see," Luke finally said.

Kayla looked at him and said, "You got that?"

"Yeah," he said. "I did. He's my brother." He looked at Travis. "Takes a lot to shake Cal up."

"Yep," Travis said. "I'll bet it does. He's Cal Jackson. The Seahawks quarterback."

"Oh," Rochelle said. "I forgot that you wouldn't know who he was."

"Took me a minute to place him, in the context," Travis said. "I knew he wasn't playing anymore. Didn't realize he was farming. But I'm sure it does take a lot to shake him up. Famously cool under pressure."

"Different kind of pressure," Luke said. "Cal's pretty protective."

"I got that, too," Travis said.

ALL KINDS OF
READJUSTMENTS

Rochelle sat still, and so did everybody else. It was as if Cal had left behind a disturbance in the very air of this serene spot, a reminder not only of this latest violence, but also of all the violence that had come before. She knew without asking that everyone here was feeling it. Everyone but Travis, though he was quiet as well, his expression thoughtful. But then, it had been obvious in the elevator that he was a lot more sensitive than he let on.

"Well," Luke said after a second, "so much for dessert. I've lost my appetite. I don't know about you all. You OK?" he asked Kayla.

"Yes," she said, then got up from the table. "I'll just go check on Eli."

Luke watched her go with a frown on his good-looking face. Once she was inside, he told Travis, "Violence upsets her. Especially this kind of thing."

"Well, yeah," Travis said. "I can imagine."

Rochelle shook herself, stood up, and began to gather dishes. "We'll get out of here in a minute and let you guys regroup. Wow, what a day. Sorry, Travis. Maybe not quite what you had in mind."

He stood with her and pitched right in clearing the table. "I'm thinking maybe my original idea for the afternoon might work, though. For everybody, even."

"What's that?" Rochelle asked.

"I was going to go check out Elk Creek Reservoir. Swimming outdoors sounds real good right now. Wash the taste of this away. Plus, it's hot. Just for an hour or two. Who's in?"

"Up there in the trees," Luke said. "Great idea. Let me go check with Kayla."

He took off after his wife, and Rochelle carried a load of dishes into the house and started loading the dishwasher. Travis brought in the salad bowl and the plate of sandwiches, leaned against the counter, and said, when she didn't speak, "What? No good? Don't like to swim? Or was all that too upsetting?"

"No." She pulled out a plastic container and began to transfer the salad into it. "I mean, it's upsetting, sure. Really upsetting. But bad things happen. I know they do."

"They do." He was standing still, as usual. Watchful. Travis didn't fidget, she realized. "So . . . what?"

"Would you go get the glasses, please?"

He turned without a word and went out for them, and she tried to have a talk with herself and pretty much failed miserably.

"Right. What?" he asked when he'd brought the glasses back in and, without her asking, started loading the dishwasher himself. Which was a promising thing to see.

"Maybe I'm just thinking that swimsuits aren't the best option," she finally said. It wasn't her only reservation, of course. The truth was, she was all over the map. The elevator, Cal, that poor girl dumped in a ditch. It had been too much emotion, so much more than she wanted to show Travis. Than she wanted to show anybody. She needed to be cool to deal with him. She needed to be in control, and she was nowhere close.

His face cleared, though, and that half smile appeared. "Ah. Well, yeah. If we're going to jump back into life here—yeah. I could say I hadn't imagined what kind of suit you might have and how you might look in it, but I'd be lying. Please tell me it isn't some kind of racing tank."

She had to smile herself. "I've got more than one." Back to flirting, and back to life. She'd keep it here. She'd keep it light.

"You're just torturing me now," he said, and she laughed and felt so much better.

"Chaperones," he suggested. "Family outing, assuming the others come. We can take your sister, too, if you want. How PG can you get?"

"And you're not going to be thinking about me naked?"

"Hey. There's a limit."

◆ ◆ ◆

She wasn't able to convince Stacy to come, though.

She'd told her sister about Cal's discovery. No way to keep that quiet, not in Paradise.

"Who was it?" Stacy asked. She was sitting on her bed, propped against the pillows, a textbook lying on the bedspread beside her. "Was it . . . was it somebody we know?"

"Cal couldn't tell," Rochelle said. "It had been a while, and the coyotes had gotten to her."

Stacy nodded. When you grew up on a farm, you knew about death, because you saw plenty of it. Death, and its consequences. Which didn't make it easier to think about. Rochelle had to swallow hard, and she could see Stacy doing the same thing.

"He didn't say much," Rochelle went on. "But you see why I want you to be careful," she couldn't help adding. "You see why I worry about who you go out with, and what you do out there. About keeping yourself safe. And when you're not sober, you're not safe. Especially if you pass out."

"What, she made it happen?" Stacy was glowering now. "Are you *blaming* her? Somebody killed her and dumped her in a ditch, and it's her fault?"

"No," Rochelle sighed. "Of course I'm not. I'm saying, I want you to be safe. And I want you to come with me today."

"I can't. I need to stay here. I've got too much homework."

Rochelle studied her face, and Stacy's eyes slid away under her gaze. Her sister pulled her legs up and wrapped her arms around them. Not a good sign. "I need to stay here," she said again.

"I wish you'd come. It's only a couple hours." *Please don't be waiting for Shane,* Rochelle wanted to say, but didn't.

"You're the one who's been saying I need to be responsible. I know it. I'm trying. And you're going with Travis anyway. I don't care how boring and steady he is, he isn't going to want your little sister in the car."

"Boring and steady" wouldn't be exactly how Rochelle would have described Travis, but she didn't disillusion her sister. "All right, then," she said. "Salad for dinner. Too hot for anything else."

"See." Stacy picked up the heavy book beside her titled *Statistics for Scientists*. "*I'd* totally be thinking about making out on a towel if a cute guy took me up there, and you're thinking about *dinner*."

Rochelle had to laugh at that. "All right, then. See you later."

By the time they got to the park, though, she wasn't thinking about dinner.

She and Travis had made the thirty-minute drive without talking much. He'd turned the radio to a country station and cranked up the volume some, and she hadn't been able to resist slipping off her sandals, putting her bare feet up on the dash, and doing some singing along. Because she was alive, it was warm out, and she was with a big, strong man with a quiet gaze, warm eyes, and laugh lines around the corners of his mouth. Because life might not always be good, but this moment was.

When they arrived, she hopped out of the truck and led the way onto the grass. The others were already here, she saw. Kayla was all the way over on the island in the middle of the cattail-lined lake with Eli, who was throwing a stick for an exuberant Daisy, while Luke was swimming a lazy lap around the island.

First things first. Rochelle dropped her bag, crossed her arms over her body, got the hem of her T-shirt in two hands, and pulled it slowly over her head, shaking her hair free and *not* looking at Travis. Not much at all.

"Oh, yeah," he said. "That's what I'm talking about."

She smiled, and if her smile was a little seductive? Too bad. "I seriously considered a navy-blue racing tank. And then I thought . . . nah." She slipped the hair elastic from her wrist, lifted her hands behind her neck, and fastened her hair into a braid, then made an unnecessary adjustment to the halter tie of the forties-style, red-and-white-checked bikini top, and he couldn't even pretend to be staring at her face. And then she slid her skort slowly down her legs, kicked it loose, and showed him her pinup-girl bikini bottoms with the buttons in a vertical row on either side. Her stomach wasn't all that flat, and she could tell Travis didn't care one bit. So she might have had to make an adjustment at the back of those, too, and do some more wriggling around. It wasn't her very sexiest suit, but it was working.

"So," she said when she'd finished, "you planning on getting in the water yourself here? Or is this strictly a spectator sport?"

"You know," he said, "some men might take your attitude as a challenge." He pulled off his cap, tossed it onto the grass, and ran his fingers through that slightly-longer hair while she tried not to imagine her own fingers in there and failed. Then he began to pull his T-shirt over his head, and she forgot all about their sparring practice.

She'd forgotten. Or he'd changed. Or something. He was just so . . . tall. For one thing. Every inch the T-shirt rose revealed delicious new territory. A flat belly with that arrow of hair she loved, leading straight down into his waistband, plus some very nice horizontal ridges and that special diagonal line on either side. More arrows to a place she wasn't going. Probably. Hopefully. And then the broadening of his chest the higher up the shirt went. That was good, too. She hadn't remembered quite that much shoulder. Those weren't gym muscles, either. Those were *man* muscles, long and lean. How had he gotten them?

"Hey." Kayla chose that moment to arrive on shore, pick up a towel, and wrap it around herself. "The water's great. You should get in."

Travis grinned at her and said, "Yep." And then he left Rochelle there, ran down the shore and straight into the water, started swimming, and kept right on going, powering toward the distant shore.

"Wow," Kayla said. "He is *fast*. Also, um, I shouldn't look, or I shouldn't care, but . . ."

"Yep," Rochelle said. "Yep. He sure is." She walked down to the water for a swim herself, feeling, all right, just a *little* miffed that he hadn't stuck around.

She managed to forget about him, though, as she swam until she'd worked off some of her nervous energy, avoiding the overexcited Daisy, who was still paddling madly after sticks. After a while, she rolled over, floated on her back, and rested, looking at blue sky and white clouds drifting slowly overhead, the dark green of pines and firs solid and comforting at the edges of her vision, and the blue bulk of Paradise Mountain and its low sister buttes rising in the distance. Her ears were full of the excited shouts of kids and the slow slap of water against the docks, and the sun was warm on her skin. Her mind drifted to Stacy and what she might be doing, and she thought, *Macho*

Taco. Tomorrow, and then she opened her hands like starfish and let the thought go.

Bad things happened. Pain and trouble and death happened. But life was for living, surely, and moments like this were meant to be savored. No matter who was or wasn't watching.

PATIENCE

Travis hadn't counted on Rochelle totally ignoring him and taking her own long, leisurely swim, but he should have known she'd do what he least expected. If this were a game, he wasn't the one getting the moves right. But then, he wasn't much of a game player. Not with real people.

He'd needed to work out anyway, though, after all that sitting, and he'd needed to cool off, too. If driving up here with Rochelle's skirt all the way up her thighs and her pretty pink toes on his dash had been tough, watching her strip down had been tougher. But she wanted him to prove he was willing to wait for her? Then he was going to do it. For as long as it took.

He was loose, relaxed, and sitting on his towel a half hour later, with Kayla beside him reading a book while the faint buzz of insects filled the air. Kids splashed in the lake, and the occasional shout drifted over from behind them, where Luke and Eli were tossing a football with Daisy in hot pursuit. All slow, easy, and lazy-summer . . . that is, until Rochelle finally emerged from the water, her hip-first glide drawing every male eye, the water sliding down her luscious body as if it wanted to kiss every inch of it. Just like he did.

And that was before she stood in front of him and slicked her hair back with one hand, then bent down for her towel.

You've seen it all before, he reminded himself desperately as he stared down the most dangerous cleavage he'd ever had the pleasure of encountering, at the droplets of water glistening against her lightly tanned skin, just asking him to lick them off.

He'd seen it before, yeah. Didn't make him one bit less eager to see it again.

She looked at him, the gleam in her eye telling him that she knew exactly what she was doing, and purred, "Payback yet?"

"Oh, yeah. You bet." He might not be good at games—not outside the bedroom, anyway—but she was great at them.

Patience, he told himself, and looked up at her and thought, *Just you wait, baby. You'll see.*

She smiled down at him like a cat who'd found the cream, then put the tip of her tongue out and slowly licked her entire upper lip before her tongue disappeared tantalizingly into that Marilyn mouth again.

He said, "OK. The porn-star thing is carrying it a little far."

She laughed, gave it up, and sat down beside him. "I've never done that before. Just wanted to see if it worked."

"It works." He was feeling a decided need to jump back in the water again. "Stop it."

"Mm." She dried her legs, then lay down on her stomach. "Does it help if I do this? And tell you that you're one heck of a swimmer?"

"No," he said, "because your back view's almost as good as your front. And swimming's what I do. Went to college on a swimming scholarship, in fact."

"Really." She lay with her cheek on her folded hands, and her pink mouth curved in a delicious smile. "An athlete. I should've guessed."

"Southern California variety. What, you wanted football?"

"Mm. No. I'll take swimming. And now go away, please. I want to talk to Kayla."

Kayla looked up from her book and said, "Don't mind me. I'm having a good time pretending not to listen."

"Hey," Rochelle said. "Maybe I want to watch Travis run around with his shirt off."

"Works for me," he said. He sprang to his feet, jogged over to Eli and Luke, clapped his hands for the ball and made a pretty good diving catch, then turned and waved the ball at Rochelle. After that, he didn't show off. Much.

◆ ◆ ◆

Twenty minutes later, Travis was on his towel again, one lazy eye on Eli, who was back in the water. The rest of them were just hanging out, too drugged by exercise and warmth and quiet to get back in the trucks and drive home. And then Rochelle had him readjusting again.

"I've been thinking," she said, rolling over onto her back and hauling herself up to sit. "About what Cal said. There's something funky about it."

"Funky how?" Travis asked, shifting his attention with a serious effort from all that sumptuous . . . Rochelle. If there was ever a woman who'd been made to fill out a bikini, that woman was Rochelle. And if there was ever a man who was lucky to have been stuck in an elevator, that man was him.

"That girl had to be killed by somebody from right around here, I'll bet," she said. "But not anybody real familiar with farming."

She was frowning, because the discovery of the body, and the way it had affected her friends, was still getting to her. He'd seen all of them work to shake it off. He noticed that, as soon as Rochelle had mentioned it again, Luke's hand had gone out to hold Kayla's. Cal wasn't the only protective man in the Jackson family.

"She had to have been dumped there," Rochelle said again, then stopped.

"Yeah?" Luke asked. "And?"

"Well, she couldn't have been killed there. Not *right* there. She didn't stumble into that ditch and die, like Cal says. And she wasn't killed in there, either. A farm ditch . . . that's going to be narrow and two, three feet deep," she explained to Travis. "And those weeds are high. Nobody could stand in there and do that. She'd have been put there to hide her, so her body wouldn't be discovered for a while. Maybe never, who knows. Nobody's going to clean out one of those ditches. So why that field?"

"Ah," Luke said. "Ah. I'm getting it. It couldn't have been somebody familiar with crops."

"What?" Kayla asked. "Explain."

"Lentils?" Luke said. "No way."

"No way *lentils?*" Kayla's pretty face showed her bafflement. "What difference does the crop make?"

"Harvest is almost over," Rochelle explained. "Only thing left to go is the lentils and garbanzos, right?" She looked at Luke, who nodded. "The wheat and barley are done."

"I'm sorry," Kayla said. "I still don't understand, even if everybody else does."

"I don't quite," Travis said. "We don't do lentils back home. But I'm getting an idea."

Luke's gaze sharpened. "You got folks who farm?"

"Yeah. Used to."

"Right, Kayla," Rochelle said. "So if you've got some fields cut and some not, and you're dumping a body, or choosing where to kill somebody? If you want someplace remote, someplace where it won't be discovered, at least for a while, where the farmer won't be coming back for a good month or so? Where do you do it?"

"Oh," Kayla said. "Someplace that's already been harvested."

"Right. A stubble field, that's where you'd put it. And any country guy would think of that, even if he wasn't a farmer himself. He'd know it was harvest. You can't exactly miss it. He wouldn't dump the body right where the farmer would be driving through in a combine the next day, or the next week. If he wanted to hide it, and he obviously did, he wouldn't take that risk."

"So he wasn't from around here," Kayla said.

"Not quite that simple," Rochelle said. "I think he *was* from around here. Or at least that he lives here now. He knew that there were such things as farm roads and ditches, and that he could find one, and that it would be a good hiding spot. Maybe even that he could find a farm road right there. Maybe he'd driven by it before. He just didn't know *enough* about farming. Lentils are low and dry and kind of . . . raggedy-looking. They look like a stubble field, especially if they've got weeds in them. Thistles, like you get in lentils?"

"Cal's fields don't have thistles," Luke put in.

"All right. No thistles. But still," Rochelle said. "A lentil field doesn't actually look like anything's ready for harvest there, not if you don't know enough to recognize the crop. I'll bet it was somebody who *was* from around here, but not country. They couldn't tell a field of lentils from a stubble field—a cut field—especially not at night."

"Could you?" Kayla asked.

"Of course I could," Rochelle said. "If I was looking to dump a body of somebody I'd murdered? You bet I'd make sure I was really looking at a stubble field."

SOME MAN

"That was a good time," Travis told her a while later, jerking her out of her near-doze. "Just what I needed."

They were back in his pickup and headed home. He'd opened the door for her again, too. She did love a man with manners.

"Mm." He had the radio on once more, but softer this time. She swung her legs up again and crossed her ankles, then caught the glance he threw her way and wiggled her toes. "What? Bothering you? No feet allowed on your dash?"

"You can put your feet up on my dash anytime. And yeah, you're bothering me."

"Really?" she asked innocently. "And I'm not even wearing my bikini anymore."

"Noticed that, too. And that was a lot of logic you had going on back there, by the way. About the lentils."

Oh. So this wasn't going to be just flirting. Which was good, of course. Even though she wanted to flirt. She yawned, covering her mouth with her hand. "You surprised?"

"Nope." He took a sharp curve at just enough speed, not trying to show off for her. "I hope they find out who did it. It's more than dying that way. That's an . . . an indignity, to be dumped like that, left in a ditch for the animals. That's an insult."

"Yeah." She was all the way awake now, and all the way sobered, too. "Maybe that was part of it. It's probably the husband, or the boyfriend. Or the ex, more likely. That's who kills women. That doesn't take much logic at all. They'll be looking for somebody whose wife left him recently, a guy who's telling people she left town, ran off with somebody else. And I'll bet that's who it'll be. That'd be why he'd want her to be . . . insulted, too. To sort of suffer, even after she died, even though I know that makes no sense. Because he was mad. You're right, it was an angry thing to do. Like murder ever isn't angry, but still. It's what bad guys do. They think they own you. They think that if you leave them, they have a . . . a right."

He glanced at her again. "You scared of your own ex?"

"No," she said, then had to stop and think a minute. "I never was," she said slowly. "I'm pretty tough."

"Another thing I've noticed."

"But a man can change when you leave him. You never know until you break up how he's going to take it. And, yeah, he's changed. I talked to him a while back, because my sister . . . well. Anyway. I thought Stacy might have been hanging out over there, and I was upset about it. And he was . . . pretty ugly. It wasn't good."

A few beats went by, as if he were trying to decide which topic to pursue. "Has she always lived with you?" he finally asked. "Stacy?"

"No. It's only been two weeks. Because she'd gotten off track."

"And you're the one to get her back on."

"I'm living in town, and she's a junior at the university. And I'm the oldest. Of six. Fair warning. Probably why I'm not that easily intimidated."

He smiled again, just a movement at the corner of his mouth. "I've got two younger sisters myself."

"Hopeless," she said, and he laughed, then sobered.

"I was thinking about something else, too," he said. "Cal seemed to think that girl was young. Maybe too young to have an ex-husband. I wonder what made him think that, if she'd been there a while."

She considered for a minute. "That'd be an impression, wouldn't you say? Something about her build, probably. Her clothes. The long hair. Something you'd notice in an instant, without even knowing you'd noticed it."

"Bet you're right. That's logical, too."

"Well, I'm a logical girl."

"Yep. You're all kinds of things."

"This isn't the sexiest conversation we've ever had," she said. "Talking about murder. Dealing with murder. What a day."

"Like I said. You're all kinds of things."

That was good. The murder . . . it was bad. But what he'd said was good. She leaned her head back, closed her eyes, and let herself drift with the music, with the moment, as Travis steered around the curves of the quiet two-lane back toward Paradise.

She opened her eyes again when the tires were scrunching over the gravel of her street. He pulled the truck to a stop at the curb and kept the motor running.

"I'll just say again," he said, "it turned out to be a pretty good day despite everything. Thanks for going with me."

"Mm." She unfastened her seat belt, but didn't rush to hop out. "It *was* good. Because you talked to me, and you took me seriously, and you didn't grab me."

He smiled, slow and sure, and her heart skipped a beat. "Going to grab you now all the same."

He leaned over and . . . didn't grab her. Instead, his hand cradled her head, just as it had that first night. He tunneled his fingers through her still-damp hair, stroked his thumb softly over her cheek, then looked into her eyes, and she felt something pass between them, as real and strong as if he'd spoken it aloud. Her lips parted in response, and only then did he touch his mouth to hers. A soft thing. An invitation, his lips brushing lightly over hers, waking her body up, bringing her to life as surely as a prince in a fairy tale.

She had a hand behind his own head now, and at last, she was feeling his thick hair beneath her fingers again. Testing the texture and length of it, seeing whether she could hold him like that. And finding out that she could.

The kiss got hotter, then, his mouth not quite as gentle, and her lips parted more under his. Somehow, her own mouth seemed to be connected to . . . everywhere, and the flames were licking. Growing. He took the invitation, deepened the kiss, and got his other hand on her waist to pull her closer. She was falling into him, tasting the heat and the desire in him, her hand still wrapped in his hair, her body pressed back against the door. He was on her like a man ought to be, and she was making some sounds into his mouth that she couldn't help one bit. And he was taking them in and asking for more.

Until, that is, a movement in her peripheral vision had her stiffening. Dell, walking Charlie on his red leash, heading across the street in front of the truck toward home. The old lady smiled and gave the two of them a cheerful wave as she passed, and that broke the moment right up.

Travis must have seen her, too, because he took his mouth away, which made her moan in protest. Then he sat up.

"Yeah," he said. "It's still right there between us, isn't it?"

"Maybe we shouldn't . . ." She had to clear her throat. "In front of my house. During the day."

His hand came out to trace over her cheek again and tuck a strand of hair behind her ear. "I'm happy to kiss you anywhere, but you're right. I'm thinking we might need some privacy pretty soon here."

"You're still leaving in December."

"Well, there's that," he agreed, his face serious.

"If only kissing you didn't feel so good," she sighed, turning her face into his palm.

"Damn, girl. You're just put on this earth to test me, aren't you?"

"Self-control is a virtue, they say." She was getting some back herself. Except that right after that, she pressed a kiss into his palm. And then she might have bitten the meaty part a little. Just a little. Just a nip, because she needed to.

He didn't say anything. He just reached for her and, this time, pulled her over to *his* side and took her mouth hard, making her gasp. And then he pulled back and gave her a slap on the hip that made her jump.

"Then stop tempting me," he said.

"You always spank girls?" She did her best to scowl at him.

That killer half smile. "Only if I really like them. And this would be where I shift gears like I'm being spontaneous and issue a suave dinner invitation to keep the day going."

"I can't do tonight." Actually, she could have, but it was better to make sure he cared enough to come back. Even though it was tough. She didn't have that much self-control herself, it seemed. She wanted to taste him. She wanted to *feel* him. Every bit of him.

He frowned, and she thought, *You can't even wait one day?* and tried not to be unreasonably disappointed. She had nothing at stake here. Nothing at all.

"I'm leaving for San Francisco tomorrow," he said. "Won't be back until Tuesday."

"Oh. You've got a class, though."

"I'll be back for my class, boss. Flying out of Union City. I've got a meeting Monday."

"Oh," she said again. "Flying from Union City's expensive." Everyone she knew spent the extra ninety minutes and made the drive to Spokane.

"Luckily, I'm rich."

"Right." She was flustered, completely off balance. She'd managed to forget that part. "I thought you said you were done down there."

"It's a meeting about a new venture." He shot another look across at her. "Something I came up with this summer and have been messing around with some."

"Oh." She should say something besides that. "But you've got the classes this semester."

"Yep. It wouldn't be now. It's in the talking stage, that's all. What do you think about next week? Dinner? Swim? You name it."

"We'll see." December really *was* it, then. Any delusional hope she might have cherished of his sticking around was just that. Of course it was. She reached down and grabbed her bag, then hopped down from the truck, and he was already around with a hand under her elbow, helping her down.

"I've been climbing out of pickups since I was four," she told him.

"Doesn't matter. It's my excuse to touch you, and I'm taking it."

"Seems to me you already did that," she said as he gave the truck door a slam and walked up the sidewalk beside her. "And you don't have to walk me to my door."

"Well, I do if I want to kiss you good-bye."

Which he did. Broad daylight and all, and he took his time, too. When he was done, she stayed inside his arms a moment despite all her doubts, rested her cheek against his chest, and said, "Maybe next week. Maybe."

"Phone number," he said. "So I can get that in writing."

She pulled back and smiled up at him. "Think you can manage to hang on to it this time?"

"Oh," he said, "I think so."

◆   ◆   ◆

She could have gone straight into the house. She could have. Instead, she leaned against the door and watched Travis walk down the sidewalk with his loose-limbed stride, just because she liked looking at him.

He was all long legs and coordinated movement. He walked like he swam. Like he danced. Like he made love. Like he knew exactly what he was doing.

"Oh, yeah, honey," she heard from a few yards away. "That's some man."

Travis was in the truck, now, lifting a hand in farewell and heading out. Rochelle sighed and turned to Dell, who had her flowered garden gloves on and was deadheading roses. Right where the action was, as usual.

"Yeah," Rochelle said. "Probably shouldn't have let him make out with me right here, huh?"

Dell gave her deep, rich chuckle. "You just try to stop him. Of course he's going to kiss you in front of your house. That's a man thing. Letting anyone who might be sniffing around know you're taken."

"I am not taken."

"No?" Dell was in a pink flowered blouse and white capri pants today. And matching earrings, naturally. "Well, you will be pretty soon, I'll bet. What he was packing in those jeans wasn't because he was happy to see *me*."

"You are a wicked old lady," Rochelle said, trying without success not to laugh.

"I might be old, but my eyes still work fine." Dell wielded her trimmers with gusto. "I'd have been grabbing that one with both hands. Looked to me like it would *take* both hands."

"That is disgusting. And you would not have. You were happily married when you were my age."

"Like Randy always said," Dell shot back without missing a beat. "Once you've got the best, don't need the rest. But I haven't seen you getting the best. Not until now."

DEDUCTIONS

Jim Lawson sat with three other deputies and Tony DeMarco, the department's shiny-new big-city detective, in the sheriff's department's bare conference room. Monday afternoon, the temperature in the room ice cold, the AC turned too low, as usual, against the heat outside.

"No word yet on who she is," DeMarco started off. "Still waiting on the DNA, and no missing persons yet that match, not anywhere even reasonably close by. But I got the preliminary report from the pathologist this morning. He's saying she's late teens, and he's calling it manual strangulation, and two and a half weeks ago."

Jim's head came up fast at that, but all he said was, "Huh."

It wasn't what any of them had been expecting to hear. Especially if nobody had come forward to report a missing woman. A missing *girl.* No friends, no family? Her body had probably been brought to the spot from outside the area, then, but that didn't fit, either. Up a farm road, in a ditch? That sounded like somebody local.

"Yeah," DeMarco said. "Her hyoid bone wasn't broken, but that's probably because she was young, and the doc says they're less likely to break with a victim under thirty. But it was damaged, and he thinks that's enough."

Jim had been a deputy for six years now. As far as looking at dead people went, the job beat being an Army Ranger all to hell. But he'd still seen his share, and not always on the highways. He had a little girl of his own, though, and women and children—that got him every time, no matter how hard he worked to hide it.

"Domestic, then, probably," he said. "Strangulation's up close and personal." And one of the most common kinds of battery men inflicted on women. Domestic abuse was about power and control, and there was nothing more controlling than cutting off a woman's air. "But a guy doesn't usually murder his ex, or his girlfriend, up a farm road out in the fields. He does it at home and takes her out there to dump her body. But she doesn't seem to be local, so . . ."

DeMarco looked miffed that *he* wasn't the one offering the psychological insight, and Jim sighed inside. That was the problem with having a Chicago cop as your detective. He tended to think you were all a bunch of hicks who couldn't detect a gas station robbery.

"Right," DeMarco said. "It could be a serial killer, of course. Or just rough sex that went bad. She could've been a hitchhiker, something like that. Doc can't tell by the exam if she was raped, which would be useful information. She probably wasn't, though, not with her jeans fastened. We'll have to wait and hope on the DNA for that, too, and under her fingernails, in case she clawed at him. Can't tell much at all from the exam, not weeks later. Too damn many animals."

Mark Lawrence, a young deputy working his first homicide, made a faint noise in the back of his throat. He'd puked at the scene. But then, so had Jim's cousin Cal, when he'd discovered the body. Some things were never going to be easy to see.

"One other thing that makes it more likely to be domestic," DeMarco said. "Blood test says she was pregnant. Get a DNA test on that, and we'll really have something."

The room went quiet for a second. A man who'd kill a pregnant woman—that was one Jim could never wrap his mind around. Not just your partner, but your baby? If anything was lower than that, he didn't know what it would be. He looked around the table, and he could tell he wasn't the only one who felt that way. Most of these guys had kids.

Something else was hanging around at the edges of his mind. He searched for it, but he couldn't quite find it.

"Any significance in the exact location, do you think?" DeMarco asked. At least he was willing to ask. "That it was on Jackson's land? Anybody with a grudge against him that you know of? Although obviously, the mutt was trying to hide her. He didn't mean the body to be discovered at all. But that if it *had* been discovered, it would point to Jackson?"

Jim's broad hand came down so hard on the table that the coffee in his Styrofoam cup jumped, scattering a few drops. "That's it," he said. "That's what I was missing. Lentils."

LOOKING AT YOU

Three fifteen on Tuesday afternoon, and Rochelle wasn't disappointed that Travis hadn't been by to see her. Hardly at all. His class had been over for more than half an hour. She wasn't proud that she'd looked it up to make sure.

He's busy, she told herself.

Or he doesn't think there's any rush, the other half of her, the voice of experience, put in. *He's sure you'll be here waiting.* Not like she could go anywhere.

But he'd texted her while he'd been gone. He'd thought it was important then. Starting right away, on Sunday.

San Francisco's 56 degrees. Be careful what you wish for.

She'd answered him, *Talking about the weather?*

And had gotten back, *Not anymore. And forget what I said about being careful. Go ahead and wish. I know I am.*

Thought you weren't a good talker, she'd typed.

I'm working on it, he'd replied. *How'm I doing?*

She'd heard from him again on Monday morning. Before his meeting, presumably. So she'd still been on his mind, which was good to know, wasn't it?

Forgot to say. Don't go kissing anybody else while I'm gone.

And she'd texted back, after an appropriate interval, *Think you get to tell me that?*

No interval at all, then.

Oh, yeah. I think so.

Which could have had her crossing her legs under her desk.

She might have dressed with some extra . . . care today too. A pretty, slim midnight-blue skirt in soft-as-butter Tencel, with a wrap-twist waist that gave her hourglass figure some extra emphasis. And a pale-blue top over a lace-trimmed white camisole that dipped just a bit in the center in a very nice V. It didn't show anything, but it might make a man's eye travel, if he were so inclined. Women weren't the only ones who liked to follow arrows. And if she were wearing a higher-heeled sandal than normal? If she felt like putting some extra sway in her step, that was her business.

Except that he wasn't going to see it. Not if he didn't come *by.*

"This is ridiculous," she said aloud. "What are you, fourteen?"

"Sorry?" Dr. Olsen said, and she jumped. She hadn't even seen him coming out of his office. He dumped some memos into her in-box and looked at her inquiringly.

"Nothing," she said, determined not to blush. She reached into her bottom drawer and pulled out her purse and her "Back in 15 Minutes" desk sign. "I'm going on break. Back soon."

He looked at her oddly. She didn't normally announce it, or rush out on him, either.

"Remember, we've got that donor reception at five," she hurried to add. "The guest list is on your computer."

"I'm remembering," he said. "You wouldn't let me forget anyway."

She nodded, picked up her purse, and walked out.

She was hungry, that was the problem. Midafternoon was the weak time, when she always wanted a cookie. But the way Travis had looked at her in her bikini was worth a cookie or two. She'd get some trail mix instead. That would be protein, at least.

Stop thinking about him. She headed down the stairs all four flights to the faculty/staff break room in the basement. No way she was taking the elevator again. Probably *ever* again.

Down the deserted hallway, then, and through the door . . . and there he was. Leaning against the counter at the far end of the room in his Levi's and a white button-down with the sleeves rolled up, drinking a carton of milk through a straw and looking like some kind of ad for the health benefits of dairy. Talking to Wilson Chang from Mechanical Engineering.

Unfortunately, it wasn't just the two of them. Two other men were sitting at one of the small round tables next to the door. Nick Matfield, hired a couple years ago, whom she didn't know that well. And Wes King, whom she unfortunately did. Clean-cut, well dressed, good-looking, and, like Nick, an assistant professor of computer science.

Also known as Dr. Why-I-Don't-Date-Professors-Anymore.

All four men looked up when she walked in. She glanced at Travis, then away again.

"Hi," he said.

She kept her glance brief, her voice cool. "Hi," she said, then headed on over to the vending machines.

Travis had chosen to hang out here rather than come see her. That told her what she needed to know right there, and she swallowed it down and shoved it aside.

Forget it. Forget him. She hadn't lost a thing. Maybe if she said it enough, she'd even believe it.

"Hey, Rochelle," Wes said. "Did you dress to kill anybody special today? You're looking especially . . . attractive."

"Really?" she said coolly. "Huh." She looked him up and down herself, opened her mouth like she was going to say something, then shut it again. *You're not,* she telegraphed with everything she had. *Looking attractive, that is.* She gave a tiny shrug, made a business of choosing an unsweetened iced tea and a packet of trail mix, collected them, and walked out. Slowly, because she wanted to move fast. Damned if either of them was going to make her run, even though she'd been regretting the weakness that had had her choosing this outfit from the second she'd seen Wes.

Once in the corridor, she tucked the drink bottle in her arm and fumbled to open the trail mix packet, wanting a cookie more than ever. She was vulnerable because she was hungry, that was all. That was *all*.

She hadn't walked far enough, though. She froze, her hands on the open packet, at the voice. Nick's. Right there.

"Holy shit. Hotter than ever. She's divorced, isn't she? Looks to me like she's up for anything, too. I might see if I'd have a shot. Bet that'd be a wild ride."

She wanted to leave. She did. Too bad her feet wouldn't move.

And just like that, there was Wes. "You could say that. Or you could say that she's the whole damn rodeo."

"You speaking from personal experience?" Nick asked. "You get a piece of that?"

"A piece?" Wes again. "I got more than a piece. I got every single inch of that. Let's say I put her through her paces until I'd had enough. That's some pure, gold-plated tail right there. I'll put it this way, though. If her tits were brains, she'd be a rocket scientist."

She'd always prayed he hadn't talked. Now she knew. But then, it was her own bad judgment all the way around. And, of course, her own temper.

Which she wasn't going to let go of now. Not at work. When it came to fight or flight, she'd always preferred to fight. But not today. Not like this.

Her hands were shaking, and sunflower seeds and peanuts were scattering over the tiled floor. She clenched her fingers over the plastic packet, squeezed it tight in her fist, and took off.

◆　◆　◆

She should have known better. She *had* known better. Of course, normally, it was easy to know better. There'd always been plenty of prospects, sure. The College of Engineering was still overwhelmingly male, and so was its faculty. Before her divorce, though, she hadn't looked. And afterwards, there hadn't been much to see.

The problem was, she was a down-home country girl with a wild side, and she wasn't all that attracted to engineers.

Until she'd started going out with Wes the year before. He'd worn the same Dockers and blue button-downs as the others, but he'd looked good in them, and he'd looked at her with so much heat, so much purpose. He hadn't lost much time asking her out after her marriage had ended, and eventually, she'd gone for it. He'd given her the full treatment, too. Dinner, wine, flowers. And he'd talked. Had told her his ambitions, his dreams. Once he got tenure, he'd start making the move into administration. Department chair first, and then dean himself someday. Maybe even a college president. Power, and money, and a better life.

She'd thought, why not? She was a hired man's daughter, and she wasn't ashamed of it, but who said she couldn't date an educated man now? Who said she couldn't even *marry* one? Anyway, she wanted somebody serious, somebody steady. A man, not a boy.

It had lasted all of six weeks. Two weeks and four romantic dates into it, she'd been sleeping with him. It had been a long time, and kissing and making out had aroused too many feelings that had demanded satisfaction, and demanded it right now. And again, as long as they kept it discreet—why not? She hadn't needed a man, but she'd sure wanted one.

He'd enjoyed that part, for sure. He'd been a bit selfish in bed, but a whole lot better than Lake had been toward the end, and at least it had been exciting. And often. She'd forgotten how good it felt to have your man want it every time, to have him look at you with that hunger in his eyes that said you were going to be getting some tonight. And men *were* selfish. If you sometimes had to finish things off yourself because he hadn't quite gotten you there—well, welcome to the real world. She'd been working on training him with as much tact as she possessed, and it had seemed like he was willing to try.

So it had been pretty good. It had been fine. Until the night when she'd said, as casually as she could manage, "My brother Bill's home on leave from the Army, and my folks are doing a big barbecue Sunday afternoon. Would you want to come?"

He was lying beside her in the dark. At her place, because he was sharing a house with another professor. He'd never even taken her there. She hadn't wondered why at the time.

Now, he sighed, rolled over onto his back, and said, "Sorry, I can't make it. Not really a good idea anyway, you think?"

"Uh . . . why not?"

"Well . . ." He toyed with a lock of her hair. "This isn't a serious thing, is it? I wouldn't want to give your family the wrong idea."

It was warm out, but she went cold anyway. She pulled the blanket up higher and tried to tell herself that that wasn't what he'd meant. "Well, not yet, of course it isn't. My dad isn't going to be meeting you with his shotgun, if that's what you're worried about. It's just a barbecue. You met my *ex,* for Pete's sake. Why would you mind meeting my family?"

Because he *had* met Lake. Rochelle had come out of the ladies' room at The Breakfast Spot the Sunday before to see Lake sitting opposite Wes, having a cozy little talk. *That* had been a shocker. Lake had stood up when she'd approached, and not out of politeness. His face had hardened, and he hadn't even said anything. He'd just left.

Rochelle had slid into the seat Lake had vacated, wishing there'd been another choice. She hadn't even wanted to share Lake's air molecules at that point, much less his chair. She'd asked, "Why were you talking to him?" And she hadn't been able to make it casual.

"Why wouldn't I?" Wes had answered. "Just a guy I met fishing."

So then she'd had to explain, and he'd shrugged and dropped it, seeming like he didn't care one way or the other, which he probably hadn't. But now, she was confused. Wes was from Colorado. He had enough country in him to fish, at least. If he'd liked Lake enough to sit and talk to him, what was the problem with meeting her folks?

Wes sighed, sat up, and switched on the light, and she pulled herself up as well, taking the sheet with her. She had a feeling it would be better to be covered up for this.

"Rochelle," he said, his voice patient enough to make her antennae quiver, "this is a lot of fun. But obviously, it's not going to lead anywhere."

"Obviously?" She wasn't cold now. She was starting to burn.

"Well, you're not exactly . . ." He laughed a little.

"Not. Exactly. What."

He looked at her, a rueful smile on his handsome face.

"Oh, come on," she said. "Spell it out."

"I'm sorry," he said. "I thought it was understood. I've got plans for the future. I'm sure I'll settle down eventually, but . . ."

"Right." She threw the sheet back, got out of bed, and started gathering her clothes. "I'm not marriage material. The mother of your future children had better have PhD after her name."

"Well, at least a master's, I imagine," he said. "I mean, no offense, but we're not quite a match, are we? Intellectually, I mean, or—well, economically, either. There are levels. You're a fun girl, but I *do* want my kids to be . . ."

"Smart," she said. "Right. Got it. I'm good enough to screw, but your future wife isn't a thirty-year-old divorcee with a hick accent and a high school diploma and boobs two cup sizes too big for the Faculty Club."

She was dressed despite her shaking hands. Now, she stalked around to his side of the bed and grabbed his clothes. Button-down shirt, stupid boring Dockers, shoes. His socks and underwear? Maybe she'd mail them to him. Interoffice.

"What are you doing?" he asked. "Hey!" he added as she headed out to the living room with her armful of clothes.

He was out of bed, and she could hear him tripping heavily over the comforter. "By the way," she tossed back over her shoulder, "you're clumsy in bed, too. I hope that brilliant future wife of yours isn't interested in orgasms, because your sorry skills sure aren't going to get her there."

She was opening her front door on the words, hauling back, and flinging his clothes out onto Main Street with all the force she had. The Dockers sailed right past the sidewalk and into the gutter. Well, they were heavy. Wallet, keys, and all. The keys came loose along the way, too. He'd been in too much of a hurry to get her own pants off to pull anything out of his pockets. Sucked to be him.

He wasn't even talking. He had his mouth open, but no words were coming out. There was a good group across the street, too, hanging around outside the bar smoking. Bonus.

"Somebody's going to be doing the walk of shame," she told Wes. "And that somebody isn't me. Get out of my house."

"I will not," he said. "Go get my clothes. Right now."

He was looming over her, grabbing her arm, but she wasn't her daddy's girl for nothing. She swung around behind him, got both hands on his back and her shoulder into it, and gave him a hard shove like she was moving a reluctant cow out of her way. It was all in how much you meant it. The push sent him stumbling out the door and teetering at the top of the three concrete steps. She saw that before she slammed the door after him and turned the lock.

"Hey!" He pounded on the door a few times, and she could hear the laughter and shouts from across the street.

She took two fast steps to her front window, shoved it up, and watched him dash across the wide downtown sidewalk and into the street for his pants. He pulled them on, hopping on one foot when his toes caught in the leg.

"You can take your PhD," she called through the window, "and shove it up your ass. I might not have a college degree, but I know an asshole when I see one. And I'm looking at you."

You could run away from people who hurt you, or you could hit back. You could break up like a lady, or you could make him pay, no matter how much that might come back to bite you later. And somehow, with her? The fierce always won.

She might be white trash, but at least she'd go down swinging.

BAGGAGE

Travis forced his hands to relax. Because one of them was a fist, and the other one was clenched so tight around the milk carton, he was crushing it.

It had taken a second for it to filter through, because he'd been halfway listening to Chang, and halfway—well, more than halfway—getting ready to take off after Rochelle. But once he'd realized what he was hearing . . . he'd been burning.

"You know," he said, keeping his voice slow and calm, "that's interesting."

King had been annoyingly friendly, and even more annoyingly full of himself, ever since Travis had arrived on campus. Like they were colleagues, like they were both on the superstar track, even though Travis was a lecturer, not a professor. Not on the academic train, and not interested in hopping aboard. Which meant that King was looking to get in on Travis's next venture. Which wouldn't be happening.

Now, the other man turned a laughing face to him. "*Interesting* would be one word. Or you could call it, 'Hot damn, that woman can swallow you whole. And she's more than willing to do it.'"

"What I'm asking myself," Travis said, pretending he hadn't heard him, "is why a smart woman like Rochelle would mix herself up with a piece of shit like you. Which makes me think," he went on, noticing with satisfaction that King's mouth had opened in shock, "that you're lying."

King shoved his chair back and stood up, but that didn't worry Travis one bit. He stood a little taller. A little straighter. And then he set the milk carton down on the counter, dropped his hands to his sides, and flexed his fingers. Just that slight straightening and relaxation of his hands, but King saw it.

King's buddy, Matfield, had pushed the other way. Backward, into the wall.

Travis spared him a contemptuous glance. "Yeah," he said, "I'd guess that pink's a color neither of you sees much of. Offscreen, that is."

"What?" Matfield asked. "Pink?"

"Work it out," Travis said.

King's face was flushing, but he hadn't taken a step, and he wouldn't. "Hell, yeah, asshole," he said. "I see plenty of pink. I sure as hell saw all of hers. I nailed that six ways from Sunday. I can give you a blow-by-blow account. So to speak."

"Creative Writing's in another building." Travis picked up his milk carton, walked to the door without one single bit of hurry, tossed his trash, and added, "And where I come from, guys who talk that kind of smack about a woman can get their faces beaten in. Just a thought." And then he walked out and waited for the adrenaline to settle.

So much for collegiality. He might have to sit by himself at the next department meeting.

That was when he saw the nuts. Or, more accurately, felt them crunching underfoot.

It took him a second to figure it out. When he did, he closed his eyes and swore silently, then took off up the stairs, two at a time. All the way to the fourth floor.

He was still moving fast when he made it into her office, and she was already there. Of course she was. No stop in the ladies' room, not for Rochelle. She was at her computer, focusing hard. She was paler than usual and that was all.

Until she turned her head and saw him.

"No," she said. "Go away."

"Sorry you heard that," he said, stopping a couple paces from her desk.

"Yeah. I heard it. And I heard you, too. Oh, wait. I didn't."

"Ah." He breathed out the word. "You left too soon, then."

"You're telling me you didn't sit there and laugh. You're telling me you didn't *share*. I've been talked about like that my whole damn life. I know how it works. Nice club you guys belong to."

There were a few tears in her eyes now. He could see them. He could tell that she wouldn't be letting them spill over, though, because she couldn't afford to let herself feel weakness, let alone show it. Something inside him twisted at the thought.

"Hasn't anybody ever had your back?" he asked her gently.

"Lots of guys would tell you they have," she said with a choked, angry laugh. "And I'm busy. Get out. Call it another narrow escape. For both of us, because you wouldn't want to keep getting those sloppy seconds. Not a classy guy like you."

She'd kept her voice low, but the dean poked his head out of his office. "Everything all right?"

"Yep," Rochelle said tightly. "Travis was just finishing something up."

"Right, then." Dr. Olsen looked hard at Travis, then headed back into his office.

"He thinks he can look out for me," Rochelle said. "So, yes. Somebody's got my back. Somebody who's over sixty, and *kind*."

Those tears were still threatening, and she still wasn't going to give into them. "Come on," he said. "We're going to talk about this."

"I'm busy. And there's nothing to talk about. Strike one. You're out."

"*Damn* it." His hand wanted to come down hard on her desk, so he shoved it into his pocket and focused on breathing. "Have some faith. Five minutes."

She looked at him, her eyes narrowed, and he looked right back at her and didn't move. "Five minutes," he said again.

"I already took my break."

"Take another one."

◆ ◆ ◆

He walked beside her down the hall and didn't say anything, because he couldn't think of the right thing to say. But then, she didn't, either. She also didn't explain when she shoved her key into the doorknob of the Materials Science Lab and switched on the light.

"Right," she finally said once he'd shut the door behind him. She turned to face him, the heavy black tables and complicated machinery stretching on either side of her, the smell of oil hanging in the air. "Talk."

"I'm not going to talk," he said, which was probably shooting himself in the foot, but he was saying it anyway. "I already told you. I took care of it. You either trust me to tell you the truth or you don't. I can't do anything about that."

"Then why are we here?"

"So you can tell me which it is."

Her eyes searched his face, and he leaned back against a table, breathed in and out some more, and tried not to let it matter as much as it did.

"Why did you come here?" she asked. "Why this job? You said you left San Francisco. You told me why you left, too. But why here?"

"Ah. Well." It wasn't an answer to his question, but it was pretty clear that she needed her own answers. He considered how much to tell her. "It's another story, but for now—I wanted a change. Another change. I'd spent some time in Spokane, remember, and the area seemed . . . right. Quiet. Peaceful. I wanted peaceful, at the time. I looked at some pictures online, and maybe I remembered that I'd met somebody from Paradise once. Maybe."

"Somebody you hadn't looked up."

"Didn't know her name. But I thought maybe I'd find her again. And I did."

She was silent, and he stood and waited, because he was a patient man. Finally, he tried again. "If it helps, I think I get it."

"No," she said, looking him straight in the eye. "You don't. You don't know what it's like to run a gauntlet in high school every time you go to your locker. You don't know how it feels to trust that maybe this time, it'll be different, and to get it thrown back in your face. You don't know what it's like to feel like a piece of meat. A piece of ass. To know that looking good or having good sex with a man will make him think you're trash. You know one reason I stayed married as long as I did? Because at least I got some respect when I had that ring on my finger."

"You're right," he said when he could manage it. "I don't know. But that doesn't mean I'm that man."

"Why should I believe you?"

"Why shouldn't you? What have I done to make you doubt me? Besides the obvious," he said, his smile a bit painful. "But since then."

"A man will do a lot to get into my pants."

This time, he couldn't control himself. His palm came down hard on the table beside him. Which didn't help anything, so he picked his hand up again and ran it through his hair. "Right," he said. "Right." He looked down between his feet and breathed out, slow and steady, then looked back at her. "You're bitter. I get it. It sounds like you've got plenty of reason to be. But—you know, from where I sit, it looks like that bitter's trying hard to drown out all your sweetness, and that's just a crying shame. It's got to be tough to reach out and grab hold of somebody new when you're carrying all that baggage." Which he had no right to say, but once again, he was saying it anyway, because he liked her too much not to try.

She stood there, and he could see the movement in her throat as she swallowed. "But," she said, "you're leaving."

"That's true. I am. But people find ways to work things out. At least so I hear."

He waited a minute, but she didn't answer, and finally, he sighed and pushed off the table. "Hell, Rochelle. I don't know what would happen. Neither do you. All I can promise is that I'll tell you the truth."

"We're going to go slow," she said, and his heart started to hammer even harder than it had when he'd first seen her walk into the break room. When he'd first wondered why he hadn't headed up to her office the second his class had been over. And whether it was at all because he'd been scared himself. Scared of what he felt.

"You bet we are," he said. "You bet."

"And I'm not promising anything."

"Got it."

"And I've got to get back to work."

She didn't move, though, and he took one step, two, until he was almost touching her, the tips of her generous breasts nearly brushing his chest.

"Did I mention," he said quietly, "that you look beautiful today? And that I missed you?"

She swayed the tiniest bit toward him, and when her body touched his . . . that was all it took. His hands were in her hair, holding her head, and he'd backed her up against that table and was kissing her hard. Taking that lush mouth he'd been torturing himself with remembering for three days now, and devouring it. He wasn't holding back one bit, and she was opening up and urging him on. Her hands were on his shoulders, then sliding down his back and up again as if she wanted to feel him the same way he was dying to feel her.

He couldn't stand it. He dropped his head to her neck and took a bite. *There*, right at that tender spot at the side. She gasped aloud, and the fire burned hotter. One hand settled over the curve of her gorgeous ass, and he pulled her in closer, higher, harder. He was kissing her neck now, and she was making some noise.

He needed to be inside her. He needed to show her. That was all.

He didn't register the sound of the key in the door at first. It was the throat clearing that had him leaping back.

"Uh . . ." A young, bearded guy in jeans, holding a backpack. Grad student. "Sorry."

Travis had stepped instinctively in front of Rochelle, but she moved right around him, shoved her hair back from her face, nodded at the guy, said, "No problem," and walked out of the room without glancing at Travis again.

He followed her, grabbing the door as she was pulling it open and holding it for her, then heading out himself.

He should have given her a hug and left it at that. What had he been thinking? He *hadn't* been thinking, that was what. Not with his brain, anyway.

"See," she said, striding down the hall in those heels, tall and magnificent, her appearance offering no hint of the fragile, tender pieces inside, "that's exactly why I can't do this. I'm not going to be that person anymore. The one he'll tell all the other grad students about, so they'll be thinking how they'd like to do me, too. I have to live here. I have to work here. My job matters. To my family. And to me." The words were running away with her, the sentences short and choppy, not like Rochelle at all. "I've clawed my way right up from the bottom, and I'm not falling back down. That's why I tried to be careful last year with Wes. To keep it quiet. And you heard how that worked out. I can't afford this."

"Hey." He took her shoulder and swung her gently around, and she turned with him and looked straight at him, and that *was* Rochelle. "I'm sorry," he said. "I shouldn't have done that. I missed you, and . . . well. But I shouldn't have grabbed you. My fault, and I'm sorry."

Her gaze was level. Steady. "I grabbed you back. There were two of us there. There have been all along. But we've got nothing to build here. I can't do this."

No. He wasn't letting this go without a fight. "If you can't, you can't. But if that's why? Then I say, screw letting them take away our good thing. And screw letting fear do the same thing. So we go out. What's everyone going to be seeing? A guy who's crazy about a woman and is doing his best to impress her, hoping and praying she likes him half as much as he likes her, and not keeping it one bit quiet. If anybody's got something to say about us, they can say it to me, because I'm going to be standing right there beside you to hear it. And to deal with it, too. That's a promise."

"For what, three months? Three and a half? You think that's going to work?"

He reached out to touch her cheek, because he wanted to hold her so badly, and he couldn't, not there in the hallway in front of her office. She leaned her face into his palm for the barest instant, and this time, it made his heart turn over.

"Yeah," he said. "I think it is."

BACK UNDER CONTROL

Rochelle was still shaken, but she wasn't going to show it any more than she could help. The way he'd kissed her, and the look in his eyes just now . . .

"I'm so bad at slow," she said, then forced her feet to take her back into the office, where she seated herself behind her desk and stuck her sign back in the drawer. Back to work. Back under control.

"So is that a yes?" He had his thumb hooked into the front pocket of his jeans again, and one hip canted like a rodeo rider. How was she supposed to resist that?

"That's a maybe." The words came out, just like that. Because of how he'd touched her face. Because of what he'd said. *Screw letting them take away our good thing.* Those were her kind of fightin' words. And because he cared about his parents, and . . . She was going *down.* She could feel it.

He's leaving, she told herself desperately, but her sensible self was losing ground all the time.

"I'll take maybe," he said. "But if slow's really what you want, we're going to have to be creative here. I don't seem to have much restraint."

"Well," she said, firing up her computer, "I like creative."

"You're not helping."

She smiled, feeling a whole lot better. "Let's see what you've got, big boy."

"And again. Not helping."

She put her elbows on the desk, plopped her chin on her folded hands, and looked up at him. It would have given him a look down her cleavage, if she showed cleavage at work, which she didn't. But she could tell it was an effort to keep his eyes up high all the same. "Well?"

"Uh . . . dinner tonight?" he tried. "Someplace nice?"

She sighed, sat up straight, and picked up the catering list for tonight's reception. "*A*, not all that creative, and not exactly the slow lane, either. It's the way you look at me. Someplace nice? Candles? Mmm . . . too tempting, don't you think? And *B*, Dr. Olsen's got a function I have to start getting ready for in half an hour. Not tonight."

All right, she was messing with him. Too bad.

"Thought you didn't think in outline form," he said.

"Hey. I learned from the best."

"All right. Dancing Friday."

"We didn't do so well with that last time. Going-slow-wise."

"No. We didn't. Anyway, you're right, let's save that up. That's dessert. That's the prize, once we're not going slow anymore, because we're going to get there if I've got a single thing to do with it. OK, then. Saturday. I'm going to call you with the plan."

"Am I going to be impressed?"

"Well," he said, "let's hope."

◆　　◆　　◆

"A bike ride," Stacy said flatly on Friday night. "To Ithaca. Thirteen miles. And *back*."

"Yep," Rochelle said, doing her perky-cheerleader thing again. "It's a beautiful path."

"And you'd know this how?"

"All right, so I've never done it. And I don't usually ride that far. But everybody *says* it's a beautiful path, and it's not supposed to be as hot on Saturday. I'm sure it'll be great. And here's the deal. I'd like you to come."

Stacy looked up at her with the one eye that was visible. She was lying facedown on her bed after her shift working the drive-through window at Macho Taco. "No."

"Come on." Rochelle sat down beside Stacy and ran a hand over her long brunette hair, stroking her the way she had when her sister had been six. She'd been impatient plenty of times then, all the mornings she'd had to get five reluctant kids out the door and onto the school bus, resenting that it was her job, that her parents had had so many kids and so little money. Now, the impatience had turned to worry for her bright, studious little sister. "You don't have anything going on until the evening tomorrow. Why not do something healthy, instead of . . ." *Winding yourself up until you're halfway to crazy and then going out and staying gone until the bars close,* she didn't say.

It wasn't Stacy's job she was worried about, and it was only partly Stacy's classes. It was what was happening between those times.

Stacy had always had a tender heart, though. Rochelle would appeal to that. For one thing, she *did* want to spend time with her sister. And for the other, she needed reinforcements. "It would really help me if you came."

Stacy rolled over onto her back. "Really? Why?"

Rochelle shrugged. She wasn't used to showing vulnerability to her younger siblings, and it felt plenty awkward. "Because I like him too much to make good decisions, maybe."

"Huh." Stacy looked slightly more interested. "You didn't seem like you did. When he planted that bush and you kicked him out."

"I didn't kick him out. I just didn't invite him *in*. Would you come? Please?"

Stacy heaved a sigh. "OK. But *I've* ridden twenty miles lots of times. You're going to whine."

"I never whine."

"Yeah? We'll see."

"It's not that hilly. I've driven out there plenty. And we're having lunch in between. How hard could it be?"

BREAKTHROUGH

Jim Lawson's phone buzzed, and he picked it up without taking his eyes off the computer screen. "Lawson."

"It's Francine." At the front desk. "I've got a girl on the other line who wants to talk to the person in charge of the murder investigation." She didn't have to say which one. They only had one. Murder wasn't exactly common around here, especially murder with any kind of mystery attached. "I can't reach Detective DeMarco, and he's off duty. I asked about putting her through to his voice mail, but I think we could lose her. She sounds pretty skittish."

"Put her on."

A click, a pause, then another click and Francine saying, "Ma'am? You're connected to Deputy Lawson."

"Hello?" The voice was young, a little sullen, and a lot wary.

"Deputy Sheriff Lawson here, ma'am," he said. "I understand you have some information for us." He hoped so. Guys killing their exes—it wasn't exactly new territory. But that didn't make it any less evil.

Some men didn't believe in good or evil. He wasn't one of them.

"I don't want to get in any trouble," the girl was saying now.

Nobody ever did. "If you know something," he said, "please tell me. A young girl is dead here, and we'd like to catch her killer. If you're calling me, I'm guessing you'd like us to do that, too."

"I don't really *know* anything," she said, and he waited. Two beats. Three. "But I think I might know who she is."

HOW HARD COULD IT BE?

I've driven it lots of times, Rochelle had told Stacy. *How hard could it be?*
Really, really hard.

It started out just fine, with her looking Saturday-morning good
in a trim, sleeveless yellow blouse that still didn't show too much, but
could maybe get a man thinking that if she unfastened just one more
button—or he did—that situation would change. And another skort,
a dark-blue one with flowers this time, since she could tell Travis liked
looking at her legs.

He showed up right on time, and he didn't exactly look her up and
down, but he noticed. Oh, yeah. He did.

He stood on her front porch, said, "Hi," and smiled at her, slow and
sure, and she just about melted. He had the most smiling eyes she'd ever
seen, he was dressed in shorts and a gray T-shirt that stretched across
about an acre of long, lean, hard muscle, and she wanted to take a bite
out of him.

"Come on in," she managed to say. "We're almost ready."

He followed her inside and said, "We?"

"Yep," she said. "I forgot to mention, I asked Stacy if she wanted to
come along." And then she held her breath.

"This would be some more going slow, then."

"That's would it would be."

He seemed fine with that, too. If it hadn't been for the way he'd kissed her earlier in the week, she'd have thought he didn't even care.

But he *had* kissed her like that. His mouth had been so deliciously firm against hers. Before he'd bitten her neck, that is. Before he'd pressed her against the table and hauled her up with one hand, letting her know that in another thirty seconds she'd have been sitting up there with her skirt around her waist.

That was why they were riding bikes today. With her sister. Which, after the first hour, she was more than ready to be done with.

Rochelle's bike, which she'd been delighted to use for errands around town after years of living off gravel roads out in the boondocks, was fat-tired and upright, as opposed to Stacy's and Travis's much faster models. Travis, though, seemed ready to accommodate that. In fact, by the time he'd looked back to find her missing and slowed to allow her to catch up for about the twelfth time, she'd had enough. She told him, as brightly as she could manage, "You go ahead and ride with Stacy. I'm fine."

"Not really the idea," he said. "The point isn't how fast we do it. The point is doing it together."

"Thanks for not bringing the testosterone. But please. Go on. I'll meet you at the end. I'm just . . . taking in the scenery."

All right, it was true, it was beautiful. The hills rolling like an inland sea—stubble fields, now, the remnants of harvested wheat and barley— glowing gold in the sunlight. Blue sky, puffy white clouds, the buzz of insects beside the path, and the foothills rising toward the low mountains to the east.

It was home, and it was good. But "foothills" meant "hills," which were one heck of a lot steeper than they seemed in a car, even on a day that wasn't too hot. And "hills" meant hard pedaling, not to mention something you could call . . . pressure. Which she didn't need Travis to notice.

Stacy had been right. Rochelle normally didn't ride more than a few miles at a time, and she was discovering that an exercise bike at the University Fitness Center also wasn't quite the same as this. Her bike saddle, although it had plenty of padding as far as her butt was concerned, was contoured fairly . . . interestingly for the rest of her. Which she'd noticed before, and not in a bad way. Hey, a girl had to get her sexual stimulation somehow.

At first, it had felt good. Before it got to be way too much, like when you were with a guy who'd never grasped the concept of indirect contact. She wriggled and readjusted, trying to find a more comfortable position, and it only made things worse. By the time she finally rolled into the outskirts of the tiny town of Ithaca and spotted the cafe, she was hopping off the bike with two blocks still to go.

Travis, of course, climbed back onto his own bike and came looping back to her. "All right?" he asked.

He was looking worried, like this wasn't working out the way he'd planned. "Fine!" she said chirpily. "Great. It was a beautiful ride."

He looked at her more closely. "Sure? You look a bit stiff. Your seat not comfortable?"

She thought about telling him exactly what wasn't comfortable, but she wasn't supposed to be sharing anatomical details with him, so she said, "I'm fine," and tried another smile. Like a gracious beauty pageant contestant. Or an electroshock victim. One or the other.

All she needed was a break. And maybe an injection of local anesthetic.

The café was tiny, with only six wooden tables, its best feature a wide back patio shaded by a huge maple and overlooking a creek overhung with aspens and weeping willows. It was time for shade, a drink, and a sandwich. And not sitting on a bicycle seat.

She took a hasty detour to the ladies' room, doing her best not to wince at the burn from peeing on chafed lady parts, then went out to the washbasin to fix her hair and minimal makeup. At least she didn't have mascara running down her face today. And it was *nice* to have a man want to do a fun, adventurous activity with her. As opposed to the fun, adventurous activity they usually proposed.

Stacy had come in with her, and now, she propped herself against the wall beside the sink for a chat. Looking reasonably perky, so this *had* been a good idea.

"Travis is pretty great," she said. "I mean, no bad-boy vibe or anything, so I don't see why I had to come, but kinda hot for an older guy. Good arms."

He had good thighs, too. He had good everything. But no bad-boy vibe? Maybe because he didn't feel the need to share it with absolutely every woman he met. Rochelle'd gotten plenty of bad-boy off him, one way and another. But she didn't share that. "At least he's wearing regular clothes," she agreed, feeling more cheerful. "No padded shorts so tight, you could take an exact measurement of his junk. No bright-yellow spandex shirt covered with pretend-sponsor names, and he didn't spend the whole time pedaling away from us like he was trying to win the Tour de Rural Bike Path. Although I can see why people do those padded shorts now."

Stacy smiled with satisfaction. "Your butt sore?"

Second person to ask her that. "No. And I'm *not* whining, so don't get your hopes up." She tucked her comb back into her backpack and said, "Ready?"

Travis kept being nice. He bought them lunch and an extremely welcome beer, leaned back in his chair with that relaxed ease that got Rochelle every time, and talked to Stacy as if he wasn't sorry she'd come along.

"So pre-med, huh?" he asked her. "I'm impressed. What kind of doctor?"

"I don't know." Stacy took a swallow of beer. "I haven't decided. I have to get there first. I mean, it's going fine," she added hastily.

"Something giving you trouble?" Travis asked.

She shrugged. "Not too bad. I'm OK."

"Mine was English Composition," Travis said. "First semester of freshman year. It about did me in right there, before I'd even started. They wanted us to analyze the themes in these novels. How do I know? I just know if it's a good story or not. And it was usually 'not.' I barely squeaked out of that. What's yours?"

Stacy's eyes flew to his face as if she were checking whether she could trust him not to laugh at her. Rochelle knew the feeling. She sat quietly and listened, wondering if a tiny window was finally opening up to her sister's heart.

"Statistics," Stacy finally said. "I mean, lots of things are hard. Sometimes I don't think I . . ." She stopped and visibly swallowed. "But this professor . . . he doesn't explain it so I get it. Or I just don't get it." She picked up her sandwich and scrutinized it as if it were fascinating, and Rochelle saw that her hand was shaking. "I don't know. I don't . . . I don't *get* it."

"Hmm," Travis said. "What exactly? What's tough?"

"Regression analysis, right now," Stacy said reluctantly. "I know I *should* be able to understand it," she hurried on, her cheeks flushing, "but I keep getting confused. I can do the math. Calculus was fine, and lots of people think that's harder. But this . . . I don't get the *idea*."

"OK," Travis said. Calm as always, soothing some of Rochelle's own jangles at Stacy's out-of-proportion distress. "Well, fortunately, here you are, and here I am, and Rochelle isn't talking to me, because I made her ride too far, not to mention that she knows she still has to get home. So we might as well bore her to death."

"I didn't say—" Rochelle began.

"Nope," he said. "You didn't. I'm reasonably fluent in body language, though." He pulled a pen out of his pack and grabbed an extra napkin off the table. "Here we go. But we'll do something that'll keep Rochelle at least marginally interested, how's that?"

"You think?" Rochelle took another sip of her own beer. She was already getting light-headed. Alcohol, warmth, and exercise weren't the best combination. Witness her tequila-fueled error of judgment with Travis.

"You're looking at the relationship of one thing to another kind of thing, right?" Travis was explaining to Stacy like a man who'd never taken a woman right off a dance floor and into his bed. "How much you can rely on one factor predicting the other. Let's say . . . how likely it is that a professor of a certain age will be a decent guy. Say your hypothesis is that they get better as they get older. So the horizontal axis is age, and the vertical one is, let's see . . ."

He grinned at Rochelle and drew two crossing lines, labeling the bottom end of the vertical line "Dickhead" and the top end "Works for Rochelle," then crosshatching the horizontal line and labeling it with numbers in increments of five, from thirty to sixty.

"So," he said, "since this is data Rochelle would have, let's let her fill it in."

She grabbed the napkin, put a dot down near the intersection of the two lines, and labeled it "Wes." Thirty and a dickhead. And then tracked all the way over to the "sixty" and wrote in, "Dr. Olsen," nice and high. Right opposite "Works for Rochelle."

"Best over-sixty guy out there," she said. "In the college, that is. And then there's the rest of them." She drew nine or ten more dots. "Each representing a known individual. I won't write names in. I'll let you draw your own conclusions once you know them better."

"Hmm," Travis said. "Now we do the best-fit line." He turned the napkin around so it faced Stacy and handed her the pen. "What would that look like?"

She hesitated, the pen hovering over the graph, then finally drew a horizontal line and looked up at him questioningly.

He smiled at her like he'd won the lottery. "Yep. That's it. You've got a fairly random scatter there, I'd say."

"Right," Stacy said. "Which means not much slope. No correlation between age and . . ."

"Level of dickhead," Travis agreed. "The older ones aren't better?" he asked Rochelle.

"Not so much. Mostly, they're about the same guy they started out being. Nice, or not. Sometimes they get worse. They start thinking they're superior, just because they get to grade people. The line might actually look like this." She made an adjustment to her sister's line. "If I gave it some more thought, got more exact."

"It might slope down a little," Stacy said.

"But not much," Rochelle said.

"Low r value." Travis looked at Stacy. "Meaning what?"

"One doesn't predict the other. Low . . . correlation coefficient? Between age and how good a guy he is." Stacy was looking excited now.

"There are all levels of professors," Rochelle agreed. "At any age."

Travis glanced at her, then started talking to Stacy again, grabbing another napkin, assigning values and doing math, and the technical part got beyond Rochelle. Stacy was nodding, though, taking the pen and doing her own calculations, so the explanation was obviously working.

Finally, Stacy sat back with a sigh and said, "Thanks. I think I've got it. It's so easy . . . when *you* explain it." She blinked, and Rochelle could swear there were tears trying to make it out.

"No problem," Travis said. "You need anything else, just ask. Anytime. I'm pretty good with statistics. As opposed to teaching game design. I wish my students would say what you just did, but maybe it depends on how quick the student is at picking it up, too. I'll tell myself that." He looked at Rochelle, then. "And sorry. I tried to keep it entertaining, but there's only so fascinating I could make that."

"Nope," she said. "I learned something, too. Besides what 'r squared' means, and maybe even how you get the p value."

"Which you understood." His eyes were so warm, which was completely unfair.

"More or less. The major ideas, at least. As long as this isn't going to be on the test."

"Have I ever told you that you've got a fairly terrific brain yourself?" he asked her.

It was the beer, surely, that had her floating away like she was filled with helium, and she couldn't answer for a moment.

"So what else did you learn?" he asked.

She took the pen from him, and when her hand brushed his, she felt the thrill of that bit of contact all the way to her toes. It even made it past some of the numbness in her nether regions. She swiveled the napkin around to face her and drew a new dot, hanging out alone, high on the graph above the "thirty" mark and right across from "Works for Rochelle." And then she looked at him and labeled it "Travis."

He cleared his throat. "I'm thirty-five, actually. You might want to move the point to the right along the horizontal axis."

She dropped the pen. "OK. That's the last time I compliment an engineer."

GOING SLOW

The day was turning out better than Travis had feared when he'd first seen Rochelle walking stiff-legged up the bike path toward the café and had cursed himself as an idiot.

Dancing, yes. Swimming, fine. Bike riding, no. Lesson learned, but too late now.

They'd finished lunch, and Stacy was coming back from the ladies' room. *She'd* done just fine riding out here. Like that did him any good at all.

Stacy didn't sit down, though. And she was crying, but trying to hide it.

"I have to . . . I'm going," she said.

Rochelle had risen to her feet. "Sweetie. What's wrong?"

Stacy shook her head violently. "Nothing. Never mind. I have to *go*."

"It's Shane, right?" Rochelle said. "Come on. *Tell* me."

Stacy looked at Travis, wild-eyed, and he got up himself and said, "I'll just—"

Stacy didn't wait for him to leave. "He . . ." She gulped in a breath. "It's just that he can't . . ." Her chin wobbled. "See me. Tonight."

She burst into tears at that, Rochelle put her arms around her and made soothing noises, and Travis stood there and thought again about leaving. He had two younger sisters. He knew all about drama. That didn't mean he enjoyed it.

"Did he say why?" Rochelle asked, smoothing a hand over Stacy's hair.

Another hard shake of the head. "No," Stacy mumbled against Rochelle's shirt, then stood up straight and wiped the heels of her hands across her eyes. "He's busy. He can't. Never mind. I'm going home. I just . . ." Another chin wobble. "I just want to go home."

"Again?" Rochelle said. "What a jerk," and Travis couldn't argue with that.

In a flash, Stacy was scowling at her. "He is *not*. You're always against him." Her voice was rising, becoming shrill. "A guy can be busy, you know! He can have things to do!"

"Sweetie—" Rochelle began. "No. He can't. Can he, Travis?"

"No," he said bluntly. He'd never understood why women were so hell-bent on fooling themselves. "He can't. Unless he asked you about tomorrow. Did he ask you?"

Stacy shook her head wildly again and rushed out of the café so fast, she stumbled over a chair and nearly fell. And then she was on her bike, and gone.

"Huh," Travis said as they watched the lonely figure pedaling away in the sunlight. "She's . . . changeable."

"She sure is." Rochelle looked after her sister with a frown. "She didn't used to be, at least not as much. I think the pressure of school might really be getting to her. Like she finally told you, even though she's never told me. The bad boyfriend doesn't help."

"How bad?"

"Not an abuser. Not physical, anyway, from what I can see, or I'd already have . . ."

"Borrowed your dad's shotgun," he guessed.

"Who says I'd have to borrow one?"

He smiled, and she smiled reluctantly back. She sat down again, turned her beer glass in her hand, and sighed. "But he's got her off balance for sure. Hot and cold, so she doesn't know what to expect. He can be busy until the cows come home as far as I'm concerned, but . . . what kind of guy doesn't want to see you on the weekend?"

"A guy with another girlfriend."

"That's what I was thinking. Or just that he's playing games."

"Guys don't play that kind of game much. The stakes are too high. Giving up a sure thing to win some kind of points? No. If he doesn't want to be with her on the weekend, he's with another girl. If we're talking 'sex possible with both parties.'"

"Wow." She blinked. "You don't mess around."

"Well, no. Not usually. And right now, I should tell you that I'd be happy to ride back and get the truck for you and your bike. Forty-five minutes, another beer while you sit right here, and I'm driving you home."

"No. Of course not." She stood up and shook it off, because that was Rochelle. "I'm good to go."

Five miles in, he could see that she wasn't. Not at all. "So," he said, coming up beside her, "is it your legs, or the seat?"

"Oh." She smiled ruefully. Painfully, too, he could swear. "Is it that obvious?"

"Well, yeah. Sorry. You're in good shape, you swam quite a bit last week, you'd ridden your bike up to school that day, and thirteen miles isn't very far, so . . ." He cut himself off at the look on her face. "I'm digging myself in deeper, aren't I?"

"No. It was a nice idea, and good of you to be all right with Stacy coming along. Not your fault."

"You're a generous woman," he said, and maybe he wasn't just talking about Stacy. "But then, I already knew that."

"Do not even go there," she said, reading his mind. "Right now, it has zero appeal."

"Oh. Not your legs, then."

"Nope, and not my butt, either."

He suppressed a snort of laughter, and at her glare, said, "Sorry, but you see my problem. If I laugh, I'm an insensitive jerk. If I ask you questions, I'm an insensitive jerk. If I get uncomfortable and shut up, I'm a socially awkward engineer, and I lose that spot on your graph. And, yes, I put it in my pocket. I know you saw. It was a sentimental moment for me. Even though I'm not a professor."

"Close enough," she muttered.

"OK, I'm going for it. I decided that 'socially awkward engineer' is worse. You need a new seat."

"No kidding."

"I could research it, if you like."

"You going to Google 'bike seat' and 'clitoral pressure'?"

He laughed. He couldn't help it. "All right. I laughed. I'm officially an insensitive jerk. Yes, I'll look that up. Consider it my penance for putting you through this. I'll find the right seat for you, and I'll even change it out. You can't be the only one. Guys have issues, too. Bike seats are notorious."

"I noticed you weren't wearing padding."

"So rare," he said with a sigh.

"What?" A tiny smile was peeking out. He was distracting her. Good.

"That I get the opportunity to discuss our crotches with the one and only woman I'm looking to use them with. Wait," he protested when she choked back a laugh of her own. "That didn't come out quite right. It was supposed to be much smoother."

"Never mind. If you were trying to turn me on, I'm pretty sure it'll never be possible again."

"So as a going-slow technique, this worked?"

"Yeah." She shifted position once more. "Congratulations."

WAITING FOR PERFECT

When Travis had picked her up that morning, Rochelle had thought about what it would be like to kiss him good-bye. About how she might take him around the back to look at the rest of her garden first, and how he might have kissed her again the way he had in the lab. Like he couldn't get enough.

She did look at her garden, eventually. It wasn't that exciting. An hour after she'd arrived home, after she'd climbed into a nice deep bath and reluctantly out of it again. When she was turning the hose on the plants in her backyard. By herself.

She saw Charlie first. The little white terrier mix came scampering across the yard, tail wagging, and jumped out of the path of the hose as if it were attacking him.

Dell wasn't far behind. She was wearing a broad red straw sun hat today to go with her cherry-patterned blouse, and carrying a pitcher of iced tea and two glasses out to her patio table.

"Come on over and sit in the shade with me when you're done," she called.

When Rochelle had finished her watering and accepted the invitation, Dell poured her a glass of iced tea, using her special watermelon-printed patio glasses, and said, "That hydrangea in the front is looking all right. Thought it might die, planted so late and all, but it's doing real well. You're taking good care of it."

"If that was supposed to be a subtle opening," Rochelle said, "it isn't working."

"You think I'm a nosy old woman."

"I don't think. I'm sure."

Dell chuckled her low ho-ho-ho. "Now, what's got you all grumpy? Just because you came home hot and tired, and he didn't kiss you good-bye as good as you hoped? What was that peck on the cheek all about?"

"Do you see *everything*? What do you do, sit over there with a telescope?"

Dell just smiled and lifted her glass. "Honey, my entertainment sources are limited, and people are a whole lot more interesting than soap operas. You're not as good as you could be, though, I've got to say. Now, when the Kavanaughs were living next door? He'd go to work, and, oh, my." She shook her head. "Well, let's just say that I never saw one woman get so much cable TV service in my life, if you get my drift. They've each got their own place now. And today? I saw Stacy come hightailing on home and leaving again, after she started out on that bike ride with you. Was leaving the two of you alone your idea, or hers?"

Rochelle had been smiling, but now, she sobered. "Hers. She's been moody, upset about her boyfriend. And about school, I finally realized today. But Travis was being so sweet to her, took us both to lunch and was helping her with a math problem, and then . . . the boyfriend thing, and she left. Didn't leave me a note, either. Did that Shane come pick her up, by any chance?"

"Nope. She walked. Dressed to kill, too. Skirt up to her hoo-ha. You ever look in her underwear drawer?"

Rochelle blinked. "What?"

"Girls always think they're being so sneaky. And nine times out of ten, it's in their underwear drawer, whatever it is. Or under the mattress. Like nobody in the world ever thought of that hiding place."

Rochelle remembered packing up Stacy's apartment. About how her sister had emptied her sock and underwear drawers, and then had sat on the bed. Until she'd packed up her bedding.

"What do you . . ." She swallowed. "What do you think it is?"

Dell put her head on one side. "Vodka, maybe. That's usually it, because you won't smell it on 'em, and it's cheap."

"No," Rochelle said. "She's not drunk. Not when she's home, and not even when she *comes* home. At least, not bad."

The blue eyes in their web of wrinkles were sharp. "You know drunk?"

"Oh, yeah. I know drunk real well."

Dell waited, but Rochelle didn't go on. *Seems to me like that bitter's trying to drown out all your sweetness.* Her marriage was over and gone. Time to put the past behind her.

"Well, check that underwear drawer," Dell said at last.

"I will."

"And ask yourself why."

"Why what?"

"What's a pretty young girl like that so scared of? What's she got to hide away from with . . . whatever it is? With booze, or drugs, or bad boys? She's going to college, got a good family. If she's looking to drown herself in something else—why?"

"Why does anybody do anything?" Rochelle said with a sigh.

"Oh, honey," Dell said reproachfully, "you know better than that. There's always a reason. Why are you holding off that prime piece of beef like he was hamburger? Got to be a reason for that, too."

"I knew you'd get around to him."

"Well, somebody's got to. You going to be good with that, when he gives up on you and finds a woman who wants him?"

"He said—" The cold fingers were inching down Rochelle's spine. "That he was good with going slow."

"Uh-huh. For how long? Because, sweet thing . . ." Dell sighed. "There's plenty of somebodies going to be ready and willing. A fine-looking man like that? One who'll look at you the way he does, like he's got a special treat just for you, and he can't wait to give it to you? One who'll take your sister for a bike ride, and be sweet to her, too? Man who can kiss like that? Give me a time machine, and I'll take him myself."

"Well," Rochelle said, giving it her best shot, "if somebody does take him, there's only so long it would be for, no matter what. He's here teaching for one semester, and that's all. Then he's going home to San Francisco. Back to being a hotshot computer millionaire."

"I can sure see why you don't want him. Sounds like a real loser. What in the wide world are you waiting for?"

"Because I want serious," Rochelle tried to explain. "I want a future. I want the real thing. I want—all right. I want a family. And if I'm spending time with Travis, I'm ruling out finding that guy. The right guy."

"Huh." Dell sat quietly for a minute, sipped her iced tea, and stared out over her curved patch of grass, neat pea-gravel path, and the flowering plants bordering it. All the way to the weeping birch and crab apple trees at the edge of the property, and beyond, to something Rochelle couldn't see. "Well, see, I'd have said that if he wasn't the real thing, I couldn't imagine what real would look like. How do you know he's not it?"

"I told you. He's leaving."

"Did he say he wouldn't ever come back?"

Rochelle moved her legs restlessly under the table. "But—"

Dell wasn't done, though. "Planes only fly one way, then?" she asked. "Or did you make some promise to your dying grandpa saying you'd never go anywhere but here?"

"This is—this is where I live," Rochelle said. "Anyway, he never said anything like that."

"Uh-huh. See how impressed I am?" Dell said. "You saving it up until somebody catches sight of you and tells you right then and there that he wants to marry you so you can be his and only his, forever and ever? Because, honey, that might be how it happens in some book from the drugstore, but out in the real world, that isn't true love, it's somebody who's going to be looking in your kitchen windows and scaring the bejeezus out of you when you finally wise up and break it off. Normally, you find a good man, put him through his paces, see if he's willing to, oh, say, take you on a bike ride, plant your flowers, be nice to your sister, meet your folks. And then you see what happens. Might work, and it might not. If you don't give it a try, you'll never know."

"I've given it too many tries already," Rochelle said. "That's my problem."

"Your parts don't come marked off for only so many users," Dell said, and Rochelle about spit out her iced tea. "You got some number of men in your head you can't go above? Forget the number. Who do you imagine knows it besides you? Long as you've got your heart and your eyes open, whose business is it?"

"*You're* saying that?"

"I'm watching for entertainment. It's not my life. It's yours. You going to let a bunch of old biddies like me tell you how to live it?"

"All right, then," Rochelle said. "The truth? I don't want to get hurt again. I want to be sure. I want forever."

"There's only one sure way to not get hurt," Dell said. "That's never to love anybody at all. Course, that hurts, too. And, honey, you can be as sure as the day, you can be right as rain, and you can do every single thing in the world exactly perfect. And you still won't necessarily get forever. Only wrong thing Randy ever did was die on me. But the son of a bitch sure did that."

JUST A GIRL

The girl answered Jim's knock pretty quickly. But then, calling out, "Sheriff's department. Open up!" usually worked.

She was young, blonde from a bottle, and wearing too much makeup. She wasn't from around here, but Jim already knew that. Because it was the second time he'd been in her apartment.

The girl's eyes darted between Jim, in his gray deputy's uniform, and Tony DeMarco, dark and sharp in detective's plain clothes that might have worked fine in Chicago but made him stick out like a sore thumb in Paradise.

"Cheryl Hendricks?" DeMarco asked.

"Yes?"

"May we come in?"

She hesitated a moment, then she glanced down the hall, and Jim knew why. She didn't want to be seen talking to the cops in the hallway of her apartment building. Either to protect her reputation from her neighbors, or . . . to protect it the other way. Because her neighbors weren't the kind of people who'd take kindly to a resident talking to the cops. It was that kind of building.

Just as Jim had expected, she held the door a fraction wider and said, "OK. But I already told him everything I know." She jerked her head at Jim.

DeMarco moved past her and led the way into a small living room that looked out onto an alley, then asked, "May we sit down?"

"Uh . . . sure."

DeMarco sat on one end of the old flowered couch and Jim took the other, removing a small notebook and pencil from his pocket and preparing to take notes.

"Thanks for contacting us," DeMarco began. "I'm very sorry to tell you, but you were right. Your roommate Heather Jones has been positively identified as the murder victim."

The heavily mascaraed brown eyes blinked twice, and the girl picked up a cushion from beside her and hugged it without seeming to realize what she was doing. "Oh."

"And we'd like to ask you some questions about her," DeMarco said.

"I didn't say you could talk to me anymore," she said. "It was a *tip*. An anonymous tip, like on TV." She looked accusingly at Jim. And since he was the good cop, he answered.

"We appreciated your call," he said. "Like I told you, that was the first step toward catching whoever did this to her."

And if you want your tips to stay anonymous, he didn't say, *move to the big city.*

DeMarco spoke up while the girl was off balance. "We just have a few more questions, Cheryl. How long ago did Heather move in with you?"

"Uh . . ." She blinked some more. "Middle of June. Sometime. I can't remember exactly when."

"And when was the last time you saw her?"

"Uh . . . I can't say exactly. Like I told *him* before." She nodded at Jim.

"Please think," DeMarco said. "It's important."

A pause while she bit her thin lips with their heavy coating of dark pink lipstick. "I remember when she was gone for a while," she said slowly. "And I thought, damn it, she's split on me. Because the September rent was due, and I was pissed."

"Around the first, then?" DeMarco asked. "Or the thirty-first?"

"Yeah. Like I said."

"And how long would you say it took you to decide she'd . . . split?" DeMarco asked.

She put her head on one side and bit her lips some more. "About a week. I had to put up a new sign for a roommate, and I remember thinking, if she hadn't come back in a week, she wouldn't be coming back."

Ah. Jim wrote down, *23rd? 24th? 25th?* Closing in.

"How did you arrive at that figure?" DeMarco asked.

"Huh?" Cheryl blinked some more.

"A week. What made that the . . . cutoff date?"

"Oh. If you're with a guy more than a week, it'll be a while," she said matter-of-factly. "Because he wants you to stay. Or he took you somewhere else. Which was fine. I was just pissed she didn't tell me."

"Huh," DeMarco said, and Jim thought for a second about that life, going from one guy to another. "Where had she come from?"

"Seattle. Like I told him. *Already*," she said with another jerk of her head at Jim. "That was where her mom was, anyway."

Her mom—and her mom's loser boyfriend, who, by all accounts, was the reason Heather had been on her own since she'd been seventeen. Jim had seen her high school yearbook picture. Junior year. Her last year. Dark bangs brushing her eyes, long hair, hopeful smile. Jim hoped her mom was suffering over the choice that had led to her eighteen-year-old daughter lying dead in an Idaho ditch. Mothers who chose their men over their children . . . He knew what a mother was supposed to be, and it wasn't that.

"We know where she was from originally, yes," DeMarco said. "But where did she come to *you* from?" When Cheryl still looked at him uncomprehendingly, he said, "Where was she living before?"

Cheryl lifted her narrow shoulders. "With some guy, I guess. The guy she came to town with."

"Who was . . ." DeMarco said. "Who?"

Another shrug. "Some guy who was going to North Dakota, I think. For the fracking."

"So she was . . . what? Hitchhiking?"

"You know. Just . . . with him for a while. Then not. Because he left."

"Uh-huh," DeMarco said as Jim made a note. Some chance of finding *that* guy. "And he didn't come back for her, or contact her that you know of?"

"Um . . . no. I mean, she never mentioned him. She would have said, because she'd have been surprised. It wasn't, like, true love or anything. He was just a guy she was with for a while."

"Right," DeMarco said. "How did you meet her?"

"I had a sign in the Laundromat about the place. She came by. We weren't BFFs or anything. She was just a roommate." She crossed and recrossed her thin legs, shifting restlessly in her chair. "I don't know anything. I told you everything I know. You guys didn't park out front, did you?"

DeMarco ignored that. "Just a few more questions, Cheryl. Where did she get the money to move in with you? I'm guessing there was some money up front, right? How much rent were you charging?"

"Two hundred a month," Cheryl said. "How do I know where she got it? She had a job."

"What job was that?"

"Working at Macho Taco. You should ask *them* when she left. They'd have, like, records. She didn't work every day, but they'd know better than me exactly which days."

"Don't worry," DeMarco said. "We'll be talking to them. How long had she been working there?"

"I don't know. How should *I* know? Since she came, I guess. Why don't you ask them?"

"We will," DeMarco promised again. "What about a boyfriend? Who was she seeing?"

The heart of the matter. Because the DNA results had come back. Heather hadn't been in the criminal justice system. But she'd sure enough been four weeks pregnant, and the father could sure enough be identified. If they could get a match.

They'd keep the information to themselves for now. If the killer had known Heather was pregnant, and if he was the *only* one who'd known—that could be very useful indeed.

Especially since "four weeks pregnant" meant that the father wasn't the mysterious fracker. It was somebody Heather had known in Paradise. Who had just jumped up to prime-suspect level.

"I don't think she was seeing anybody in particular," Cheryl said. Which meant that finding him wouldn't be easy. But then, this one hadn't looked easy from the start. "I mean, nobody special."

"Anybody ever come here?" DeMarco asked.

"No. It was a rule. No guys here. Because it's *my* place, and I don't want some sketchy guy in here stealing my stuff."

"How about when you weren't home?"

"Then I wouldn't know, would I?"

"OK," DeMarco said. They'd ask the neighbors, of course. But the neighbors here? They wouldn't be talking. "Where did she hang out?"

"I saw her sometimes at the Back Alley, maybe," she said reluctantly. "Places like that."

"At bars," DeMarco said.

"Well, yeah. Where else? She wasn't exactly the library type."

"Who with?"

"*I* don't know. Guys."

"Anonymous guys," DeMarco said flatly. "Come on. *Which* guys?"

"I don't know, OK? No one guy. Just guys. Sometimes she came home, and sometimes she didn't. You know."

"Cheryl," Jim said. Time for Good Cop again. "One of them may have killed her. If you know, please tell us. Otherwise, you're leaving a guy out there who's willing to kill a girl and dump her like trash. And she wasn't trash."

He could see her swallow. "How do you know she wasn't?"

"Because nobody's trash," he said. "Nobody deserves that."

A moment, and then she answered. "Maybe . . . country guys, some of them."

"Anybody you know?" Jim said, since he was on a roll here. "Anybody you could describe? Please. Think back. It could be important."

"No," she said. "I didn't notice. I'm not from here, and besides, I go for college guys. You know, ones who might actually get you somewhere. Anyway, she was pretty. You don't hang around in bars with girls who are prettier than you."

"So if you didn't notice," Jim pressed, "how do you know they were country guys?"

Her brow knitted, and DeMarco and Jim sat quiet as she thought. "Chew," she finally said. "On the back pocket." She sketched a circle in the air, and Jim made a note. The round tin of chewing tobacco, always carried in that same pocket until it left a white ring on the back of your jeans. Not necessarily country guys. Plenty of college kids chewed. But those college kids were more likely to have come off of farms.

"How old were these guys?" Jim asked. "Older guys? Kids? What?"

"Not older," Cheryl said immediately. "And not kids. Twenties, thirties, maybe. Like that."

"So you *did* notice them," DeMarco pounced.

"No. Barely. Hardly at all." She was getting agitated again. "I told you. I can't help you. And you can't come back here."

DeMarco ignored that, too. They'd be coming back here. Talking to her neighbors, too. "You called us, what, almost three weeks after she disappeared? A week after the body was found. Why did you wait to report her missing?"

"Because I didn't *know* she was missing. I mean, I knew she wasn't *here,* but how was I supposed to know?" *And I didn't want to get involved,* she didn't have to say. "I thought she'd left with a guy. But then I thought . . ." Something flickered behind the brown eyes. "Maybe it was her. Because I heard, long brown hair and pink shirt. She liked pink. And she left her stuff."

"Could you show us?" DeMarco asked. "Show us her room?"

"It's *my* room. And I rented her bed already, I told you. Weeks ago. She was *gone.*"

"You didn't keep her things?"

"Well, yeah. Some of them."

To his credit, DeMarco didn't show any impatience. "Can you show us her belongings now? We'll be taking them in any case. They're evidence, and her mother will want them."

Maybe her mother would. And maybe she wouldn't.

Cheryl got up, DeMarco looked at Jim, and Jim followed Cheryl back into a tiny bedroom, filled up fairly completely by two twin beds, neither of which was made. Not much of a place. Not much of a life, but somebody's life all the same.

Cheryl got down on her knees and poked around under the far bed, the one by the window, and finally pulled out a green garbage bag.

"I put her stuff in here," she said. "In case."

"That was kind of you," Jim said, taking the bag from her.

The compliment worked, because her mouth got a tiny tremble to it, and she lost a fraction of her toughness, that shell that was probably the only defense she had. "I thought . . ." she said. "You know. In case she came back. When you don't have much, and what you have isn't that great—some people think you wouldn't care, but it's all you *have,* you know?"

"Yeah. I know. Come on." Jim gestured toward the door and followed her out.

She sat in her chair again, and Jim sat on the couch and emptied the bag onto the coffee table.

Cheryl said, "Hey!"

Jim looked up at her. "Sorry. But we want you to go through these things with us, in case any of them are significant." Which they didn't look to be. Jeans, shorts, tops. A pair of high-heeled sandals, a cheap short black dress with spaghetti straps. A tangle of bras, some underwear. And a bear.

A raggedy, floppy thing, its chest replaced with some ancient flowered material, buttons sewn in place of its eyes, and its paws rubbed until they were nothing but a checkerboard of threads.

"No purse," DeMarco said. "No cosmetics. No shampoo. Where's the rest?"

"I didn't save everything," Cheryl said. "I mean, she didn't come back. And I had to rent the place."

She'd used the shampoo, Jim guessed, and maybe even the makeup.

"What about her purse?" DeMarco pressed.

"It wasn't with her? I mean, when they . . ." Her throat worked. "Found her?"

DeMarco ignored that. "She use drugs?" he asked without looking up.

Jim was watching Cheryl. The purse part had rung true. The purse was really missing, then. Well, a woman always took her purse, which made it recognizable. Anybody who'd bothered to hide a body would have disposed of the purse. Where? Anywhere. It was a big county.

He saw Cheryl's eyes shift to the side before she said, "I don't know. It was none of my business."

"But she drank in bars," DeMarco said. "And smoked."

"How do you know?"

DeMarco lifted a flowered top to his nose and took a sniff. "I know. And even if I didn't, the lab will be able to tell us exactly what she smoked, and what other residue is on these clothes. So if that residue isn't yours, you'd better tell us, because otherwise, we might be thinking it came from you."

Cheryl was looking wild-eyed now. "Maybe," she said. "Maybe she did. I wouldn't really know."

"What?" DeMarco asked. "What are we going to find on her clothes that we *wouldn't* find if we, say, searched your apartment? Meth?"

"No," Cheryl said, more alarmed than ever. She made a convulsive movement as if she were going to stand, then clearly thought better of it. "Not meth. *No.* I would have known *that.*"

"Uh-huh. She leave anything behind?"

"I told you. I tossed everything except what's in there."

"Uh-huh. You tossed her drugs. How much weed was it?" DeMarco asked.

"It wasn't—" Cheryl began to say, then clamped her mouth shut.

"We can't help you unless you tell us," Jim said. "If you tell us, you've got nothing to worry about. Like you say—it's nothing to do with you." Cheryl had taken the drugs herself, or she'd sold them. Depending on what they were.

"Maybe . . ." Cheryl hesitated.

"If you remember," Jim said, "tell us. We don't care what you use or don't. We care about finding out who killed her. She didn't have money for drugs, it sounds like." He looked at the pathetic pile of clothes on the coffee table. "Sounds like she was barely hanging on. If we knew what kind of drugs she left behind, it could bring us that much closer to finding her killer. I'm guessing somebody gave them to her. Or that she . . . traded for them, maybe. What do you think? Which one would be more likely?"

Cheryl tucked her arms and legs closer to her body. Drawing in tight, like a crab going into its shell. "Maybe . . . pills," she whispered. "Vikes. And I don't know how she got them. I *don't.*"

Vicodin. Prescription pain medicine. Opiates. The fastest-growing drug problem in North Idaho, and one of the most deceptively addictive. Not a surprise, not in a college town. And the first real break they'd had.

Jim tried some more, and then DeMarco did, but when Cheryl didn't say anything else, just kept looking resolutely at her feet and shaking her head, they gave it up. For today. Jim handed over his card. "I have a daughter myself," he told Cheryl. "I want to find out who did this. This shouldn't have happened. Heather didn't deserve it. She was just a girl with a rough life, trying to get by. That's why you called us, because you cared. And so do we."

Cheryl picked up the ragged bear from the coffee table, rubbing its paw between finger and thumb. "That *is* why I called you," she said. "I know you guys don't believe me, but that's why. I didn't think she'd leave her bear. She slept with it. I bet she'd had it since she was little. I didn't want to call you. I knew I'd get in trouble. But I did." Her eyes were suddenly fierce. "What you said," she told Jim. "She wasn't trash. She was just a girl who'd had a hard time. People do. Girls do."

"Yeah," Jim said. "They do."

"And I thought . . ." Her face worked, her mouth twisting up tight. She'd lost her tough edge, and for a moment, Jim could see the girl she'd been even through the heavy makeup. *Just a girl who'd had a hard time.*

"If it was her," she said, still rubbing the bear's threadbare paw, "I wanted you to know. I thought—" She looked down at the tattered thing, and when she spoke again, her voice was soft. "She was scared of the dark. She should at least be able to be buried with her bear."

NOT SO SLOW

Rochelle expected Travis to call her on Sunday, but he didn't. Instead, she got another text.

Recovered?

She thought a moment, then typed,

In what sense?

She could almost see that smile curling up one corner of his mouth before the words appeared on the screen.

Oh, come on, baby. You know the answer to that.

Not slow, she typed.

Right.

And that was it. All day. He might be willing to go slow, but she wasn't sure she was, because it was just about killing her.

He didn't show up, in fact, until Tuesday afternoon, when he sauntered into her office and dropped into her visitor's chair.

She propped her elbows on the desk, set her chin on her folded hands, and eyed him. Blue button-down shirt with the sleeves rolled up, Levi's, one ankle crossed over the other. Absolutely average, and not one single bit average.

"So," he said. "Adequately casual amount of time elapsed?"

"Maybe," she said, trying so hard not to smile.

"Good. Then let's have dinner. And forget the not-slow element of that. You're working all day, I'm working all day, and I don't want to wait until the weekend for a recreational activity that either frustrates me to the point of actual pain or injures critically important parts of you. Dinner."

"My." She opened her eyes wide. "Somebody woke up bossy this morning."

"Let's call it decisive," he said.

"Oh, let's. When?"

"I don't care. Today. Tomorrow. Soon as I can get it. Dinner, out where everybody sees us and everybody knows us and everybody can think what they like, because I'll be thinking the exact same thing. I want to see you wearing something really good just to tease me. I want to get that testing thing where you dare me not to look and I have to sneak a peek anyway, because I can't help it."

She was smiling. She was totally helpless not to. "Tomorrow. Don't wear khaki Dockers."

He stood up. "I'll pick you up at six thirty. And I don't own any Dockers."

◆   ◆   ◆

The minute she opened the door, she saw that they weren't Dockers. They were some kind of slim summer-weight black wool trousers, because the weather had turned hot again, one of those blasts of Indian summer that so often happened when harvest was over, as if Nature knew that the farmers needed to have their own chance at lazy summer days. Travis was wearing them with a short-sleeved soft-blue knit shirt that showed off the corded muscles of his forearms and the very satisfactory bulge of biceps and triceps. All the appropriate arm muscles, all fully present and accounted for. And when he stood on her porch and looked at her in her blue flower-print halter-top sundress and high heels, he sighed, said, "You know what? Screw going slow," put one hand on her waist and the other on her shoulder, pulled her up close, and kissed her breathless.

He lifted his mouth from hers at last, brushed his lips across her cheek, making her shudder, and murmured into her ear, close enough that she felt all the shivery heat of it, "I'd say, 'Screw dinner,' too, but I might be pushing my luck. What do you think?"

"Mm." She kissed *him* this time, because his mouth was firm and warm and so delicious. He smelled faintly of pine and leather. He smelled like a cowboy ought to and never actually did, so she buried her face in his neck, breathed him in, and then kissed him there, too, just because he had such a wonderfully strong throat, and he'd obviously shaved before he'd come over. A man deserved some kind of reward for that, didn't he?

She got a sharp inhalation for her pains, and a tightening of his hands on her body that didn't feel bad at all, before he said, "You've got five seconds to say, 'Let's go out.'"

She pulled his head down for one more soft, sweet kiss, smiled into his eyes, and said, "Let's go out."

◆　　◆　　◆

Travis sat on the patio of Paradise's newest and finest restaurant, La Traviata, and looked at Rochelle some more.

Paradise's finest had turned out to be a pizza place. Of course it had. But it had a weathered brick façade, candles on the tables, and a great wine list, and he didn't care anyway. He liked pizza, and he liked Rochelle. He'd especially liked swinging her down from the truck with two hands around her waist, which had been absolutely unnecessary, and totally necessary all the same. Not to mention the feeling of warm, bare skin under his palm when he'd put a hand on her back to escort her into the restaurant. If he could have, he'd have traced right up the line of her shoulder blade with one slow thumb. That hadn't been an option, but he'd felt the tiny ripple that went through her at his touch, and his body had responded to it like it was wired straight to hers.

They'd eaten dinner in the last warmth of the setting sun, and then she'd reached for her cropped white sweater, and he'd put a hand out to help her on with it. He'd watched her button it slowly, from bottom to top. She'd known he was watching, and she hadn't minded a bit.

The other part of his plan had gone well, too. He'd seen a few people he knew while they'd been sitting here on a warm September night on one of the busiest corners in town, and she'd seen more. He hoped they all spread it around. Suited him fine.

"You know what I want to know about you?" she asked him now, running a slow fingertip around the rim of her wineglass in the soft glow of candlelight and driving him crazy.

"Mm," he said, still watching that finger.

"How'd you get those muscles?"

He laughed, feeling ridiculously gratified. "I told you. I was a swimmer. Still am. A mile first thing every morning in the university's pool, and more on the weekend."

"Maybe." She looked at him from under her lashes. "That's not all, though. You've got *man* muscles. More than you did before. And man hands."

"Hope so." He'd forgotten about his own wine. He took a sip, but the buzz he was feeling wasn't coming from the alcohol.

"You did something that changed you these past months," she said. "I can tell. You're . . . patient."

"Not that patient."

"Yeah. I noticed. So what happened? After your dad died?"

"Man," he said, "I shared a *lot* in that elevator, didn't I?"

"Good thing, too, or we wouldn't be here. So what was it? You went . . . mountain climbing? Or on a three-month Buddhist retreat that included lots of gym time? What?"

"I built houses."

She blinked. "What?"

"For Habitat for Humanity, down near home. My dad's farm used a lot of migrant workers. All that agriculture down there does. It's hand cultivation, not like here. And their housing is . . . you could call it substandard."

"At your parents' place?"

"Nope. They'd moved off the farm, remember? Anyway, my folks did things right. My mom wouldn't have had it any other way, even if my dad would've. Which he wouldn't. But when I was looking in the mirror after we put my dad in the ground, and not much liking the man looking back at me . . . I wanted to do something that wasn't about me. Something hard. Something at home. Something that mattered. That was what I came up with. It worked all right."

"For how long?"

"Five months. Until the foreman took me aside one day and said, 'Whatever you were running away from, don't you think it's time to head on back and face it?' That sounded like good advice to me. Decided I'd take it."

"But you didn't. You came here."

"Nope. Went back to San Francisco. Thought about doing something new, something in the business. Had some ideas, too, but I couldn't settle. I'd gotten used to being outside more, I guess. Having some space and some quiet. And then I saw the ad for this job, and it didn't sound bad, as a transition. You asked me about that, remember? Maybe I remembered something about that town, too. That it had somebody in it I wanted to see again. So I came to Paradise, took a job that's kicking my butt, and found a girl I used to know. And that part," he told her, "would be the bonus."

"I bet your mom's proud of you," she said.

He had to look away at that. "I hope so."

In fact, his mom *had* been proud of him. When he'd come up halfway through his stint to spend the weekend, once he'd felt like he could look her in the face again, she'd let him know it.

That was when he'd finally had the guts to say, after dinner on that Saturday night, while they were still sitting at a kitchen table that had one too few people at it, "I did the wrong thing, not coming home when Dad was sick. And I'm sorry. I wish I could tell Dad so."

They'd been some of the hardest words he'd ever spoken. The tears had risen in her eyes, and seeing them had made his own throat close up.

"Oh, baby," she'd said, her hand coming out to clasp his and holding it hard, as hard as she'd hugged him when he'd arrived. Like she needed to hold him, or like she knew how much he needed her to do it, or maybe both. "Your dad knew you your whole life, remember? He had plenty of time to know the man you grew up to be. Just like I have. He lived proud of you, and he died proud of you. Don't you worry."

He might have shed a couple of tears himself that night. But there were some things that were too much for a man to bear.

"She said she was, didn't she?" Rochelle asked now. "Proud?"

He breathed out slowly. "Do you have to keep messing with my head?" She laughed in surprise, and he gave her a rueful smile and said, "You just can't help but make this real, can you?"

"No," she said, "I think that's coming from you," and just like that, he was taking her hand across the table. Taking it, and holding it, rubbing a thumb over the sensitive palm and watching her eyes darken. With passion, maybe, and with something else, too. With emotion.

"Hey, guys."

He didn't drop Rochelle's hand. He just turned to see Stacy, in a red T-shirt and khaki shorts, standing beside them holding the handlebars of her bike.

"Hey," he said. "How're you doing?"

She looked between him and Rochelle. "Want me to go?"

"No," Rochelle said, withdrawing her hand hastily, and Travis sighed and thought, *Damn.*

"Of course not," Rochelle went on. "Sit down. You want some pizza? We've got quite a bit left."

"Ugh." Stacy made a face. "Sorry," she added hastily. "It's just—No, thanks."

Once Stacy had parked her bike and joined them, Travis lifted a hand for the waitress and asked her, "Would you like something to drink? A salad?"

"Well, thanks." She looked surprised. "Just a Coke, maybe."

"Something's wrong," Rochelle said when the Coke had been ordered. "What?"

Stacy shrugged and sat, her shoulders slumped.

"Is it school?" Rochelle pressed. "Or—" She glanced at Travis. "Shane? Come on and tell us. Or just tell Travis. He kind of specializes in defending women's honor."

"Only Marks women," he said with a smile for Stacy. "But I'm not too bad at that. Say the word."

"What? No," she said distractedly. She pulled her dark hair back from her face, then let it fall. "It was just . . . they found out who that girl was, the one Cal Jackson found. Did you hear?"

"Yeah," Rochelle said, and just like that, all the magic was gone. "I heard. It's really upsetting. Poor thing."

"Well, a bunch of guys from the sheriff's department were out at Macho Taco today," Stacy said. "They were . . . questioning everybody. And I found out that she had my job. I mean, my *exact* job. She worked the drive-through at Macho Taco. That was probably why there was an opening. And I kept thinking, tonight . . . what if she met the guy there? I kept looking at all the guys coming through the line tonight and . . . *wondering.* She was only eighteen. Could one of those guys have done that to her? Was I looking right at him? She even looked like me. What if . . . what if he picked her up after her shift, or something? And then . . ."

That one made Travis's blood run cold. That girl had worked where Stacy was now? That wasn't good. *Probably somebody the girl was dating,* he told himself. *Probably nothing to do with it.* But still. There Stacy was, working that window, riding her bike home alone. It just didn't feel . . . safe.

He saw something flicker across Rochelle's face. Concern. Alarm. And then she was holding Stacy's hand, and he could all but see her shoving her own feelings back and focusing on her sister.

"Not likely," she said robustly. "How many of them have *you* gone out with? Thirty seconds to pick up his tacos—not gonna happen. It would have been somebody she met in a bar, something like that, because those uniforms aren't that flattering. I think it's the hat."

Stacy's eyes flew up to meet her sister's, and Rochelle's hand gripped hers more tightly.

"Hey," Rochelle said gently. "It's going to be OK. They'll find out who did it. It's *one* guy. Probably somebody she was seeing, somebody completely unconnected to where she worked. It won't turn out to be that complicated."

Travis sure hoped she was right.

THE WORKS OF SATAN

Stacy had been working the drive-through with half her attention. In between customers, she was listening to Jim Lawson questioning the other girls. The sharp-dressed guy without a uniform was in the manager's office, and Mark Lawrence, the younger deputy, was in a corner taking notes.

It was exciting, like a cop show. At first.

"So did Heather talk to anybody in particular?" Jim was asking. "Any regulars who'd spend a little extra time at the window when she was working it?"

"We're supposed to move them through fast." That was Tammy Armstrong, a thin brunette who always wore her hair scraped painfully tightly into a bun and seemed to have come from a family so religious, she'd probably never broken a rule in her life. Not even 'no chewing gum.'

Jim scratched the back of his head and looked around at the rest of the girls. "Well, yeah. But you know, guys might sometimes hang around an extra minute or two and pass the time of day. And if you're not busy . . . Was she the kind of girl they'd do that with?"

His gaze landed on Emily Yarborough, who'd been a few years ahead of Stacy in school. "Yeah?" Jim asked her, because he must have seen something on Emily's round, sweet face. "She was?"

"I didn't notice much," Emily said. "But sometimes . . . Maybe."

"Hmm," he said. "Anybody you knew?"

"Well," she said, "maybe that's why I noticed them in particular, because I knew them."

"Who did you recognize?" he asked.

"I don't want to get them in trouble," she said. "I mean, nobody *did* anything. They just talked to her, maybe. Like you said. Just for a minute."

"Sure," he said easily. "We're just trying to get a picture of her life. Find out who she knew."

No, you aren't, Stacy thought. *You're looking for the guy who murdered her and dumped her body in Cal Jackson's ditch.* That was when it stopped being exciting and became something else.

"Well," Emily said. "Maybe Dave Harris. Danny Boyle. Like that. They're married, I know," she hastened to say. "It was nothing, just talking. And they didn't come in that often anyway, because it was summer."

Stacy froze. *No.* It couldn't be those guys. She *knew* those guys. *No.*

It wouldn't be them, though. They wouldn't have had time to see even their families, let alone . . . somebody else. Not during harvest, and the busy weeks leading up to it. Not during the season when anyone working on a farm had the least free time.

"Anybody else?" Jim asked. Emily hesitated, and Jim asked again, "Who? You're not accusing them of anything. You're just giving us a starting point."

Like hell, Stacy thought. *No.*

"Maybe . . . Miles Kimberling," Emily said reluctantly, a fiery blush traveling up her pale skin. She had a crush on him, Stacy realized. Miles wasn't married, and he wasn't a hired man like the other two. His dad was one of the big farmers, friends with Cal and Luke Jackson's dad. Miles had a wild side, though, and a reputation. But Miles was . . . he was *nice*. And she *knew* him. Better than the others, because he was younger, between her age and Rochelle's.

Dave Harris . . . Miles . . . She saw their faces in her mind, drifting in and out. In . . . in flashes.

A car pulled up, and she was turning back to the window and taking the order, trying hard to get herself under control, not to shake.

The pansies. Rochelle's shower curtain, mildewed now, because Rochelle hadn't taken it when she'd left Lake.

The night when she'd woken up in the ER without remembering . . . it had to have been that night.

Another flash. Somebody had been laughing, saying, *". . . like 'em that way. If they're not conscious, they can't bitch about what you do. Good times."*

That had been Dave Harris. She knew it. At Lake's.

Rochelle would kill her.

All Stacy had to do was not tell that one piece, though, and Rochelle would never know. Stacy would never go out there again. She'd keep out of it.

The customer pulled away, and she tried not to listen, but she couldn't help it. "What about her behavior?" Jim was asking. "Anything you noticed? She ever complain about anything? Seem troubled? Call in sick?"

Emily looked at the other girls, opened her mouth, then closed it again. Stacy hadn't known Heather, but she'd heard things. She held still, tried to shrink into herself so nobody would notice her, and waited for what the girls would say.

"You can't get her in trouble now," Jim said. "We're trying to catch her killer. Whatever she did, she didn't deserve to die for it."

Tammy said impatiently, "Well, maybe. But maybe she did things that made her more likely to get killed."

Stacy went even more rigid at that, but so did everyone else. That was just . . . mean. That was just *wrong*.

Jim didn't seem surprised, though. He looked at Tammy. "What kinds of things?" he asked her.

"None of us knew her that well," Tammy said. "She wasn't here that long, and she was pretty trashy."

Like it had been Heather's fault. Like nothing bad could happen to Tammy, because she was good. But it didn't work that way. Stacy might feel like she didn't know anything half the time, but at least she knew that.

"All I can tell you is," Tammy went on, "she took a lot of bathroom breaks. Way more than she was entitled to. *And* that one day, that last day she worked? When I went in there after her? There was something in the garbage."

"How did you find that?" That was Angie Johnson, who was a little older, a lot tougher, and reminded Stacy of Rochelle. "You snooped through the trash? Nice."

"Of course I didn't." There were two spots of color high up on Tammy's thin cheeks now. "I was . . . I had to throw something away." She glanced at Jim, then away again.

"Just say you had your period," Angie said with disgust. "All right, you're pure. We get it."

"What did you see?" Jim asked. "And was this . . ." He flipped back through his notebook. "August twenty-second, Saturday?"

"*I* don't know what day," Tammy said. "The last day she worked, because I remember afterwards thinking, maybe that was why she didn't come back. And I never said it was hers. I just said I *saw* it. We're required to cooperate, and *I'm* cooperating. Unlike *some* people."

"*What* did you see?" Angie said. "A fifth of whisky? A Baggie of white powder labeled 'Cocaine'? A copy of the *Works of Satan*? What?"

Tammy glared at Angie. "A pregnancy test, that's what. And the line was blue."

Long seconds ticked by before Emily said in a small voice, "She said something. That night. When we were closing."

"What did she say?" Jim asked. When she hesitated, he added, "As exactly as you can remember it. The exact words can help."

"I didn't know what it meant at the time," Emily said. "She was leaving. We were walking out."

"And what did she say?" Jim asked again.

"She said . . ." Emily took a deep breath. "Something like, 'That bastard is going to get me out of this. He can't afford *not* to, and I'm going to tell him so.' I didn't know she was . . . pregnant. I thought she just meant out of *here,* you know. Not working here anymore. She told me she was only going to be staying for a while. At first. She was really cheerful at first. Normal. And then, at the end . . . she wasn't. I thought . . . I thought the same thing as Tammy, afterwards, sort of. That that was why she didn't come back, that she'd found something better, or it was about that guy." She looked at Jim, then. "Do you think the guy was . . . do you think he might have been married?"

CHOICES

Rochelle sat and listened while Stacy told a halting story. About the girl who'd worked the drive-through. Who might have been pregnant, and who might have been killed for it, and her baby along with her.

To find out a woman was pregnant with your baby, and to kill both of them? How could a man do that? Rochelle knew how. She knew better. She knew a man could do worse than that, and still, it shook her to the bone.

"Whoa," she said when Stacy had finished telling them the story. "That's . . . that's terrible." It was an inadequate response, and she knew it, but she didn't trust herself to say more.

"Do you think . . ." Stacy hugged herself, "that's who killed her? The baby's father? If she really *was* pregnant?" It had shaken Stacy as much as Rochelle. At *least* as much, because she'd heard it. Rochelle put an arm around her little sister and tried to think what to say.

"Sounds likely," Travis said.

"And those guys Emily mentioned," Stacy said. "Those are . . ."

"Yeah," Rochelle said, and took a breath. "They sure are." She told Travis, "They're some of my ex's buddies."

"But nobody said *his* name," Stacy said. "Lake's. Nobody said anything about *him*."

"Well, that's good," Rochelle said. *Get it together. For Stacy.* "But not too surprising. He doesn't like Mexican food. Too many suspicious ingredients."

Travis glanced at her in surprise, and she explained, "You know. Cumin. Cilantro. Scary herbs and spices."

He smiled at that, and she went on for Stacy's benefit, "And like I said, somebody flirting a little at the drive-through? What does *that* prove? Just about nothing. I'm sure that's what Jim Lawson's thinking."

Still, it was . . . it was awful to think that somebody you'd known—or even somebody you'd barely met—could be a murderer.

It couldn't be, though. It had to be somebody else, because she *knew* those guys.

They sat another minute while Rochelle tried to think of something else to say, something more comforting, but she hadn't thought of it yet when Travis said, "You're cold, Stacy. We should go."

He was right. The night was still plenty warm, but Stacy was definitely shivering. Travis signed the receipt, closed the leather envelope over it, and tucked his credit card back into his wallet. "You know that thing about me defending the Marks sisters' honor?" he said. "I'm also pretty good at putting their bikes in the back of my truck and driving them home. You get almost as many points for that, and it's so much easier."

Which made Stacy smile, and which was nice of him, especially considering that this was the second time his date with Rochelle had ended up including her sister.

Stacy didn't say much during the drive, and when Travis had pulled to a stop outside the house and had lifted her bike out of the truck, she shivered, said, "Thanks. I'm going to go take a shower," and wheeled it around to the back of the house without another word.

Rochelle stood and looked after her, then said, "I need to talk to her. And this would be a good night to have a talk about birth control, maybe. After that shower."

She'd looked in Stacy's underwear drawer the previous weekend, and her sock drawer and bedside table, too, and hadn't found anything but underwear and socks. She hadn't found birth control pills, either. Could *that* be the reason for Stacy's moodiness? *Oh, no.*

"I'd say you're right," Travis said. "And this is where I count myself lucky that my parents took care of all of this . . . well, *parenting,* for lack of a better word, for my younger sisters. Remind me again why you're in charge."

"You're wondering if I've told my folks I'm worried about her." She leaned against the side of the truck, and he leaned back beside her, seemingly content to stay there. Standing still, as always. There was no fidget to Travis. "No," she said. "I haven't. They know that she's moved in with me, but I didn't tell them why. That she . . ." She took a breath, then admitted it, what she hadn't told anybody. "She overdosed, the night before I met you again. Pills and alcohol. Bad enough for the ER."

Silence for a moment, then, "That's not good."

"No. She said it was one time, but I doubt it."

"Yeah, right," he said. "Words to cling to. 'I'll pull out,' and 'It was just one time.'"

She smiled in spite of her concern. "So if you say that, I shouldn't believe you?"

"Definitely not. Because I'll be lying for sure. No way I'd be able to do that."

"Just . . ." *Hold that thought,* she didn't say. "Anyway. She lost her great job, too, and she didn't seem worried enough about it. Maybe I overreacted, but I don't think so. She seems awfully shaky. Also, as you know, I hate her boyfriend. Slimy SOB."

"Don't hold back. Let it out."

"Thanks. I believe I will."

"But," he said, "you haven't mentioned any of that to your folks."

"No. Because . . ." He was standing so close, both of them turned a bit toward each other, and now, she reached out a hand and drew the backs of her fingers a couple inches down his chest. Just wanting to touch him, to . . . ground herself. She looked at her hand without really seeing it and said, "It's my dad, mostly. He'll be so disappointed if she doesn't make it. And the overdose . . . no. She's the smart one. She's the hope."

"Oh, I wouldn't say that," he said, his voice deep and quiet in the darkness. Despite the lingering heat, there were clouds across the moon tonight, and a heaviness in the air that spoke of rain coming, the kind of cloudburst that would have been a threat during harvest, but was a welcome relief now.

"Well, thanks," she said. "But let's say that college didn't seem like an option for me."

"You said six of you. And I'm trying to talk about this, by the way. Even though you've got your hand on me."

"Oh." She took it off, and his own hand shot out and trapped it there.

"No," he said. "Leave it. I'm loving it. And tell me. Six of you."

Most men wouldn't have stood outside her house in the dark and asked her to recite her list of siblings, but then, Travis wasn't most men. She'd already figured that out. So she obliged.

"One other sister," she said. "Faye, next oldest to me. The one who's in town, but that doesn't help much. She worked to put her husband through school, and now she's enjoying the benefits. Nice house, nice car, and one son who has way too much of her focus and way too many video games. That boy's going to be a lawyer or a doctor, or maybe a dope fiend if she pushes him over the edge. She's not going to look out for Stacy. Not a chance."

He didn't say anything, and she went on. "And then the twins. They joined the Army together after high school. One's a staff sergeant now." Her palm was flat on Travis's chest now, and his own hand lay over hers, holding it there. "That's Bill. He's like you. Solid. I missed him like hell when he left. Then there's Aaron. He joined up because Bill did, because the two of them were tight like that. Aaron . . ." She took a ragged breath. "He was going to go to college, but he didn't make it home from Afghanistan. The Army was supposed to be his ticket, but it punched it instead."

"I'm sorry," Travis said. His chest was warm, and so was his hand, and she kept going.

"Bill's career military," she said, "and it kills my folks, but they're so proud of him. And then there's Mike, just older than Stacy, who's working on a farm over near Yakima right now. He turned out a bit . . . wild. Hard to control, always. So you see how Stacy's it. Stacy and Bill."

"And you," he said.

She swallowed over the lump in her throat. Too much emotion tonight, too much worry. And touching Travis, talking to Travis, was too much comfort. She couldn't keep it cool. She couldn't keep her distance. "Oh, well, I'm a little disappointing, too. Divorced, you know. Bill's married. Got two kids."

"Do your folks really think it's a competition?" he asked. "Because mine wouldn't."

"No," she said. "No. Of course not. But you don't know." No question, the tears were there, now, right behind her eyes. "How hard they worked. How hard they tried. How my dad would change into his church clothes before every single parent-teacher conference for sixsix kids, slick down his hair, go in, and ask all those questions. The doctors and lawyers didn't always go for their kids, but my parents did. You don't know how much they wanted us to have a chance to do better, and how proud they were when Stacy graduated from high school with that scholarship. If she doesn't make it . . ." She had to breathe the thought back. "It'll break their hearts. Especially my dad's. I can't let that happen. And I can't give them something else to worry about. Not if I can help it."

His voice was quiet. Deep as the night. "Your folks aren't the only ones who try hard."

"I guess," she said, the thud of his heartbeat steady against her palm. For once, she couldn't be smart, and she couldn't be snarky. It was too real, and too raw. "But I know how I disappointed myself, and how upset they were for me. And I don't want Stacy to go through that. I pulled myself up from my mistakes, but it wasn't easy. And I'm . . ."

"Strong," he said.

"Yes." She knew she was. No point in denying it. "And what Stacy told us tonight about that girl. She made some bad choices, picked the wrong guy, and look at the price she paid. It's too easy. It happens too much."

"That wasn't Stacy, though. Maybe Stacy's stronger than you think. If she's anything like her sister . . . I think so. And she's got something you didn't have."

"What's that?"

"She's got you."

They were both quiet for a minute, then, because Rochelle had to let that one soak in. "So," she finally said. "We keep showing each other our tender places, don't we?"

She was afraid he'd make some cheesy comment in response to that, and she couldn't have stood it. But all he said was, "Yep. We sure do. And it doesn't make me want to kiss you one bit less."

She swayed into him, and he let her hand go at last, then put his own hand around her head, his thumb stroking her jaw, and lifted her face to his.

"Damn," he breathed. "It's that mouth." And then he kissed her.

It wasn't hard, it wasn't rough, and it wasn't fast. It was slow, and thorough, and oh, so hot. The wine was sweet on their tongues, the air was warm and heavy, and Travis was all over her. Somehow, he had her backed up against the truck with one hand at her waist pulling her close, the other on her shoulder. That maddeningly slow thumb traced the edge of her halter neckline, sending a tingling message all the way down her body. He angled his mouth over hers, took it more deeply, and she was melting.

He must have felt her response, but he still wasn't rushing. Not a bit. His body said, *We've got all night,* and all her body wanted to say back was, *Cowboy, take me home.*

His lips were drifting over her cheek now, moving all the way to her ear until he took hold of her earlobe with his teeth and bit down, and she heard herself whimpering and couldn't stop it. She had hold of him, too, had one hand caressing the back of his neck, the other grabbing his shoulder, pulling him closer. She needed all that hardness against her, inside her. She needed it *now.*

His mouth moved slowly back to her own, and he gave her another kiss that was hot enough and hard enough to steal her breath. She was making some noise, leaning back farther against the truck, willing his hand to move, because she needed it. And then he was breaking the kiss and stepping back.

"Yeah," he said, sounding shaken. "So much for kissing you goodnight."

"Travis . . ." She didn't move. She wasn't sure she could.

"Two choices," he said. "*A,* you invite me in, but you won't, because of Stacy. *B,* you come home with me and know that I'm going to be walking you backward all the way into my bed. If we make it farther than the door, because the way I feel right now, it'd be up against the wall."

That one sent a tremor through her, and for once, she couldn't answer.

"Or there's *C*." His hand was on her face again as if he couldn't stand not to hold her. "You get back in this truck and let me touch you everywhere I need to."

"You're doing it again," she managed to say. "Outline form."

She wanted *C*, and she wanted it right now. She wanted to fog up the windows. She wanted those hard hands all over her body. She wanted . . . she *needed* to let go. She needed to turn it loose, and to feel him do it, too. She needed to climb on board and ride that train all the way down. But she didn't need to do it at nine o'clock at night in front of all her neighbors, and she *did* need to talk to Stacy.

"Come on, baby," Travis said, his hand in her hair now. "Choose."

"*D,*" she said, with the greatest effort of her life. "To be continued."

UPS AND DOWNS

Her sacrifice looked like it was going to be in vain, because at first, Stacy refused to talk to her.

"What?" her sister said when Rochelle knocked on her bedroom door and went in to find Stacy in her underwear and a T-shirt, sitting on the edge of the bed and rubbing lotion into her legs. "I'm *pregnant* now? Would you *stop*, please? I mean, yay for free rent, but seriously, Ro, you need to get a grip."

"Well," Rochelle said, off balance once more, "I just thought I'd check. Because you seemed so upset tonight."

"Because somebody *died*. Because a girl who looked like me and had my job was *murdered* and dumped in a ditch. Not because I'm wondering how I'll raise my love child." Stacy lifted the hem of her T-shirt. "Look. Flat stomach. I'd show you the *real* evidence, but there's a limit to sharing, you know?" She leaned closer and whispered, "But if you're counting the tampons, too? I'm making a dent."

A snort of laughter escaped Rochelle, and she sat down beside her sister, took Stacy's bottle of lotion from her, and started doing her own legs. "You're right. We'll stick with the stomach. Yours is sure flatter than mine."

"And note," Stacy said, "that I didn't ask *you* whether you've been slacking off on the sit-ups, or maybe making a cozy home for my future niece or nephew. I'm also not moving on from there to ask what you're using to keep Mr. Irresistible's little swimmers from slamming their tiny heads into your plump, juicy ovum. Because that would be *your* business."

"*Ick,*" Rochelle said, but she had to laugh. This was Stacy sounding like Stacy at last.

"Hey. Bio major. I can't help it."

"Anyway," Rochelle said, "that'd be a boring conversation either way, because Mr. Irresistible and I aren't doing the deed."

"Well, *that's* tragic." Stacy rolled over onto her stomach and stuffed the pillow under her cheek. "Watch and learn: I'm not even going to ask how come. I could guess, but . . ." She paused to consider. "Nah. He's tall, he's hot, and he was holding your hand and staring into your eyes before I showed up tonight and wrecked it. I got nothin'."

Rochelle slapped her sister's butt, and Stacy jumped and laughed.

"All right," Rochelle said, feeling much more cheerful. "Congratulations on your restraint. And for the record? Birth control pills, for no other reason lately than a stubborn refusal to admit defeat, because I sure haven't been needing them. Or you could be nice and call it an optimistic nature."

"I know," Stacy said. "About the pills. I live here. I open the medicine cabinet. And for *my* record . . . IUD. Happy?"

"Well," Rochelle said, "getting there, anyway. Thanks, sweetie." She bent and kissed Stacy's cheek, and her sister put an arm around her neck and held her there for a moment.

"Thanks," Stacy said, her voice muffled by the pillow. "For bringing me home tonight. I kinda needed you to, you know?"

"I know." Rochelle kissed her sister again. "Love you, babe."

"Love you, too."

◆ ◆ ◆

So Wednesday was what you'd call a mixed bag. Some very bad, and some very, very good.

Thursday, on the other hand, was just plain awful.

The day dawned hot, muggy, and overcast. Stacy woke up blurry eyed and grouchy, they'd run out of milk, and the "Check Engine" light came on when Rochelle pulled out of the driveway. By the time she'd dropped the car off and hiked up to the university, she was dripping with sweat. Add being late into the office, and having Dr. Halvorsen, her least favorite department head, already in there frowning and looking at his watch?

Yeah. It was one of those days where it got really hard to count your blessings. Until it finally got better.

ONE HELL OF A RIDE

Either Travis was going to have sex with Rochelle sometime in this calendar year, or he was going to die. He was pretty sure it was going to be one or the other.

He made it through Thursday. And then he turned the computer off and did something about it.

She was in her front yard when he pulled up. Dressed to kill—him, anyway—in khaki shorts, a white V-necked T-shirt, and work boots, swinging a hoe for all she was worth despite the heat, a baseball cap pulled low on her head and her hair back in a knot. She looked hot, she looked grumpy, and she looked like exactly what he wanted.

He could be a good guy and help her with her garden. Or he could be the man he thought she needed right now and pull her out of it. He knew which one he was going for.

He didn't even get out of the truck. When she looked up at the crunch of gravel from his tires, he leaned over and said through the open passenger window, "Hey, pretty girl. Want to go for a ride?"

She stood, the hoe in one hand, drew a forearm across her face, and said, "Where to?"

"You're going to have to find that out for yourself. Got a cooler in the back full of ice and Corona. Climb on in, put those pretty toes up on my dash, and let's see where we get."

She dropped her hoe into the dirt and swayed her way over to him, working it in that way she should have a patent on. When she got there, she put her forearms on the rolled-down window and gave him a sneak preview of paradise right down that shirt.

"A girl could get in trouble accepting that kind of invitation," she told him. Those blue eyes were sparkling, the full lips were curving, and he was already starting to burn.

"Yep." For once, he wasn't trying not to look. He was going ahead and looking. Tonight, they were going to be throwing the rule book out the window. "She sure could. Least that's what I'm hoping."

"You know what?" she said. "I've been awfully good for an awfully long time."

"Sure seems like it to me," he said. "Being in charge all the time's got to get old, too. Maybe you could step back and give somebody else a chance."

She cocked her head and looked at him from under the brim of her ball cap. "And would that somebody be you?"

"One way to find out."

And then he waited while his heart beat so loud he'd swear he could hear it. Until she pulled the door open, climbed on up, and said, "Well, hell, boy. Let's go."

◆　◆　◆

She was in Travis's truck, headed for who-knew-where, with her laundry still tumbling in the dryer and her yard half weeded. And she didn't care. She'd borrowed his phone to text Stacy, and that was it. She was done.

She started out by unlacing her boots and pulling off her socks, and then, yes, she put her feet up on his dash. He started to roll up the windows, but she said, "Nah. Leave them down. I like the wind," and he obliged.

There was a hint of a breeze now, the stultifying heaviness of the day promising to break. Threatening to pour down over them, to pummel them delirious, and she wanted to be out here to feel it.

She reached behind her head, pulled out the two sticks that had been holding her hair, and let it fall. It instantly began flying around her head, restrained only by the ball cap, and she laughed. "Feels good."

"Now, see," he said. "That's the kind of picture I had in my head all day."

"You did?"

"Oh, yeah. You can't kiss me like that and not leave me thinking."

"I thought you were the one kissing *me*. Sure felt like it."

"Good." He turned onto the county road on the east side of town and headed north, the low hump of Paradise Mountain rising farther to the east.

"We going hiking?" she asked lazily, her elbow on the open window matching his own. He was dressed like her. Shorts and T-shirt, running shoes without socks. "Going to have to put my boots back on, then."

"Thought I told you to wait and see."

She turned her head to look at him and saw his half smile. "Anybody ever tell you that you're a miserable failure at being a New Age man?"

"Aw, baby," he said. "Now you've gone and hurt my feelings."

They were in the foothills now. The fields not yet plowed, glowing yellow in the evening light with the remnants of the harvest. Hay bales lying round and golden against a background of higher hills dotted with evergreens, with the humped gray cloud banks looming beyond. And then Travis slowed and made a right, and they were heading to the mountain.

When he turned off onto the gravel road and raised the windows against the dust, she said, "Oh, yeah. I think I'm getting a clue. But then, you like to swim. I haven't been out *here* in a while."

"I do. Like to swim, that is. And why haven't you been out here? You seem to like to swim yourself."

"More of a high school thing. And I was busy. All that life stuff. All that being in charge, like you said. I do have a story, though."

"Let's hear it," he said, heading around a corner. Not too fast, because Travis knew how to drive in gravel. Surprise.

"First time I was here? Kegger. Fifteen years old, told my folks I was spending the night with a girlfriend, and they found out. I'll never know how." She laughed, remembering. "There I was, sitting around a campfire with a bunch of other kids, all of us out to be wild and crazy, drinking my very first beer and thinking how bad it tasted. Stuart Landford with his arm around me and his hand getting closer, thinking it was his lucky night, when there came my dad."

"Ah," Travis said. "Haven't had the pleasure of meeting your dad yet, but I'm imagining he's a powerful force."

"He sure was that night. Looming up into the light like something in a campfire horror story, looking right at me, saying, 'Rochelle Amanda Marks,' like it was being pronounced from the pulpit. I thought I'd keel over dead of a heart attack right there, and you never saw anything faster in your life than the way Stuart's hand whipped off of me."

"That cure you of being a bad girl?"

"I think you know the answer to that. I still had plenty of lessons to learn. I should've listened to my dad a *lot* more than I did. Had a thing for bad boys for way too long."

"Maybe," he said, swinging around another turn, "you just need the right guy to be bad with."

"A good, strong man with some bad boy in him? That's the idea. Haven't found one like that yet, though." She shifted her feet on the dash, curled her toes, took off her ball cap, lifted her hair in both hands, and pulled it over one shoulder.

"You think?" he said. "And here I thought maybe your search was over."

"You that guy?" She slid her eyes on over to him, then left them there, because he was worth watching. Sitting so still, nothing but one hand moving, turning the steering wheel.

"I sure hope so," he said. "I know I'm a guy who wants a good woman with some bad girl in her. What's life without a little adventure?"

Her breath had been coming harder ever since she'd hopped up into his truck, and now . . . well, she hoped nobody was going to be taking her pulse anytime soon. "We done going slow, then?"

"Far as I'm concerned? From tonight on, we're in the fast lane, pedal to the metal and pushing it all the way. That's the way I want it, anyway. Fast and bumpy and scary as hell."

"I hope so," she said, "because if you're looking for smooth, I'm not it. I've got all that complication going on, and so do you. It's not going to be easy."

He pulled over, then, at a place she wouldn't have been able to find, all this time later. Nothing but a wide spot in the road and some tire tracks, and a path leading into the cedars.

He pulled the key out and tossed it under the seat. Idaho security. He didn't say anything for a minute, and she waited.

"I don't want easy," he finally said. "I've had easy. I don't want pretty good, and I sure as hell don't want close enough. I want all the way. I want crazy-about-you. I want can't-get-enough. I want to get a ticket next time I drive home from the airport because I couldn't go another minute without being with you. And I want to know you feel the same way about me. I want you, and that's it."

"You're talking about sex." She couldn't get her breath. She couldn't still her heart.

"You think so? I'd say I'm talking about everything. I'm talking forget being careful. Forget being safe. Hold my hand and jump off that cliff with me. Eyes wide open."

"You think we'll work?"

"Second time you've asked me that. I don't know if we'll work. We could go down in flames. But I'm betting it'll be one hell of a ride."

STORM DAMAGE

She was off balance. He could see it. Not answering, just looking at him. And then she shoved her door open and hopped down, and he followed her, stopping to pull the seat forward and grab the compact Styrofoam cooler and the big lantern-style flashlight.

The crunch of the doors shutting set a crow cawing from somewhere overhead, a harsh sound quickly taken up by another bird, then dying away to silence. Gravel shifted under his feet, and ahead of him, Rochelle quick-stepped over it onto the dirt path that led into the woods.

The sun was beginning to tint the clouds to the west with pink, the insects buzzed in the undergrowth, and the scent of cedars hung nearly palpably in the warm air. A breeze gusted, lifting his hair, letting him know that the storm would be breaking soon. And he followed Rochelle into the trees as she climbed the dirt path in her bare feet. Up and over the little rise, and there it was.

The first and biggest of the three dredge ponds, like teardrops carved out of the mountain, relics of long-ago mining. The water lay deep and still, inviting in the twilight, its shimmering depths edged by huge, tumbled slabs of stone. The buzz of insects was stronger now, and

Rochelle was standing on one of the flat stones at the edge, looking out over the water.

He stopped about ten feet from her, set down the cooler, and kicked off his shoes. She didn't say anything, just turned and looked at him. And then she got her hands on the hem of that white tee and pulled it over her head, the same way she'd done at the reservoir, and he was staring in exactly the same way he'd done then.

No red-checked bikini. A pale-pink bra, cut low. Then her hands were on the snap of her shorts, and those were getting tossed with her T-shirt.

Bikini underwear that matched the bra. Just those couple pieces of fabric between his hands and every luscious bit of her.

"You didn't tell me to bring my suit," she said.

"Nope." He pulled his own shirt over his head and dropped it on top of his shoes. "I figured your underwear would be good enough. And I was right."

"Really? I thought this was pedal to the metal." And just like that, she had her hands behind her back, and that bra was coming *off*.

Oh, yeah.

Another flick of her thumbs, and the final scrap of pink was falling at her feet and getting kicked aside. And there she was. Every glorious inch of her, rich and full and all for him.

"What do you think, big boy?" she asked him. "Ready to put your money where your mouth is?"

She didn't wait to take his hand. She just turned around and jumped straight into the water.

◆　◆　◆

Rochelle dropped, and her stomach dropped with her. The water hit her like a punch in the face, cold enough to make her gasp once she rose to the surface and headed across the pool.

She didn't look back for him. She heard the splash behind her and smiled, the water cold against her teeth. And she increased her pace. She was warming up now, stroking hard and kicking harder, curving around the shore, knowing he was behind her, and knowing exactly how fast he was, too.

Which didn't make it any less of a shock to be caught. She was being pulled straight across the water by one leg, gliding right into his arms, rolling half onto her back as she went. And then taken in a rescuer's sidestroke, his arm across her chest, her back against his front, feeling him kicking strongly beneath her, his single arm carrying them closer to shore.

His feet touched bottom before hers did, and he was rising with her, both arms around her now, holding her tight, turning her in the water until she faced him.

She slid her way down his body, gasping at the shock of that, too. He had a hand under her, was pulling her up high, onto her toes, and he was kissing her.

If he'd been maddeningly slow the night before, that was gone. This man wasn't patient, and he wasn't gentle. He wasn't asking anymore, either. He was telling, and she loved it, so she got her hands around his head and kissed him right back. But he didn't stay there. His mouth dropped to her neck, and he bit her, the same way he had that day in the lab. His hand was on her breast, cool against her skin, and her nipple, already hardened by the cold water, tightened to an aching point as his thumb flicked across it.

He moved his head down to the spot where her neck met her shoulder, bit again, kept that thumb rubbing over her, until he trapped her sensitized nipple between two fingers and began a gentle squeeze and release that had her moaning.

They'd barely started, and she was ready to do it right now. Right here. That was when the sky opened up.

It wasn't "rain." It was more like "flood." She was being swallowed by water. Drowned.

"Whoa," Travis gasped. "Back to the truck." He let her go, and she settled back down into the water—the water beneath them, that is, because it was raining so hard, the drops bouncing against the surface of the pond and rising again, that it was as if the whole world were liquid.

He stayed behind her all the way across. Watching, she registered in some dim corner of her mind, to see that she made it. It was true: the sheet of rain made the shape of the pond and even direction confusing, but she was at the other side—what she thought was the other side—finding a level spot between the rocks and climbing out. He had hold of her hand then, and was pulling her with him. The sky had darkened, the world gone gray. She stumbled, he slowed to allow her to regain her footing, and then they were moving through the deluge again.

A white shape appeared in front of them, and just as she registered it as his ice chest, Travis dropped down and felt around on the ground. Then a wide white circle of light appeared, silver streaks of rain shining in its beam.

Flashlight.

"All right?" he asked, gasping against the force of the downpour.

"Fine," she said, her teeth beginning to chatter. He grabbed her hand again, moved the flashlight around until the beam of light picked up the trail, then they were nearly running, following that white circle up over the hill and out to the road. Travis pulled the truck's passenger door open, lifted her up, and threw her bodily in. Then he was around the other side, turning the flashlight off, pulling the seat forward, and grabbing a couple towels from behind it. He tossed one to her, finally climbed in himself, and slammed the door. And they were safe.

She was laughing now, overwhelmed by the night, by the rain, by the dash through the water and the woods, and he was laughing along with her, toweling her hair dry while she rubbed at her body and felt the tingle of warmth returning. And something else, too, as she scrubbed at his own short hair, then moved on down to his broad chest. He was taking the towel out of her hands, dropping it behind her, pulling her into him again, and kissing her, and neither of them was laughing now. The rain beat against the roof like a hail of bullets, the truck was rocking with the force of the wind, and then there was a flash so bright, it lit the whole cab, followed almost immediately by a clap of thunder that rattled their teeth. Which was when the hail started.

The noise was surrounding them, pounding them, and Rochelle was back against the door, somehow, the glass of the window cold against the back of her head, Travis's mouth hot and hard on the side of her neck, his hand on her breast, teasing the nipple until she was moaning.

"Travis . . ." she managed to say, but he wasn't listening. His mouth had moved farther down, his lips had closed around the hardened peak, and her hips were lifting, straining toward him. His other hand was stroking down her body, over her hip, down to her thigh, and then he'd grabbed hold of her leg and was shoving it all the way up and over the back of the seat, was pushing the other leg down until her foot hit the floor.

Another flash of lightning lit his body up, showed it stark and vivid. Bending over her, so big, so strong, like an image from a dream, or the best fantasy ever. The cab wasn't nearly big enough, and it didn't matter. The hail was drumming, the truck was rocking, and inside, Travis was moving down, and down some more, and her hands were grasping. Flailing. Coming around behind her and holding the grab bar at the top of the door, hanging on while her hips rose desperately into the air.

He didn't ask, and he didn't wait. He had one hand on her other thigh, holding her legs open, and his fingers inside her, thrusting hard, finding the spot. His fingers were so long, and that was so good. And then he put his mouth to her as the lightning flashed and the thunder rocked and rolled around the truck. The hair on the back of her neck was standing up straight, and she was crying out, barely hanging on. Caught up in the storm, the bolts going straight through her body, hard as iron, sharp as sin.

There was no patience at all in that mouth, those hands. Her upper body jerked forward from the door, and she was straining, climbing, starting to wail. Until she was there. Convulsing again and again. Struck by the lightning, free-falling as the thunder rolled over her, around her, through her. All the way gone.

◆　◆　◆

The hail stopped as abruptly as it had started, and all Travis could see was Rochelle lying under his hands, her body lush and pale as some night-blooming flower. She was shaking, her panting breath loud in the sudden silence.

"Uhh . . ." she said, and that was all.

"Come on." He sat up, pulled her leg down, then reached across her and opened the glove compartment, grateful beyond measure that he'd tossed the condoms into the truck and not the cooler.

Her hair was tumbled, she was trembling, and he had to have her. Right now.

"Wait," he told her, handing her the condom packet.

"What?" She blinked at him and pushed herself up to sitting.

"Wait," he said again. He opened the door, climbed down, barely feeling the gravel under his bare feet, and grabbed the sleeping bag from behind the seat, then ran around to the back of the truck and opened the tailgate. He swept at the hail with an arm, then gave it up, opened the sleeping bag, and tossed it down. Close enough.

She was climbing down when he got back to her.

"I told you to wait," he said. "Gravel's too sharp."

"Travis. I—" she began, but she didn't get the rest out, because he had an arm under her hips, another under her shoulders, and was carrying her to the back of the truck and setting her on the edge of the tailgate, on top of the sleeping bag. The open door of the truck cast a glow that lit up her hair and the rich curves of her body, and he stood over her, got a hard rush, and welcomed it.

He said, "Lie down, baby," saw the shudder run through her, and that was another rush. Then she was easing back, lying down on her elbows until she was flat on her back. He was pulling her forward so her hips were at the edge of the tailgate, taking the condom from her with the absolute screaming last of his self-control, and shoving her thighs apart.

A single hard thrust, and he was all the way inside her. And it was almost too much right there.

He'd had a plan for this. A plan to go slowly, to make it last, to do all the things he'd imagined. And he wasn't doing a bit of it. She had her legs pulled up high, wrapped around his back, and there was going to be nothing in the world slow or subtle or easy about any of it.

He needed more, though. He needed it all. He got his hands on her knees and shoved them up until her heels rested on his shoulders. She whimpered, and just like that, he was all the way from 'hard' to 'savage.' She was crying out, taking him so deep, and he was lost. His fingers dug into her thighs and hips, holding her in place for him, holding her down. She was bucking, her rich body laid out before him, her arms flung out behind her, and the roaring in his head was louder than any storm.

"Travis," she gasped. "Harder. More. Please. *Hard.*"

So he gave it to her the way she wanted it. The way he needed to do it. He gave it to her hard. He gave her everything he had, and he took her right along with him, trembling and shaking, lying underneath him and begging him, exactly the way she needed to be. The desire had its claws in him, raking him, shaking him loose from his foundations. Until, at the end, he threw his head back, gritted his teeth, and let it all go.

AFTERMATH

Rochelle was back in the cab at last, because he'd *carried* her there. Nobody had ever done that, because frankly, nobody had ever been big and strong enough to manage it. But Travis was both, and no question, it thrilled her.

Right now, he was driving down the mountain again. He'd had to run back through the mud for the cooler and their sodden clothes first, though. She'd offered to help, he'd refused, and she had to admit that it felt absolutely terrific to have somebody else carrying the competence banner for once and letting her relax.

Now, he had his soaking-wet shorts back on, and that was all. And as for her—well, she had the sleeping bag pulled over her torso, at least. And if she were sitting right beside Travis with her hand up on his leg? Maybe that was because she needed to touch him some more.

"That wasn't exactly what I meant to do," he said, pulling onto the county road again and heading toward town.

"No?" She stretched, her body utterly relaxed, cocooned in well-being, and sent her hand down the inside of his thigh. "Now, see, I would've sworn that that was *exactly* what you meant to do. And that you meant it when you did it, too. I'm going to have some interesting bruises tomorrow."

He glanced sharply across at her. "What? I hurt you?"

"If you're going to grab that hard . . ." She sighed. "Well, I guess there are worse things than a few fingerprints to remind me of how much you wanted it. Besides, sometimes you just need that throwdown. And, boy, you can throw a woman *down*."

He took one hand off the steering wheel and took hers. "So you're not sorry?"

Her own smile felt as slow and lazy as a summer day on the river. "I'll let you know after you do it again. I'm a slow learner, I guess."

"Come lie down on my bed," he said, his hand holding hers to his thigh, "and I'll do my best to convince you. I'm prepared to give the matter my undivided attention. You'd better be planning to spend the night, because I'm thinking it could take a while. But I *won't* be hurting you again. That's a promise."

The pulse had started its heavy, low thrum all the way back before she'd hopped into his truck, as if her heart were beating from a whole new spot. Now, it picked right up again. "What about if you need to bite me some more?" she asked, and if her hand had moved up his leg some? Well, you could hardly blame her. He had a lot of hard muscle on that thigh, and she hadn't felt it nearly enough. "I noticed you enjoy that."

He groaned. "We're going to crash. I hope you realize that."

"Oh," she purred, "I have faith in you." Her sleeping bag might have slipped, and she knew he'd noticed, so she didn't make one single effort to pull it back up. "I think you're going to get us there, because I think you need to."

"Yeah," he said, then had to clear his throat. "You could be right."

Time to torture him some more. She put a hand to her wet hair and said, "On the other hand—I have to work in the morning. I need a shower, too."

"I've got a shower. Only one thing wrong with it."

"What's that?" She was still playing, and so glad to be able to do it. "I'd say I've had enough cold water tonight."

"It hasn't had you in it. And don't worry, it's going to be plenty hot in there. I know some things showers are good for."

"Getting clean?" She was giving it her best shot, but her brain cells didn't have much to work with, not with him diverting her blood to the exact opposite place.

"Oh, no," he promised. "It's not going to be clean. We're going to be getting down and dirty. I've got plans."

"And you get to say that?" She was still in there swinging, at least.

"I get to say it." He braked for the stop sign that marked the city limits. "And you get to say yes or no."

He might have felt her shiver, because he turned his head to smile at her, then took his hand off hers for the first of the turns that would lead back to his place. When she tugged the sleeping bag up, though, his hand shot back out to grab her own. "Leave it. Nothing says, 'Welcome to Paradise' like the naked woman of my dreams snuggled up next to me with her hands all over me, headed straight for my bed."

"Somebody could see," she said, slapping his hand away and laughing, then yanking up the sodden fabric.

He sighed. "I was having a precious moment. You had to rain on my parade, didn't you?"

When he pulled up in front of Carol Ritter's big white-frame house, though, it wasn't quite that sexy. Rochelle wrapped the soaked sleeping bag around herself and stepped down as best she could, holding her boots in one hand, while Travis followed behind her with an armful of wet clothes and the ice chest.

It would have been just fine if Carol hadn't been out in her back-yard, sweeping her patio. At *night*, because heaven forbid that Carol would wake up to wet leaves on her pristine flagstones.

Rochelle rocked to a stop when Carol stopped sweeping to stare at her, and could sense Travis stopping right behind her.

"Hey, Carol," Rochelle said, trying to pretend that she wasn't quite so obviously naked. "We finally got that storm, huh?"

Carol's eyes went from her to Travis, but it was Travis who spoke next. "I took Rochelle for a swim," he said. "Worked out a little differently than we expected."

"Uh-huh," Carol said.

"She's cold now, though," Travis said. "Got to get her inside and warm her up. When you finally get the girl, you've got to take care of her, or she could change her mind. At least that's what my mom always told me."

He stepped around Rochelle, set down his ice chest in front of the door of the white cottage, opened the door, and said, "And my mom was usually right. Come on, baby. Let's go."

As Rochelle stepped through the door ahead of him, she heard him say, "Night, Carol."

Now everyone would know. And she couldn't even be sorry.

◆ ◆ ◆

"I need to ask you a favor," Rochelle said, coming out of his bathroom at six the next morning and distracting him.

He dumped the pile of dry, wrinkled clothes onto the bed he'd made while she'd been in there. "I thought it was fairly obvious that I'm willing to do you any favors you might need."

She smiled, her tousled hair falling down over one blue eye, and picked through the pile for her underwear. "This one might not be quite as much fun, though. My car's in the shop. Has been since yesterday, actually, because they couldn't get to it until today. You willing to hang around my place while I get a little less obviously, umm . . . ?"

"Oh, go on, baby," he said. "You can say the word. Seems to me you said it last night. I could swear I remember that. Turns out I loved hearing it, too. Guess it's all about the context."

When she'd been on her hands and knees on the floor, that is, because they hadn't made it to the bed after all, once they'd finally turned off the shower. Her head had been down, the rasp of her breath hard in his ears, her wet hair hanging around her face. The marks of his fingertips from the first time had showed livid against the white skin on the sides of her hips and backs of her thighs, and that had excited him even more. It was wrong, and he'd known it, and he hadn't cared. He'd been holding her hips again, careful not to bruise her this time, but not one bit careful about anything else. And she'd been moaning out the words, her arms shaking so much that she'd finally collapsed onto her elbows and buried her face in her hands as he'd buried himself in her body. Deep, hard, and all the way home.

"Oh, God. Travis. Yes. Please. More. Fuck me harder."

And when he'd gotten a hand around in front of her and begun to stroke, and she'd gone up like a rocket, calling out loud until she'd lost her words and had started to wail . . . When the contractions had been so strong around him that he'd actually thought he couldn't stand it, and had pulled him into an orgasm so intense, it had just about broken him . . .

Oh, yeah. Her saying the word had worked just fine for him. It would work just fine right now. He'd happily do that to her any day of the week, and hear that from her, too.

Now, she scowled at him, and he put the idea aside. For now.

"Quit it," she said. "Stay focused. Would you be able to give me a ride to work?"

"Of course I would." Walk into the building with her? You bet he'd do that. "I'll pick you up tonight, too." And if she had to come by the Computer Science department to tell him she was ready to go? That would suit him fine. Wes's office was two doors down. A hand on

Rochelle's back, a dismissive glance . . . Oh, yeah. That worked. "But wait a minute." He sat on the edge of the bed and looked at her, which wasn't exactly a hardship. There was a whole lot of Rochelle, and every inch of it was terrific.

He forced himself to concentrate on the matter at hand. "Your car's in the shop? How did you get home after work yesterday?"

"Walked, of course," she said, stepping into her underwear and pulling it up over her hips. "It was hot as hell, too."

"Why didn't you call me for a ride?"

She was leaning over to pick up her bra now, and he might have gotten distracted again. He'd looked at her naked for half the night, but apparently he wasn't tired of it yet. Looking wasn't enough, though. His hands needed to be all over her. Right now.

"What?" she said. "I should have assumed that you'd be happy to drop everything and drive me home?"

"Yep. You should have." She'd managed to destroy the last remnants of his self-control, because he reached for her waist, pulled her over to him, and tugged gently until she was sitting in his lap with a knee on either side of his hips. And then he might have had to spend some time kissing her, not to mention filling both palms with those luscious breasts.

"Travis," she gasped. "Work."

"Mm," he answered, sending a sneaky hand down to stroke her through that pale-pink fabric, feeling the dampness there with a thrill that wasn't one bit lessened by the number of times he'd had her last night. "You sure? There's such a thing as calling in sick. And right now, I've got a real bad fever."

"Except that I'd be the one who was supposed to be sick," she said, then squirmed and made a tiny sound of protest as his mouth found a rosy nipple he hadn't had nearly enough of yet, and his hand slipped inside those tiny pale-pink bikinis.

Oh, yeah. Oh, *yeah*. That felt *good*.

"Travis," she moaned. "No." But then she wriggled, and he was just about too far gone. "Tonight. *Wait.*"

"Right," he said, not willing to let her go quite yet. "Does this mean you're going to go dancing with me again, finally? We'd better have pulled into the fast lane now."

"*Yes.* Geez, you're going to be a demanding boyfriend."

He laughed, gave her a slap on the butt that felt just fine, too, and said, "Oh, baby. You know it."

◆ ◆ ◆

Carol wasn't outside when they left, which made Travis a little sad, because he'd have liked to have said good morning. On the other hand, when they arrived at Rochelle's house, Rochelle's neighbor was out sweeping her front steps, her little dog sniffing around the garden and lifting his leg on a rosebush. If you had a secret, this town might not be the easiest place to keep it.

"Morning, Dell," Rochelle said.

"Well, good morning to *you*," the old lady said, walking down the steps and coming across the yard. "Have we finally made it to the formal introduction stage?" Her sharp gaze took in Rochelle's rumpled appearance, the stubble on Travis's jaw.

"You could say that," Travis said. "Morning. Travis Cochran."

She pulled off her pink flowered gardening glove and shook his hand. She was wearing a blue muumuu today with earrings to match, the biggest ones yet. "Dell Sawyer. Pleased to meet you. We going to be seeing more of you around here?"

"Yes, ma'am," he said. "That's my plan."

"I need to go get ready for work," Rochelle said. "Come on in and make yourself some breakfast, Travis."

"You not cooking for him?" Dell asked.

"Nope," Rochelle said. "Not this morning, anyway." She didn't explain any more than that, just took off into the house, and Dell looked speculatively at Travis again.

"Well, good for her," Dell said. "You let a man get too comfortable, he starts thinking he owns the place, and you right along with it."

Travis laughed out loud. "Probably so. We'll see if I can talk her into taking turns. What do you think?"

"Honey," Dell said, "I think you're on the right track."

DIGGING DEEPER

As far as Jim was concerned, a few days after the three deputies had questioned the girls in Macho Taco, the pieces were definitely *not* falling into place. He sat at the conference table and frowned down at his hands while DeMarco talked.

"So what have we got?" the detective asked. "A pregnancy, maybe a married guy. Somebody with something to lose. Pills. And too many suspects, with the evidence pointing in two main directions. *Opposite* directions. We heard some of the same names at the taco place and the bar. Those guys with the chew in their back pockets. Call them Group One. And the guys from town. Group Two. Which looks like a more likely direction on the one hand, because the only place I've heard much about pills is on campus. And we haven't heard about anybody dealing at all, not in pills. But she got them somewhere, and she couldn't have afforded to buy them."

"Campus is where that mostly goes on," Jim said, "and they get it the old-fashioned way—from their parents' medicine cabinets, and their friends. We've talked to the university cops and the city cops and heard the same thing. Yeah, they're up there, all around. Passed around at parties, mostly, and friend to friend. We don't even have proof Heather had a habit. No residue in her body, nothing on her clothes. All we have is her roommate's hint that she was using Vicodin, but I think we can believe that. I'm thinking amateur prostitution, feeding that habit."

"Anyway," Mark Lawrence said, speaking up for once, and Jim looked at him to encourage him to go on. Lawrence had grown up on a farm and was years younger than Jim, and both things could be helpful here. "For the country boys, it's more about drinking and weed, unless you're talking meth, and we're not, not with that crowd. And also—the city guys, the college guys—they're just . . . random, right? I mean, no connections. Not to each other, and not to drugs, either."

He shut up, then, flushing a bit under DeMarco's scrutiny, and Jim picked it up. "Yep. Nothing tying any of those guys together at all. Just a group of individuals. But those country boys . . ." He stared out the window at the scene along Pine Street without really seeing anything. "When do you talk to this many guys who know each other, play them off against each other like we have, and nobody wants to rule himself out? The town guys—they caved right in, gave us those DNA swabs. It was the country boys who didn't. Like they're hanging together, like they all decided not to talk. But why? For nothing I know of. No tie I can think of that should be that strong. Not like we've got organized crime out here, and if we did, those boys wouldn't be the ones doing it. And the lentils. It's the farm boys who aren't talking, but those lentils . . ." He shook his head. "Doesn't fit. Two opposite directions, like you said. The pills and the lentils on one hand, which says 'town' to me. Or 'university,' more likely. And the not-talking on the other."

DeMarco said, "You keep talking about those lentils. I don't buy it. A field's a field at night. You said it'd look the same."

"No," Jim said. "I said it'd look the same if you didn't know farming."

"All right, then," DeMarco said. "Assuming you're right about that. Everything makes sense, right? If it isn't making sense to us, it's because we're looking at it the wrong way around."

"Right," Jim said. "And?" They'd gone over this again and again, of course. This shouldn't have been so hard, unless the girl actually *had* been picked up by somebody random. Somebody passing through. Picked up off the street. But it didn't smell like that to either of them.

It was the alibis. They had six country boys giving each other alibis for Sunday night, because they'd all been at the same party. In and out, though, there and gone, and none of them admitting to seeing the girl there. A party, they'd all said. Just some music and a lot of beer. Just Sunday night with the guys. Which was likely enough, if it hadn't been for the refusal to get swabbed.

They'd narrowed the probable time of the murder down to sometime between Sunday afternoon, when Cheryl had finally remembered last seeing Heather, and Monday morning, when Heather hadn't showed up to work. Almost all those boys had been working on Sunday, and all of them had been at the party, and none of them had admitted to seeing Heather at all.

A party, though. A bunch of low-caliber guys drinking, out in a lonely house in the country? On the same night when a girl had gone missing, the night she'd most likely been murdered, with her body dumped out there? A girl who'd been seen with some of those guys? Any cop's nose would've twitched at that.

Too many miles of back road, though, that was the problem. Everybody driving fifteen, twenty minutes to get back to his own place from wherever he'd been, and even farther to town. Everybody working by himself, moving from field to field, dirt farm roads and gravel back roads and paved highways. As an investigation, it was pretty much a nightmare.

"So," DeMarco said, running through it one more time, because that was what you did. And to give him credit, DeMarco didn't just talk. He listened. "If we're thinking it's the farm boys who know something, because they're the ones who aren't cooperating? Then let's go back to square one. If it doesn't make sense one way, it has to make sense another. Maybe the lentils mean something else."

Jim frowned down at the table. "You're talking about Cal Jackson."

"Who *did* let us swab his cheek," DeMarco said. "And who came up negative as the father, *and* who was home with his wife and new baby on the nights in question. In the fields during the day, but then where did the girl come from?" He shook his head. "Although his baby would've been, what? Ten days old? I've got a kid. I could've been dancing on the bar with a Hooters waitress for an hour when my kid was ten days old, and I don't think my wife would even have noticed I was gone. But Jackson found the body, and he told us. All he had to do was leave it there. So unless he's a stone-cold psychopath who'd get off on 'discovering' the body and fooling us—"

"Which he isn't," Jim said. "I'd know. He's my cousin, and besides, he played in the NFL for almost ten years. If you're a stone-cold psychopath, your teammates are going to know it. He's not stepping out on Zoe, either. You want DNA? Cal's got 'loyal' stamped right into his. You and I both know you never can tell. Except I can. It's not him."

Mark nodded. "I agree. Not him. I'd have said, not possible."

"Or, if it *is* one of those guys, the farm guys," DeMarco went on. Not dropping it, not quite. They had to find out who'd done this, because otherwise, that little bit of cloud was going to hang over Cal forever, and Jim thought Cal knew it. "If it was a guy who'd know lentils, like you said, then he dumped her there for a reason. *Because* it was Jackson's field. So I'll ask what I asked you before. Who hated him?"

"*Hated,*" Jim said slowly, "that's a strong word. Cal's a hard guy not to like. Jealous, maybe, though—a few people. Probably quite a few. But that could be anybody. Cal's been a star his whole life. I was jealous of him a time or two myself, growing up. And I'm his cousin." Until he *had* grown up, enough to realize that having it all wasn't all it was cracked up to be, and to know the man inside. Cal felt hurt like anybody else, and he'd felt it plenty.

"Who'd be jealous enough to dump a body on his land?" DeMarco pressed.

"Hard to say," Jim said, "because it still seems stupid. Unless somebody wanted it found, like you said. Unless somebody was sitting back enjoying the drama. A stone-cold psychopath."

"Or somebody who got carried away," DeMarco said. "Who thought it seemed like a good idea at the time. Probably not quite a domestic, like we said. Not really premeditated, either. Crime of opportunity. Because she's pregnant, or just a fight. He's going to pull off the road somewhere. Sees Jackson's road, knows it's his. He's not even thinking he'll kill her, maybe. A fight, or scaring her, or even rough sex in the bed of the pickup, where you said that would happen."

"If it was outdoors, yeah, probably in the bed. But her jeans were fastened," Jim reminded DeMarco.

"Still possible. But probably not. So say he hates Jackson, and he's hating the girl, or he's not hating her, but he's been too rough and he's been drinking. And he thinks, 'I'll dump it here. That'll show him.' Who's that guy? Of those six guys who are hanging together, refusing those swabs. Who's that guy?"

"I don't know," Jim said. "They've all got a reckless streak. All got quite a bit of the underachiever about them. That's why they're friends. I'd ask, who would they be scared of? Or just who's the leader? Because somebody's telling them not to talk, and somebody's backing that up."

"And who's that?" DeMarco asked.

"Couple guys," Jim said. "Dave Harris. And maybe Lake Farnsworth, of course. The party was at his place, which made him the most noticed there. Everybody would give him an alibi, even if he wasn't there every minute. Everybody would think he had been."

"Harris is married," DeMarco said. "Something to lose. And the meanest, I'd say. The hardest."

"Agreed," Jim said. "And Farnsworth is barely on our list. Never seen with the girl. Never danced with her. Never left with her. Nothing to do with her."

Lake Farnsworth had been questioned, just like everybody else who'd been seen in the bar when the girl had been there. But nobody had ever seen him at Macho Taco, or even talking to Heather, and other than the party being at his house—they had nothing. Jim got a tingle all the same, just the trace of it up his arms. "He's real tight with that group, though," he said slowly. "Good-time boy, not much mean to him, I'd have said. A fighting side after a few, yeah, but that's about it."

"A fighting side after a few," DeMarco repeated.

"Yeah, which makes it possible. Hot blood, yes. The heat of the moment, I could see that. Maybe. But what would be the motive? Divorced, doesn't have two cents to rub together. Spends his pay-check down at the bar, and always has. Never hit his wife when he was married that I know of, and with Rochelle?" Jim smiled. "You'd know, because she'd have clocked *him* with her frying pan and walked out the door. Count on it. What kind of threat would that girl be to him?"

"The rough sex, maybe," DeMarco suggested.

"Maybe," Jim said dubiously. "I'd peg Harris more for that, both ways. But Rochelle—" He sat up a little straighter, and the tingle got stronger. "His ex. She works up at the university. Always has. He'd know people up there. There's that connection."

"You saying Rochelle's in it?" Lawrence said. "They didn't have what you'd call a friendly split. And Rochelle's pretty straight."

"No," Jim said. "I'm saying he could have university connections. Pills—distribution—you're talking about the university." He shook his head in frustration. "Just a thought. Just a flash."

"Right." DeMarco shoved back from the table. "We talk to all of them again, that's all. Especially Farnsworth. We start over. We put enough heat on, and somebody's going to crack. Somebody always does."

A TWISTY MIND

The man's phone buzzed, and he glanced at the number. *Restricted call.* He pushed the button and said, "Yeah."

No preamble on the other end. "This is getting way too close."

"And once again, I'm working. As I've mentioned. I'll call you later."

"You told me there was nothing to worry about. I'm not stupid. There's something to worry about."

"No. There really isn't. So a girl died. Very sad. She was a girl a lot of guys danced with, and some of them might even have been seen leaving a bar with her, too. A drifter with a low-rent job and a low-rent life who met a sad end. Unless the cops get a hot tip, that's where it's going to stay. And they're not going to get a hot tip. All my guys want to keep earning that extra tax-free income, and they might be scared of what might happen to them if they talked. And that might be wise. I'm not worried, and if I'm not worried, you shouldn't be worried, either."

"That's right," the voice said. Ah, trying a shift in tactics now. "I don't have to worry. All I'm doing is scribbling on prescription pads. I'm not the one juggling a workforce of however many runners, with a biker gang I don't even want to know about on the other end. And I won't be the one holding the bag if it goes south."

"That's right. You won't. I will. You're getting fifty percent of the take just for scribbling. I'm doing everything else, and it's under control."

His partner was still harping. "Fifty percent of what you *tell* me the take is. You don't exactly give me itemized receipts. Don't think I haven't noticed that."

It had only been six months, and his so-called partner already had delusions of grandeur. Entrepreneurship had its downside, for sure. Which was why he was busy scouting out a new partner, and a new network, too. Away from here. A shark had to keep swimming or die, right?

The best defense was a good offense, and it was past time to remind his partner who had the upper hand. "You saying you want to get more involved?" he asked. "Or do you want me to send over one of those bikers to run the numbers for you?"

"No!"

"Thought not." It wasn't really a biker gang, actually. It was a couple bartenders all the way up in Spokane, each with a busy trade and every opportunity to hand something extra across the bar along with a cocktail napkin. Far from Paradise, across the state line, and no connection to him at all. And it was true: the receipts weren't nearly as low as reported. A bartender took one hell of a smaller cut than a biker gang would have, and was a whole lot less dangerous, too.

There were benefits to having a twisty mind. Always stay two steps ahead, that was his motto. Which was why he was moving up. He was a shark, and he was always swimming.

"Keep scribbling," he advised his partner now. "And don't worry. I've got this."

He did. Or he would. Whatever he had to do to get there, he'd do. Ambition had built this country, they said. And it was going to build his future.

NIGHT OUT

As kickoffs went, Rochelle's first weekend with Travis was pretty much the best ever. It started with him, true to his word, taking her dancing on Friday night. And when she was walking into the Cowboy Bar with a long, lean hunk of testosterone in jeans and boots and shoulders that wouldn't quit, a man who proceeded to spend the entire evening letting everyone there know that she was the only woman he wanted? That part wasn't bad at all, ego-boost-wise.

"I ever tell you that I like the way you dance?" she asked him over the wail of the guitar, the insistent beat of the drums. Her boots were sliding over the hardwood in exact time with his, and his hand was steering her with perfect authority, letting her relax and go with the music. To go with him, as if the same energy were running through both of them, a stream of silver flowing from his hand straight into her body.

"I ever tell you that dancing with you is like making love standing up?" he answered, then added, "Twirling you," and did. Twice.

She was laughing when she came back into his arms. "Really? I'm not sure you'd be doing exactly that, though."

She saw that delicious twitch at the corner of his mouth. "No?" he said. "Seems to me I turned you around pretty good last night. I think you liked it, too."

"That's right," she said, somehow managing to keep on dancing and breathing. "You told me once that you couldn't decide which view was your favorite. Guess I'll have to help you choose again tonight. Maybe we'd better leave a light on so you can find your way. What do you think?"

"See, now," he sighed, "this is why I love you. Because you always say the right thing. You bet we're going to leave the light on, because I'm watching that. And I'll give you some practice right now. Twirling you again."

This is why I love you. A few words, so casually spoken, and she wasn't going to believe he meant them. But she was going to hold them close all the same, pressed into her hand like pieces of beach glass, the kind you had to turn in your fingers just so you could feel their smoothness, the kind you had to sneak a peek at now and then just because they were so pretty, and you'd found them for yourself.

It was quite a contrast to what Lake had said, the last time she'd asked him to take her dancing. After he'd looked at her like she was nuts.

"The only reason to ask a girl to dance," he'd said, "is to find out her name. And I already know your name."

Now she thought, *Ha. Joke's on you.* All Lake would have had to do was take her out and say something like Travis just had, and he could have written his ticket. But then, he wouldn't have said something like that, and he hadn't cared that much about his ticket. Her body had been a convenience to him, and that was about it.

She didn't want to think about Lake tonight, though, so she thrust the memory aside and kept dancing with Travis. Pressed up close to his chest during the slow ones, his lips brushing over her temple, murmuring sweet suggestions into her ear. Both of them knowing exactly what they had to look forward to, and both wanting to wait for it until they couldn't wait a single minute more.

Sliding over beside him again in his rig then, for the drive home. Having him turn at the stoplight and kiss her, long and slow, his hand slipping inside her shirt like he had to do it. She'd worn an apricot top with a wide V-neck, knowing he'd be sneaking peeks down it all evening, and wanting him to.

"Damn, baby," he said, his breath warm in her ear, his hand hard and hot against her skin. "You turn me on so much. You've got me aching for it." Which wasn't "I love you," but it worked for her.

And then they got to his house, and he set about fulfilling every single promise his body had made to hers.

He did leave a light on. And then he laid her down on his bed and undressed her with aching slowness. Pushing the apricot top off one shoulder, her own startled intake of breath loud in her ears as his lips brushed the tender spot just beneath the outer edge of her collarbone, then made their slow way down until he was kissing the swells of her breasts, one hand beneath each full mound, raising them for his eager mouth. His hands so firm, but not the least bit rough, not tonight. Velvet over steel. At last, he was pushing her top up with his thumbs, inch by slow inch, with his mouth right behind it. He was pulling it over her head then, revealing the satin and lace of her strapless bra, which he got rid of with one quick flick of his fingers.

"Ah," he breathed, and then he was on her. The same urgency as the night before, but not one single bit of rush. His hands strong and sure and still so deliciously slow, his mouth hard and hot, kissing, sucking, biting gently, until she was moving restlessly under him.

"Travis," she said. "Travis." And he didn't answer, but one of his hands was skimming up her thigh, now, making its leisurely way higher and higher. His mouth on hers, stealing her kisses, stealing her breath. Until his questing fingers found the tiny strap, and his hand stilled.

"Mm." She felt the vibration of the word against her. He rubbed his face between her breasts, then caught a nipple between his teeth, making her shudder. "You're wearing a thong."

"Well, yeah. It's been known to happen." She was still going for smart-ass, but it was getting harder.

He sighed with pure satisfaction. "Let's leave that on, then. But we'll take this little skirt off, how about that?"

"Well, you're the boss," she managed to say, and his hand, which had been tracing the strip of lace over her hip bone, stopped again.

"Now, if you're going to say stuff like that," he said, "you're just asking for it."

"I am asking for it," she said. "Haven't you noticed? You going to give it to me?"

"Oh, yeah." His hand was moving again, stroking down that line of elastic, closer and closer. "I'm going to give it to you. You just wait."

And "wait" was what he meant. His hand hadn't reached the right spot for a long time, no matter how eagerly her own hands had slipped under his T-shirt, pulled it over his head, stroked over his chest, down his abdomen, over his back. No matter how slowly and seductively she'd unbuckled his belt and unbuttoned his jeans.

There'd be another night when she was in charge, she promised herself right before she gave it up, the same way she had on the dance floor, and surrendered to those demanding hands.

The hands that had turned her over, finally, exactly the way he'd promised. Had known precisely where they'd wanted to go, and had gone there, followed by his mouth. He'd kissed his way down her spine one vertebra at a time, and who'd known a back could feel like that? And while he'd been doing that, his hands had been sliding up the backs of her thighs. Sliding up, and sliding them apart.

"You're so gorgeous," she heard, though things were getting a bit hazy now. "So I'm just going to do this." His thumbs were moving along the sensitive line where her thighs began, then diving down, tracing it farther. So close and still so far, until she was wriggling, until she was moaning, her face pressed into the mattress. And then, when she couldn't have stood it a moment longer, he was shoving a pillow beneath her hips and delving down to touch her where she needed him, using the fabric of the thong as a plaything, rubbing her with it, up and down and around and, finally, inside her, which was the worst, and the best, too. Over and over, until her hips were leaving the bed and she was rising onto her knees.

"Travis," she moaned, her head turning from side to side. "Please. Come on. I need you."

"No," he said. "Not yet."

He was turning her again, then at last, taking the strap of her thong in both hands and pulling it down her legs, freeing her from it. He left her hips propped high on the pillow, though, and then he was pushing her legs up next to her head with a palm on the back of each thigh while she panted and called out.

"Let's hear you beg again," he said. "Let's hear it, Rochelle."

"Oh, please," she said, because it seemed she didn't have any pride left. "Please. Come on. Please."

She knew he was smiling, and she didn't care. When his tongue finally flicked over the aching, sensitized nub, she might have made some noise. And after that . . . she might have made even more.

And still he kept it slow. His hands on her legs were hard, but the rest of him was so patient. He worked her over like he'd never heard of "hurry," like he'd never heard of "bored," like he'd never, ever heard of "enough." Until she was shaking. Until she was crazy. Until she was, finally, over the top, calling out and bucking against him, racked with the spasms that shook her again and again.

And that had just been the foreplay.

ANOTHER SATURDAY NIGHT

On Saturday night, Miles Kimberling knocked once, then walked on into the house in the country with none of his normal pleasurable shiver of danger and excitement. This wasn't a game anymore, and it sure as hell wasn't fun.

The usual party, for the usual purpose. They'd been back to Saturdays for the past few weeks, ever since harvest had ended and the farmers among them weren't in the fields until ten o'clock on Saturday nights.

Most . . . groups . . . handled their transactions in mall parking lots, Miles had been told. They counted on the anonymity of acres of blacktop and rows of cars. Week after week, in the same public places.

Most people were fools. That was why they got caught. He'd been told that, too.

It wasn't that Paradise didn't have a mall. It was a big one, stretching along the highway for a good half mile. And, yeah, the Walmart parking lot was good-sized. But it wasn't anonymous, not in a town this size. A bunch of good ol' boys getting together after the work-week, though, blowing off smoke out in the country? What could be more natural?

It had seemed so easy when he'd first heard about it. All he had to do was walk into a different pharmacy every day or two, one town or another, one state or another—easy to do here, near the border of Washington, Idaho, and Oregon, with Montana not too far away, either—and hand over a few prescriptions. Piece of cake. In return, he got great parties, and the kind of payoff that made his girlfriends happy to see him, and ready and willing to show it. Both of them.

He didn't need money, not really. He needed excitement, the edge his boring-ass life had never provided. He'd been getting it now, and then some. And he didn't have to do anything really bad for it, nothing he'd lost any sleep over. So a bunch of college kids had a pharm party. That wasn't his doing, and anyway, it wasn't like anybody was cooking meth here.

But he hadn't been counting on this. He hadn't been counting on murder.

The energy level was off the charts tonight, like always. Payday, and collection day. But this time, the tone was wrong, and he wasn't the only one feeling it. Nobody was hanging around. Most of the guys had handed in their goods, taken their stack of prescription slips and the Baggie or the bills that constituted tonight's pay, and headed right out again. Only a few of them remained now, and all the others were antsy, too. The difference was, they were willing to say something about it, because they were the ones who'd started out with the boss, the same way Miles had.

The boss had said that, too. Not to use his name. To think of him as "the boss," and to refer to him that way, if they had to talk about him at all. Which had seemed stupid, but exciting. Kind of like being a spy, or part of some organized-crime syndicate, instead of a guy who was turning into a few drugstore parking lots and standing in line at a few counters.

"All this isn't doing me one bit of good," Danny Boyle was saying now. "My boss heard that the cops were talking to me. That was bad enough. And then my wife did."

"She still enjoying those fringe benefits?" the boss asked. Danny was another one who took his pay in pills. "Tell her there's nothing in this, other than every single guy at the bar getting questioned. Which is the truth."

"If they force me to give a sample, though . . ." Danny said. "Thing is—it *could* have been me."

The reason for the DNA test was common knowledge around town now. As always, Miles's mind skittered away from the implications. *DNA* was an easier word than *baby*, or even *fetus*.

Embryo, he told himself desperately. *Ball of cells.* No matter how he thought about it, the idea made him sick, as it had ever since he'd heard. And not just because of the danger to himself.

Mostly the danger to himself, though. That DNA was like a bullet in a game of Russian roulette. You were spinning the chamber every time, knowing that eventually, the trigger wouldn't click on empty. Somebody had been the father, and given Heather's habit, it was likely to be one of them. That was why it was so important, they'd all been told, that nobody rule himself out. Every time you took a man out of the mix, you shortened the odds on everybody else. And you shortened the odds that somebody would talk, too, that one of them would rat the rest out.

"It could have been anybody," the boss said. "That's the point. That's our loophole. They can't force you to give that sample, not without a judge's order, and for that, they'd need hard evidence. Which they don't have. They've asked just about all of you, and plenty of other guys, too. Anybody they heard she danced with, or left with. Ol' Heather got around, and that's what's going to save everybody here. As long as nobody lets them swab his cheek, as long as everybody keeps quiet, everybody's all right. Hang together, or hang separately."

He looked around the circle of faces. Some men stared back at him, while others looked into their plastic cups. When the glance came his way, Miles looked down. He didn't know who'd done it. He didn't want to know. He didn't even want to think about it.

Some random guy, he told himself. *Some guy she met.* The cops hadn't even pinned it down to a single night. They were asking about Saturday and Sunday. Which meant it could have been anybody. Except he didn't think so.

The boss didn't raise his voice. He lowered it. "And I mean just exactly that. You give them that sample? I'm going to find out about it. So don't do it. If you do? Your paycheck isn't the only thing you'll lose."

Almost everyone looked away, then. Miles could see that with a quick glance to either side beneath his lowered eyelids. "Just ask cute little Heather," the boss continued. "Oh, wait. You can't."

◆　　◆　　◆

Miles hung around for another half hour, even though all he wanted to do was to get out. At last, though, the screen door finally banged behind Dave Harris, and the boss was looking at Miles sideways, like he was wondering what he was still doing there.

"Time to go," he said. "Party's over."

"Yeah." Miles reached a hand into his back pocket and pulled out the prescription slips. "I just wanted to tell you—I'm out."

Silence, and Miles started getting nervous. *More* nervous. "Hey," he said. "I get that it's leaving you a guy short. So, here." He pulled the bag of pills from his front pocket and handed them over. Tiffany and Amber were both going to be pissed, but all of a sudden, that didn't matter. "Look, you can have these back. I wasn't counting on all this. It was just for fun, you know? But my old man—" He was sweating now. "You know. He could kick me out. He's already said some things. Too much to lose, man. I didn't even sleep with that girl. I couldn't be the father, and this is way past what I thought it would be. I wasn't counting on this," he repeated.

"You've got a whole lot *more* to lose if you talk," the boss said. "You do get that, right?"

"Hey, man." Miles was backing away a couple paces now. "I get it."

"You go getting your cheek swabbed, and it's not going to be a secret. Everybody's a friend here. That's how this all started, right? You don't want to make enemies. You'll be out there all alone, and you'll be in a very bad spot."

"I won't," Miles said. "I'm not. It's just . . . I'm getting a lot of pressure, man. And I'm done."

CHANGE OF PLAN

Unfortunately, Rochelle only had two weekends with Travis, and a couple of work weeks during which she tried not to let herself get carried away and pretty much failed miserably. And then, on Saturday, he took off for San Francisco again.

"Sorry," he told her as she stood in the circle of his arms at her front door on Saturday morning. He'd just spent a good five minutes kissing her good-bye, and she was already missing him. "It's going to take a couple days, this go-round. We're talking money, and as you know, that takes time."

"Mm." She had one hand on the ridge of muscle along one shoulder, the other one splayed across his chest. Now, she kissed him on the neck, bit down just to hear him suck in his breath, and smiled. "Come back to me."

"Oh, you know it." One hand had drifted perilously low on her back, the fingertips resting lightly on the uppermost swell of her bottom, his sneaky thumb finding the edge of her shirt and burrowing under it to stroke the sensitive skin just above her waistband, as if he hadn't noticed that Ken Johnson was washing his car across the street with half his attention, and watching Rochelle get kissed with the other half. Or as if he had.

"Not like I could stay away if I tried," Travis told her. "You could say you've got me hooked, and you'd be right. You want me to bring you back a present?"

"No," she said. "I just want you." Then she put both hands around his head and pulled it down for another long kiss.

He texted her from the airport an hour later. *Next time, remind me not to get out of the truck. Almost missed my plane. Where'd you get that mouth?*

She smiled a secret little smile and texted him back. *Same place I got that rear end you like so much. Got them both from my mama.*

He answered right away, as if he'd been watching his screen. *Well, she did a real good job on both. I guess I'd better not tell her so,* which made her laugh.

She'd gone to work on Monday, and she'd gone to work on Tuesday, too, and had tried to pretend she hadn't been waiting for him to come back. Until he'd sauntered into her office early Tuesday afternoon, all hips and grin, sat on the edge of her desk like he belonged there, and said, "Hey, pretty lady. Miss me?"

"Unprofessional," she said, trying to frown at him. "Not to mention cocky."

He lifted one dark eyebrow. "All righty, then. We playing hard to get?" He took a seat in the visitor's chair. "Better?"

"Well, no," she conceded. She looked around to check that the other doors were closed. They weren't, so she lowered her voice. "I kind of like it when you try to look down my shirt. And I think you've figured out that I'm not that hard for you to get. You can pretty much have it. Any way you want it."

He leaned his head back for a moment and let out a low groan, and she had to smile. "So," he said. "Tonight. Dinner, or what?"

She twirled her pen, and he watched her. "What," she finally said. "First. And then dinner. If I get to choose, and tonight?" She lowered her voice even more, so he had to lean across the desk to hear her. "I'd better get to choose. You've had it all your own way up to now, and if I don't take the reins pretty soon, we're going to have a power imbalance. And I know you wouldn't want that."

His eyes were gleaming now, and he'd just opened his mouth to say something that she devoutly hoped was going to have her crossing her legs and fighting a telltale shudder, when Dr. Olsen came out of his office.

"Well, hello, Travis," he said with obvious surprise. "Need something?"

"Nope," he said, standing up. "Just bothering Rochelle, I'm afraid. Got a class, though. See you later."

Dr. Olsen watched him go with a frown on his normally good-natured face, his old-fashioned gray buzz cut uncharacteristically bristling. "He pestering you?" he asked Rochelle. "Because I can do something about that."

She made a business of straightening the already-straight folders in her vertical file. "Nope. It's fine. We're going out, actually."

His voice gentled. "You sure?"

She felt the unaccustomed color creeping up her neck, a rising tide of heat. She never blushed, but she was doing it now. She'd hoped he hadn't heard about Wes. Well, it wasn't the first hope she'd ever had dashed. "Who knows," she said. "But at least he's not going to be slut-shaming me to the whole College. Which will be a step up, obviously."

He nodded. "You have any trouble, tell me this time."

"I won't," she said. "I'll keep it professional. But thanks." And then she had to fight not just the blush, but a tiny bit of choking up, too.

Travis was messing with her mind and no mistake. And that was before she got the text ten minutes later.

Consider me ready to let you take the reins. Hope that means what I think it means.

She texted back, *Let's say that your head's the one that's going to be banging tonight. OK if we don't make it out of the truck for a while? Think I've got a favor to repay. Maybe we could find someplace dark and private. I might know a spot.*

She waited until the words appeared on her screen, and then the smile bloomed. *Damn you, woman. I have to teach a class in 15 minutes. You had to leave me with that image?*

I have to do a lot of things, she typed. *Wait and see.*

◆　◆　◆

Except that he hadn't gotten to see anything, because when she'd arrived home that evening, ready to take a long hot bath, rub her entire body with her silkiest lotion, and generally prepare to make Travis lose his mind? The duplex had been dark and quiet, but not quiet enough.

She'd gone to the door of Stacy's room, knocked, and said, "Stace?"

"No," the muffled voice said.

More moodiness, but for some reason, the alarm bells were ringing. "What's going on?" She tried the doorknob. Unlocked, thank goodness. She went inside and found Stacy, not in bed as she'd imagined, but on the floor, wedged into a corner, her arms wrapped around her legs and her head buried in her folded arms, rocking back and forth in distress.

"Baby." Rochelle was there in an instant. "What?"

A violent shake of the head was her answer.

"*What?*" Rochelle asked again. She tried to get an arm around Stacy, but her sister shrugged her off. "Shane? What?"

"*No.* Go *away.* You can't help." Stacy whirled and faced the wall.

"Sweetie, please," Rochelle said. "Tell me. Nothing's so bad that we can't deal with it."

Stacy shook her head again. Both hands were on her head now, her elbows together, her body curled into itself like a snail going into its shell, racked with sobs that shook Rochelle as if they'd come from her own body.

What had her sister done? Or what had somebody done to her? She'd been driving Stacy back and forth to work for her evening shifts. She hadn't wanted her riding her bike in the dark, not anymore. But something had happened? What? And why hadn't Rochelle done more? She should have done more.

She looked around the room for clues, spotted Stacy's backpack thrown into the opposite corner, went over to it, and opened it. The first thing she saw was the blue book.

She was pulling it out when Stacy came scrambling over the floor like a crab and tried to grab it from her. *"No,"* her sister wailed. "That's private!"

Rochelle held the blue book up out of Stacy's reach and looked at the circled number on the front. Seventy-nine. The relief weakened her knees, followed instantly by puzzlement.

"You got a, what?" she asked. "A C-plus? In what?" She didn't know what she'd feared. It had seemed *bad.* All this over a bad grade?

"You don't *get* it." Stacy had sunk back to the ground again, and was rocking again. Like she had when she was little, when the other kids had been mean to her because she was too smart. "I can't . . . It's so . . ."

"Right," Rochelle said, keeping it matter-of-fact. "It's just the midterm, though. *One* midterm. What grade do you have to have?"

"An A." Stacy's voice had risen to a near-hysterical pitch. "I have to have an A. It's my *major.* It's *medical school.*"

"And isn't it possible to get an A, still? Hard, maybe, but possible? You get some tutoring, ace the final and the labs—you're all good. As long as everything else is going all right." She looked at her sister. *"Is* it going all right?"

But Stacy just cried, and nothing Rochelle could say could get an answer until she said, "All right. This is past me. I don't know what to do here. I'm calling the folks."

Stacy finally looked up, the black eyeliner running in twin streaks down her blotched face. "No!" She scrambled up from the floor and grabbed the blue book out of Rochelle's hands. "No. Please. Please don't tell them. Don't tell . . ." She was crying hard again. "Please, Ro. Don't tell Daddy. I can't *stand* it."

"But, sweetie, don't you see?" Rochelle tried to explain. "This is over the top. You're always so good in school, and now you're not, and you're having some kind of . . . what, breakdown? You *have* to get help, and I don't know how to help you."

"I'll go to . . . to . . ." Stacy said.

"The right answer would be, 'I'll go to the counseling center,'" Rochelle said. "The only thing that's going to help here is you saying, 'I'll call tomorrow morning and make an appointment.'"

"I'll do it," Stacy said. "I promise." But her eyes were sliding away even as she said it.

"I'm going to ask you for proof," Rochelle said. "And you need to get tutoring if you're having trouble. I'm going to ask you for proof of that, too. I know you can do this. But you need *help*. Everybody needs help sometimes. This is your time, that's all."

Why? she wondered. The classes were hard, sure. But Stacy had always aced them. Especially in her major.

"If I don't see proof of an appointment," she said, "it's the folks." Who could do . . . what? Not much. They didn't know much about college. Rochelle's mother hadn't even graduated from high school, because by the time graduation had come around, she'd already had Rochelle. Which was why it mattered so much to both of them that Stacy do this.

"I promise," Stacy said again.

"All right, then," Rochelle smoothed Stacy's matted hair back from her wet face. "Go take a shower, and we'll have some soup. Because have you eaten?"

Stacy shrugged miserably and shook her head.

"Right," Rochelle said. "Shower. Change. Soup. And then we sit with this test book, and you tell me what went wrong. You can't fix things if you don't look straight at them. So that's what we're going to do. Look straight at it, and then once you know what's wrong, you're going to fix it."

She wasn't sure how much she'd helped, but at least she'd gotten Stacy out of the corner. But she couldn't leave her alone and risk her ending up there again. Not even for Travis.

SURPRISE APPEARANCE

Rochelle was writing up the minutes from the Jackson Foundation's latest meeting the next day, her gaze somewhere in the distance as she tried to distill ten minutes of academic-speak into a few cogent sentences, when the woman breezed into the office.

Not an engineering student, because Rochelle would have remembered her. Long and lean as a racehorse, her dark hair cut short and choppy, three piercings in each ear, plus one in a nostril displaying a tiny piece of turquoise. No makeup, but then, her strong, dark features didn't require any. A short-sleeved, embroidered blouse revealing a tattoo in some sort of swirling tribal design on one upper arm, skinny indigo jeans tucked into low boots, and a canvas backpack slung over one shoulder.

Not a kid, either. Midtwenties, maybe, and with a life force that radiated out of her. More interesting than almost anybody who'd showed up in this office lately. Besides Travis, of course.

"Can I help you?" Rochelle asked.

"Yeah, thanks." As if Rochelle's thought had conjured it up, the woman asked, "Can you tell me how to find Travis Cochran? He works here, doesn't he? Is he around today, do you know? I tried him earlier, but I couldn't reach him. Or maybe you can give me his address. I came up kind of impulsively," she explained, without explaining at all.

"I'm sorry," Rochelle said. "No, I can't give out his address." Her heart had started to pound, a steady thud that somehow spelled *doom*. Because the woman hadn't said *Wayne*. She'd said *Travis*. And that meant something. "I believe he will have just gotten out of class," she added. She didn't *believe*, actually. She knew. "He may be back in his office now. That's down on the third floor."

"Could I call him from your phone and see?" The woman glanced out the window. "My phone's dead, and I need to get in touch with him and get back out there. The light's going to be perfect in half an hour."

The *light*? Rochelle picked up the phone and prepared to dial Travis's extension. She didn't have to look that up, either. "I'll call down there for you," she said. "Can I tell him who's asking?"

The red lips curved into a smile. "Sure. Tell him it's his wife."

Rochelle sat without moving for a couple long seconds. Without breathing. The sickness rose, and she forced it back. And then she set the phone into its cradle with exaggerated care and stood up. She might not be able to feel her legs, but that didn't matter one bit. "You know what?" she told the woman, keeping her voice absolutely, positively steady. "I'll take you down there myself. Come on. Let's go find him."

Some women ran away from things that hurt—and from people who hurt them. Rochelle ran straight at them. Did it hurt just as much? You bet it did. That didn't mean she had to lie down and take it.

◆　◆　◆

Travis took the stairs to the third floor two at a time, swinging his laptop case. He'd dump it in the office and go check out Rochelle, that was the plan. Was it stupid to need to see her face again before tonight? Yeah, it was. And he had to do it anyway.

But right now, there was a girl hunched up on the floor outside his office, her knees pulled up tight, one arm wrapped around them, and he sighed. Not office hours, but he wasn't that good at saying no to students, especially not when their body language spelled "distress." Her dark hair was falling over her face, her fingers flying over her phone.

It wasn't until he got there that he realized it was Stacy.

"Well, hey," he said, stopping a couple feet from her.

She had her hand over the phone before she even looked up, and then it was back in her backpack and she was standing.

"Hi," she said, her cheeks flushed pink. "Um, you said . . . if I needed help. Do you think . . . would you have time? The midterm's on Friday, and . . . I . . . I . . ." She stopped talking and gulped in a breath. "If you have time. If you think . . . if you could."

"Of course I have time," he said, pulling out his key and unlocking the door. And abandoning Rochelle with an inward sigh of resignation. He knew where her own priorities would have been. "Come on in and tell me what the problem is."

He couldn't have said if he hoped this was just about statistics, or that she'd ask him about something else. She needed help, he was surer than ever of that after the quick phone call from Rochelle the night before. He just wasn't sure that he was the person to give it.

It wasn't that he wasn't an expert on men behaving badly. It was that he probably was.

They didn't get into that right away, of course. In fact, he wasn't quite sure how he was supposed to go from "analysis of variance" to "why some men enjoy being dirty lying dogs and jerking you around." He was still trying to work that out when Rochelle came into his office.

Well, "came in" would be one way of putting it. She'd always knocked, on the rare occasions when he'd gotten her down here. Today, she was in the door like a blast of winter wind. And she wasn't alone, he registered a second later. She had Zora with her. *What?*

Stacy had swiveled around the second Rochelle had come in. Travis was standing up, just starting to say, "Hey," but Rochelle beat him to the punch. Just about literally. The woman who'd woken in his bed before dawn on Saturday morning, uncurling and stretching those long limbs like a sleek, satisfied Siamese, was gone. This right here? This was a tiger. The kind that some fool might think he'd tamed, right up until the moment when he realized his disastrous mistake.

"I brought you a visitor," she said, and you could have frozen icicles on that voice. "All the way from California, I'm guessing. And here I thought I was so much smarter than Stacy. I knew better. I knew *so* much better, and I still fell for it."

Stacy had her mouth open now the same way Travis did, he registered in one tiny, unpreoccupied corner of his mind. But Rochelle didn't give either of them a chance to speak. "What kind of guy doesn't want to see a girl on the weekend?" she mimicked savagely. "'A guy with another girlfriend,' somebody once told me. Or how about this? How about a guy with a *wife*? A guy who's flying off for 'meetings' that last for days? On the *weekends*. You sneaking, lying, cheating son of a *bitch*."

She wasn't slapping him. That, he might have been able to handle. Instead, she was just standing there, the contempt and anger radiating off her. He was struck dumb, but at the same time—he was burning.

"Wait." That was Zora. Half laughing, half horrified. "Wait, wait, wait. My bad. I'm sorry. I didn't realize—*No*. I'm not his wife. I'm his *sister*."

Travis finally had his voice back. "Yes. She is. My little sister Zora, who I'm not one bit glad to see. What the *hell*—" He broke off, because that wasn't the part that mattered. "But why would you . . . why would you even—" He tried to find the words, ran a hand through his hair in frustration. "OK. I see why you would. Maybe. But—no. *No*. Don't you know me by now? Don't you know me at *all*?"

"Hey. Wait. Both of you." Zora was still trying to explain herself to Rochelle, as if that were going to be possible. "I was just trying to

give him a little scare. What can I say? I got a wild hair. It happens."
She lifted one slender shoulder in an extravagant shrug. "He's always
so serious, it's like I just *have* to get up in there and rattle his cage, you
know? I didn't realize I was messing with his good thing. But no way."
She laughed, a sudden musical peal that was completely inappropriate
under the circumstances, a sound that some people said they found
infectious. Some people who weren't Travis. "Really. Trust me. No. I'm
nothing like his wife. I hope."

NOT WITHOUT A FIGHT

Rochelle stood on the spot, staring at Travis. Her heart had lifted. And then it had plunged. It wasn't hot blood she was feeling anymore, either. It was pure ice-cold rage.

She *didn't* hit him. She'd decided a while back that if violence wasn't OK for men, it wasn't OK for women, either. But, *man,* was that hard to remember right now. Her hand ached to hit him. Her hand *burned* to hit him.

Stacy was still standing there, too, and Rochelle could see how miserable she was at being caught up in this. Part of Rochelle wanted to stop, to take care of her sister, but most of her needed to keep going. Needed to *know.* However bad it was—nothing was worse than not knowing. Nothing was more damaging than not facing the truth.

"So this is your sister," she said to Travis, amazed that she could still keep her voice level. "Who is nothing like your wife."

"Not my wife. My ex." His moment of uncertainty and indecision was gone, and he was Travis again, standing still and solid and telling her straight out. Like he was trustworthy. Except that maybe he wasn't. "She's saying she's nothing like my ex-wife. Although actually, if you ask me, there are similarities."

"You were married before," Rochelle said, ignoring that. "And you didn't tell me."

"You were quoting me a while ago, right?" he said. "OK, now I'll quote you. What kind of person hasn't made mistakes by this point? Yeah, I was married. For three years. It's been over for seven. It was a long time ago."

"You still should have told me."

"Yeah. I should have. I guess I'd confessed so much by then, I was afraid to pile on any more. And it was so long ago, I told myself it didn't matter. Does that make me a stand-up guy?" he said, before she could. "No. It doesn't. And we can talk about all of this, but I'd rather do it alone with you. And I'd like the alone part to start right now."

"Nice," Zora said. "And what did you confess? What did you *do?* Inquiring minds want to know."

He looked at her. "Do not push me," he warned. "And why are you even here?"

"Nice again," she said, not a bit daunted. "It's a story. It's because of the hills. I wanted to shoot them."

Huh?

"Well, don't tell me the story now," Travis said with a ruthlessness that could only come from a brother, so that was what he had to be. Which still left the matter of the wife he hadn't told her about. "Tell me some other time when you haven't just torpedoed my hard-won love life, and I might be interested. I assume this is, what? A quick visit?"

"Yes, because I have to go back to my boring-ass job on Monday," Zora said. "I came by to ask if I could sleep on your couch."

"No," he said at once. "At least—" He blew out a breath. "Look. I'll tell you, in case you haven't figured it out. You're thirty seconds away from walking out of here with Stacy. And, oh. This other person standing here? This innocent passerby caught in the crossfire? She's *Rochelle's* little sister. Her name's Stacy, and she's a very nice girl who's going to come back in, oh—" He looked at Rochelle, then back at Stacy. "Half an hour, so I can help her with her statistics class. But right now, both of you are going to do something for me. Make friends, and then, Zora, you can ask to sleep on *Stacy's* couch. Or get her to go with you to my place and stay there. Because at the moment, I've got one priority, and that's convincing Rochelle to do some making up tonight. And I've got a very small place."

"You do not get to say that, bud," Rochelle said. "*Any* of it."

"I don't get to announce that that's what we'll be doing," he said. "You bet I get to say that that's what I'm aiming for. And I get to get my sister out of the way while I do it, too. And, no," he said when Rochelle would have protested, "I'm not just talking about sex. I'm talking about talking. I'm talking about us getting through this one, too. Together. It's been too hard to get here, and I'm not letting it go without a fight."

"*Nice,*" Zora said again. "No, literally, bro. That was pretty hot. Very decisive and alpha. But man, I'd forgotten how bossy you can be. I guess that works on women, huh? So weird to think about my brother's sex life. You're right—I don't want to know." She looked at Stacy. "Got a couch?"

Rochelle was the one who wanted to pull at her hair now. "I have to get back to work," she said. "I don't leave my desk. I'm professional. That's my deal. So, Stacy, you go on and stay here, and Travis, I'll see you tonight. Maybe. Because ever since I met you? I'm so messed up."

"Well, baby," he said, "that makes two of us."

◆　◆　◆

For all his brave talk, Travis was . . . well, all right, he was nervous when he pulled up outside Rochelle's house that evening. No use pretending otherwise.

She hadn't stuck around this afternoon. She'd headed right back upstairs, and the look she'd shot him had told him that he wasn't invited to follow her.

I'm professional. That's my deal. She couldn't afford to have personal crises at work. He got it. He'd never been the type to do that, either. It seemed that things had changed, though, because he would have given just about anything to be able to talk it over right then.

Now, it was six thirty, and he was ringing her doorbell, not sure what to expect. At least Dell wasn't outside, for once. He supposed she couldn't pretend to be watering her garden in the near-dark. Besides, there would be nothing to see. He hoped.

He waited a minute, the door opened, and it wasn't Rochelle. It was Stacy, with Zora right behind her, chewing on a carrot and looking as inquisitive and bright-eyed as a chipmunk.

"Hi," Stacy said.

She looked a whole lot better than she had this afternoon. You could even say she was bouncing. She and Zora must be getting along. Which was the least of his worries right now.

"Hi," he said. "Rochelle ready?"

"Nope," Stacy said. "I think she's going to make you wait. Want to come in?"

"Sure." He stepped inside and, at Stacy's invitation, sat on the living-room couch.

"We'd hang out," Stacy said, "but we're in the middle of making dinner."

Zora raised her carrot at him in a sort of rodent salute. "You could come into the kitchen," she said, "but you don't want to. Because we're talking about you."

She walked out, and Stacy looked at her, then back at Travis, and ended up following his sister. Which suited him. He didn't need anyone to watch him pretending to be calm.

He looked around, since this was the first time he'd sat down in here. Rochelle had gone to quite a bit of effort, he suspected. The walls were painted in some kind of . . . blotchy way, a sort of variegated yellow-gold that reminded him of Italy. That style had a name and was supposed to be artistic, he was fairly sure. She had a round oak dining table with mismatched chairs decorated with seat cushions in different striped and flowered patterns, and the table was set with a vase of hydrangeas from the plant he'd given her. That made him feel a little better. If she'd decided to break up with him, she would have tossed his flowers. There were some framed pictures on the wall, family photographs and art prints, mostly Van Gogh. Rural landscapes made up of the same sorts of greens and golds you saw around here, and one of irises that he liked a lot.

It all spelled 'Rochelle': neat, practical, and feminine, but a little bit exotic, too. A little bit unexpected, a little bit exciting. He liked it.

He was looking at his watch for about the fifth time when he heard a door opening somewhere in the back of the house. A few seconds later, Rochelle walked into the room, and he stood up without knowing what he was doing. Her hair was mussed in a way that set his heart pounding, her makeup was soft and sultry, and she was wearing skinny jeans, low-heeled boots, and a cream-colored top with a sort of ruffled neckline along the draped V. Nothing that wasn't classy. And nothing that wasn't sexy. Which was *very* good news.

She stopped a few feet away, picked up a soft brown leather bag and a long sweater from a chair by the door, and said, "So what do you think?"

"I think," he said, "that you're trying to blow my mind. As usual. Either you're trying to make me really, really sorry to lose you, or really, really glad not to. Which is it?"

She tossed her hair back over one shoulder, shrugged into the sweater, and said, "Kinda depends on you, doesn't it?"

"Then," he said, "let's go for a drive."

◆ ◆ ◆

He headed out of town toward Ithaca. Looking for subconscious better memories, maybe, or just a long, lonely stretch of winding rural highway. Easier to talk when you were sitting side by side, he figured. He turned the radio to a country station, because she liked that, but kept the music low. And then he waited.

"So," she said as he turned left at the stoplight and onto the highway. "Divorced."

"Yep."

He could feel her eyes on him, and he said, "What?"

"What do you mean, 'What?' Tell me the story, of course. Tell me why you didn't tell me. Tell me whether you've got . . ." She waved a hand, but her voice didn't sound one bit casual. "Kids. That's the one I really want to know. Tell me."

"No," he said. "No kids. I'd have told you *that*. She was . . . Kim was . . . the last person to have kids." He laughed, but it didn't come out too good. No surprise. "Free spirit. Saving the world. Kids don't tend to figure into a life like that."

"That the kind of woman you want?" she asked. "Is that why you like me? Free spirit?"

"Yes. No." He sighed and piloted the car around a long, smooth curve. Almost nobody else out here. Nothing going on. Just the two of them, driving on into the darkness. "I want to know what the right answer is. Want to give me a hint?"

"The true answer," she said at once. "That's the right one."

"The true answer," he said, "is that I don't want a 'kind of woman.' I want you."

Silence for a long moment, and then she said, her voice a little unsteady, "Do not try to sidetrack me, buster. Because that was killer. Tell me the story."

"All right, but it's not pretty."

"Hey. You're talking to the woman who sent her bridal gown up in smoke in the dead of winter, stomping around the backyard in a fuzzy bathrobe and boots and a temperature of a hundred and one, crying all the makeup off her face. I know ugly. Tell me the story."

He took a moment to put it together, and she sat there and waited for it. What was this, the second (third?) time he'd bared his soul? Why? Maybe because she *had* burned her bridal gown. Maybe because she'd listened every other time he'd talked. Maybe.

"Kim," he finally began. "That was her name. Wait. I already said that. Anyway, we met in college, had moved in together by senior year. She was very bright, very passionate. I was steady, and she was exciting, and that seemed to work pretty well. She liked running off to different places to do . . . good deeds, I guess, and having me to come back to. She didn't make much, because she worked for nonprofits, in between the running off. Passionate, like I said."

"So what happened?"

He shrugged. "So we got married, the way people do when they've been together for four years. And I told myself I didn't want my dad's life anyway."

"Let me guess," she said. "You didn't get married in church."

"Nope. At the beach. Barefoot. In a pagan ceremony. Which was stupid, as far as I was concerned, and more than that as far as my folks were, but you could call it a compromise. Because guess which one of us wanted to get married."

"You."

"And you'd be right. So we got married. And eventually, 'steady' probably became 'boring,' in her case, and 'exciting' maybe became 'flaky' in mine. Also the way people do. Mismatch. Nobody's fault. Except it was. At least that's the way I saw it."

"Why?" she asked.

He glanced across at her, hesitated, then said, "I'd sure like it if you'd slide on over beside me while I told you this. It's not that easy to talk about. Which is why I don't. I told my dad the whole story, and that's about it. My mom probably knows, but if she does, she's never said."

She didn't play coy, and she didn't say anything cute. She just unbuckled her seat belt, slid on over, and buckled herself in again. He felt her there, warm and fragrant, and something settled into place inside him, just like that.

And he felt better. Just like that.

"I was a nice guy then," he finally went on.

"You still are."

He shook his head. "No. Not that nice."

"Travis." She had her hand on his knee again, but for nothing but comfort this time. "Tell me."

He was still driving, and he was remembering, and telling her. It didn't come out easy, but it came.

Kim had been in Chile, because they'd had a big quake there, and she'd been volunteering. Gone for nearly three months while he'd earned money, had tried to be glad that he could support her in her dream, and tried not to resent that she hadn't been there to support him in his. She was doing what mattered to her, they were both independent adults with independent lives, and money wasn't an issue. That was the good thing about working in tech.

He'd gone out to SFO to pick her up that night. Eleven thirty p.m. by the time the plane had come in, and he hadn't cared. He'd gotten there early so he'd be sure to spot her, had stood there holding a bunch of pink roses like the sap he'd been. She'd come running through the security gate to him, and he'd picked her right up off the ground and swung her in a circle and laughed out loud, and so had she. Somebody had even taken a picture, he'd noticed out of the corner of his eye, probably because they were so cute, and so in love.

And then he'd driven her home, parked the car, and walked with her to the apartment in the Mission that was still barely furnished, because she didn't care and he didn't have time. Their arms around each other, her talking a mile a minute, him listening and smiling and waiting for the moment when they'd climbed the three flights of stairs. After he'd opened the door, because she'd lost her keys, of course, and he was picking her up again to kiss her for real.

She'd dropped the flowers, and he still remembered seeing them fall onto the hardwood floor. Bouncing, like it was slow motion, the moment frozen in his memory, frozen in time. The last beautiful thing. Before he'd scooped her into his arms, had stepped on a rose and crushed it, and hadn't cared a bit. He'd carried her into the bedroom and laid her down on the bed, and she'd pulled at his shirt and he'd pulled at hers, and they'd made laughing, reckless, desperate, half-dressed love, gasping and stroking and kissing.

Afterwards, he'd rolled to his back, held her over him, kissed her again, and said, "I love you, I ever tell you that? And I missed you. Don't be gone so long next time, OK?"

She'd wriggled down, put her head on his chest, stroked his shoulder, and said, "Yeah. Well. I might not be, because I have something to tell you." She'd laughed again, an uncertain sound this time. "I guess there's only one way to say this. I'm pregnant."

The shock had frozen him for a second, and he literally hadn't been able to speak. And then he'd said, "Whoa," in a voice that hadn't even sounded like his. "Whoa," he'd said again, and laughed. "Whoa, baby." He'd held her closer, hugged her to him, and laughed again. "Wow."

"Wayne. Wait. There's more."

It had been something in the way she'd said it. His arms had still been around her, but his whole body had gone still. "What . . ." He'd swallowed. "What's the more?"

"It isn't yours."

◆　　◆　　◆

"Wow," Rochelle said quietly. "That sucks."

"It wasn't my favorite moment of all time, no."

"So let me guess. Some other guy down there saving the world?"

"Yep. He didn't matter, of course. He wasn't important. It was just one of those things. 'It's like a war zone, Wayne,'" he quoted, and no matter how long it had been, the anger was still right there. "Like she couldn't help herself, but it didn't matter, because it was just 'release of tension,' and fidelity was an archaic construct anyway. I told her that if she'd thought it was an archaic construct, maybe she could've clued me in before she'd married me, and she just sighed like I was hopeless. Like it was my problem."

He was going a little fast, so he eased up on the gas, relaxed his hands on the wheel. "Sorry. It was a long time ago. Shouldn't matter now."

"Of course it should," she said. "So what happened?"

"Well, see, that was the other part that made it OK. To her. Because she decided to have an abortion, in the end, and then we'd be back to normal. But she hadn't wanted to sneak around on me, because she believed in honesty."

"Just not fidelity."

"Right. It was just a big ol' mess all around. I knew I didn't have a right to tell her what to do. It wasn't my body, and it wasn't even my baby, but the whole thing . . ." He swallowed. "It made me sick. That she could do it in the first place like it didn't matter—"

"Like *you* didn't matter," Rochelle said. "Yeah. Been there."

He glanced at her. Her hand was still strong on his leg, and it still felt good. "Yep. And then that she could get rid of the pregnancy like *that* didn't matter, either. She told me it was good that it had happened, in fact, because it had forced her to really look at whether she wanted kids. And to realize that she didn't. 'There are so many more important things happening in the world than one person's children.' That's what she said. That if you had them, you cared about them more than the rest of the world, and it wasn't right. Attachment as the root of evil, and all that."

"Seems to me," Rochelle said slowly, "that that's about the most important thing of all. But that might just be me. I'd say that caring about people, *individual* people, is pretty much the biggest part of being a human being. Maybe the best part."

"Well, that's how I saw it, too. Still do, I suppose. Which made it the kind of divorce you'd call 'irreconcilable differences.' And maybe you can see why I didn't feel like telling you all about it. It wasn't the kind of thing that fills a man with pride. Put me in a pretty dark place for quite a while, if you want to know the truth. And maybe I came out of it not quite such a nice guy."

She was quiet for a long minute, and then she said, "Guess I'm not the only one who's complicated."

"Nope. But it's like I told you. I don't want easy. Except, you know—I lied."

She took her hand off his knee in shock, and he reached his own hand out and set it back there again. "I mean," he said, "that we're complicated, sure, but it's easy, too. Having you here . . . it fits. It's easy. Like when you work and work at a jigsaw puzzle, trying to fit pieces in. Then you find the right piece, and it just slips on in. So easy. And that's not about sex," he added. "Although I wouldn't mind that, either."

She laughed, sounding a little breathless, and he said, "So what do you think? Ready to turn around and go home? Or out to dinner? Because I'm hungry and you're beautiful, and I'd sure love to take you out and show you off, if that isn't an archaic construct itself. I'm probably betraying my unevolved nature again, talking like you're mine. Even though I like to think of you that way. Since I'm confessing and all."

"I don't know," she said. "I'm still trying to wrap my head around the image of you doing a jigsaw puzzle."

He smiled, feeling so much lighter. "I had to go back a few decades for that one. So what do you say?"

She sighed. "You're going to make me give up all my mad, aren't you? And it was such a good one, too. If we don't fight, does that mean we don't get make-up sex?"

This, he was completely sure about. No question at all. "Oh, yeah," he told her. "We get make-up sex. In fact, didn't you have some things in mind you wanted to do? Assuming you don't think fidelity's an archaic construct, because that one's a deal-breaker."

"Mm." She'd snuggled a little closer, had switched hands so she had one free to stroke the back of his neck. The other hand was moving up his thigh, and he had a feeling that he was going to be one hell of a happy man tonight.

"If it's an archaic construct," she said, her mouth at his ear and both hands going places they shouldn't, not while a man was trying to keep a truck on the road, "it's one of my favorites."

BY ACCIDENT

The dust bloomed out behind the pickup as the man took a curve in the gravel road at practiced speed. Another turn, and he was bumping up a rutted side road that was going to be nasty in the rain. But the man at the other end of the road wasn't going to have to worry about that.

He pulled over halfway up in the shadow of a cut bank and parked. Blocking half the road, but nobody was going to know. He ran down the road a couple hundred yards to check. His truck wasn't visible from below. Good.

The air was autumn-cool today at last, a low massing of gray clouds promising rain within a few hours, making the man grateful for his jacket, although he was pumped enough on adrenaline right now that he probably wouldn't have felt the cold anyway. And rain was good. Rain was perfect. Rain would wash away any tracks he or his truck had made in the gravel, if anybody cared to check for them.

Slow, he reminded himself, heading up the hill again. *Methodical.* Which was easy, because he'd thought this out. But now, it was time to act.

The harder you work, the luckier you get. He hadn't often been accused of working hard in the past, but then, he hadn't had nearly as much incentive. There was another one like that, too. What was it? *Fortune favors the bold.* Yeah, that was it. He wasn't about to wait around and have his fate taken out of his hands.

He passed his truck and pressed on. Two more curves, and the little blue-and-white single-wide came into view, a dusty truck parked outside next to a metal shop. And in front of the open shop door, on the concrete slab? An old black Camaro, at an angle now, its front jacked up, its tail facing the road. The shriek of heavy metal shattering the country quiet. And a pair of blue-jeaned legs ending in work boots extending out from under the car.

Best of all? Those legs were lying on top of a rolling creeper. Which would raise the man's head a good six inches off the ground.

Miles Kimberling. Spending a Saturday afternoon working on his car. Alone.

It was almost too much to hope for. The man approached cautiously all the same, his steps even quieter now. No dog barking, but then, if Miles had had a dog, the plan would have been different.

His thought had been to get Miles to collect his own semiautomatic, then get him up in his own truck with a story about needing a driver. Miles would have been too scared to say no, he knew. Pussy. As if he'd ever take somebody like that into any sort of sticky situation. He'd have had Miles set the gun down on the seat, and then he'd have taken him out to the lonely stretches beside the Clearwater River, where Miles would have had an accident. An accident called, "Shooting himself in the head and rolling into the river." Because he'd been worried about the girl. Best case? Because he'd been ridden by guilt over what he'd done to her. He was the type who'd be guilt-ridden, for sure. Anybody would say so. The weak, pathetic type with a guilty conscience that would weigh him down and never let him get away with a thing.

Miles had said he hadn't slept with Heather. How likely was that? Nobody turned it down when it was free. Or almost free. Anybody could have had her for a pill, and for a few of them? She'd been willing to do anything. He'd put that to the test himself often enough.

And with the kind of extra luck that came to guys who took it, Miles would even turn out to be the father. Case closed.

Nothing like water to conceal fingerprints that would tell another story. Could be the body would never be found. It was a tricky river.

But he wasn't going to have to do all that, not if he was lucky. And he was always lucky these days. He'd have to cancel his ride out, which was already in place, but that was better, too. Another person who wouldn't be getting cold feet and a conscience.

Was it risky? Sure it was. But doing nothing was riskier. Act now, and act fast. Because Miles was losing his nerve. One more visit from the cops, and who knew what he'd be saying? He suspected that Miles wasn't high on the cops' list right now, which would make this two birds with one stone. A suspect revealed, and then a solution. And a sure-enough warning to all the others. They'd know. They'd all know.

Fortune favors the bold.

He was inching along now, not that Miles could have heard him, not with Metallica blaring a few feet from his head. "Fade to Black." Appropriate.

The man stopped at the back of the car and paused for a couple seconds, assessing. No chocks under the back wheels. How easy was this?

He lifted both hands into the air, heaved in a huge breath, and coiled the dark energy within himself like a spring. And then he released it. He shoved with both gloved hands at the trunk of the Camaro, putting all his body weight behind it. The car rocked forward, then slipped off the jack and crashed down hard. The front bounced once, twice, then came to rest on the concrete.

The man pulled his work gloves off and stuffed them into his jacket pockets. He didn't walk around the car. He didn't have to. The legs had jerked once, but now, they weren't moving. That told the story. And, even as he watched, a thin crimson trail appeared from beneath the car and snaked its way onward, bright across the white concrete.

"Should have chocked the tires, man," he said aloud. "Safety doesn't happen by accident."

THUNDERSTORM

The rain started on Saturday night, and it started with a bang. Travis was at the pizza place with Rochelle again, because he'd wanted to give her a romantic evening, and he wasn't a great cook. His sister was still staying with Stacy, Rochelle was still staying with him, and that arrangement suited him fine. Tonight, they were here drinking wine, talking a little and being quiet a little, and he was enjoying all of it.

It was what he'd said. Easy.

When the first drops of rain pattered against the window beside them, a sudden gust of wind shaking the frame, she looked out at it and said, "Supposed to get a thunderstorm."

"I heard," he said.

Her slowest, sultriest smile bloomed, then, and he watched the candlelight flicker over her face, on her throat, over the soft skin to that dangerous valley his undisciplined eyes kept trying to fall into. She'd chosen to wear that red wrap sweater tonight, the one he hadn't seen since their first time together, and he was deeply and profoundly grateful for her decision. As he lost the battle not to stare, she smiled some more, took a leisurely sip of wine, and swallowed it down.

"Know what's fun to do in a thunderstorm?" she asked him, setting her glass down but not releasing it, her fingers still caressing its stem.

"No, what?" he asked, although the thud of his heart was giving him a clue. His eyes were torn, now, between her neckline, that smile, and that hand.

"Somebody gave me the ride of my life in one of those storms a while back, as I recall," she mused, looking past him at the reflections in the watery window glass, her face soft with the memory. "Lit me right up while the thunder rolled over me, and, man, did that ever feel good. I'd kinda like to do it to him, you know? If he had any desire to lean back in the seat of a pickup, give up some of that power of his, and let a woman have her way with him. Because when the windows are steamed all the way up and the radio's playing way down low, when the lightning strikes and you get that flash, when you get to look down at her head in your lap and your hands all tangled up in her hair, and . . ." She took a final swallow of rich red wine, draining her glass, and shrugged. "Well. You know. I'm thinking that if you wanted to put me in that truck of yours and drive me up above the golf course, we could find a place to park and see if it's something you could handle. Or . . ." Another hypnotically slow stroke of a crimson-tipped finger around the rim of her glass. "Not. Whichever you like. *Whatever* you like. You know. Whatever you like."

He was raising his hand for the check before she'd finished talking, and he didn't think he'd ever signed his name that fast.

And, no, it hadn't been something he could handle. The truck had rocked and swayed in the wind and the rain, and so had he. She'd made him slide over on the bench seat "to give me room," and then she'd climbed over him, changed her mind halfway across, taken his head in both hands, and taken his mouth like it was hers. Like there was nothing on earth she'd rather do, like she was going to suck his soul right out of his body. All the promise of the night in that one kiss, and he was already gone.

He'd managed to get his hands on some of his favorite parts of her, because that wrap sweater had surely been made for his hand to slide inside, and straddling him had made her skirt ride right up her thighs, and that was all more than good. But that was about as far as he'd gotten, because once she'd set in to rock his world for real, his mind had gone on vacation, and the rest of him had been fully occupied.

There were women who didn't enjoy oral sex, he knew. Rochelle wasn't one of them. Tonight, she'd given it her all, and Rochelle's all was something else again. She wasn't shy, she wasn't squeamish, and she'd been right. When the flash of lightning lit up the truck, showed him his hands twisted in her hair and her gorgeous mouth around him . . . he'd been gasping, and she'd had to slow down, or it would have been over right then.

But she *had* slowed down. She'd made it last until, finally, his head had been back, his eyes had been squeezed shut, his ears had been filled with the pounding rain and the keening wind, the slow soft music and his own harsh breath, and he'd had both arms stretched out, gripping the seat back for all he was worth, just trying to hang on. All he'd been able to do was feel, and climb, and try to breathe.

And by the time she was taking him all the way there? The truck could have blown down the hill, the flood could have carried them away, and he wouldn't have been able to do a thing to stop it. There'd been no place but this cab, nothing in the world but her mouth, and no force on earth that could have held him back.

Afterwards, she'd scooted over behind the wheel and driven them back to his place through the rain, because he might still have been a little shaky. By the time they'd gotten home, though, he'd recovered. And then he'd set out to show her how grateful he was.

Some people said the first time was the best, and no question, the first time had been spectacular. He wasn't sure which time this had been, because he'd lost count, but it had been right up there. He wasn't sure they'd gotten to "best" yet, either, but one thing you could say about

Rochelle—she was a very, very hard worker. He'd be willing to bet they still had some milestones to hit.

On Sunday morning, he drove her home with a stop at the grocery store, and they cooked breakfast together and ate it with Stacy and Zora. Family time, and some more coming up, because he was going to meet her parents today. And all of that worked for him, too. He was pretty far gone.

Stacy seemed to have perked up since their tutoring session. She'd come by his office again on Thursday afternoon, and they'd worked a little more. She was plenty bright, just panicked right now for some reason, that's what he'd say. It wasn't that uncommon, and he didn't quite see what Rochelle was so worried about. Although he'd never have said that.

Well, maybe being around Zora had helped. His sister had enough breezy attitude to rub off on anybody.

He asked, once they were sitting around the table and he had his coffee in front of him, "So how did the midterm go, Stacy? That was Friday, right? You nail that ANOVA?"

"I think so," she said. "I think I did all right. Thanks a lot for your help."

"Anything else you need," he said, "just ask. I'm not so good with the life sciences, maybe, but that math and physics stuff? I'm your man."

"He is," Zora said. "If it's boring, he's got it."

He lifted his coffee cup in ironic salute. "My epitaph."

"So," Zora said as she attacked her French toast and grilled bananas with an enthusiastic sigh, because Zora had the metabolism of a hummingbird. "Much as I appreciate the awesome accommodation, you do realize, Travis, that you haven't even asked me why I'm here. Pretty sad performance for your girlfriend, don't you think?"

"Ah . . ." he said. "In what sense would that be?"

She sighed. "Thought I told you. I do not want to know. But as a brother, maybe? I mean—" She gestured to Stacy. "Here's Rochelle, *living* with her beloved little sister. And you can barely be troubled to say hello to yours."

"I'll take that," Stacy muttered.

Zora said, "Quiet. You're messing with my point," and Stacy smiled.

"Right." Travis took another sip of coffee and eyed Zora. "So, in my persona as a concerned, loving brother, what are you doing here? Oh, wait, I remember. It's because of the hills. Which I know you're going to tell me about, since you basically came out of the womb talking and haven't shut up since."

"Nice," Zora said, not the least bit abashed. "Yep. Mom told me where you were, what you were doing, and I looked it up, and there are some *amazing* shadows here. Some amazing colors. So I came," she said simply.

"She takes pictures," Travis told Rochelle.

"I am a photographer," Zora said loftily. "Well, normally I'm a temp, but if we're counting hours spent, I'm a photographer."

"Hey," Stacy said, "at least you don't work the drive-through at Macho Taco. Count your blessings."

"And I have a brother who could totally be supporting the arts right now," Zora said. "Want to buy my plane ticket home, Travis?"

"Nope," he said, cutting himself another bite of French toast. "You want the nine-to-five, though, I might have a spot for you coming up."

"Yeah?" She eyed him dubiously. "Doing what? I cannot wait. Maid?"

"No," he said calmly. "Graphic artist. Got a new project starting up this winter, and we're going to be hiring pretty soon. You want to brush up on those computer graphics skills, and we'll get a little nepotism going."

"With two weeks of vacation a year," she said.

"That's the idea."

She sighed. "No, thanks." She reached for another slice of bacon. "See," she told Stacy, "it *looks* like a good deal, and it sucks your soul."

Travis smiled. "Yeah, regular jobs are like that, huh, Rochelle?"

"You do tend to have to go to them every day, yes." She poured herself another cup of coffee. "So how's the new project going?"

She was asking for once, and he knew that wasn't easy for her. Thinking about his life after December, because just maybe, she was starting to believe that she'd be part of it.

He smiled at her. "You mean those weekends with my wife? If my 'wife' has a gut, a beard, and an alarming amount of body hair, that is. It's going good. This baby is going to *fly*." He laughed, suddenly filled with surging optimism. "Wait and see."

"Yeah?" she asked. "That's great. Really." And then she dropped her eyes and stared down at her coffee cup.

Zora was looking back and forth between them. "What?"

"Rochelle thinks I'm going to leave her," he said, and Rochelle's hand jerked, the coffee splashing out of her cup and spilling across the table. She uttered an exclamation, set her cup down, and jumped up for a sponge.

"Rochelle," he said. "Wait."

She sat down again. "Never mind. Eyes wide open here, like you said. We're all good."

He exhaled. "San Francisco isn't the moon."

"Right," she said. "I know. That faith thing. I'm working on it."

"Oh," Zora said. "Got it. And let's see. We're going to meet her parents today?"

"Yep," Travis said. He took Rochelle's hand. "You and me both. And I'm pretty excited about it, too."

FOOTBALL AND FISHING

Which was why, that afternoon, he was on the highway with Rochelle and headed south. In her car this time, with her driving. She'd gotten in on the driver's side with a little bit of bravado, and he'd just looked at her, smiled, climbed into the passenger seat, said, "Hey. Your car. And I am secure in my masculinity," and had even made her laugh.

His short-term status, though, hung over them like the clouds that were still massed low in the sky. He was going out to meet her folks, and he was leaving. Both things were true. He wasn't going to make her promises he couldn't keep, not after a couple of months. Being with her felt so right, but was it? He didn't know, and neither did she, and they'd both been burned too badly before. And meanwhile, his time here was running out like calendar leaves flying away in a movie montage. What had started out as four months was now less than two, and every day, he got a little better understanding of how deeply Rochelle was rooted to this place.

Programming problems had solutions. Relationship problems sometimes didn't. That was why he'd always preferred programming.

She slowed, after twenty minutes or so, for the barely-there town of Kernville. The rain had stopped while they'd been driving, but the gray skies didn't help the looks of anything around them. Which were some grain elevators, a gas station, a barbershop, and a beauty salon, followed by a post office, a café, a thrift store, and an ancient grocery store whose faded signs and boarded-up windows spoke of a long-ago closure and nobody to take over the retail space. The ground rose to the right side of the highway, with a few nice-looking frame houses sitting perched on the hill, and fell into a hollow to the left before rising again to a much lower elevation.

A right side of the highway, and a left side, and a great big difference between them. And Rochelle turned left.

The narrow blacktop dipped down past one of the sorriest-looking trailer parks Travis had ever seen, then climbed the hill. A town of a few blocks, some of them better than others, none of them anything to write home about.

He knew all about this kind of town. He'd grown up near a few.

Rochelle stopped in front of a modest frame house, painted blue, with a white picket fence surrounding a small, neatly trimmed lawn edged by shrubs.

"Ha," Travis said, unfolding himself from the compact car. It had stopped raining, at least temporarily. "Score one for me."

"What?" Rochelle asked, coming around the car.

He pointed. "Hydrangeas." Looking a little desolate now that their flowering was over, with the water dripping mournfully off their leaves.

"You think I'm easy?" she said with a toss of her head.

"Nope," he said, taking her hand, "I know you're not."

She squeezed his hand and said, "Ready?"

"Who's more nervous?" he asked, but absently, because his attention had been caught by something else. By the sodden yellow ribbons still managing to flutter in the chilly wind, one attached to each handrail of the porch steps. And by the red-bordered banner hanging on a dowel from the front window: one blue star below, and one gold star above.

Two sons. One coming home, if the ribbons could will him there. And one who never would.

Rochelle saw the direction of his gaze and squeezed his hand again. "It's good to be proud," she said quietly.

"Yeah," he said, and thought about six kids minus one, and how it didn't matter how many you had left, losing one would hurt just as much. Thought about Cal Jackson, the new father, finding the body of that young girl in his ditch.

I kept thinking . . . her folks.

That was why, when the door opened and Rochelle's dad—because that had to be Rochelle's dad, Larry—came out onto the porch, Travis's expression was probably a little serious.

Which matched Larry's own expression perfectly. Only a couple inches shorter than Travis, broad shouldered, lean as whipcord, and ramrod straight, his graying brown hair cut uncompromisingly short and a lifetime of outdoor work in the lines around his eyes.

He came down the steps to join them, and Travis caught the force of him in a heartbeat. His own dad had been tough, and tough-minded, too. Rochelle's dad was more so.

The other man put out a broad hand. "Larry Marks," he said, still without a smile. "You're Travis, I presume."

"Yes, sir." As always, under pressure, Travis slowed down instead of speeding up. He put out his own hand and shook the older man's. Nothing weak, but not a pissing contest, either. "Travis Cochran."

Rochelle's dad stood still a minute, the deep blue eyes evaluating him, and Travis looked straight back and got even stiller, until he heard Rochelle say from beside him, her tone dry as dust, "You won't get him that way, Dad. I think he might be as tough as you."

A reluctant grin split the weathered cheeks, and Larry dropped Travis's hand and asked him, "That so?"

"No, sir," Travis said. "But I'm working on it. Rochelle's a pretty good test."

That got more of a grin, and Larry said, "Well, a woman can do that to you." He looked Travis over. "Huh. Rochelle says you're not such a city boy. That right?"

"Not originally, anyway," Travis said. "Softened up some, probably, these days."

"You fish? Do any hunting?"

"Dad," Rochelle said, "he's not even in the *house*. And he's a computer guy from San Francisco."

"What did I do?" Larry asked in genuine surprise. "Asked the man a simple question. And, what? Computer guys can't fish?"

Travis was grinning now himself, all his nerves banished. This, he got. This was just a dad of daughters being a dad. Sizing him up. "Fish, yes, when I get a chance. You see some city guys up here fishing from time to time, though, I'm guessing, so I'm not sure that says much."

"You're right about that," Larry said. "Every gadget in the book, the price tags still practically hanging off their fancy new waders, and not catching a dang thing. Can't buy smarts or skills, can you?" The sharp eyes were still assessing. "But you don't hunt."

"Not anymore, no. I went out with my dad some when I was younger, but seems I don't much care for it."

"Don't like to kill things," Larry guessed.

Travis looked him in the eye. "Nope. I don't. Not unless they're trying to kill me."

Larry laughed at that, gave Travis a quick pat on the back, and told Rochelle. "All right. He'll do. Come on inside and meet Rochelle's mom."

"Sorry," Rochelle muttered as they went up the stairs behind her dad.

"Nah," Travis said. "At least he wasn't sitting up on the porch cleaning his gun."

He heard the bark of laughter from ahead of them, and Larry turned around at the top of the stairs to say, "I won't say I never thought about it. You could say I'm sorry I didn't think about it more."

"And that," Rochelle said in resignation, "would be a not-too-subtle reference to Lake. Travis doesn't believe in cheating, Dad. Good news."

"Nobody believes in it when somebody's doing it to them," Larry said. "Doesn't say much."

"Another good point," Travis said. "I suppose we'll just have to wait and see how it works out."

"We'll do that," Larry said. The level blue eyes told Travis, *Don't screw up, boy.* And he wouldn't have liked to be Lake.

Into the house, then, after a whole lot of wiping of feet. The living room was small, but that was no surprise. The whole house was small and neat as a pin, the furniture shabby. A dark brown couch bought to hide the wear, a recliner that had "man of the house" written all over it, a dining area with its table set with a flowered cloth. And a woman coming forward to meet them, body thickened with age and six children, face worn by time and pain, but a smile on her face and a hug for Rochelle. Her mom, Valerie.

"Both of you here, *and* Stacy," she said. "During midterms, that's what she said." She chuckled. "She'll be distracted about that, but I'm just happy to see her. She's always studying," she told Travis. "Ever since she was a little girl."

He shot a glance at Rochelle, saw her looking back at him, and thought, *not anymore.*

He said, "Nice to meet you, ma'am. I hope it's all right with you that my sister's coming out, too, at least once she and Stacy finish driving all over the countryside taking pictures. I guess Rochelle told you that Zora's a photographer. At least, she'd like to be a photographer."

"Oh, sure," Valerie said. "Can't wait to meet her. And we get lots of those. It's the light or something. The shape of the hills, I guess. The clouds. We get them out here in all seasons. Right now, though, when most of the fields are plowed and there's not much to see but brown dirt? Doesn't look like much to me, tell you the truth, especially in the rain. I wouldn't hang that on my wall, but then, nobody asked me to. Come on in the kitchen and help me out, Rochelle."

Which left Travis there with her dad, but there was a Seahawks game on the TV, and Larry was sitting in the recliner now and picking up the remote, so Travis wasn't too worried.

Football and fishing. He could do football and fishing.

FISHTAIL

Stacy was up. Pumped. So she hadn't heard from Shane for two days. So what? She'd had a good time with Zora the night before, and she was all set for the week. He'd helped with that, at least, before he'd disappeared on her again.

Too bad. Let him miss *her* for a change, she thought recklessly, taking a curve fast, feeling the truck fishtail a bit amid the gravel spray. She wasn't going to call him. She was going to be Rochelle from now on. She was going to be a badass. The music was blasting from the open windows, and she was flying.

"Whoa," Zora shouted over the wail of guitars. She was laughing, but sounding a little alarmed, too. "Maybe we shouldn't put Travis's truck in the ditch. He's attached to it. Oh, look," she added, craning her neck to see up a hill. "Go up there. Wow. Cloud *city*. Let's drive up where I can see out. Can you?"

They'd been out here for more than an hour now, taking the back roads, Stacy finding the high points for Zora, for her pictures. Stacy was driving—and pulling over every time Zora yelled, "Stop!" Which was a lot. The storm had broken, at least for the time being, but the clouds were moving fast. Some blue sky, shafts of sunlight beaming down over the hills, lighting up the earth and the sky behind it. All brown, gold, and blue, and that rich, clear quality of light you got after a storm. At least Stacy guessed that was the idea.

She braked hard at a mailbox stuck askew onto a post. *Kimberling.* Miles's place. His dad's was farther along. This road was steep, and Zora would have a good view from up there. She swung off the road, a little too fast again. Another fishtail, then she straightened the truck out and began to climb.

"Yeah," Zora said as the panorama spread out beneath them. "This is *it.* Worth it. Keep going up. Top of the hill."

The road was muddy up here, the gravel spread too thin. The big wheels spun out hard, and Stacy gave it more gas. The tires bit, and then the truck surged forward. Stacy spun the wheel to get them around the curve and pressed hard on the gas. The tires were sliding in the mud, slipping, and then the skid took them over. The rear end was swinging out behind, and they were revolving, the nose pointed downhill, and past it. Another lurch, a hard bang, the nose coming up, and they were headed backward, straight into the ditch, hitting the bank hard. Her torso jolted against her seat belt, then back again, and her neck whipped backward. And then there was just the music. Loud. Wailing like the scream trying to get out from inside her.

Her shaking hand felt for the key and turned it off. The music died, the cooling engine ticked over, and, finally, she dared to look.

Please, she thought. *Please.* And there was Zora, stabbing at her own seat belt, eyes wide with shock, and speaking at last.

"Whoa." Zora's voice was shaking. "Whoa." She grabbed at the seat for her camera, dove down to the floor, her hand groping, searching, then picked it up and examined it. She took a deep breath. "It's all right. You OK?"

"Yeah." The word came out reedy, too thin, and Stacy tried again. "Fine." The high was gone, and she was sick. Cold. She opened the door and climbed out, hanging on to the door to keep from sliding down the steep bank, then edged her way down to check out the back.

Stuck, that was all. Just a couple dents in the bumper, she thought desperately, and it was an old truck with its share of scrapes. An easy tow, too.

But she was going to have to tell Travis, who'd been so nice to her. The sickness rose again at the thought, and she swallowed it back.

Sliding off a muddy road happened, though, right? He wouldn't be too mad. Rochelle wouldn't . . . Her mind skittered away from the thought of Rochelle. And her parents.

Zora was out of the truck, too, looking at the rear end from the other side. "Not too bad," she said, echoing Stacy's thoughts. "We just need a tow, I'd say." She had her phone out. "I'll call Travis and tell him. I'll bet he and your dad could get us out."

"No!" It came out too loud, and Stacy moderated her tone. "No. Let's walk up the road. We should be able to get a tow here." Maybe there wouldn't be much damage, and nobody would have to see the truck actually in the ditch. Nobody but Zora. Or Rochelle and Travis, if Stacy had to. Just not her dad.

Zora shrugged and nodded. "You say so." She was from the country, too, Stacy remembered. She knew that where there was a farmer, there'd be a tow strap. It was going to be all right. It *had* to be all right.

"I have to leave by three thirty, that's all," Zora said. "To catch my flight home, so faster's better, as far as I'm concerned."

Stacy felt sick again, with guilt this time at messing up Zora's day. She'd wanted to be a badass, and all she'd done was screw up. Again. She wanted to run away, but she couldn't. Not from this. She had to get the truck out of the ditch, and then she had to drive back home and tell Travis. And then she'd have to pay for the damage. The hysteria wanted to rise again at the thought, but there was no escaping it. She'd have to pay.

She started walking up the road, and Zora followed without speaking. Stacy's chest ached a little from where the seat belt had caught her, and her head hurt, too. She massaged her shoulder and asked Zora, "You sore?"

Zora rolled her own neck. "A little. I'll live." She wasn't berating Stacy, even though she must have known it had all been Stacy's fault. Stacy was glad, because otherwise, she would have cried.

They kept walking, and then it got worse, because the rain started again. A few big drops, and then the thunder rolled, the lightning lit up the landscape below, making a barn flash vivid red, the contours of the hills jump out in stark relief. Just that fast, it started to pour, the thunder grumbling overhead.

They were running now. "Should have stayed in the truck," Zora gasped, but she was laughing.

Nothing stuck to her, Stacy thought miserably, whereas *everything* stuck to Stacy.

"I wish I'd had a shot of that just now," Zora added. "That lightning flash. That was *something*." Like to her, this was all a big adventure. But then, *she* wasn't the one who'd put the truck in the ditch.

Around a broad curve, and there, just off the road in front of them, was the blue-and-white trailer, the black car next to it in the driveway. There was a light shining through the mobile home's window. Somebody was home, then.

Just let there be no bad damage to the truck, Stacy prayed. *Just let the truck be OK.*

They were running now, slipping a little in the gravel, trying to get out of the downpour, their coats held over their heads. Up the gravel driveway and onto the concrete slab.

There were legs sticking out from under the black car, she realized with a jolt. Legs in blue jeans, ending in work boots. A normal sight. But the jeans were soaked, the water running in rivulets down the creases. The boots, too, were dark with water. But nobody would be doing that. Nobody would be out here in this.

And the legs were still.

Stacy's steps slowed, but she walked closer. The man was on a creeper, but surely there wasn't enough space for one under there, not without a jack. She got closer still, forcing her feet to move until she was standing over him, part of her mind trying to spiral away, trying to go higher, into the clouds, away from here. She pulled it ruthlessly back down.

Focus. Deal.

She bent down, put a hand on an ice-cold, soaking-wet calf, and said, "Hey."

The calf didn't move, and there was no sound but the rain hitting the metal roof of the trailer. She'd dropped her jacket from over her head at some point, and the water was streaming through her hair, over her face, but she didn't notice. Because the leg she was touching was stiff. She swallowed, then touched it again to make sure. She tried to shake it. And she couldn't move it.

Rigor mortis.

It seemed to take forever for her head to swing around to face Zora, standing a little bit behind her, her eyes and mouth dark holes in her face.

Stacy stood up and pulled her phone out of her pack. Her organic chemistry book was in there getting soaked, she registered vaguely. She pushed buttons, and waited.

"Hi," she said when the official voice answered. "I'm out at, uh, Kimberling's place. Uh, Miles. And I think he's . . . someone's . . ." Her voice shook, but she forced herself to be precise. "Someone is, anyway. Someone's dead."

THE FIXERS

Rochelle was in the kitchen, just starting to wonder what was keeping Stacy and Zora, when she got the call. Travis had said his sister was a fanatic about her photography, but Stacy knew her parents always started meals on time. When you were one of six kids and you were poor, you showed up when dinner started, or you didn't eat.

Travis brought her purse to her in the kitchen on the heels of the thought, holding the bag out while her phone buzzed inside like an angry wasp.

She pulled the phone out and pushed the button. "Stacy. Finally. Where are you?"

And then she put out a hand for Travis, and he stopped on his way to the door. Stopped and stood.

"What?" she said into the phone. "Say it again."

She could barely understand the voice at the other end. It sounded as if Stacy's teeth were chattering.

"He's dead," she heard. "And the truck . . . the truck's crashed."

"Oh, my God." Rochelle had grabbed Travis's arm, and her mother had stopped in the act of stirring the stew, the wooden spoon dripping rich brown gravy back into the cast-iron pot. *Plop. Plop. Plop.* Her eyes were on Rochelle.

"Stacy," Rochelle said, keeping her voice calm even as she wanted to scream. "Did you hit somebody? Did you . . ." *Kill somebody,* she didn't say, because she couldn't stand to think it.

"No." It was a sob. Rochelle sagged a little, and Travis put a hand out to steady her. "But the truck went into the ditch, and . . . and . . . he's dead. The sheriff's here, and I need you to come get me. Please, Ro. Come get me."

"Where are you?" Rochelle demanded.

"Miles . . . Miles Kimberling's. Up there. On his road."

"And somebody's dead?" Rochelle pressed. Her mother was white, now, and Travis had gone rigid, was mouthing, "Zora."

"Stacy," Rochelle said. "Is Zora all right?"

"What? Yes," Stacy said, and Rochelle breathed out, said, "Yes," to Travis, and saw him close his eyes for a moment.

"But I need you to come," Stacy said again. "Because Miles . . . he's dead."

Rochelle's father was in the kitchen now, too, his face hard and alert, the little room steamy and crowded with people and tension.

"We're on our way," Rochelle told her sister, and hung up. She'd go get Stacy. They'd sort out the rest after that.

In the end, after a brief discussion, they took two rigs. Travis and her dad in her dad's truck, and Rochelle and her mom in Rochelle's car.

Rochelle's mother said, when they were in the car, "Miles Kimberling. Oh, poor Pam."

Her voice was bleak, and Rochelle knew how doubly hard that blow was falling. A son lost, and Stacy . . .

Please, God, she prayed, *let Stacy not have done something really wrong. Let her not have hit him. Let her not have to live with that.*

The drive seemed to last forever, following her dad's rig, the windshield wipers slapping time. In fact, it was only fifteen minutes before they came around the curve and saw them. The sheriff's vehicle blocking the road, the white SUV with its light bars rotating, flashing red and blue through the rain. And Travis's pickup, tail down in the ditch.

Jim Lawson got out of the SUV as they approached, rain streaming off his Smokey Bear hat, a slicker doing an inadequate job of protecting his broad-shouldered frame. He put a hand up, but it wasn't necessary. Neither Rochelle nor her father needed telling. They stopped, and Rochelle was out of the car and racing to the SUV, because she could see the figures inside it.

She made it at the same time as her dad. Her mom puffed up a second later, and Stacy was tumbling out of the SUV and throwing herself into her mother's arms.

There were no bodies. There was no ambulance. Because Stacy hadn't killed anybody.

$$\blacklozenge \quad \blacklozenge \quad \blacklozenge$$

After that, it was just a matter of organization. Rochelle and her mom getting Stacy and Zora into Rochelle's car, while her dad maneuvered his pickup nose-to-nose with Travis's rig. By the time Rochelle had backed, turned, and headed down the road again, she could see Travis in the rearview mirror, going headfirst on his back under his truck with the tow strap.

Zora in the front with Rochelle, Stacy in the back with her mother. Valerie holding her daughter, strong and silent. Taking care of her youngest child as she'd taken care of them all, and thinking about that other mother, Rochelle knew. That mother who was finding out that she'd just become a member of the least popular club on earth.

Then they were back at home, and Rochelle was shepherding Zora and Stacy into the house and helping her mother find dry clothes, because the girls were soaked. The men arrived a few minutes later, her father grim-faced, Travis quiet and solid, his clothes caked with mud.

"Your truck," Rochelle said to Travis once he'd accepted the loan of dry clothes from her dad and gotten changed. She gestured him to a seat in the living room. He might as well get comfortable while they waited for their much-delayed lunch. Once again, their day out hadn't gone anywhere close to plan.

"A couple dents," he said. "It's fine."

"Who was driving?" she asked. The question had nagged at her even as she'd listened to Zora's quiet, shocked explanation of what they'd found at Miles's house.

He shrugged. "Don't know. Doesn't matter."

"I saw the marks," she said. The clear indications of a skid, dug into the gravel and the mud. "They took that corner way too fast."

Zora had come into the living room to sit with them, the light within her subdued for once, and Rochelle looked at her. "Who was driving?" she demanded.

Zora hesitated, and that told the story. "I thought so," Rochelle said. "Stacy." She squared her shoulders and told Travis, "I'll pay to get it fixed. She can pay me back."

"No," he said, "you won't. It's a couple dents. No need to bang out a couple dents on a work truck."

"Travis—" she said.

He looked at her, and she recoiled a little, because for once, he looked . . . angry. With her. "Do you think that matters to me right now?" he asked her. "Do you imagine I give a damn?"

"No," she said, willing her voice not to tremble. "But I do. It doesn't do a bit of good not to have to pay for your mistakes. You know that as well as I do."

He said, "Whatever. We'll talk about it later."

They ate a lunch, then, that nobody had much appetite for. With her dad gone quiet, her mom's eyes gone red, and Stacy gone white.

Finally, they were driving back to Paradise, and Zora said, "I missed my plane."

Travis said, "Yeah. I'll buy you a ticket home for the morning." He looked at Rochelle. "I'll come in for a minute and take care of that."

"Sure," she said.

It was five by the time they got back to her house, and the continuing rain had brought an early gloom to the day. True to his word, Travis came in and took care of Zora's ticket. Of course he did, because Travis was focused. And Rochelle set her alarm clock for three so she could wake Zora up in time for the drive to Spokane to catch the six o'clock plane, because she was focused, too. And then Zora and Stacy were on the couch, wrapped in afghans and watching a movie, and Rochelle and Travis were sitting at the kitchen table warming their hands around cups of tea. Rochelle had taken tea out to the others as well. Tea seemed like a better idea than vodka.

"Rough day," Travis said.

"Yeah." Just like that, the tears rose, threatening to choke her. She looked down and took a sip of tea, and Travis's hand was around hers. Nothing but comfort, and she sat for a moment and breathed it in.

"Your folks," he said. "That's a rough thing, too."

"Yes," she said, so grateful that she didn't have to explain, that Travis was a . . . a grown-up. That he might be able to guess with what stoicism her parents would go to Miles's funeral, and that her mother would be delivering a casserole to Miles's mother as her neighbors had done for her after the military officers had appeared on her doorstep. And not just this week. Her mother would be doing it next week, and the week after that. A month from now, when the comfort and the understanding had disappeared from everywhere else. When the shock had worn off and the grinding pain of a new reality had set in. That's when her mother would be there.

Miles hadn't been much to write home about, not so far. But he hadn't been bad, either, not really. He was like Lake, that was all. Convinced that there was a more exciting life he should be living, and always chasing it. And whatever he'd been, he'd been his parents' child.

His loss would open all the old wounds for her parents as well, because that was how it worked. And they'd cope the same way they always had. They'd endure, and they'd reach out to help somebody else through it.

She didn't say all that to Travis, though. She was too tired. And maybe she didn't need to. Maybe he knew.

"Zora will be all right," he said. "But Stacy's pretty shook up."

"Sorry again about your truck," she said. "Sorry about Zora missing her flight, too." The weight of it all tried to crush her for just a moment, and she set her shoulders under it, as always, and pushed back up. "Another thing you had to take care of."

"You'll be the one getting her on the road, though. Somebody's always the fixer, aren't they? It's you, just like it's me." He stood up then, and said, "I'll go. Long day for both of us. But if you need me, you know where I am."

She got up herself, went to him, and put her arms around him, and he wrapped her up, held her close, and rocked a little. Then he kissed her on top of her head, and she had to squeeze her eyes shut against the tenderness of it.

She held the front door open for a minute when he'd gone, after a quiet word and a hug for Zora, and watched him loping across the sidewalk through the rain that had started up again as if it would never stop, as if the world were made of rain after the heat of the summer.

He hopped into his truck, raised a hand to her, and pulled out. And Rochelle thought, *I need you now.*

A DANGEROUS PROFESSION

Jim Lawson sat in the little conference room with DeMarco and Mark Lawrence and looked through the various printouts. Ten shades of nothing, right there.

"Yeah," DeMarco said, leaning back in his chair and flipping a pencil in his hand. Point end tapping, then eraser end, over and over against the laminated wood. "Car fell off the jack. Looks like an accident, pure and simple."

"I could swear, though," Jim said, "that he was antsy. That he wanted to talk. Now he's dead, and that's just way too much of a coincidence for me. Falling off the jack with the car on a concrete slab? Not the best concrete job I ever saw, but not the worst, either. It happened before it started raining, too." He shrugged a shoulder. "Could happen, of course. Happens somewhere every other week, probably." He shuffled through the papers again. "Too much rain to show any tire marks on the road, too. It'd be nice if Stacy Marks hadn't gone into the ditch right below the house. Muddied things up, so to speak. But it probably didn't make any difference." He sighed, knocked the papers together, and set them down. "Nope. You're getting the go-ahead for the DNA match if you can, I assume."

"Already asked his parents for the permission," DeMarco said. "You think he could have gotten careless because of the investigation?"

Jim sighed and scratched the back of his head. "Nah," he finally said. "Or maybe yeah. Upset, for sure. Obviously, he was upset. At being a suspect, and I'd say that was it. I still say the same thing I said before. I wouldn't peg him for this. He's a follower, not a leader, always has been. No real badass to him. Get a girl pregnant, lure her out into a field, strangle her, and hide her in a ditch? And then shut up about it and not fall apart?" He shook his head. "Not where my money would be. My money would've been on him knowing something, being pressured not to tell, and caving anyway. Wherever the pressure was coming from at the moment, that would be the way Miles would jump. Which is why I don't believe his car fell off the jack."

"You think somebody shut him up." DeMarco's pencil was moving faster than ever. Eraser. Point. Eraser. Point. "So," he said, running through it one more time, because that was what you did. "If it's the country boys who are at the heart of it, and this Kimberling is either the one who was scared, the one somebody shut up before he could talk, or the one who did it? And don't tell me he wasn't a badass," he added. "A weak guy, a guy whose dad's leaning on him already to straighten up? Who's afraid he's going to get dumped on his ass out of his inheritance, or whatever a farm is?"

"Not quite an inheritance," Jim said. "Too much work for that. But his future. Call it that."

"All right. Guy like that. Get him cornered. Druggie girl, runaway type, she's pregnant and he's Catholic. She says she'll go to his dad. You think he couldn't get his hands around her throat?"

"Sure he could," Jim said. "But if he had, he wouldn't have seemed like he was dying to say, 'Hit me with that Q-Tip.' And he did."

"Granted," DeMarco said. "Unless he knew he wasn't the father, but he *was* the killer."

"No," Jim said. "Like I said. I don't buy it. And nobody else is going to be clamming up, scared to rule himself out for fear of Miles Kimberling. Or for love of him, either. He wasn't what you'd call magnetic with other guys. No kind of an alpha male."

Lawrence nodded at that.

"Back to square one, then," DeMarco said, because he'd met Miles, too. "Back to personalities. If Kimberling's death wasn't an accident, we've got hot blood—maybe—with Heather's murder, and cold blood with Kimberling's for sure. And a country boy for sure, too. We're closing in on that. Not two directions anymore. One direction."

"Yep," Jim said.

"Farnsworth. The party was at his house. Kimberling was his friend. You said he had a fighting side after a few."

"Murder in cold blood, though?" Jim shook his head. "Not so much. Harris is meaner, like we said. And Farnsworth's never been what you'd call a big planner."

"Well," DeMarco said, shoving himself back from the table, "we'll get him in here again. We'll get them *all* in here again and put the heat on. If they think we're moving in on them, and if we tell them we know why Kimberling died? Somebody's going to cave."

"If that's why he died," Jim said, "then nobody's going to talk. If we bring them in and they clam up even more? Then that's why he died."

"How many accidents can one guy arrange?" DeMarco asked. "Before somebody says, 'Hell with this, I want out.'"

"I wouldn't want to bet," Jim said. "Farming's a dangerous profession."

ANOTHER MONKEY WRENCH

Rochelle knew Travis was frustrated, even though he hadn't said so. She'd spent every night at home this week, not wanting to leave Stacy, who seemed more fragile than ever since the events of Sunday. Her sister would come home and go straight to her room like a teenager, and Rochelle wasn't sure what to do about it. She had a feeling, though, that it was better to be home in case Stacy did want to talk.

She and Travis had made dinner together at his house a couple nights during the week, but she'd been home by eleven both times. He'd gotten out of bed and kissed her good-bye at the door without a word, but as whirlwind romances went, he was probably thinking that it wasn't the most spontaneous and carefree thing he'd ever experienced.

She wished, selfishly, that Zora had stuck around, so she could have left Stacy with her. Besides, she liked Travis's sister, and she thought her relaxed attitude would be good for Stacy right now. The two of them had shared that experience, which always helped. But it was true that you had to show up for jobs if you wanted to keep them. She wished Travis didn't have to go back to San Francisco on Sunday, too, speaking of that. She wished he didn't have to go back at all.

This one's going to fly. I know it.

He'd looked so excited when he'd said it. So alive. It was his future, and his passion, and he was going to pursue it. In San Francisco. And there was nothing wrong with that.

Dell's words came back to her then. *You can be as sure as the day, you can be right as rain, and you can do every single thing in the world exactly perfect. And you still won't necessarily get forever.*

Anybody who'd been married and wasn't anymore knew that was true. *It is what it is.* She had a toothbrush at his place, some clothes in his closet, and a key to his house, and all those things had been his idea. She wasn't going to wreck this by looking past December and wondering what would happen then, or by being dissatisfied with the time they had now. She'd found out she could have a decent relationship, that she could recognize a decent guy. That was important, going forward. And going forward was what it was all about.

And then Travis came by the office on Thursday, sat down in the visitor's chair, looked at her soberly, and said, "Tell me we get all night tomorrow," and she threw another monkey wrench into the mix.

"Sure," she said, then picked up her pen and fiddled with it. "Maybe you'd help me with something first, though. Right after work, as soon as I change my clothes. It'll take about an hour, and I'm afraid it isn't all that fun. And then—whatever, though."

"Uh-huh," he said. "I've just resigned myself. This is my patient face. What is it?"

"I'd like it if you'd drive me out to Lake's and hang around with me while I do something."

"We talking arson?" he said. "I thought we were both letting the past go."

She had to laugh. "No. It's my bulbs."

"Christmas, or otherwise?"

That won him another reluctant smile. "Of the flower variety. It took me a long time to get those tulips and irises together, all the ones

I wanted, and I can't stand to think of them coming up another spring at his place and getting . . . ignored. Or trampled, probably. I can just see his boot coming down on them." Her fingers curled more tightly around her pen at the thought. "I should've taken them at the time, but it was winter. Snow, you know. And I didn't think of asking for them in the settlement. I wasn't at my best. Anyway, I'm . . . attached, I guess. I want *those* ones. And now's the time to plant them."

"Well, if there's one thing I've learned from my mother," he said, "it's that there's no arguing with a gardener. Sure. If you have to go, I'm there."

"I know it isn't great to ask you," she said. "But I'm a little nervous about it. I could call Lake and ask him, but you know . . . I think he'd say no. In fact, I have half a feeling that he'd dig them up himself and throw them in the burn barrel just to spite me, especially if he was drunk. So I'm going to sneak in there and get them. He always goes to the bar after work on Friday. On that, he's totally reliable." That had come out bitter, so she kept going, trying for matter-of-fact. "It'll be fine, but I'd rather not do it alone. My dad would go with me, but that might not end well."

"No," Travis said, "I can imagine it wouldn't. Having met your dad."

"Plus, I want to take a vehicle that his neighbors won't recognize."

"You don't have to give me all these reasons, you know," he said. "You could assume that you could ask for what you need from me, and I'd do my best to say yes."

That brought her up short. "Well . . ." She tried to laugh. "My sister just wrecked your truck, remember? And favors aren't my expectation."

"Yeah." His expression might have been called . . . grim. "I noticed." He stood up. "And I'll do it anyway."

So on Friday at five thirty, instead of fixing a steak dinner at his place and then going dancing—which was the plan at the end of this— they were turning off the highway, and, stupid as it was to care anymore, her stomach was plummeting. It got worse with every rotation of the wheels, until finally, Travis was pulling into Lake's driveway.

The sun would be setting soon, but this wouldn't take long. She concentrated on that, because she didn't want to think about anything else. The little white house looked shabbier than ever in the bleak light of autumn. Something was funky about the screen door, too. A wide rip in the mesh about a foot off the ground, like somebody had put his boot through it. Which he probably had.

She wasn't looking at the house. Not anymore. She was here for a reason—a reason that wasn't seeming like a great idea right now.

They were here, though. *Get in, do it, get out.* "Pull around behind the shop," she told Travis.

He glanced at her, then rolled slowly over the weed-choked gravel and came to a stop behind the metal shop, out of sight of the road.

She hopped out, grabbing two trowels, a couple paper bags, and her gardening gloves along the way, and Travis followed after her. She rocked to a stop, though, before she'd taken three steps.

"Well," she said, "that didn't take long."

Travis was at her side, looking at the cornstalks, dried now, in the garden plot. Growing vegetables wasn't like Lake, and judging from the unharvested ears on every plant, he hadn't had any changes of heart. The point was what lay behind the corn. A row of marijuana plants, low to the ground from recent harvesting. At least twenty of them.

"He tried that when we were married," she said, shaking it off and heading for the front of the yard. "Planted them farther from the house, of course. Way out by the back fence, thinking I wouldn't see. I found them anyway, of course. Dug them up and burned them the moment I saw them. Those were the first precious things of his I dumped into that burn barrel. I thought he was going to hit me that night for sure. That night almost did us in. It should have, probably, but I was still in there trying, and I guess he was, too."

She stopped near the fence bordering the road, said, "Here. Along in a row. The bulbs should be right down here," and stuck the trowel down into the weedy earth.

"He hit you?" Travis asked, crouching down and beginning to dig a couple yards away.

"No. He didn't get there, or he stopped first. Whichever." Her trowel hit something, and she dug gently around it, found the knobby root, and pulled it up. "Ah," she said. "Yep. Here we go," She tossed it into a bag and kept digging.

"He swung me around by the arm," she continued at last. "Shoved me up against the kitchen wall while he shouted at me. First time he ever called me a fucking bitch, but not the last." She looked up at Travis. "Don't ever call me that."

"Don't worry," Travis said, and she'd call that look . . . hard. "I won't."

"Funny," she said, "I haven't thought about that in a long time. Blocked it out, I guess. I was actually scared for a moment."

"Well, yeah. I'd imagine. What happened?"

She let out a huff of laughter, tossed a couple more bulbs into the bag from the growing trench, and said, "I looked him in the eye and said, 'If you hit me, you'd better enjoy it, because it'll be the last thing you do. You've got to sleep sometime.' I meant it, too. Nobody hits me."

She wouldn't have described the twist of Travis's mouth as a smile. He was making good progress on his end of the trench, though. "Sounds about right. What did he do?"

"Let me go and stormed out, stayed gone all day and all night. Showed up again the next day with an armful of flowers and an apology, sweet and sorry like he did so well, and I let it go, because he'd never been violent before. And give him credit, he never was again. And maybe I shouldn't have done it myself—burned his plants. I suppose I felt bad that I'd reacted like that instead of talking to him about it. But I never liked having all that weed in the house anyway, and growing it? That made me crazy. I saw the SWAT team, you know. Saw myself in a jumpsuit and a jail cell, up on distribution charges. A bit dramatic, maybe, but the laws were tougher then, especially for that much of it. Not personal use, you know. And my job's important to me."

"And your reputation," Travis said.

"Yeah. That, too." They were moving fast, the recent rain having softened the ground. Halfway across the yard, which was good, because the light was fading.

Just as she was thinking it, she dug her trowel into the earth, and the handle snapped off.

"Shoot," she said. Travis looked up, and she held up the blade. "I'll go get a shovel."

She headed across the yard, grabbed the knob of the shop door, and bounced right off it. She hadn't expected it to be locked.

"Well, that's stupid," she said aloud. She reached up under the eaves of the overhang, felt along the board, and found the key, then opened the door and reached for the light.

She blinked, as much in surprise as at the sudden brightness. Lake had always been a slob, and the back of the building was as messy as she remembered. A wheelbarrow and garden tools shoved into one corner, all mixed up with a lawn mower and a concrete mixer. Bags of fertilizer tossed back there, too. For the marijuana, probably, because he'd never cared enough about the lawn to go to extremes like actual fertilizer. She'd done the mowing, in fact, because he wouldn't have bothered until the grass was knee-deep.

The front of the shop, though, was clear, with a new line of shelving containing a neat row of cardboard boxes. An open container of snack-sized Ziploc bags sat beside a full carton of the same thing. There was a bottle of Canadian whisky and a stack of plastic glasses, too. A folding table was set up on the cement floor, with chairs on two sides and a couple more folded against the wall. As if there were a regular poker game happening out here, but why on earth would Lake be playing poker with his buddies out in his drafty, spidery shop? Not like he didn't have the house to himself.

Well, it wasn't her problem. She went across to the garden tools and grabbed a spade, then left the building. Which was when she heard the engine.

COMPANY

The daylight was even dimmer than before, and the truck had its headlights on. She didn't have to see it to recognize it, though. The low grumble of the old Ford's engine would have told her. She knew the sound of Lake's rig.

She didn't rush. No point. She hung up the key again under the eaves and went out to join Travis.

The truck stopped at the entrance to the driveway, and the window slowly lowered. Lake had somebody with him, a passenger she couldn't make out in the gloom. A girl, probably. The only reason she could think of that he wouldn't be at the bar.

"What the hell are you doing here?" he asked. Which was a reasonable question.

Travis reached out and took the shovel from Rochelle, and she let him have it and said, "Getting my bulbs. I figured you'd be out, and you wouldn't care anyway."

Lake left the truck standing where it was and climbed down, and on the other side, his passenger did, too.

It wasn't a girl. It was Shane, which was a shock. Rochelle hadn't realized they knew each other. Had Stacy known? If so, why hadn't she told Rochelle?

Shane came around the front of the truck, Lake stood still, and then both men were standing in front of the driver's door. The headlights were still on, casting a faint glow over the scene, and beside her, Travis was moving. He took one step forward and to the left, ending up slightly in front of Rochelle. He had both hands on the shovel, had shifted it around so it was held down and to his right.

The hair on the back of her neck was standing up. There was a menace in the air that she'd never felt with Lake, not even on that night she'd just been remembering.

Shane still hadn't said anything. He just stood there, a step behind Lake. *Not such a tough guy, are you?* Rochelle thought.

"You were wrong," Lake said. "I care. You don't have any right to be here, and you sure as hell don't have a right to get into my shop. You read the sign?" He gestured toward the fence. "Trespassers will be shot."

Rochelle laughed, and at that moment, she meant it. "I was there when you nailed that sign to the post, remember? You going to start your killing career with me? Come on, Lake. I took my bulbs, that's all. Most of them. You don't want my flowers anyway."

"Everything here is mine," he said. "Everything."

"Yep," she said, "and trust me, I don't want any of it. Anything but this. So if you'll quit acting like Arnold Schwarzenegger on a testosterone mission and pull your rig in so we can get out, we'll be on our way."

It was a standoff, then, and she didn't want to admit how fast her pulse was racing. Travis hadn't moved, but she could feel the tension vibrating in him as if he were standing on his toes, his entire body on a hair trigger. That shovel ready to swing.

Ten seconds passed. Twenty, while they all stood frozen. Finally, Lake said, "Get out of here, then."

Rochelle bent for her paper bags, and Lake said, "No."

"Lake . . ." She sighed. "That's just silly. You don't want them."

"No," he said again.

She shrugged, said, "Fine," and looked at Travis. His face was carved from granite, and he hadn't lowered his shovel one inch. "Come on," she told him.

"Get back in your truck," Travis told Lake, his voice low, but not the least bit soft. "Move it out of the way, and we'll leave."

"Or what?" Lake laughed, and the sound rang out as harsh as the caw of a crow. "You'll hit me with my shovel?"

"That's right," Travis said.

"Two of us," Lake said.

"I'm fast," Travis said. "Try me." He jerked his head at Rochelle, but his eyes didn't leave Lake. "Get your bulbs."

She did it. Fast as she could, grabbing first one paper bag, then the other, clutching them to her.

Lake and Shane stood still a moment more, then Lake shrugged and said, "Fine. Too much trouble anyway. I sure as hell don't need her white-trash father after me like a rabid dog."

The red mist descended over Rochelle's vision, and it took everything she had to stand still, not to rush Lake and go for his eyes. But she did stand still, and after another moment, Lake and Shane climbed back up into the truck, its engine still grumbling.

"We're walking to my truck," Travis told her quietly. "Now. Go."

She nodded once, short and jerky. Every muscle was rigid as she took the twenty steps to the shop, expecting to hear the truck shift into gear at any second, the revving of the engine. Travis stayed a pace behind her, still to her right. She knew he was poised to shove her out of the way if Lake tried to run them down. She knew it like it had already happened.

The second they were behind the shop, out of sight of the two men, Travis was running. Pulling the passenger door open and throwing her inside with her paper bags, then around to his side, leaping in, handing her the shovel, shoving the key in the ignition. And then he was around the building. Face-to-face with the other truck.

Two engines rumbling, and then Lake revved his.

"Put your seat belt on," Travis said, and she did it.

Lake's rig moved, and she tensed even more. But he went to their left, pulled up onto the concrete in front of the shop, and stopped, and Travis was giving his truck gas and heading out. Not fast, and not slow. And then he was turning onto the road. Still not fast. Until they were around the corner, and he put the hammer down and kicked up some dust.

She didn't think she breathed until they'd turned onto the highway. Travis drove to the next turnoff, then pulled off the road and turned the key with a hand that trembled.

She had her seat belt unfastened and was in his arms in an instant. He grabbed her hard and held her close, and she took a few deep breaths and felt him doing the same.

"Wow," she said when she could speak again. "Wow. I didn't—I'm so sorry."

"No," he said, his voice unsteady. "No. You didn't know, or you wouldn't have gone. I'll just say one thing, and then I'll shut up. Do not ever go out there again, you hear?"

"This is where I say something kick-ass," she said, wishing her voice weren't shaking. "But I can't. I'm just going to say—thanks. Thanks for making him let me take my . . . my bulbs. They'd better bloom now, that's all I have to say. They'd damn well . . . better."

"That was . . . pretty kick-ass right there," he said. "What you said. That wasn't bad at all."

DIE TRYING

Travis's shakes subsided only gradually, and he could tell it was the same for Rochelle.

Halfway to town, she stirred herself and said, "I didn't know that Shane knew Lake. Or the other way around. That doesn't feel like good news."

"Shane?" Travis said. "Who's Shane? Oh. The bad boyfriend. That was him? That's . . . odd."

"Yeah." She pulled out her phone, dialed, grimaced, and said, "It's me. Ro. Call me when you can," and hung up. "She was going out tonight," she told Travis. "With her girlfriends, which I was glad of. Entering the land of the living again, I thought. I know it was a shock, finding the body and everything, but her reaction's so . . . over the top. She's been going to the counseling center, but I'm not sure it's helping. And tonight . . . I hope she's not going to see him. I know she hasn't this week, because I've been there. She's been so low, and he hasn't been around. Tells you something. Well, tells *you* something, and tells *me* something. Doesn't tell Stacy anything, apparently." She shrugged, a weary motion. "I don't even know what to say. 'Don't go out with that guy, because I don't think he's any better than the guy I actually *married?*'"

"Easy to give advice," Travis said. "Hard to take it."

"Yep." She pulled a hand through her hair and sighed. "I'll talk to her tomorrow anyway. I'll try again."

And then she put the phone away and was quiet, and Travis thought, *Yes, you will.* Rochelle would always try again. "Quit" wasn't in her vocabulary, or her nature. Except maybe with him, and even there—she was trying.

She was so tough, and so tender, too. So afraid to show her soft places, thinking that if she did, somebody would stomp them. The same way Lake would have tossed her bulbs into the burn barrel, just because they were precious to her.

Lake might never have hit her, maybe. That didn't mean he hadn't hurt her.

When he pulled up outside his house, he said, "Let's make dinner," and she nodded. So they went inside, and they did. Steak. Potatoes in the microwave, salad, a beer. When they'd eaten, he felt better, and he thought she did, too. They loaded the dishwasher, and he said, "Come on. Let's take a shower."

There would be no jumping anyone, not tonight. They stood under the warm spray, and he took the soap and a cloth and washed her body like he could wash the pain and the fear away, the shock of thinking that somebody you'd loved could want to hurt you. His touch was gentle over her arms, her neck, down to her breasts, and beyond, and she stood, her eyes closed, and let him do it.

He wanted his hands to be the ones she thought about tonight, his voice the one she heard when she fell asleep, his arms the ones she would dream about. He wanted to be the strength that kept away her nightmares.

When he finished, she took the soap and the cloth from him and did it all to him. Still not speaking, but her eyes steady on his now, her hands firm, but gentle, too, as if she knew how much he needed her. As if she knew how afraid he'd been, and she wanted to make it better, the same way he did for her. Then she put the soap away, and they stepped out, dried each other off, and went into the bedroom. They pulled the covers back, climbed in, and made a nest. A haven where nothing could threaten them, because they were together.

No rushing, not tonight. Slow touches, soft murmurs, kisses so tender that his heart ached with it. A long, slow, sweet build, and then he was rocking her, slow and deep and steady, her breath in his ears, her hands clutching his shoulders, sliding down his arms, hanging on tight. Her heart pounding beneath him, and his pounding, too. Until she was climbing, and he was going right along with her. Until they went over the top together, shuddering and sighing, then held each other close during the whole ride down.

When they'd finished, he rolled to his back, and she lay beside him. Nothing touching but the hand he held, his fingers threaded through hers. And the connection running strong all the same. Peace stealing over him, warm as the blankets that covered them, quiet as the wind sighing through the trees.

He was letting himself drift off to sleep when she spoke and jolted him awake again.

"It's hard to jump in with both feet," she said, her voice quiet in the darkness, "when you've got one foot out the door."

He'd been running his thumb over her knuckles. Now, everything in him stilled. "What?"

"The way I felt tonight . . . out there. I knew you were there for me. I knew you were never going to run. I knew you'd . . ." She stopped again. "I knew you'd die trying."

"Yeah," he said, the relief swamping him, making him weak. "Yeah. You were right. I would have."

He'd told her dad that he didn't like killing things, not unless they were trying to kill him. He'd have to amend that now, because he'd been willing to do it tonight. He'd known it down in some dark place at the very bottom of his soul. And it hadn't been to save himself.

It wasn't just who he was willing to kill for, either. It was who he was willing to die for.

When they'd had their backs turned . . . he'd been rehearsing it. The second he'd heard that engine roar, he'd have been shoving her to the left with all his might, pushing her out of the truck's path. There'd been no doubt. No hesitation. No second thoughts. He'd *known*.

He was still trying to work out how to say all that when she spoke. "So I'm thinking," she said, "if you've got that kind of guts? If you were ready to put it on the line for me? What I am doing being such a wuss? Here I've got what I always wanted, and I'm scared to reach out and go for it."

She'd rolled to face him now, and he was barely breathing. "And in case you haven't figured it out," she said, "that's you. So I'm going to cowboy up and tell you. You haven't said the words. You might not be where I am. But I'm going to say it anyway. I'm going to jump in with both feet, with my arms and my eyes wide open. I'm going to grab my good thing. I'm going to tell you . . ." She took a breath, and he heard it. The fear, and the certainty. Both right there, no holds barred. Nothing but pure, shining courage. Nothing but Rochelle. "I'm going to tell you," she said again, "that I'm in. I'm going to love you, and it doesn't matter what you do about it. I'm going to die trying."

"Oh, baby," he said over the lump in his throat. "Rochelle. I—" Now *he* was the one who was floundering. "If somebody here hasn't got guts, that somebody isn't you." He had to hold her then. He had to kiss her, and stroke his hand over her hair.

"Not an . . . answer," she said against his shoulder.

"No. So how about this." He took a breath, and he did it. He jumped. "How about if I tell you that I'm crazy in love with you. That I would've done anything to keep you safe tonight, because it was all that mattered to me. That deciding to take this job is looking like the best choice I ever made, and being with you is the best I've ever felt. Does that work?"

He was choking up. He was free-falling. He smoothed a hand over her hair again, down her back, and felt her heart beating against his chest, strong and steady and sure. "I love you so much," he told her. "I just wish I had better words to tell you."

"Well," she said, with a laugh that didn't sound much steadier than he was feeling, "I'd say that was pretty good. I'd say, I'll take it."

WHAT'S WORTH IT

Rochelle woke slowly the next morning. No nightmares to trouble her, because when she'd rolled over in the night, Travis had been there to touch, and that had been pure comfort.

And he loved her, too. He'd told her so. He'd told her, and kissed her, and fallen asleep holding her. And she could believe it, because if there was one thing Travis was, it was solid.

She got up, now, moving quietly so as not to wake him. He was sleeping on his stomach, one arm flung out across her pillow, his hand around it like he was still hanging on to her. He might not have slept as easily as she had, she suspected. He might have been feeling protective. And as somebody who'd taken care of herself and everyone around her for just about forever, that didn't feel bad at all.

She was in the kitchen, drinking a cup of coffee and looking out the window at Carol's fruit trees, when he came in. Blue jeans and bare feet, buttoning a flannel shirt over a sleeveless white undershirt. Looking good.

"Morning," he said, bending down to give her a quick kiss. "You made coffee."

"Yep. Called Stacy again, too, but she didn't answer again. Still asleep, probably."

"Hmm." He pulled out a mug and poured his own.

"Carol has cherries," she remarked absently.

"Huh?"

She gestured out the window with her mug. "Plum tree, and sour cherry tree." Their branches barer, now, in the aftermath of the storm. "They can make a mess for sure if you don't keep up with them, but you get pie."

"That so? That come with the tree?"

She smiled. "You have to make them. And to pit the fruit, too, which is a job. But it's worth it. Real's always worth it."

"Ah," he said. "Trees. But when you plant trees, you'll have hung it up."

"Kind of pessimistic. Maybe I should have said that when I plant trees, I'll be putting down my roots. Sounds better, huh? It's my life, and nobody else's." She finished off her coffee and stood up. "How about breakfast?"

◆　　◆　　◆

And later that morning, after they'd eaten breakfast and gone back to bed again, because it was chilly outside and so warm under the blankets, Travis offered to help her plant her bulbs.

"It's the least I can do," he said, one slow thumb running down her spine, "seeing as how I didn't dig fast enough to get all of them for you."

"You just want me to fix you lunch," she said lazily. She stretched in satisfaction, nearly purring at the sensation of his hand barely grazing her back, his fingernails scraping so lightly over her skin. She stayed sprawled on her stomach, the sheet all the way down to her thighs, not worrying one bit about how she looked in the full light of morning. She knew she looked just fine to him. She knew it because he'd told her, and he'd showed her. Because he loved to watch, whether he was over her, or whether, like this morning, she was over him, riding him slow and easy while he caressed her everywhere he could reach. And Travis had a very good reach.

"You've got some kind of magic in your fingers, you know that?" she told him. His palm was smoothing over the curves of her behind, now, sliding down her thighs, and she shivered. "You sure know how to touch me."

"Maybe it's not just lunch I want," he said, coming up over her and pressing a kiss between her shoulder blades, which felt fine, too. "It gets lonesome in this bed at night, you know? You help me sleep."

She smiled. "Nice one. Come on. Bulbs."

He gave her a good slap on the butt. "Then you'd better get dressed and quit tempting me."

She didn't, though. Instead, she smiled wickedly at him and said, "Is that a hint of what you want in exchange?"

He laughed, and he didn't look shocked, either. He looked nothing but thrilled. "Is that an offer?"

She rolled over, pulled him on top of her, kissed him until she could swear his eyes crossed, and said, "Nope. That's a promise."

Love was good. And love with Travis was the best.

◆　◆　◆

Dell was out front cleaning up her yard when Travis pulled up in front of Rochelle's house. Rochelle led him up the walk, so damn happy to have him behind her. Charlie pattered over to say hello, and Rochelle bent down to give him a scratch behind a fluffy white ear, then said, "Morning."

"*Good* morning," Dell said, leaning on her rake. All in yellow today, as cheerful as the blue sky, the puffy clouds, the shining clarity of the air. "You two look pretty happy."

Travis laughed. "Yep. Going to help Rochelle with her gardening today, and that's a guaranteed good time. And if you've got some man jobs yourself, you let me know. Rochelle says she loves a man who can do man jobs, and you know I want that."

"Watch out," Dell said. "I might take you up on that. And you might want to check on Stacy," she told Rochelle. "She had the music cranked up last night."

"Oh, I'm sorry," Rochelle said. Dell never complained. It must have been extreme.

Dell made an impatient gesture. "I'm not worried about that. Hell, I'm old. I don't sleep anyway. But it was that breakup sound, where you play those sad, wailing, somebody-done-me-wrong songs until you find the best one, then you play it over and over. Get it good and loud and sing along, start drinking the wine from the bottle because you spilled the last time you tried to pour."

"Well," Rochelle said, "that might not be such bad news."

"I'd say you're right." The spidery webs beside Dell's eyes and mouth creased with her smile. "The ones you get that messed up over—they're always the ones you're better off without, aren't they? The ones that jerk you around like you're on their string, where you think afterwards, should've sent him a thank-you note. Better she gets it over with now than when she's thirty-five and got two kids with him, anyway. I came on over to tell her so, in fact. Thought we could sit on the couch and have that glass of wine together, talk about what sorry pieces of work men can be." She glanced at Travis. "Present company excepted, of course."

"Don't worry about me," he said. "I've got the picture."

"Not that men have any exclusive on that," she said. "I've known some men who could tell a tale or two along those lines. But anyway, I figured at least I could've poured. She wouldn't let me come in, though." She shook her head, then resumed her raking. "But a little heartbreak never killed anyone, and you know you gotta hit bottom before you can come up again."

"Well, thanks," Rochelle said, her hand already on the doorknob. "She didn't go out today?"

"Nope," Dell said. "Sleeping it off."

The house was quiet, murky-dark despite the brightness outside, when Rochelle stepped inside with Travis behind her. All the curtains still drawn, even though it was nearly ten.

Well, if Stacy had been up half the night playing sad songs, she could easily still be sleeping. Sometimes you just wanted to escape, and drinking yourself into oblivion could seem like the best way. It might not help anything, but at least it stopped the hurting. It beat going to a bar and taking a stranger home, anyway.

That was what Rochelle told herself as she knocked on the door of Stacy's room. She didn't start worrying until she knocked again more loudly, called her sister's name, and got no answer. And until she tried the doorknob, and it was locked.

"Travis," she called, and he was there. Right there, like he'd been waiting for her to call.

"Got a key?" he asked as she rattled the doorknob.

"Uh . . ." She tried to think. "Stacy!" she called again, pounding with the heel of her hand. "No. I don't."

"Stand back," he said, and she stepped a couple paces away in the narrow hallway. Not enough room to get a run at it, but Travis didn't need one. He hauled in a breath, and then his booted foot came up and smashed into the wood beside the doorknob, faster than she could blink. The door slammed open with a splintering crash, hit the wall, and bounced back, and Travis had the heel of his hand against it on the bounce, was shoving it open and heading inside. And Rochelle was right behind him.

Stacy was on the bed. And she wasn't moving.

Rochelle didn't even know how she made it to her sister's side. She was just there, her hand on Stacy's face. It wasn't cold, it was warm, and Rochelle was barely breathing herself as she fumbled beneath Stacy's chin, tried to still her own heart enough to focus, to feel for a pulse.

Slow. But it was there, and Rochelle's fingers were shaking against Stacy's skin.

She saw the wine bottle, then. Empty. Knocked over, a few drops having spilled on the gray carpeting beneath the bedside table. A prescription bottle with some pills inside. And an empty half-size Ziploc bag beside it.

"Not just drunk," she told Travis, because he was right there. "You don't pass out this bad from one bottle of wine."

She had her hand in her purse, pulling out her phone, but Travis was handing her his keys and lifting Stacy in his arms. "We can get her there faster," he said. "Let's go. You drive. You'll know where the emergency entrance is. And take the . . ." He gestured with his head. "The pills."

Stacy was limp when he put her in the truck, and limp when he lifted her out of it, once Rochelle had pulled the truck to a rocking stop in front of the emergency entrance of Hillman Hospital.

"Go," she said, but she didn't have to tell him, because he was already out, Stacy in his arms, and she was parking and racing in after him.

By the time she got inside, Stacy was gone, and Travis was standing at the admissions desk.

Rochelle hauled up beside him and answered the question the nurse was asking, even though she was having trouble getting her breath. "Wine," she told the woman. "And pills, I think. Some kind of pills."

"Was she on any prescription medication?" the nurse asked calmly.

"I think so." Rochelle handed over the pill bottle, and then, after some hesitation, the plastic bag as well. "I think there could have been something in here, too. I think . . ." She swallowed. "It could have been more than one thing. Plus a bottle of wine."

"When did she take these?" the nurse asked.

"I don't know," Rochelle said. "Hours ago, I'd guess. Sometime in the night." When Rochelle should have been *home*. She'd known Stacy was having trouble. She should have been home.

She was shaking on the thought, and Travis had seen it, had his arm around her. The nurse nodded, handed Rochelle a clipboard with forms attached, and said, "Please fill these out."

"Can I talk to a doctor?" Rochelle asked.

"They'll be working on her," the nurse said. "What's your relation?"

"Sister."

"Name?"

Rochelle gave it to her, and the nurse said, "When there's something to tell you, they'll let you know. Now, please." She gestured to the clipboard. "Take a seat and fill those out. That's how you can help."

FIXABLE

Travis held her hand, once she was finished with the forms and had made the call she should have made weeks ago, the one to her parents. He waited beside her, and when she muttered, "I shouldn't have left. I shouldn't have," he said, "Of course you should have. This isn't your fault."

"Then whose is it?" she asked.

"It's his," he said. "That guy who hurt her because he could. That's what I'm betting. And it's life. It's hard times, and looking for an out, a way to feel better any way there is."

"If she'd told me," Rochelle said wretchedly. "If she'd *said*."

"She's telling you now. She's telling all of you. She's saying she can't do it alone anymore."

That was when the doctor appeared and called her name, and Rochelle went to him. And Travis held her hand for that, too.

It was a younger man this time, his face not as impatient, not as judgmental as the doctor from Stacy's first trip here. And Rochelle held her breath.

"We've put her in intensive care," he said, and when Rochelle stiffened, he added, "to monitor her. She'll be there some hours, I'd guess."

"Is she . . ." Rochelle swallowed. "Going to get better?"

"If she'd taken enough to kill her straight out," he said, "she'd be dead already. She's coming around now. What we're doing is supportive care, and some decontamination, too. Activated charcoal and intravenous sodium bicarbonate. And, yes," he said with a bit of a smile, "that's baking soda. Otherwise—checking her, that's all. Supportive care means supporting all her systems until her body flushes the toxins out."

"What did she take?" Travis asked.

"A few extra antidepressants, looks like," the doctor said. "The toxic dose of tricyclics—the kind she was prescribed—isn't too far from the clinical one. Which means a person can feel extra depressed and think, if one's good, three or four must be better. And if you combine them with a bottle of wine and a few Vicodin, it's not good. Where did she get pain medication?"

"I . . ." Rochelle said. "I don't . . ."

"She take it from you? An old prescription, maybe?"

"No. I've never taken pain medication."

"Hmm. Has she?"

"Yes." Rochelle breathed out. "Yes. She broke her ankle last spring. She was taking it then, I know, for quite a while. She had to have a second surgery. But that was a *long* time ago. Uh . . ." She tried to think. "She must have been all done with that by April, I'd have thought. May at the latest."

"Hmm," he said again, making a note on the clipboard he held. "You have any reason to think she could have a problem?"

"I . . ." she started to say, and then she looked him in the eye and said, "Yes. I do. What do I do about that?"

He flipped the papers over on his clipboard. "Get her help."

He left, then, and she and Travis moved to the waiting room for the intensive care unit. She got to hold Stacy's hand for fifteen minutes in there, while her sister blinked groggily at her from above an oxygen mask, an IV running into her arm and a blood pressure monitor on her finger, an array of screens behind her, and Rochelle kept it together because there was no choice. Until she had to leave again.

And then there was the harder thing. When her parents showed up, and she had to explain it all to them. Her mother's face strained and gray, her father's set.

"I'm sorry," Rochelle said wretchedly when she'd finished the all-too-short account, everything she knew. "I should have told you. I didn't want you to worry."

"Not sure what we could have done that you didn't," her dad said. "You made her get help, didn't you? You took her home with you."

"I should have looked in her purse," Rochelle said. "I checked the other places, but I didn't check there. I should have . . ."

"No," her mother said. "This isn't your fault. You can't fix everything."

Rochelle felt her throat closing, and she couldn't stop it. She didn't cry, she thought wonderingly, even as she felt the hot tears spilling over. She never cried, because it didn't help.

She'd hadn't even cried on the day of her brother's funeral, because she'd been holding Stacy. She'd cried the day she'd known her marriage was over, and that was all. She'd cried because she'd failed. She'd never cried since, but she was crying now, because she'd failed again.

"But I wanted to," she said miserably. "Oh, Mom. I wanted to fix it so bad. I wanted to . . . to . . ."

"Oh, baby," her mother said, folding her into her arms, "I know. I know you wanted to. You did your best. All you can do is your best."

◆　◆　◆

Stacy spent more than twelve hours in the hospital, as it turned out, and it was well after midnight by the time Rochelle's parents put their youngest child into her dad's pickup, tucked safely between them, and drove her home to Kernville with Rochelle and Travis following behind.

"You don't have to come," Rochelle told Travis. She was dull with fatigue, everything seeming to take an extra second to register, her very words not forming quite fast enough on her tongue. "I can drive, if you take me home for my car."

"No, you can't. And sure I do," he said, as if there were no argument possible.

"But you're supposed to . . ." The white line in the highway was hypnotizing her, and she was staring at it, her vision starting to blur. "You're supposed to leave tomorrow. Today. Whatever."

"Yeah, right. You remember that thing we said about love? What do you imagine it means?"

"I don't . . ." She couldn't seem to finish a sentence.

"Means I'm not going to San Francisco tomorrow. Today. Whatever. Means I'm staying here as long as you need me."

"Oh," she said. "Well . . . thanks." And then she leaned against his big body, closed her eyes, and might have fallen asleep. Just for a minute.

She remembered climbing into the narrow twin bed in the tiny room she'd left so many years ago, and after that, it seemed like barely any time had passed before she was stirring, rolling over, and blinking in incomprehension at the white-painted ceiling. Slowly, the events of the day before came back to her, and she sat up and saw Stacy across from her, sitting up in bed, a cup of something in her hand.

"Hi," Rochelle said, still feeling fuzzy.

Stacy looked down at her mug. "Hi. I can't believe you're here. I'm sorry."

Rochelle pushed herself farther up in bed and shoved the pillow behind her. "No. Don't be sorry. Be glad that you finally did something desperate enough for us to notice, so we can help."

Stacy huffed out a laugh. "Yeah, right. Make an excuse for me."

"I'm not going to make an excuse." Rochelle wasn't sure what she'd thought she'd say to Stacy this morning, but it didn't matter. Seemed she was saying this. "The hell with that. I'm going to hold your feet to the fire and make you take this on. You've been running away because you don't think you can face it. But I know you can. You've done a whole lot of things, and you can do this. You're going to have all the help there is. You've got this, and you're going to do it."

"No," Stacy said. "That's you. I'm not you."

Just like that, Rochelle was done feeling guilty. Now, she was mad. A much more familiar sensation. "What, because it's easy for me? Who ever said it was easy for anyone? I said you could do it. I didn't say it'd be easy. Getting off those pills, all that stuff you've been taking, *whatever* you've been taking? It's going to be hard. And you're going to do it like you've done everything else. Like you went to college, and you stuck it out, even though you cried the first day, and probably a lot of days. And I know," she continued when Stacy stared at her, "because I saw you. I knew when you'd been crying. And I admired you, because you stuck it out anyway. Just like you sucked it up in fifth grade when Marlene Thompson made fun of your clothes and your weight and your hair every single day. You didn't quit then, and you're not going to quit now."

"But you can *do* those things," Rochelle could see the tears hovering at the edges of Stacy's lids now, hear the wobble in her voice, and she hardened her heart against them. "You're never scared. I'm so . . . I'm so *scared,* Ro. I was so scared, and it was the only thing that helped."

"What was?"

"When I . . ." Stacy took a breath. "When I broke my ankle. I was so scared I'd flunk out. It hurt, and I missed school, and I . . ." Her chin trembled some more. "I wasn't sure I could make it. And the pills made me feel better. They made it so I could do it."

"Did they make you smarter?" Rochelle asked. "I don't think so. I bet they made you dumber. They just took the fear away, that was all. But the smarts, and the work? That was all you."

"But the fear," Stacy tried to explain, sounding desperate. "It just . . . it smothered everything else. But if I took the pills, I could do it. Don't you *see?*"

"So you told the doctor that you needed more. You told him it still hurt."

Stacy looked away again. "Yeah," she whispered.

"But that couldn't last forever. So what happened then?"

Stacy was picking at the red yarn of the hand-tied quilt covering her bed. "You can get them," she said reluctantly.

"Uh-huh. Shane."

"It was harder, before. To buy them, I mean. I was so afraid I'd get caught, that you'd all find out, that Mom and Dad . . ." The hand tugging at the yarn was shaking now. "But he always had them, and he sold them to me, extra cheap, because he liked me. He said it was fine. That lots of people took them, and if you could feel bad or you could feel good, why wouldn't you feel good? And that made sense, because I was so *tired* of it. I got so tired of feeling bad all the time. I just wanted to feel *good.*"

"And he had more pills, too," Rochelle said. "Whatever you were taking that first night, at that party."

"I hardly ever did that," Desperate sincerity in Stacy's voice, on her face. "It was just the Vicodin. Really, Ro. It wasn't for . . . for partying. It was just to feel *better.* If I don't take them . . . I feel so . . . bad. So scared. Because what about now? I'm way behind. I've got a lab due, and homework for Stats, and . . . and . . ." She was grabbing a fistful of quilt, squeezing it. "And he said . . . Shane said . . . I couldn't get them from him anymore. That he didn't want to . . ." Her shoulders were heaving. "See me," she whispered. "Because I was too . . . he said I was . . ." She stopped, the tears dripping onto the quilt, and if Shane had been there, Rochelle wouldn't have answered for her actions.

"Stacy." Rochelle had swung around and put her feet on the floor. She was in her underwear and a T-shirt, and the floor was chilly, so she pulled the quilt around herself. "You almost died the other night. You almost *died*. That matters so much more than Stats, or whatever horrible thing Shane said. It wasn't true anyway. He's a user, and he was saying what would hurt you most, because that's what users do."

"No," Stacy said miserably. "He doesn't take them. He never does. He's . . . he's strong."

"No, he's not." Of that, Rochelle was absolutely sure. "He's weak. He's the kind of person who feeds off other people's weaknesses. He's a vampire. That's his addiction, and that's not one bit strong. And he doesn't matter anyway." She still didn't know how to do this, what was the right thing to say, but she was tired of waiting for Stacy to open up. She was going to go for it. "He's all mixed up with the pills for you. That's what I think. With you trying to be a different person. Which is stupid, because the person you are is fine. The person you are is *great*. So he said you were . . . what? Too needy. Too pushy. Too whatever it is, so you'd be on the defensive all the time, thinking it was you. It wasn't you. It was him." She started to say more, then stopped.

"What?" Stacy said.

There were times to project strength, and times to admit weakness. And right now, it was time for Rochelle to get over herself and tell Stacy how it worked down at the bottom of the hole. "That's the way bad relationships go. It's like boiling a frog."

"It's like *what?*"

At least Stacy wasn't crying anymore. "If you drop a frog into hot water," Rochelle explained, "he'll hop right out again. You put him in cold water, though, then turn that stove on? He stays right there. The water starts warming up, and he starts getting cozy. You've changed his . . . his environment, and he feels like it's normal. By the time he's cooking? Too late then."

Stacy shook her head violently, and Rochelle said, "Not pretty, but that's the truth. You take a little, then you take a little more, and before you know it, you're taking way too much. I ought to know. I sat in that pot for years and got boiled. Just like Shane was doing to you."

"I thought Lake cheated on you," Stacy said. "I thought that was it."

"That was just the last thing. Relationships don't end over the last thing. It's only the last thing because it's the thing that happens right before you've had enough. My marriage ended, and that was the best thing that ever happened to me, and *this* is going to be the best thing that ever happened to *you*. You're going to get over this, which has just about *nothing* to do with Shane, even though it feels like it. *Trust* me," she said when Stacy shook her head again. "It's going to be hard work, and at the end of it? You're going to be stronger, and better, and you're going to be out of that pot. And meanwhile, if you have to . . . whatever. Take a medical break from school? Get some incompletes? Go into your advisor's office and explain, with a note from a doctor? A *real* doctor, who's helping you get over this instead of just writing you a prescription for more and more of it? You face up to it, you explain, you start to *deal*. Things happen. Accommodations are *possible*. Didn't you know?"

"They . . . they are?" Stacy asked.

Rochelle exhaled. "Of course they are. Things happen to people. Everybody knows that."

The force of it hit her, then. She could have smacked herself in the forehead. How hadn't she seen it? "That's why," she said slowly. "You *don't* know it. You think if you disappoint anybody, anybody at all . . . it's the end of the world. That it'll all come crashing down."

Stacy wasn't just *starting* to cry now. She was crying, full out. "I can't . . ." she managed to say. "I can't stand to . . . Mom. Daddy. I'm so . . . I'm so . . . ashamed." The word was a sob. "All this time. I've been so ashamed of what you'd all think if you knew. I just . . . I always screw up. I always screw *up*."

Rochelle was over on the other bed, gathering her sister into her arms. "No. No. You don't. You don't have to be perfect. Nobody's expecting you to be perfect."

"What if I'm . . ." Stacy's nose was streaming, and she wiped her hand under it like the little girl she'd been, and Rochelle's heart turned over. "What if I'm not a doctor?" she whispered. "What if I can't . . . I can't get in?"

"Then you go to plan B." That one, Rochelle was sure of. "There's always a plan B. Always. And if that doesn't work? You go to plan C. You know how many plans I'm on? Working my way through the alphabet, that's what. Life's all about falling and getting up again. This is your low point. Time to get up again. Because how many people do everything right? Nobody, that's who. Nobody. The only way you fail is if you give up. You've got people all around you who aren't going to give up on you. We don't care if you're a doctor. We care about *you*. And we're not going to let you give up on yourself, either. Because we love you."

"I don't know why," Stacy said in a small voice, sounding so broken. But she was fixable. Rochelle knew it. She was fixable. "I don't see why."

"Oh, baby." Rochelle hugged her, helpless with it. "Because we do. Because you're ours. *All* of ours. Because you're worth the effort. You're worth our effort, and you're worth yours."

◆ ◆ ◆

She left Stacy after another few minutes. Left her wiping her eyes, but the tears this time were the healing kind, she hoped. The problem was out there now, at least, and out was better than in.

She ducked into the bathroom, then went in search of clothes, ending up with a flannel shirt borrowed from her dad, thrown over yesterday's jeans. And then she went into the kitchen to find her mom, who was cooking breakfast, and to fill her in.

"Well," Valerie said when Rochelle had finished, "I guess we do that, then. Find a doctor, and do what he says. At least we know what we're dealing with now. There are plenty of families around here who've made it through this kind of trouble. If she wants to change, if she wants to get better—that's the main thing."

"A doctor, or a therapist, or whatever—they might want to do some family counseling, I'll bet," Rochelle said. "I suspect there are some things Stacy's going to have to hear a few times from you and Dad before they sink in."

"Whatever it takes," her mother said. "I'll go talk to her right now, and get her up, too. No problem ever got solved by lying in bed, fretting about it. Finish making breakfast, will you, sweetie?"

With that, she handed Rochelle the spatula and left the kitchen, and Rochelle pulled the bacon out of the fridge, started laying strips of it on the heated griddle, and felt some of the weight leaving her shoulders at last.

She hadn't wanted to tell her parents about Stacy, and she'd been wrong, because they would deal. They'd already started. Travis had been right. She should have had more faith.

Her early life might not have been so rich on the money side, she thought as the bacon began to curl and sizzle on the griddle, but if she'd absorbed half of her parents' coping skills along the way, that wasn't too bad an inheritance at all.

What she'd told Stacy had been true. She'd been at the bottom of the pot, but her frog had hopped out anyway. She was never going in there again, and she was going to help tip Stacy's pot right *over.*

Shane be damned, she thought ferociously as she stabbed at the bacon and flipped it with too much force. *Bad boyfriends be damned.* Women were stronger than that.

She got thrown out of her mad a minute later, when Travis came in the door from the mud room behind her dad, both of them shedding shoes and jackets along the way.

"Oh," she said blankly. "You're here. I didn't realize you'd stayed over."

"Aw, baby," Travis said. "That could've come out better. I could leave if you want."

Just like that, her heart was lifting, and her day was turning around. Travis did that to her, it seemed. "What do you think, Dad?" she asked, turning her bacon again, but without quite so much violence. "Should I make him leave?"

"Oh, I don't know," her father said. "He doesn't seem too bad to me so far. Drove you home at two in the morning, got up early, went out with me to feed the stock. Even knew how to do it. Maybe you could give him breakfast first, anyway."

"Maybe so," she said. "Besides, I need a ride home."

"How's Stacy?" Travis asked, and she sobered.

"Better." She listened, heard her mom's voice and Stacy's quieter one. "Tell you later, all right?" She jerked her head toward the other side of the room. "Coffee cups to the left of the sink," she told Travis, "and French toast and bacon coming up. We'll see if we can keep it relatively drama-free this morning, how's that? I keep testing him, Dad," she explained. "One adventure after another. You haven't seen the half of it."

"Didn't I say," Travis said, pulling down a mug and pouring from the simple countertop coffeemaker, "that I liked my life with a little adventure?"

"You did," she said, "but I'm not sure you were counting on this much of it."

"That's the thing about adventures, though," he said. "You don't always get to choose them. We could try building ourselves some kind of stable platform to work from, maybe. What do you think?"

"Funny," she said, "I was just thinking something like that myself."

She smiled at him, and he smiled back, and her dad poured his own coffee and didn't say anything. But he might have been smiling, too.

CHOICES

Travis drove Rochelle home, eventually, because that was what he could do, and he had to do something. He helped her pack up Stacy's things, and drove her out to her parents' again to deliver them. She told him he didn't have to, of course, and he did it anyway. At least he could drive her. By then, it was lunchtime, and he took her out to the Breakfast Spot for a sandwich. And that was half their Sunday.

"Wow," she said when he pulled up outside her house, the fatigue evident in her voice. "One o'clock already. I had a lot of plans for this weekend."

"Me too. Guess that's the way it goes."

"Sorry about that. Your trip and everything. Call me tomorrow, maybe?"

That had sounded too far away, but they were both tired, and they both did have too much to do, so he left her and went home again. It felt a whole lot different walking into his cottage alone than it had walking out of it with Rochelle barely twenty-four hours earlier, though. Not as good, that was for sure.

And finally, he called his partner again.

"About time," Jed complained. "You on your way?"

"No. I'll change it around to next week, or the one after."

"We're going to lose this," Jed said. "Venture capital doesn't grow on trees."

Jed had been Travis's chief programmer at the company that was no longer his. Travis had lured him away without much difficulty, because he'd been right—things weren't going all that well there. It was Jed's first time not working for a payroll, though, and he was nervous.

"We aren't going to lose it," Travis said. "If it's good enough, they'll want it."

"Nobody's going to go for it, man," Jed said, "if you aren't all the way in. You're too far away, and part-time is no time. Six more weeks, right? You need to *get* here."

"Quit worrying. You're doing your part. Let me do mine."

He hung up, then sat a minute before making his next call, to begin to reschedule the meetings that had been meant to be lining up the rest of their team. He rested an elbow on his knee and scrubbed a hand over his unshaven jaw, suddenly weary.

The measure of a man is in the choices he makes.

He shook his head irritably. *Thanks, Dad. Way to get into my head. How about if you can't even see your choices clearly? Or if none of them will work?*

Then think them through again.

All right. Choice A: Stay here and do . . . something. Some teaching or lecturing, some lower-level programming. Work for somebody else, because it didn't matter how much money you had, a man still needed to work. And give up his project.

The interactive orienteering game had come to him during a long mountain bike ride through the hills of the East Bay on a foggy summer day, with the misty tendrils drifting between redwood trunks and welcome silence surrounding him. He'd seen it mapped out, because that was what it would be. Mapped out. Competition and virtual teams, all tethered to their phones, the GPS holding them accountable. Anywhere in the world you could map. In Toronto or London, the Colorado mountains or the Palouse hills.

It was all there in his head, and it would work. He could feel it. But it was going to take a serious team of computing firepower. It was going to take marketing and finance and all the rest of it. He wanted to do it, and he wanted to run it.

Choice B, then: Convince Rochelle to leave her home town, her family, and her job, every one of them precious to her, and move to San Francisco with him. That looked just about as difficult, in a whole different way. He didn't think Rochelle would grow that well in the city. Her roots here went too deep.

After thirty-five years of nowhere close, he'd finally found the woman he needed. Loving, strong, and loyal to the bone. The joke was on him, though, because those loyalties cut both ways.

Or a third choice. Go back without her, which was the only reasonable answer, and didn't feel like a choice at all, not anymore. Even though all along, he'd thought, *Hey, plenty of people make long-distance relationships work, at least for a while.*

My eggs are drying up by the day, she'd said. *I don't have time to mess around.*

He didn't think she'd go for it, not for any length of time, not without a plan for how it would end. And he knew he didn't want to. Hell, he hadn't wanted to leave for the weekend. He hadn't even wanted to leave her for tonight.

It was all too much to think about, so as usual, he set it aside, opened his computer, and got into his to-do list, which started with those calls. He'd do better after a full night's sleep.

But it would have been easier to sleep with her there.

FALLING INTO PLACE

Seven thirty on Monday evening, and Rochelle was sitting on the couch, watching a movie and, frankly, waiting for Travis to come over so she could fall asleep with her head on his shoulder, then go to bed with him holding her.

It wasn't about sex, not tonight. It was just about him being there. And he'd do it. She knew it.

Her phone buzzed, and she reached for it with a lazy hand, her mouth already curving in anticipation.

It wasn't him. It was Stacy.

"Ro?"

Rochelle couldn't help a sigh. She and her mom had taken Stacy to the doctor that morning, had gotten a referral to a psychiatrist and an emergency appointment for Wednesday, and then Rochelle had gone with Stacy to see her advisor. Stacy had been silent, white, and exhausted when they'd finished, and by the time Rochelle had driven Stacy back to her parents' and gone to work all afternoon, she hadn't been at her best herself.

She didn't want to talk to her sister tonight. But she'd said she'd be there for her, and that started right now.

"Hey." She tried to inject some energy into it. "How you doing?"

"Um . . ." Stacy's voice was trembling. "Did you see my text?"

"Uh . . . hang on." Rochelle scrolled, and froze.

Forwarded. *Hey know what got some stuff for you. Call me.*

She was back on the call so fast, she almost dropped the phone. "What the *hell*," she said, so angry she could barely speak.

"I wanted to . . ." Stacy said. "I wanted to call. I wanted to go. I was thinking, I could go out the back, take Mom's keys off the hook later, once they go to bed. And then I thought, I *can't*. I don't want to *do* this anymore. I don't want to do it to them, and I don't want to do it for . . . for me. And he's trying to put me back in the pot. Isn't he?"

"You bet he is," Rochelle managed to say. "You bet."

"But it's so *hard*," Stacy said. "It's so hard not to go, because I *want* them. I want them so bad. Can you help me? Please? I know I don't deserve it. But . . . please?"

"You bet I can. But hey, baby. Put Mom on the phone now, OK?"

"Are you going to tell her?"

"Yep." No point in lying. That was what this was all about. About telling the truth. "I'm going to tell her, and she's going to sit on the couch with you until I get there. She's going to be proud of you for calling me instead of calling him back, just like I am."

How could Shane *dare* to do that? Break up with her, then yank that chain some more, suck her back in just when Stacy was pulling herself out of this? He was jerking her around, and Rochelle knew—she *knew*—that he was doing it on purpose. She'd *kill* him.

"I have to tell you something else first," Stacy said. "You've been so good to me, and I . . . I haven't told you all of it."

"What?" *Oh, God. What now?*

"It's Lake," Stacy said. "It's . . . that I think things happen at Lake's."

The cold dread was rising through Rochelle's body so fast, it was like she'd jumped into a freezing river. "Explain."

"You remember that first night? When I was in the ER? And I told you I didn't remember?"

"Of course I remember. You're saying you remember, too."

"I remembered a . . . a while ago," Stacy said. "I wanted to tell you, but I couldn't. I couldn't tell you without telling you about . . . about me," she continued miserably. "About the pills, and Shane, and . . . everything. I couldn't tell you."

"Stacy. I don't care about that. You're telling me now. Good for you. So tell me everything. Right now. You're telling me that party was at Lake's."

Your place, Stacy had told her on the phone that night.

Is my sister here? she'd asked Dave Harris, and he'd asked, *Which one?* With that same look on his face he'd used to have when he'd seen her after some "hunting trip" when Lake had come home wasted.

And Lake hadn't been there. Where had he been?

"I only went that one time," Stacy said. "But they were going into the back room. And there were . . . there were lots of drugs, Ro. *Lots* of drugs. Pills, like the ones I took that night. Party pills. And everybody was really . . . pumped. I think . . . I think he's dealing. Lake. I think he is. I think all those guys are . . . whatever it is, they're all doing it. All his friends, you know? Dave Harris, and Danny Boyle, and all of them. And . . ." Her voice shook. "Miles. He was there, too. I think something's going on. I saw pill bottles, and I saw . . ." It was a whisper now. "Prescriptions. Slips."

It all slotted into place in Rochelle's head, like a roulette ball falling into the one and only spot it would land. The Ziploc bag on Stacy's night table. The pills, and Shane being with Lake the other night, and Lake's friends in his living room, too late on a Sunday night during harvest. The card table, the Canadian whisky. And the snack-sized Ziploc bags.

But her sister. Her little sister. How *could* he? How could Lake have hurt her sister?

"How many times did you see it?" she asked Stacy.

"Only then," Stacy said. "Only that night. After that . . . Shane didn't take me there again, and I wouldn't have wanted to go anyway. Because I was scared. I don't remember. I really don't," she burst out. "But I know I was scared. Somebody was saying something. A girl. I remember that, and being scared, but I don't remember what she was saying."

"OK." Rochelle took a breath. "OK. Now, listen. Thanks for telling me. You did good, OK? You called me, and you told me. You did so good. Now put Mom on, all right? And I'll be there later."

When she'd hung up, she clicked the remote and turned off her movie, then sat still and thought it through until she had to move. She stood up, paced the room with her arms wrapped around herself, and thought some more. She thought about everything Stacy had said. About a girl everybody had been questioned about, a girl Miles and Danny and Dave had talked to out at Macho Taco, a girl they'd danced with at the Back Alley. About the other night at Lake's. What she'd seen, and what she'd felt.

She thought about Miles Kimberling, about the sweet little boy she'd used to babysit. About how he'd followed the older boys around, and how he'd been following Lake ever since. About his car falling off the jack, onto a level concrete driveway.

There was something she had to do. She had to take care of this. She was sure she was right. But just in case she was wrong . . . she'd be prepared for that, too.

◆　◆　◆

She was stopped by a red light at the highway. A semi blew by, rocking her car in the wake of its passage. It was a black night, the moon behind clouds, the air autumn-chilly and the wind picking up. Bleak. Spooky, even. The thought that had nagged at her popped up again. She sighed, backed, pulled over, and called Travis.

She wasn't used to asking for help, but that wasn't what she was doing, exactly. Just another precaution.

Voice mail, but maybe that was better.

She left a quick message and hung up, the light turned green, and she pulled out and turned left onto the highway toward Union City.

Twenty minutes to think it through, to make sure she'd been right. Twenty minutes to rehearse it.

And when the phone rang, she ignored it. She'd call back later, once she was done.

Lake's rig was out in front of the shop instead of behind it tonight, for some reason, and lights were glowing through the front windows. Of course he'd be home, eight o'clock on Monday night. She got out of the car before she could change her mind, climbed up the splintery stairs to the porch, pulled back the screen door with the hole through the bottom . . . and didn't have to knock. Because the porch light had come on, and the door was already opening, Lake alerted by the sound of her car out here in the quiet of the country.

He stood in the doorway, stared at her hard and cold, and said, "Go away."

Not the best start. Well, she didn't have a burning desire to see the filthy inside of her former home anyway. It was freezing out here, but who cared? She wasn't staying long.

"Did you know Stacy almost died the other night?" she asked him.

"What?" Something flickered across his face. Still good-looking, but the weakness in it so apparent to her now.

"She was in intensive care for hours. Seems she took a whole bunch of drugs. Just like she did that other night, the night she was out here. You almost killed my sister, Lake. Twice. And you're in so much trouble."

"You need to leave," he said. "Right now. This is none of your business, and you need to stay out of it." He shifted his weight, moved forward, forcing her back a step, and pulled the door shut behind him. "You can't come to my house and tell me what to do. I told you the other night, remember? You don't live here anymore, and I'm not that pussy you used to kick out of the house when I got drunk. You're the one who'll be in trouble if you don't get out of here."

Maybe I've changed, he'd said that night on the phone. *You might be surprised.*

People didn't change, though. Lake was the man he'd always been. Good-natured most of the time, unless he was drunk. Good at making friends, and keeping them, too, such as they were. Loyal in his fashion, at least to his buddies. And lazy right down to his bones. Sure that there should have been a way for him to end up on top, and that other people had been given an easier path.

And no kind of a criminal mastermind.

"I'm not going to leave," she said. "I know what's going on. I know you've gotten in way over your head, too. You're going to end up holding the bag, Lake. You need to get out of it now, and tell the cops what you know."

He started to laugh. Dismissing her, like he'd always used to do, once things had gone bad between them. "You got a whole theory going here? That powerful brain of yours tell you so?"

She held her temper, and she held her ground. "I know what they're doing. I know that your friends are the ones getting the pills. Getting prescriptions filled, or whatever it is." She didn't know, actually. She was guessing, but she was pretty sure she was right. "I think the . . . the distribution happens here, because you're single, and you don't have neighbors. I think you've been letting somebody use your shop to package the pills, and I'll bet you're getting rid of the bottles in the burn barrel. Somebody's selling those packages, but that somebody isn't you. All you're getting is a cut."

"How do you know?" He looked . . . offended, now. Like he'd used to look when she'd made a suggestion about how he might get ahead. Like she was insulting his competence. At what? At crime?

She went on and insulted it some more. "Because if it *was* you," she said, "if you'd been getting the big bucks? You'd have bought a new rig already, or a boat, or both, even if you were trying to hide it, parking it behind the shop. And you haven't. You're probably saving up until you can pay cash, because you wouldn't be able to get a loan." She could see from the startled expression on his face that she was right, so she pressed on. "You've been suckered into all of it, and you have to get out. The cops are going to know everything soon. They're not stupid. Even if you don't care about yourself, what's that going to do to your folks?"

Lake's expression changed again. Alert. Alarmed, maybe. "Yeah," she told him. "I know all about it. I think that's why that girl died, too. I think she was pregnant, and she knew what was going on, because she slept with too many guys, and guys talk to women they sleep with. They brag to them, and I'll bet all your buddies bragged to her. I'm guessing she came out here and said she was going to talk about what she knew unless somebody paid her off, and she got killed for it. But you wouldn't have done that. You never hit me, even at the end."

She didn't tell him that Stacy had been the one to help her connect the dots, because it didn't feel like a good idea. Two things had happened on the same August weekend, though. Stacy had taken too many prescription drugs at Lake's house at a party with a bunch of his friends, and a girl had been killed. A girl who'd dated a bunch of Lake's friends, had walked out of her job on that last day knowing she was pregnant, and saying, "That bastard is going to get me out of this. He can't afford not to."

Somebody was saying something. A girl. And I was scared. It didn't take a huge leap to figure out that it might have been the same girl.

"You need to leave," Lake said, "or I'll hit you right now. And I won't stop." He took a short step forward, and she still didn't move back.

"All your buddies have been questioned about her, haven't they?" she asked him. "That's no secret. And you know who did it. You *have* to know. He killed a pregnant woman and dumped her body, and that isn't you, Lake. It isn't *you*. You can't be part of that. Miles Kimberling, too. You went to *school* with Miles. He followed you around like a puppy his whole life. Now he's dead, just like that girl's dead. Why?"

"Because his car fell off the jack."

"Really? You really think that? I don't. I think somebody shoved his car off that jack while he was working on it. I think it was the same person who killed that girl and put her in Cal Jackson's ditch, and I know that person wasn't you. At first I couldn't figure out who it was. I thought it could be Dave, but he'd know a lentil field when he saw one, as well as you would. And then I realized that there was one person at that party who probably wouldn't know that. One person who wasn't there when I showed up, but who was there earlier. One person who I bet has been in this thing all along. I think he's dragged you into this, and he's going to drag you right down with him unless you do something about it."

"You need to shut *up*. You need to keep out of it. I'm warning you."

The skin was prickling at the back of her neck, the same cold menace she'd felt out here before. Turned on like a faucet. Could she have been wrong? Not just wrong. *Horribly* wrong.

"I won't keep out of it," she said, working hard to keep her voice from trembling, "because I *know* this isn't the man you are. When I had that miscarriage—" Her throat wanted to close at that, but she forced herself to keep going. "You cried. And you loved Stacy," she went on in a hurry. Why had she even said that? Maybe because she wanted to remember Lake differently from this. To remember the man she'd fallen in love with, and not the man who was looking at her with that . . . that glazed expression, like he was checking out, like he wasn't even hearing her. "You used to give her piggyback rides," she said desperately. "I'll bet you told him not to bring her back to your house, because you didn't want her mixed up with this, but she's mixed up anyway. She's so mixed up, Lake. So messed up. You're not a bad person, I know you're not, but you're ruining all these lives. I know it sounded like parties, and recreation, and nobody gets hurt, but Stacy almost died, and that other girl *did*. And so did Miles."

It wasn't working. Why wasn't it working? "I know you didn't expect all this," she said, not willing to believe it, not able to accept that she'd read him so wrong. "This can't have been what you signed up for. You thought it'd be easy money, and it'd be exciting, and it's turned so bad. If you go to Jim Lawson and tell him what you know, it'll help you, and it'll end all this. Otherwise, you're going to go to prison, and you have to know it. Accessory to murder, and all the rest of it. But if you give them up? The person who got you into this, and whoever's writing the prescriptions, or however it's happening? If you say what you know? You can make it easier on yourself, and your friends, too, and I know that matters to you. You can keep it from getting any worse."

The voice came from behind her, out of the darkness. "No. He can't. And neither can you."

THE BOGEYMAN

Rochelle whirled, and her right hand went to the soft leather bag that hung over her shoulder. She was groping, but he was already up the stairs.

Shane. Who wouldn't have recognized a lentil field if it had bitten him in the butt. The cold coming off him in waves.

Not a bad boy. A bad man.

He'd been in the house, and he'd come around the back. And he'd heard.

He grabbed her wrist right out of the bag and pulled her back by it, then yanked it up, twisting it behind her back until she cried out. He reached inside her purse himself and felt around. And she saw the smile.

"Oh, yeah," he said, pulling out her .38. "Too easy."

"*No.*" It was Lake. He was launching himself, and Rochelle was gasping, pain blooming in her shoulder, as Shane jerked her around by her wrist.

It seemed like she saw it even before she heard the explosion. The dark spot appearing on Lake's gray T-shirt, and then the barking report of the revolver. Her ears were ringing, and Lake was swaying, then sinking to his knees. Shane was kicking him on the shoulder, shoving him to one side even as he spun Rochelle around and shoved the gun into her ribs, under the arm he was still pulling back.

"Didn't you hear your hubby?" he said. "He told you to leave. Told you about five times. You're divorced, you're nothing but trouble, and he still wanted to protect you from the bogeyman at the bottom of the stairs. He even took a bullet for you. That's what I call sweet."

"Go to hell," Rochelle gasped. "I'm going to kill you."

"Oh, no. I'm going to kill *you*. Or, correction. You're going to kill yourself. Came out to confront hubby, because he's been supplying your sweet, stupid little sister with all that stuff she loves." He made a tsk-tsk noise. "Things got heated, you being so protective and all, and you shot him. Oh, dear. What have you done? Murder One? Orange *so* isn't your color. Only one way out."

Rochelle stared wildly at Lake. Sprawled on his side, a horrible sucking, gurgling noise coming from his chest, red blood bubbling from his mouth. *Alive.*

"Whoops," Shane said. "You're a lousy shot, sweetheart." He raised the gun again, and Rochelle flung herself sideways, heedless of the pain from her shoulder, knocking herself into him, kicking back with one heel at his shin.

He fired, but the shot went wild, straight through the house, and she was still kicking. But he was yanking harder at her arm, and now, the gun was at her temple. The pain in her shoulder was making her gasp again, and the ringing in her ears was so loud.

"*Shit,*" Shane said as light washed over them. Headlights, appearing then disappearing. Somebody coming up the road.

Travis, Rochelle thought in despair. *No.*

Shane had her down the stairs, the muzzle against her breast again, and she stumbled, crying out against the pain in her arm. Shane pushed her around her car to the passenger side, pulled the door open, and thrust her inside.

"Into the car." He was getting in right beside her, shoving her across the gearshift. "Start it up. Turn around. Head to the highway." She hesitated, and he said, "Now. Or I'll blow your head off right here."

The gun was at her head again, digging into her temple, and she turned the key with fingers that trembled with rage. At herself. At him.

The truck was slowing now, preparing to turn into the driveway, and Rochelle backed up and swung the car around. If Travis got here while she was sitting with Shane? Shane would shoot him. She knew it.

She lurched forward, her tires spinning for a moment before they bit, and then she was down the driveway just as Travis turned into it, out, and down the road.

She caught one brief glimpse of Travis turning to look at her as they went past, saw the horror of recognition in his face, and then she was down the gravel road and leaving him behind.

Don't follow me, she prayed, even though she knew it was hopeless. There was no way Travis wouldn't follow her. That would be like asking the sun not to rise.

Shane wasn't going to kill him, though, not if she could help it. She might have a gun on her, but she was behind the wheel of a three-thousand-pound guided missile, and she was going to use it.

The seat belt warning was chiming away, and Shane said, "Put on your seat belt. Safety first."

He lowered the gun until it was pressed into her ribs, just beneath her arm, and she reached up with her left hand, pulled her seat belt across her body, and fastened it, because there was no choice.

Which made her plan harder, but not impossible. This wasn't the spot. The slope was too gentle, their speed too slow. *Head to the highway,* he'd said. Highway speed, a good enough downgrade? She'd find a way. She might be going tonight, but she wasn't going alone. And if she could manage it, she was going to survive, too. All Shane had to do was miss.

She put her foot down and got the car taking the curves of the side road as fast as she dared. She'd get him used to it, put some distance between herself and Travis. Maybe they could get to the highway before he caught up, and he'd choose the wrong direction. Maybe.

She caught the flash of lights in the rearview mirror and forced herself not to move, not even her eyes. But Shane must have seen it, too, because he was swiveling around, the muzzle still pressing painfully into her side.

"Well, look at that," he said, twisting the rearview mirror around so only he could see it. "Do I dare to hope that's the boyfriend? You've got just all kinds of heroes willing to take one in the heart for you, don't you, sweetheart? That's going to save me a whole lot of trouble." He kept the gun tight against her ribs as he bent down for the purse that had fallen from her arm as she'd scrambled across the seats. "Cell phone," he muttered. "My, you're organized. Got a pocket for everything."

"Eat shit and die," she said.

"And, again," he said, "that would be you. Let's see now. Last call made? Ah, yes. Travis. How convenient."

The ringing came in over the car's speakers, and as soon as it stopped, she shouted, "Travis! Hang up!"

"Good idea," Shane said. "If you want her to die right now."

"You'll die, too," she said, even as Travis said, "No." Low and calm.

"Ah, but will I?" Shane asked. Talking to both of them. "Turn left," he told her, as conversational as if they'd been out for a Sunday drive, because they were approaching the highway. "So often, car accidents are survivable, aren't they?"

That's it, she realized as she looked for traffic, saw nothing, and swung out across the lane. *That's how I do it, if it comes to that.* Air bags and seat belts were one thing, but going under a semi? There was no air bag in the world that could protect you against that.

Shane was talking again, though, and she focused. "So, Rochelle's New Boyfriend," he said. "Travis what?"

"You don't need to know my name," Travis said. "Just think of me as the guy who's going to kill you."

Shane sighed. "You don't listen too well, do you? I noticed that with Lake the other night. But I bet you'll listen to me better. I'm more persuasive, don't you think? Lake had such a good time being the leader of Dangerous Men. That's what he called himself. 'The boss.' Like a title. Isn't that about the stupidest thing you ever heard? He never even guessed that he was only there to take the fall for me. And now he has. Accessory to murder? Don't make me laugh. He never even wanted to know. Never wanted to ask, even after I did him that great big favor."

"What favor would that be?" Travis asked.

"Little Heather thought he should pay up, since he was the boss and all. Poor ol' Lake didn't know what to do. He'd never even nailed her himself, and here he was going to be in so much trouble. So I took care of it. I let him take his adorable little passed-out sister on home for me, too, get her out of the way, and I'll bet he didn't take advantage of that either. Pussy."

"Yeah," Travis said, while Rochelle forced her hands, shaking with rage, to stay on the wheel. "A conscience can be a real liability, I hear."

"Don't I know it," Shane said. "And after I took care of the Heather situation for him, did he even ask me about it? No. Probably told himself she went to live on a farm. Well, she kind of did, didn't she?" He shook his head. "Too dumb for the job, that's what it amounts to. Put that on the certificate. 'Cause of Death: Stupidity.' Not to mention that he didn't bother to tell me that Stacy was his ex-wife's sister until halfway through that party. Don't you think that was a serious omission? He deserved to die just for that."

"Pretty stupid of you to keep seeing her after that," Rochelle said. "Maybe you aren't quite as smart as you think you are."

She got a dig in the ribs with the gun for that. "Didn't see her that much, though, did I? Kept her begging for it, did you notice? That's always fun. Besides—risk is what lets you know you're alive. And a cute little straight girl going over to the Dark Side? She was always so . . . *shocked.*" He laughed, and Rochelle wished there'd been a semi coming right now.

They were at the top of the grade into Union City, the lights spread out below her, and she took the first curve and thought, *Thelma and Louise style, if I have to.*

"What do you want?" Travis asked.

"Well, let's see," Shane said. "Right now, I want to kill your girl-friend. And then I want to kill you. How's that? Oh, and by the way? I want you not to call the cops. That's what we'll call a nonnegotiable demand."

SEIZE THE MOMENT

Too bad he already had.

He'd walked in from the showers tonight, opened his locker, pulled out his stuff, and finally noticed the voice mail from Rochelle. He'd missed her by ten minutes.

Thirty seconds later, he was flying out of the gym, pounding through the parking lot to his truck, and throwing himself inside. Pressing the redial number and putting her on speaker even as he peeled out of the lot. No answer, and he'd hit the highway ten miles over the limit already and putting his foot down.

"Hey," the message had said. "I'm going out to Lake's. I found out that he's got something to do with those pills Stacy's been taking, and I need to talk to him about it. And I know you'd say to wait and go with you, or not to go at all. He won't talk if somebody else is there, though, and I need him to talk, and to listen to me. He wasn't a great husband, but he *was* my husband, and we had some . . ." A breath out. "Some better times. I owe him this much, and he's not going to hurt me. I'm letting you know, though. Points for that."

When he'd gotten to Lake's house at last, had seen her car reversing and turning, he'd been weak with relief. She'd been there, she'd talked to Lake, she'd left. He was going to have . . . words with her, though. He was going to have *serious* words.

And then he'd gotten closer. He'd seen that she wasn't alone. And when he'd been level with her . . . he'd seen the gun to her head, and he'd seen who'd been holding it.

He'd called 911, and he'd even remembered the name. Jim Lawson. Somebody he'd met. Somebody he could trust to handle this right.

He hoped.

Since then, he'd been concentrating on keeping up, because Rochelle was *flying*. On seeing where they went so he could tell Jim. He'd put Jim on hold so he could answer, and right now, he was wishing desperately that he could have patched Jim into the call.

"So what will you do," he said now, "if I call the cops? Purely as a matter of interest." He still slowed down under pressure, but the calm had never come harder.

"What will I do?" The voice came, happy and buzzed, over the phone lying on the seat beside him, and if Travis could have, he'd have reached right through that phone and strangled him. Just like that. "Let me make myself very, very clear. If I see a single blue light flash? If I hear a siren? If I get worried one single bit? I'll shoot her right here. You'd better pray I don't run across an ambulance."

"Well," Travis said, "*you* might think it's a great idea to shoot somebody who's driving sixty miles an hour. Can't say I would."

"Thanks for the tip," he heard. "I've actually got a plan for that, but you can watch and see. As for shooting her? I was thinking in the heart, but you know—she's got such spectacular tits, I kinda hate to ruin them. Her head doesn't excite me too much. Guess I'll do it there. And then I'll wait for you and shoot you. How does that sound?"

Travis's hands had tightened on the steering wheel, and now, he loosened them deliberately. Shane was trying to goad him. Time to goad right back, get him off balance. Give Rochelle a chance.

"You've forgotten," he said. "You're doing that because a siren's headed your way. And how's your, what? Murder-suicide? How's it going to look then? What was that Rochelle said? Not quite as smart as you think you are, are you?"

He needed to get off the phone so he could call Jim back, and he needed to do it now.

"Like a tragic love triangle, that's what," Shane said. "It's a sad moment for a man when he finds out his girlfriend's still banging her ex, isn't it? Could even drive him to murder. Not to mention that I will have won. Can't put a price on that."

Travis considered pointing out that it would be pretty hard to do the "tragic love triangle" deal if the cops showed up and found you standing next to two dead bodies, but he didn't. *He's batshit crazy,* he thought. *He's not going to listen.* So instead, he said, "What? You're breaking up. I can't hear you." And then he picked up his phone and hit the button to call Lawson back.

◆　◆　◆

Rochelle had reached the bottom of the grade. She hadn't driven off the road, and she hadn't driven under a semi. Blame her optimistic nature, or a survival instinct bred into her by generations of dirt-poor farm workers doing what they had to do to make it through to tomorrow. Her left hand had come down under cover of darkness as Shane talked to Travis, had searched, and had closed around something small, something she'd forgotten she even had. Something she needed.

"Well, that's sad," Shane said when the phone went dead. "I was kinda enjoying Boyfriend. Take a right. We'll take a romantic drive along the river."

"My car's going to run out of gas pretty soon," she said. "Sadly for you, I only started with a quarter tank."

"Thanks for telling me, sweetheart. You know what you haven't asked me yet?"

"No, what's that? Seems like you've told me everything. Boy, do you love to talk. Boring as hell, too."

"Tough girl, aren't you? Makes me sadder than ever that I never got you and Stacy together."

"Dream on."

"And now I never will," he went on as if she hadn't spoken. "Life's just full of tragedy. Which brings me to my point. Let's see. Lake's dead by now, and you and Boyfriend are going to be dead real soon, too. Almost all my liabilities. The cops can put everything on Lake, wrap it all up in a bow, and off I go to start my next adventure, because I was barely a bystander."

"Maybe I didn't ask you because I don't care. What do you want me to do, admire your criminal mind?"

"Well, it'd be nice. Not many guys could pull off running a whole enterprise and not having anyone know they're doing it. I don't even have to worry about distribution."

"Do tell. So I can admire and all."

He smiled. "This is like in the movies, huh? Where the killer confesses everything, and then he's captured? You wearing a wire, sweetheart? How well does it work underwater?"

She shrugged. "Suit yourself." *You're not going to be captured,* she promised him with everything she had. *You're going to be dead.*

There was still traffic on the road, this close to the city. The river was a dark expanse to their right, here below the dam. To the other side was nothing.

"Well, I'll tell you," Shane said. "Just because we're passing the time and all until I seize my moment."

No, she thought, *because you can't stand that I said I didn't care and didn't want to know.*

He was still talking. Of course he was. "*Carpe diem,* that's what they say. Seize the day. And that's me. Your hubby between me and all those weakest links, and a bartender in Spokane taking care of the distribution a nice safe hundred miles from me. Big sports bar? Simplest thing in the world to hand over a bag of pills with somebody's drink and have them add a fifty-dollar tip. No biker gangs, no unreliable college students to manage. No muss, no fuss. Pretty much genius."

She didn't even bother to answer that. *Seize the moment.* Worked for her. She was swinging fast around the curves, Travis's lights hard on her tail.

"But that thing you haven't asked me," he said. "Why hasn't Stacy called me back yet? That wouldn't have something to do with you, would it? My last loose end, and here I'd been planning on tying it up tonight. Oh, well. Tomorrow's another day."

The chill was running down her arms, and she forced her voice into calm as she answered. "Stacy's not going to call you back."

"No? We'll see. Without you there? I think she will. Sounds like she got pretty distraught the other night. She loves me, you see, and she loves you. She just goes around loving everybody, doesn't she? You might have clued her in on how good an idea that is."

"Loving a piece of shit like you?" she said. "Yeah, I might have. Oh, wait. I did."

"She might get so distraught," he went on, "that she'd drive into a tree on the way home from my place. Or just go to sleep and never wake up. Pills and alcohol. Dangerous combination, especially when you don't know what you're taking, because somebody's dropped them in your drink and sent you on home with a Baggie full of more. Stacy's got a real bad habit. Bad habits can kill you, you know. Make a note."

"She doesn't know anything," Rochelle managed to say. She'd been berating herself for going to Lake's, for endangering not just herself but Travis, too. But if she hadn't done that . . . if this didn't work . . . *Oh, no. Not Stacy.*

"She knows me," Shane said. "And nobody's allowed to know me. I'm just a guy hanging around sometimes. No," he sighed. "I'm afraid I'd already decided that Stacy has to go. She was a loose end, and now you are, too. You've slowed me down, but it doesn't really matter, does it? Tonight, tomorrow. Same difference. Turn in here."

A boat launch.

"Stop at the top of the ramp," Shane said. He was lifting the gun from her side now, moving it up. To her head.

How well does it work underwater? He was going to shoot her, then shove the car into the river.

Like hell he was. Her revolver needed a long, hard pull, and she was betting he didn't know it. He'd be a semiautomatic guy all the way. Always taking the easy route.

She didn't stop. Instead, she gunned the engine, then shifted her foot fast and braked with all her might. And the moment she did it, her hand was swinging around, her finger pressing down on the tiny can of pepper spray she'd bought almost a year ago, when another predator was threatening women in Paradise. Had bought, and then had nearly forgotten.

Nearly forgotten, but not quite. She emptied the entire can into Shane's face.

A whole lot of things happened at once, and they were all bad. Her face was on fire, her eyes had closed, and she couldn't breathe. The car was lurching forward, then they were flying, and there was a noise like a cannon blast. The pain—*more* pain—bloomed in her head, spiky, red, and burning hot.

She couldn't hear. She couldn't see. And her head was on fire. The next instant, the car slammed down like it was hitting concrete, jolting her against her seat belt even as she screamed with the pain. Screamed, but she couldn't hear it, because she was deaf. And she was dying.

ICE COLD

Travis was right behind them, turning off into the boat-launch area. His heart was racing, his breath coming hard and fast, and his mind considering scenarios, then rejecting them.

The cops weren't here. They were back there somewhere, but they weren't here.

That was when he heard the shot. *Oh, God. Oh, no.* And Rochelle's car, sailing into the river and smashing down hard. Floating. For now.

He didn't think. He was out of the truck, kicking off his running shoes, throwing himself into the water, and swimming hard for the car.

She's not dead, he told himself desperately. *She can't be dead. Not Rochelle.*

Five or six yards, that was all. The water was bitterly cold, numbing him, taking his breath. But he was at the driver's window and grabbing the door handle.

Locked.

The moon came out from behind the clouds, and he saw it. A dark spiderweb on the glass. *The shot.* He punched at the window, kernels of safety glass were falling away, and he could see.

Rochelle, right there. Wheezing. Gasping. Darkness covering her face. Blood. And beyond her, more gasping and coughing, but he barely noticed it.

He grabbed her shoulder, and she turned that terrible face toward him.

"Rochelle," he shouted. "Punch your seat belt. Punch it."

He said it again, but she still wasn't doing anything. She couldn't hear, he realized. The gunshot. And she couldn't see. The blood.

He pulled himself farther into the car, heaving his entire body over her. Something burned his throat, tried to suck his breath, stung his eyes. He fought the sensation, reached for her side, and fumbled. At last, he felt the button, and he was stabbing at it, then pulling the seat belt back.

The car was sinking lower. Water was pouring in the side window now, tilting the car toward him. His head went under, but the freezing water washed his eyes and took the sting away. He came up again and saw the angle. His weight, the weight of the water, all of it threatening to tip the car.

Get her out. He shoved himself back out of the window, pulling her with him. One hand on the window frame to hold him there, the other one reaching in, around her side, yanking hard.

"Baby." His teeth were chattering, his entire body shivering. "Move toward me. Come on. Move."

She couldn't hear him, he knew, but she was moving toward him anyway, instinctively, maybe, and he was pulling her.

She wasn't coming, though. She was stuck.

The car tilted again, the moonlight shone more strongly, and he saw it. Shane, grabbing Rochelle's ankle, pulling her down.

Travis forgot about holding on to the side of the car. He got both hands under Rochelle's arms and his stockinged feet against the car door, heaved with everything he had, and she came loose like a cork from a bottle.

Shane was still grabbing, still flailing, and the car was even lower now, the water rushing in. But Travis didn't care about the car. He was treading water with his legs and one arm, hanging on to Rochelle with the other hand, being dragged downstream with the current, and it was cold. So cold.

She went under, came up choking. She was stunned, still. Disoriented. She wasn't going to make it.

I'm going to die trying, she'd said. And so was he. Right now, if he had to. Do it, or die trying. He grabbed her with his left arm across her chest, hauled her in tight against him, and focused on the shore.

Five or six yards. Piece of cake.

His entire body was shaking with cold now, but he struck out in a diagonal path all the same. Farther to swim, but so much easier than straight across the current, and his strength was ebbing too fast.

There were lights flashing on shore. Red and blue. Headlights illuminating the water far to the left of him, where the car was. He couldn't hear anything above the rush of the river, and his progress was so slow. Too slow, and getting slower. He was shutting down.

No. Move. Swim.

He'd trained for the Olympics once. He hadn't made it. He'd trained his heart out and swum his guts out, and he hadn't made it.

Swim.

Rochelle was gasping, choking out a word. "What . . . what . . ."

Hold still, he thought. *I need to swim.* He forced his legs to keep moving.

Die trying.

The shore was closer now, the lights swinging around, shining on the water next to him. Shouts, and something dark hitting the water. A person, and then another.

Two more strokes. Three. Four. His foot hit something, but it took a moment for the message to get through his foggy brain.

Touch bottom. Stand up.

He got his feet under him, stood, and fell over, somehow managing to keep hold of Rochelle. A figure materialized ahead of him, holding out a strap.

"Hang on," a male voice said.

Travis shook his head, and with the last of his strength, shoved Rochelle at the rescuer. And then he fell again.

◆　◆　◆

He was shaking worse than ever. He tried to move his arms, and he couldn't, and the panic filled him.

Drowning. He was drowning.

"Stay still," a voice above him said. "Hold still."

He opened his eyes. His entire body was jerking, shuddering, and he was still trying to move his arms, and he still couldn't.

Ambulance, he realized fuzzily. His arms and legs were fastened down, he was dry, and there was warmth on his stomach, his groin, his armpits. And he was shaking so hard.

His mind wanted to skitter down into dark panic. *Why?* And then the coldest thing yet.

Rochelle.

He'd dropped her. He'd said he'd die trying, or he'd thought it. Something. And he'd dropped her.

"R-Rochelle," he said.

Just like that, she was there. Her hand on his chest, her face in his vision. Her hair plastered to her, her body wrapped in blankets like that other time, that time in his truck. Something wrong with her head, though. The whole top of it covered with white. *Bandage.*

"Wha . . . what . . .?" he asked. He couldn't get it out. He couldn't say it.

She seemed to understand him, though. "I pepper-sprayed . . . the bastard," she said, although her voice wasn't right, either. Not at all.

"And he . . . shot me. Luckily . . . he's a crappy shot. Just gave me a new part."

Where was Shane? Travis needed to get *out*. He was trapped. What if Shane came back?

"Hold still," the paramedic said. "You're losing heat. Hold still."

Travis tried to explain that he needed to not be trapped. In case. In case Shane came back.

Rochelle was saying something else now. "Let me," she told the paramedic beside her. "Please. Let me warm him up."

The straps holding Travis down were coming loose at last, and he was trying to get up, but Rochelle put a hand on his chest and said, "Travis. Baby. Lie down. Wait for me."

Her voice was trembling, and she needed him to wait, so he did. She stood up and dropped her own blankets.

She was naked. He wanted to tell her not to do that, but he couldn't get the words out. She pulled his blankets back and straddled him, and he wanted to tell her not to do that, either, not in front of that guy. And then she lay down on top of him on the narrow stretcher, her head against his neck, her full breasts pressed into his chest. The blankets were coming over them, and her arms were wrapped around him, and she was talking.

"Stay with me," she said. "Let me warm you up. Stay with me."

She was asking, so he tried, and she lay over him and held him. He was still shaking hard, but she was holding on anyway.

A minute later, or forever, and she was talking again, so he tried to listen.

"Know what I used to think?" she asked him.

He didn't answer, because he couldn't, but she didn't wait anyway. "I used to think, I'm holding out for a full-grown man. I'm holding out for a hero, and I just might be holding out forever. But you know what happened?"

"Wh-what?" he managed to say.

"My hero came along." Her mouth was at his neck, her breath warming him there, and he felt the vibration of her voice all the way from her chest into his own, like her body and his were the same. "I held out, and there he came, riding into my life like it was meant to be. He came along, and he saved me. He saved me in all kinds of ways."

"G-good," he said, and then he said it again. "Good."

"And he's you," she said, and she was crying. "Travis . . . he's you."

◆　◆　◆

Gradually, his shakes subsided to trembles, and his mind got clearer, like coming out of a dream. Or a nightmare. Rochelle didn't move, though, and he didn't want her to. He had his arms around her, too, now. It was everything he could do just to lift them, but he lifted them anyway.

"That's better," she said when he'd done it. "It's always better when you hold me."

"Yeah." His brain was still fuzzy, and his entire body was so beat, it was like he'd been hit with a bag of rocks.

"I need to tell the cops about Lake," she said, and that took him a long couple of seconds to process. "He wasn't dead. I need to tell them. He tried to save me, and Shane shot him."

"I told them . . . it was . . . his house. I think . . . they went." He hoped she understood, because it was too much to explain.

"Oh." She sighed. "Good."

If Lake had tried to save Rochelle, that was good, but Lake was the one who'd put her in danger in the first place. Travis remembered that much.

"You shouldn't have gone," he said.

"If I hadn't, Shane would have killed Stacy. He was going to make her OD again. Worse."

He didn't have an answer for that, and he was too tired anyway, so he lay there and didn't say anything.

The ambulance was slowing now. Turning, then turning again. A hospital, surely. And Rochelle was talking some more.

"I knew I'd kill Shane," she said. "But I knew you'd save me, too. I'm not sure if I killed him, but you sure enough saved me. Although I saved you, too."

"Huh?" He didn't remember that. Should he?

"I know you're going to make a crack sometime here about my boobs being life preservers," she said. "I'm just saving you . . ."

Her voice broke, and he tightened his arms around her. Holding her tight. Holding her close.

She took a breath and finished. Tough right up to the end. Strong and loving, fierce and tender. His perfect match. His perfect woman. "I'm just saving you the trouble."

THAT PERSON

Thanksgiving had come and gone, and Travis was in his truck on a Saturday morning in early December, driving to Rochelle's house once again. Driving carefully, just like that first day with his hydrangea, trying not to tip his cargo over in the bed of the truck.

It wasn't hot today, of course. There was that. It had been hot in Brawley, though, when he'd taken Rochelle to his mother's ten days ago for a second Thanksgiving dinner. After they'd had their first at her parents', because the near miss had been too close for her folks, and they'd needed Rochelle with them.

Two daughters nearly lost in the space of a few days . . . it had taxed even their stoicism. Both daughters had been restored, though, thanks to Rochelle. Who never gave in, and never gave up.

What did you do when you found a woman like that? You held on to her, that was what. You held on to her, and you didn't let her go.

Farmers hold on, he'd told her back in that elevator. He wasn't a farmer, but he'd known one. He'd learned how to hold on from the best. And anytime he needed a reminder, Rochelle's dad would be there to give it to him.

He pulled up on the gravel outside her house and hopped down. Snow tonight, they'd said, and it felt like it. But then, it seemed like every momentous event in his and Rochelle's life had had something to do with water, so that was fair enough.

His heart was going like a runaway train by the time he headed up her walk. Dell was outside, fastening Charlie's red leash to his collar, wrapped in a voluminous, extravagantly hooded wool coat. No puffy jackets for Dell.

"Well, good morning, sunshine," she said. "What's that you've got in your truck? Kinda out of season, aren't you?"

"You could call it a statement," he said.

"Hmm." Her eyes shone bright under the hood. "Can't wait to hear. But I'm guessing I might have to wait to do that."

"You'd be guessing right."

He was up on the porch now, ringing the doorbell. Stacy answered it. She'd been back with Rochelle for a few weeks now, and she was doing all right.

"Hi," he said. "How's it going?"

"Not too bad," she said. "Studying. Come on in."

She'd been coming by his office a couple times a week to work on her Stats homework, even though she didn't really need it. Her brain was just fine. It was only her confidence that needed a boost. That had been shaken to the core, there was no doubt, but there was nothing like making it through something tough and coming out stronger on the other side to restore your confidence. It might not be her best academic semester ever, but she was making it through.

It also didn't hurt to have the people gone who'd been sapping your confidence, and nothing was more gone than dead. Shane had died that night, before the rescuers could get to him, and Lake hadn't. Lake had survived to tell his story to the sheriff's office, and Rochelle had told the rest of it.

It was a fairly interesting story, too. It turned out that Shane's real partner hadn't been a doctor at all, but the office manager for a pain clinic up in Spokane. Across state lines, making tracing prescriptions harder, especially when you could divide them up among three doctors and forge all of their signatures. Especially when you were the one ordering the prescription pads.

Shane had been smart, all right, making sure the distribution of the pills happened far away, keeping the network under the radar. He just hadn't been as smart as he'd thought he was, with Heather's pregnancy being one prime example, not to mention having four men witnessing him leave Lake's house with her on the night she'd disappeared. Once the dam of silence had burst, it had all come out, and thanks to Jim Lawson, Travis and Rochelle had gotten an early rundown on the whole sad story.

And as for Lake—he was probably going to jail, no hope for that. On probation for a good long time at the very least, despite his cooperation, but Rochelle hadn't seemed to lose too much sleep over that.

"He was always going to go to jail," she'd told Travis's mom after dinner on that Saturday night after Thanksgiving, when the three of them, plus an uncharacteristically subdued Zora, had been taking a walk around town. "It was just a matter of time. Shortcuts always seem to turn into dead ends, don't they? But Lake never figured that out. Maybe he'll know now. I hope so."

"That's pretty forgiving," Zora had said.

"Hey," Rochelle had answered, squeezing Travis's hand, "forgiving is what it's all about. Somebody helped me realize recently that when you hang on to the bitter, it doesn't hurt anyone but yourself. I think Lake tried to protect Stacy, and he definitely tried to protect me. He was wrong, and he was weak, but he wasn't evil."

And if that wasn't forgiving, Travis didn't know what was.

Now, the woman herself was coming out of the kitchen, wiping her hands on a dish towel.

"Hi," she said. "I thought you weren't coming by until tonight."

"Surprise. I wanted you to go look at something with me."

She studied his face, seeming to read the suppressed emotion perfectly. "You've got that look. This isn't the car again, is it? Because I have a car."

He sighed. "It isn't the car."

She had a lousy car, that was what, a car she'd bought with the pitiful insurance money and too much of her savings. He'd tried to argue that he'd been in the whole thing with her, that it had been half his responsibility that she'd gone into the river, but she'd just looked at him, her eyes narrowed, and said, "Nice try, buster."

All of a sudden, he got the answer to that one, and almost laughed out loud. His next trip to San Francisco? He was tacking on another visit to the Imperial Valley, he was buying his mom something she'd actually like, and then he was driving back in Rochelle's car. Which was a black Mustang ragtop with a black leather interior. A down-home flashy muscle car for a down-home flashy girl. It was the car of his teenage dreams, and since she was pretty much the woman of them? That worked.

And her own car could go to Stacy. That worked, too.

"You're doing it again," she said. "What are you cooking up?"

He grinned. He couldn't help it. "Take a ride with me and see."

She hesitated a moment longer, then flipped the dish towel to Stacy, who was sitting at the dining table, pretending to work and actually listening hard, because she caught the towel in midair.

"Right," Rochelle said. "This a surprise?"

"You could say that."

"My birthday isn't for two weeks."

"Call it an early present. Or a present for me, maybe. Whichever."

"If it's black underwear," she said, "you've got no imagination."

Stacy snorted, and Travis grinned again. "Seems like I asked you sometime or other," he said, "if it didn't get old to be in charge all the time. If you'd ever thought about giving somebody else a chance."

He got a toss of the blonde head for that. Damn, but he loved this woman. That tough, and that tender? Yeah, he'd take her.

"I've given you a chance, buddy," she said. "And thanks for the slutty talk in front of my sister."

"No," Stacy said, not even pretending not to listen anymore. "You're my role model, Ro. Totally. I'm just soaking it up over here."

Travis waited, because he was a patient man, and after a minute, Rochelle sighed and said, "Now you've got me all curious. OK. You win."

"See, baby," he said, "that's why I love you. Because you tell me what I want to hear."

◆   ◆   ◆

Rochelle was still going for tough, maybe just because Travis loved it, but the attitude was getting pretty hard to maintain.

She rocked to a stop on the walkway. "That's a tree. In your truck."

"Yep," he said. "Good eyes. That's what it is, all right. It's a sour cherry tree, in fact. I hear they're messy, but you can make pie, so I thought, what the hell. Real's always worth it."

"Is that the surprise?"

"Well, yeah."

"Oh." She swallowed. "It's winter, though. Ground's frozen." He'd bought her a *tree?* She'd been wishing, she admitted to herself, for something else. She'd been wishing for something ridiculous.

"You can keep them in a container over the winter. I looked it up. And remember that in-charge thing I mentioned?" He pulled open the passenger door. "Hop in."

"We going to take it somewhere else?" she asked, climbing into the truck. "All right. I'm officially confused."

"Good." He was slamming her door, going to his side, and jumping in. That air of excitement right there, so strong she could nearly touch it. "It's not a long ride. And I've got this speech planned for while we take it, so shut up, please, and listen."

"Well, if you ask that nicely, how can I refuse?" She didn't want to admit how short of breath she was. How much her defenses were being stripped away, every last one of them.

Please, she thought. Begging it of her life, maybe. She took what she was given, and she made the best of it, but this . . . she needed it so badly. She needed *him. Please.*

He pulled to a stop at the end of the street, then made a careful right on Fourth. Not rocking the tree in the back. "Sometimes," he said, "you meet the exact right person at the exact wrong time. And there's no help for it, because you aren't in the right place. That's what happened to us, and I think it messed you up, and for that, I'm sorry."

He was heading north. Five blocks. Six. Toward his house, in the good part of town.

"Don't be," she said. "I'm not. If I hadn't met you then, and I hadn't walked off that dance floor with you? We wouldn't be here. Sometimes, mistakes are the only way to get where you need to go, and you were the best mistake I ever made."

"You're right," he said. "But then, you usually are."

He smiled at her, and she said, "You remember that," and did her best to maintain.

"And maybe once in your life," he went on after a moment, swinging his truck left onto the wide, stately, maple-lined quiet of D Street, "if you're luckier than you deserve, you meet exactly the right person at exactly the right time. Maybe you're even lucky enough, and smart enough, and ready enough, to recognize it. And that's what's happened to me. I've met exactly the right person, and I know it."

He pulled to a stop in front of the house Rochelle had told him once was her favorite, the blue one on the corner lot with the tower on one side and the huge garden surrounding it. The one that had belonged to the Stevensons forever and ever, where you could see Margie Stevenson working for hours every morning of the year. And never mind that Margie was over eighty, or that Harry couldn't help her anymore, not since his back surgery.

"I met that person," Travis continued. "And I met her at exactly the right time, too. For me."

He was climbing out, and she was climbing out, too. And he was lifting his tree out of the truck and walking toward the front gate. "And if you tell me it's exactly the right time for you and put me out of my misery," he said, "then I'll spend the rest of my life trying to show you that you weren't wrong."

"You . . ." She was still trying to process. "Where are we going?"

"I bought a house," he said. "I've never owned a house, and I don't know what I'm doing. I'm hoping you'll help me figure it out. Probably needs remodeling or something. I don't know much about that, either, but I do know this really competent woman."

He stopped, she opened the gate, he led the way through with his tree, and she followed him. Helpless.

"But . . . this house belongs to the Stevensons," she said.

"Ah," he said. "Ah. Well, seems they decided to sell. I managed to hear about it early, because I had this deal with a Realtor, you see. And the minute I took a look, I thought, this is it. So I did something impulsive. You could say that I jumped off that cliff with my eyes wide open. You could say that."

"You bought a house," she said again. "But . . . San Francisco."

"Yeah." He'd reached the huge weathered brick patio, now, and he set the tree down, opened the back door, and led the way into a sun porch. A sun porch that could be filled with flowering plants and wicker furniture. Maybe. Someday. "I thought about choices A, B, and C. Stay here with you and give up my dream. Try to get you to move with me. Or leave you and do a long-distance deal. And then I remembered."

"Remembered what?" She was barely managing to speak now.

"Choice D. To be continued. I thought, it's a brave new world out there. Who says I have to be in San Francisco? A house this big's bound to have room for a home office, don't you think?"

"Didn't you . . . didn't you even *look* at it?"

"Barely. Mostly, I looked at the outside. I figured you could help me get the inside right. Maybe. Hopefully. So anyway, I thought I could do some back and forth. And maybe I could convince you to go back and forth a little, too. You might like San Francisco. It's a nice place to visit, even if you don't want to live there. Although, you know . . ." His voice didn't sound entirely strong anymore. It was downright shaky, in fact. "Maybe you'd do some *real* back and forth with me at some point. I do have a condo. It's got three bedrooms. One of them could even be a nursery. If a person was taking maternity leave, for example."

"You're . . ." She put a hand to her head and tried to think. "I have to say . . . I have to tell you." It was the hardest thing she'd ever said, and she said it anyway. "I don't know if I can have a baby. I'm turning thirty-two, and I . . . I had a miscarriage before."

She tried not to let it matter, tried to hope it wouldn't matter to him, but she had to say it, because they had to tell the truth, no matter what.

He paused a moment, and she waited and tried to breathe. "Well," he said, "we'll give it our best shot, how's that? We'll try our best. Because, you know, trying's all we've got."

She never cried. Never. But the tears were there, and they weren't going to stay inside. "Travis," she said. "I just—I just—"

"I know this isn't a diamond ring," he said, starting to smile. Starting to light up, exactly the same way she was. Because this mattered to him exactly as much as it mattered to her. "I wasn't sure I could buy the right ring, though. I was pretty sure I could buy the right house."

He took her hand, and then . . . It was an old-fashioned thing, but he was an old-fashioned guy. He dropped to a knee, right there on the bricks, and she was crying for real now. Nothing held back, and no holds barred. She was his, and that was all there was to it.

"So, Rochelle Marks," he said, "I'm asking you to marry me. I'm asking you to hold my hand and jump off this cliff with me. Eyes wide open."

"Arms wide open." Somehow, she got the words out. And then she was pulling him to his feet, throwing herself into his arms, laughing and crying and burying her face in his neck while he stood, solid and strong, and held her. Held her so tight, like he'd never let her go. Because he wouldn't, and she knew it, like she knew him. All the way down to the bone.

"And I'm answering you," she told him. "I'm saying, you bet your life. You can bet your heart, because I'm betting mine. I'm betting it forever. I'm saying yes."

AUTHOR'S NOTE

Abuse of prescription drugs can seem harmless—and that's the issue. In fact, prescription drug abuse is second only to marijuana as the nation's largest illicit drug problem, and is especially severe in the western states. Young people are particularly likely to abuse prescription drugs because they are easy to obtain from friends or relatives, whether knowingly supplied or taken from medicine cabinets. These drugs are seen as legal, "not that serious," and "safer" than nonprescription drugs, and many teenagers and young adults, like Stacy, view them as study aids.

Some facts:

Safer? No. More people die from overdoses of prescription opioids than from all other drugs combined, including heroin and cocaine. These drugs are especially dangerous when taken with alcohol, or when two or more types of drugs are taken together—the kinds of things Stacy does.

Opioid pain relievers (the kind Stacy takes) attach to the same cell receptors targeted by heroin.

In 2011, 52 million people in the US age 12+ had used prescription drugs nonmedically at least once in their lifetime, 6.2 million in the past month. One in twenty-two people aged twelve and over had used prescription drugs nonmedically in the past year.

The most commonly abused prescription drugs are painkillers (5.1 million abusers), tranquilizers (2.2 million abusers), and stimulants (1.1 million abusers).

Idaho has the fourth-highest rate of prescription drug abuse in the United States. Seven out of the ten states with the highest rates of abuse of these drugs are located in the West.

Source: National Institute on Drug Abuse; National Institutes of Health; U.S. Department of Health and Human Services

Learn more:

http://www.drugabuse.gov/related-topics/trends-statistics/infographics/popping-pills-prescription-drug-abuse-in-america
http://www.drugabuse.gov/publications/drugfacts/prescription-over-counter-medications

ACKNOWLEDGMENTS

Many people helped with the research for this book. Any errors or omissions, however, are my own.

My thanks go to, in alphabetical order: The Honorable Barbara Buchanan, Rick Dalessio, Jake Druffel, Shane L. Greenbank, and Erika Iiams, for their help with country life, farming, drug-abuse issues, and legal issues. Thanks especially to Erika for the lentils.

As always, thanks to my awesome critique team: Barbara Buchanan, Carol Chappell, Anne Forell, Mary Guidry, Leslie Harlib, Kathy Harward, and Bob Pryor, for helping whip the book into shape.

And to my editors at Montlake Romance, Maria Gomez and Charlotte Herscher, for their assistance.

Finally, to my husband, Rick Nolting, and my sons, James Nolting and Sam Nolting, for helping me believe that I could and would write this book.

ABOUT THE AUTHOR

Photo © 2015 Shoey Sindel

Rosalind James, a publishing-industry veteran and former marketing executive, is the author of contemporary romance and romantic suspense novels published both independently and through Montlake Romance. She started writing down one of the stories in her head on a whim four years ago while living in Auckland, New Zealand. Within six weeks, she had finished the book, thrown a lifetime of caution to the wind, and quit her day job. She and her husband live in Berkeley, California, with a Labrador retriever named Charlie.

Made in the USA
Monee, IL
03 August 2020

37562398R00215